RECKLESS

AN OPTION ZERO NOVEL

CHRISTY REECE

Reckless
An Option Zero Novel
Published by Christy Reece
Cover Art by Kelly A. Martin of KAM Design
Image Credits:
Tylinek /DepositPhotos, remusrigo.DepositPhotos, PeopleImages.com/DepositPhotos,mast3r/DepositPhotos, f11photo/DepositPhotos
Copyright 2024 by Christy Reece
ISBN: 979-8-9886772-3-9

To obtain permission to excerpt portions of the text, please contact the author at *Christy@christyreece.com.*

Closely held secrets can have deadly consequences

Family is everything to OZ operative Jazz McAlister, who once lost everyone and everything she loved. The mysterious disappearance of her brother years ago left a deep ache in her heart that she's never forgotten. When circumstances bring him abruptly back into her life, Jazz will do anything to find out the truth of where he's been and what happened to him. Revealing her plans to Xavier Quinn, her OZ partner and best friend, is out of the question. He would never understand. This is something she must do on her own.

Xavier has been in covert ops a long time, but he's never had a partner like Jazz. She's smart, brave, and fiercely loyal, and with one look, she can melt his heart of stone. Together, they make a formidable partnership, and it's one he treasures, which is why he's stunned when she goes out on her own without any explanation.

Jazz thought she had a plan, but how could she forget that life can turn on a dime? When her life is upended once again, Xavier and her OZ teammates are the only ones she trusts to help her. If only her recklessness hadn't put her in the crosshairs of a sadistic predator bent on stealing her life.

As the Option Zero team rush to save Jazz, forces no one could ever have predicted will do everything within their power to see that Jazz and her team are destroyed forever.

But love is stronger than hate, and family is often more of the heart than blood, proving once again that evil cannot win.

For Jackie.
I miss you.

To us, family means putting your arms around each other and being there.
~Barbara Bush

CHAPTER ONE

Nineteen Years Ago
Chicago, Illinois

"Stop. Stop. Stop."

Crouched behind thick, green bushes, ten-year-old Jasmine McAlister whisper-screamed the words. Her thin body trembled, her shoulders tense with misery. She wanted to put her hands over her ears to cut off the sounds but refused to give herself the comfort. If Brody had to endure this pain because of her, then she would endure the sounds of his agony for him.

If she had just done what she'd been told to do, none of this would be happening. They knew that punishing Brody would always hurt more than if she took the blows herself. It didn't help that Brody was more than willing to take the pain for her. He thought it was his duty to protect her, and as much as she didn't want to hurt, she hated seeing him in pain.

It lasted only five minutes or so, but it felt like a lifetime before Brody came around the corner. She watched him for a second to see how badly he'd been hurt. His mouth was set in a grim line, but the instant he saw her, he gave her a quick, wry smile. "Arthur may look like a gorilla, but he hits like a kitten."

Jazz swallowed back a sob. She knew that wasn't true. She'd been on the receiving end of Arthur's giant hands on more than one occasion. The hits hurt all the way to the bone. However, after he'd left a bruise on her that had lasted over two weeks, he'd limited his meanness to mostly nasty words and mean looks. And when he really wanted to hurt her, he took out her punishment on her big brother.

"I'm sorry, Brody," Jazz whispered. "I'll try to be better."

"You be you, Jazzy. Arthur's gonna hit me every day, no matter what. Might as well be for a good cause."

She knew he was only trying to make her feel better, but there was no denying that this was her fault. Next time Arthur told her to do something, she would do it, no matter how gross it was. Cleaning up a bathroom where he and his drinking buddies had vomited all over the floor would be a small price to pay compared with having Brody take punishment for her disobedience.

"Thank you for protecting me."

"It's what big brothers do."

Despite her sorrow, she couldn't help but smile. Brody was big—there was no denying that. At fourteen, he was already over six feet tall, had wide shoulders and hands almost as large as Arthur's. If he wanted to, he could beat up Arthur, but if he did, they both knew what would happen. Brody would be put in juvenile detention, and she would be at the mercy of Arthur and his friends.

And he was her brother. Maybe not by blood. His daddy had married her mama when Jazz was four, but that didn't matter. From the day he and Connor McAlister had walked in the door, they had become her family and Brody had become her protector.

For six years, they had been the perfect family. Her mama and Connor, aka Papa Mac, had been the best mommy and daddy in the world. Then one day, the police had shown up at her school and told her that her home had exploded due to a faulty gas line. Her mom and Papa Mac were gone, and she and Brody had nothing but each other. Their parents, their home, and all their possessions were gone. The next day, she and her brother had been bundled onto a bus in Atlanta and had arrived in Chicago late at night. Arthur Kelly had met them at the bus depot. Neither of them knew him, but they'd been told he was the only relative—a distant cousin of Jazz's mother—who would agree to take them together. They hadn't protested, because the last thing they wanted was to be separated.

Brody was all she had left in the world, and it terrified her that he would be taken from her, too.

That's why she needed to behave and do whatever they told her to do. What would she do if they punished her by taking Brody away? She couldn't let that happen. She wouldn't survive without her big brother.

CHAPTER TWO

Four Years Later
Indianapolis, Indiana

Huddled beneath a thin blanket, Jazz peered out the window into the inky darkness. It was well past midnight, and though the streets weren't empty, the people who occupied them now either walked furtively or drunkenly. In this neighborhood, being outside at this time of night was dangerous.

Brody was out there somewhere. Was he trying to get home to her? He had been gone for over twenty-four hours now. He'd left yesterday afternoon with over a hundred dollars in his pocket to buy food. She was used to being left alone for long periods of time, but this was the longest he'd ever been away.

Had Arthur found them? Two years ago, they'd snuck out in the middle of the night and had traveled as far as they could with the money they'd managed to pilfer from the jar Arthur kept above the fridge. Seventy-seven dollars didn't take them very far. Two bus tickets to Indianapolis had used up half their money. The rest had been spent on a skanky motel room, along with a jar of peanut butter and a loaf of bread.

Over the past two years, their circumstances had improved. Brody had gotten a job as a bouncer at a strip joint. Even though he was still technically a minor, his size gave him an advantage. Well over six feet, with broad shoulders and an impressive scowl, he had managed to finagle his way into various jobs. Getting paid in cash was the ideal way when you were in hiding. No messy paperwork or identification needed. Show up, do the job, and keep your mouth shut. Brody had become an expert at that.

This last job, at the strip joint, had come with less money, but as incentive, the owner had given Brody an apartment on the top floor. It wasn't much more than a room with a single bed, a ratty sofa, and a small fridge and microwave, but it was more than they'd had before.

No one knew that she lived here, too. Brody wanted to keep her as hidden as possible. She didn't fully know the reason why. She knew his employer might not want a teenage girl living above a nudie bar—at least that's what Brody had said. But Jazz knew it was more than that.

Why they'd snuck out of Arthur's house in the middle of the night was still a bit of a mystery. Brody had woken her up, told her to grab her clothes, put on her shoes, and to be as quiet as possible. She hadn't questioned him. She never questioned her big brother. He was the only one who looked out for her. She owed him everything.

She knew Brody had overheard something that scared him. And though he never said, she knew it had something to do with her. She had asked him numerous times, and he had skirted the issue, telling her that he'd just had enough. That was understandable. In the two years they'd been with Arthur, Brody had received the brunt of his abuse. She'd taken some, but there was something about Brody that made Arthur enjoy hurting him.

There was more to the story than Brody would give her, though. On occasion, she'd seen Arthur's friends give her looks that creeped her out. She didn't quite know what those looks meant, but she did know that they made her scared and uncomfortable.

A strong breeze rattled the window, and icy air crept through the windowsill. Jazz pulled the blanket tighter over her body and continued her vigil. She tried to will her eyes to see Brody's tall, athletic frame amble down the street, just as she'd seen it so many times before. A sick feeling in the pit of her stomach told her that wasn't going to happen this time.

Where could he have gone? The grocery store he usually went to was only three blocks away. With their limited funds, it rarely took him longer than half an hour to purchase their food and come home. So making herself believe that something awful hadn't befallen him just wasn't going to happen.

Wiping the tears streaming from her eyes, she knew she had no choice but to face the facts. Something terrible had happened, and her brother wasn't coming back.

COVERED from top to toe in black, Jazz opened the apartment door and stuck her head out. She rarely walked outside this door. She knew Brody only wanted to protect her, but the fear of stepping outside sent nervous sweat rolling down her back. Everything looked so dark and forbidding. She had waited until the strip joint had closed down and the streets outside were mostly empty. As small as she was and in dark clothing, she hoped to be able to sneak out without being seen at all.

Not going out was no longer an option. She had finished the last of the bread this morning. There were maybe a couple ounces of milk left, a half sleeve of saltines, and a dented can of tuna. That was enough to get her through another day, but after that, there would be nothing left. Brody had taken most of their money with him, but she had found a twenty-dollar bill he'd given her for her birthday last year. Since she never went out, there had been nothing to use it on. Now it was all she had.

She put one foot outside the door and then peered over her shoulder one last time at the note she'd left for Brody on the counter. If he came home and found her gone, he would be terrified. She knew he'd come looking for her, so she'd explained in detail the route she would take to the small twenty-four-hour market four blocks over. Her hope was to get there and back within half an hour. That might be pushing it, but she figured if she ran all the way there and walked quickly back, she could do it.

Taking a deep breath, she straightened her shoulders and stepped into the dim hallway. Her eyes focused on the door that led outside, Jazz ground her teeth as she forced her trembling legs to move. The instant she touched the doorknob, a sense of dread filled her. What if Brody returned and didn't see the note? Had she put it in a place he would immediately see? Should she wait until tomorrow to go out? She had crackers and tuna. She didn't absolutely need anything. Maybe if she waited another day...

No. She had to go. Even though Brody had told her to never leave, his absence gave her no choice. This was her best chance to get what she needed without anyone seeing her. He would understand.

She opened the door and gasped as icy-cold air stole her breath. It was always cold in the apartment, but compared with outside, the temperature inside was downright balmy. The sweatshirt and light jacket, along with the baseball cap, weren't going to keep this coldness at bay, but she had come this far. She refused to stop now.

Taking the outside stairway, she zipped down to the side yard and sprinted toward the sidewalk. If she kept to the shadows, she should be able to zoom straight to the market without a soul seeing her.

It had been almost two years since she'd been outside the apartment. Remembering where the market was located might have been a problem if not for her special gift. Brody had told her she was never to tell anyone about it, because someone might try to use it against her. She didn't understand what he'd meant by that, but when Brody told her something, she rarely argued with him. Telling anyone she had a photographic memory and never forgot anything would remain her secret. In this instance, she was grateful for the gift.

She ran down the empty sidewalk. When her ears picked up a strange sound, she stopped abruptly and melted into the darkness, waiting. When nothing happened and no other noise sounded, she took off again. By the time she made it to the market, she was sweating and panting. Staying indoors, with no regular exercise had turned her into a weak-kneed, out-of-shape pansy. She promised herself that when Brody came back, she would persuade him to let her at least run around the block at night to regain her strength.

The parking lot of the store was well lit, which made her uncomfortable. Being seen by anyone was almost as terrifying as leaving the apartment. It did, however, make her feel better that she could see if danger came her way.

She pushed the door open and breathed in a sigh. The warmth of the store, along with the fragrance of fresh produce, felt like coming home. If she'd had time and wasn't terrified of being seen, she would have liked to walk up and down each aisle and enjoy this rare experience. Since that couldn't happen, she quickly grabbed a small basket by the door and sped through the store. Five minutes later, the basket was filled with a carton of milk, a jar of peanut butter, a loaf of bread, a half-dozen eggs, two cans of soup, and a jar of multivitamins.

Carefully calculating the items in her head, she anticipated a bill of just over sixteen dollars. It was much more than she wanted to spend, but if she was careful, the food could last her at least a couple of weeks, if not more.

The sleepy-looking, young cashier didn't seem the least bit curious about her, which was a relief. Even though she was almost fifteen years old, she had a delicate frame that had yet to produce even the slightest of feminine curves. She often lamented the lack of a figure, but sometimes, like now, it came in handy.

Should she ask him if he'd seen anyone around that looked like Brody? With his large build and distinctive green eyes, her brother would be memorable to most people. When the clerk glanced up at her with a cold sneer, she quickly changed her mind. He didn't look as though he would lift a finger to help anyone. Besides, the last thing she needed was to call attention to herself.

Stacking the items on the counter, she felt her heart pound as her items were scanned. When the bill came to just over twenty-one dollars, her eyes bugged out. How had she miscalculated?

She gnawed her lip, knowing she had to put some items back. With reluctance, her face most likely the color of the tomato soup she'd picked up, she said gruffly, "I've changed my mind. I don't want the soup or vitamins."

With an irritated glare, the cashier grabbed the items she had rejected, rescanned them, and snarled the new amount. "Seventeen oh two."

Totally intimidated by the scowl and humiliated to boot,

Jazz shoved the twenty across the counter. When he just continued to scowl at her, she said softly, "What's wrong?"

"You ain't got two pennies?"

"No."

"Whatever." He opened the cash register and counted out the change. Practically throwing the money on the counter, he sat on a wooden stool and started reading his phone.

"Um… Can I have a bag?"

As if he didn't hear her, he didn't bother to raise his head.

Fighting tears, Jazz pocketed the change and then grabbed her grocery items. If she'd had larger pockets in her jacket, she wouldn't have as much of a problem, but she had no choice but to try to carry all the items in her arms. She was halfway to the door when a voice inside her head that sounded just like Brody's stopped her. *Hey, Little Mighty, just what the hell are you doing? Tell that jerk to get you a sack, or you're going to kick his ass.*

Remembering the nickname Brody had given her caused a grin to tug at her mouth. Having no human interaction other than with her brother for two years had made her timid and afraid of everything. Once, those words—*timid* and *afraid*—had not even been in her vocabulary. The very fact that this jerk had made her feel less than human reignited the spitfire she'd once been.

Turning back, she stalked back to the counter and snapped, "Hey, dirtwad, give me a bag."

The kid's head jerked up, and he glared at her. "What did you say?"

"I said give me a bag. I paid for these things, and I need something to carry them."

"I don't have to give you shit."

Setting the items on the counter, Jazz leaned forward and growled, "Either give me a bag, or I'm coming across this counter. You don't want that. Trust me."

Her glaring eyes locked with his. In spite of the fact that he was twice as big as she was and could clearly have knocked her into next year, he backed away. Grabbing a plastic bag, he threw her items into it and shoved it toward her. "There. Happy?"

Taking it from him, she replied quietly, "No."

She walked out the door, her dignity restored. However, the instant she was outside, the anxiety returned. So much for not wanting to call attention to herself. What if he called the police on her? What if there were cameras in the store and someone somewhere recognized her? Brody had told her that Arthur was likely looking for them.

Cursing her temper, she zoomed down the sidewalk toward the apartment. It was almost four in the morning. People would soon be on the streets. If she was caught, there was no telling where she would end up. Brody would never be able to find her.

As if all the devils in hell were after her, Jazz raced home. She tried her best to keep to the shadows, but her biggest priority was getting back to the apartment as quickly as possible. Since most of her money had been used for this one small trip, she needn't worry about leaving the apartment again. Hopefully, Brody would be back soon, and everything could get back to normal.

The thought that he might have come back while she was gone made her run even faster. Suddenly convinced that Brody had returned home, she became more excited the closer she got. He must be so worried about her.

Heart racing, Jazz reached the strip joint and flew up the steps to the apartment. Her hand shaking with excitement, it took three tries before she could get the key into the lock. When she finally turned the doorknob, she had a huge smile on her face, somehow sure that Brody had indeed come home.

The instant she stepped inside, she knew all the excitement had been for nothing. The room was empty. The note she'd put on the counter was untouched. Silence permeated the small area, and Jazz had never felt more alone in her entire life.

∼

TEN DAYS LATER, she was back at the store with her measly two dollars and ninety-eight cents clutched tightly in her hand. She had deliberately gone on a different night than before in hopes that the same clerk wouldn't be working. No such luck.

This time, though, he seemed much more interested in her than before. She was hyperalert already, and every one of her senses was telling her to leave. Problem was, she had no food left. She told herself if she hurried, it wouldn't be an issue. Besides, with the small amount of cash she had, she couldn't buy much anyway.

"Anything I can help you find?"

In the midst of reaching for a pint of milk, Jazz froze. Why was the clerk suddenly so helpful?

Without looking at him, she said, "No, thanks."

Hurriedly grabbing the milk, she figured she had just enough money for a small bag of rice. Probably not the most nutritional thing to eat, but if she limited herself to a small bowl a day with a few ounces of milk, she figured she could go at least another week before things became dire.

She put her two items on the counter and waited for the clerk to ring them up. He picked up each item and examined them as if he'd never seen them before.

"Is something wrong?"

"No." He grinned, showing off stained, yellow teeth. "Just making sure there aren't any defects. You never know."

"Can you hurry up?"

"Sure. Sure." He rang up the milk and then slowly slipped it into a bag. "You need another bag for the rice?"

"No. One bag will do."

"Okay. Let's see. That'll be two dollars and twenty-seven cents."

Jazz quickly placed the money on the counter and then went to take grab the bag. The clerk held it away from her and said, "Let me get you your ticket."

"Not necessary." She grabbed the bag from him and ran out of the store. His helpful attitude had been way too weird. She hadn't wanted to wait around to see how much weirder he could get.

She took off at a run and immediately slammed into a giant, hard chest. Bouncing backward, she looked up into the face of the scariest-looking man she'd ever seen.

"Hey there, little girl. Where you going?"

She took in his appearance all at once—beady brown eyes, pockmarked face, thick lips, his body the size of a gorilla.

If he got hold of her, she wouldn't be getting away from him. She did the only thing she knew to do—what Brody had instructed her to do if any man ever grabbed her. Thankful for her thick running shoes and her ability to move quickly, Jazz backed up and gave his crotch the hardest kick she could manage.

Agony on his face, the man dropped like a stone. Jazz didn't wait around to see what he would do next. She zoomed around the corner and stopped short. Two men stood before her, blocking her way.

This was no random attack. These men were here *for her*.

She knew if she turned around, the man she'd kicked would have recovered enough to capture her. With nowhere else to go, she darted to the left.

Heavy feet pounded behind her. Grateful for her speed, she sprinted away. She was deliberately going in the opposite direction of the apartment. If they found where she lived, she would never be able to go back. She would find a place to hide for a few hours and then head back home.

She rounded a corner, sure that they were no longer behind her. Spotting a giant garbage bin, she took a step toward it. Agony seared her scalp, and her body jerked backward. One of the men had grabbed her braid and was pulling her toward him. She knew she'd have only one chance to get this right. Pulling the knife from the sheath at her waist, she struck out, slicing the braid in two. A few months ago, when Brody had given her the long, slender knife, she had laughed at the ridiculous thought of ever having to use it. Now, she couldn't be more grateful. Free again, she took off, faster than she'd ever run before.

She had no idea where she was going, but if she stopped, they would take her. Was Arthur behind this? Was this what had happened to Brody? If so, what had they done to him? The wild thought hit her that maybe she should let them catch her. If they took her to where Brody was, maybe they could escape together, like they had from Arthur. She discarded the thought immediately as insane and then poured on the speed.

When the sound of footsteps behind her dimmed, she knew she had lost them, if only temporarily. Breath wheezed from her lungs, and her legs were shaking. She couldn't keep going. Daring a glance over her shoulder, she saw no one, but when she heard a shout, she knew they hadn't stopped chasing her.

She was in a residential area now. Cars were parked on the sides of the road in front of houses. Doing the only thing that made sense to her, Jazz scooted underneath one of the vehicles. Barely a second later, she heard their footsteps again and saw two pairs of legs. Whoever these men were, they were persistent.

Thankful for her dark clothing and small body, she lay still, determined to wait them out. As long as she remained hidden, she was safe. They would eventually give up and go away. Once she was safe, she would return home and decide what she needed to do.

The last man joined them, and as if a higher power were giving her the information she needed, they stopped beside the car she was hiding under and began to talk. As she listened, ice entered her veins.

"I can't run no more, man," one of them panted.

"We can't stop now," another one said. "I know it's the girl they're looking for."

"Maybe so," his companion wheezed, "but she's gone now. We can come back."

"Okay, yeah," another one said. "But I ain't giving up. I don't care if I have to walk these streets day and night. She must live around here somewhere. She's gotta come back out sometime. We see her, we grab her. Understand?"

"Yeah," his friend said, "we won't give up."

Knowledge set in, and Jazz knew one immutable truth. She had no choice but to disappear. That meant leaving Indianapolis and going somewhere no one could find her. Not even Brody.

A COUPLE HOURS LATER, she was on her way out of town. A few minutes after she'd heard the men's conversation, they had departed. She had waited another half hour, and then, just before the sun rose, she'd found her way home. How she'd done that, she wasn't quite sure. Nothing had looked familiar. After roaming around for a while, she'd just happened upon the strip joint and known she'd never seen a sweeter sight. With no time to waste, she'd dashed upstairs and gathered her meager belongings. Other than one of Brody's favorite sweatshirts and one of his ball caps, she had left his things alone.

She prayed he would return home soon, but she had little hope that he would be able to find her. She hadn't left a note this time. Even though she had no idea where she was going, she'd wanted to leave no evidence that she had been here, just in case they somehow figured out a way to track her.

With determination and absolutely no skill, she had grabbed a pair of scissors from the kitchen drawer and cut what was left of her hair. Her scalp was sore from having had her hair almost pulled out at the roots, and though tears had welled in her eyes, she had refused to shed even one of them. Losing her long hair was a small thing compared with all the other stuff. When she'd finished, she had only a few inches left and looked like the young boy she'd sometimes been mistaken for. She told herself that was a good thing. They were looking for a girl, not a young boy.

Then with a heavy heart, she walked out the door without a backward glance. The pawnshop a couple of streets over gave her two hundred fifty dollars for the only piece of jewelry of monetary value she owned. The dainty diamond and ruby necklace had been a gift from her mama and Papa Mac on her tenth birthday. She had treasured it and sworn she would never let it go. Though it broke her heart, she'd had no choice but to sell it. She was sure it was worth much more than the amount she'd sold it for, but she hadn't had the heart or the time to haggle.

Her only other piece of jewelry was a heart-shaped locket with a photo of her mama, Papa Mac, Brody, and herself. It didn't have as much value as the necklace, but to Jazz, it meant everything. She swore she would die before she ever let it go.

She now stood in the middle of the busy bus station and weighed her options. Even though she had identification, she couldn't risk using it to purchase a ticket. Not only was she a minor traveling alone, she wanted no record of where she was headed. She had no idea how difficult it would be to gain access to a passenger list, but if they found out she'd left the city, she would never be safe.

The station was huge, and there were dozens of people going to and fro, all seeming to know exactly where they were going, without all the doubts that seemed to be crashing upon her. She took note of a group of people lining up to get on a bus. A man stood at the doorway and took each ticket as the person boarded. Sneaking onto a bus seemed almost impossible.

And then, once again, her prayers were answered in the noisiest way possible. A group of rowdy preteens, accompanied by only two adults, came dashing into the station. The kids acted as if they'd been let out of a zoo, and the adults wore expressions of defeat and weariness. From their backpacks and chatter about their trip, she discerned they were headed to Chicago for some kind of school-related event. That there were only two adults with them seemed odd, but for her purposes, they were a prayer answered. If she could finagle her way into the group, she could pretend to be one of them until she was on the bus.

Going back to Chicago, where Arthur lived, was admittedly dangerous. But if the goons who'd almost nabbed her earlier reported that she had been seen in Indianapolis, then Chicago would be the last place they would look.

Okay, yes, it seemed chancy at best, but it was her only option. Taking a deep breath, she pulled her cap down tighter and stood behind the group. When one of the kids made an off-color comment, she, like all the other kids, joined in the laughter. They all moved as one toward the bus, and Jazz went right along with them. One of the harried adults in charge shoved a handful of boarding passes at the ticket-taking man. He gave an eye roll at all the kids and then, with a slump of his shoulders, moved aside. The group moved en masse onto the bus, shoving at one another and giggling as they made their way down the aisle. Jazz was right there with them.

As they filtered into seats, she separated herself from the group. She would have liked to stay with them, because not only did they give her cover, she'd feel safer in a group. However, someone at some point was bound to notice that she didn't belong and would start asking questions. She preferred not to take that risk.

She moved to the very back of the bus and scrunched into the corner. Since the bus was only half full, she was one lone figure in the dark, and she wanted to stay that way.

About ten minutes after the bus pulled away from the station, Jazz began to breathe normally again. With that relaxation came the grief she had buried. She looked out the back window at what she was leaving behind. It wasn't the city, the ratty little apartment, or even the few good memories she and Brody had made there. It was the sorrow of leaving behind the only person she loved. Her beloved brother was somewhere out there. What had happened to him? Had he been taken by the same men? Had something awful happened to him? She didn't know. But as the bus moved down the highway and her heart solidified into stone, Jazz swore with all the fervency she had left inside her, that someday, some way, she would find Brody again. He was all she had left.

CHAPTER THREE

Present Day
Seattle, Washington

X avier Quinn frowned as he reviewed the information on his phone. It'd been a while since he'd used this particular alias, and now he remembered why. He hated the guy, even if he existed only on paper.

For this OZ op, he was Oliver Jackson, age thirty-four, a perpetual womanizer. Ollie was still living off his inheritance and seemed to have no goal other than partying and sleeping with as many women as he could before he died.

Xavier shook his head. Yeah, definitely not his favorite role.

A grin kicked up on his face when he thought about how Jazz wouldn't like her alias any better. If he was a sleaze, then she was one of his many one-night stands. That was likely the most unrealistic thing about their entire cover. There were a lot of descriptions he could come up with for Jasmine McAlister, but a one-night stand would not be one of them.

Intelligent, fiercely independent, stubborn, and loyal to a

fault were just a few ways he would describe his beautiful partner. After what they'd learned about her brother last year, she had not changed her mind one iota about him. She loved Brody McAlister, wanted to find him, and that was that. Xavier, on the other hand, wanted to beat him within an inch of his life for abandoning his fourteen-year-old sister, leaving her to survive on her own, as if she meant nothing to him.

Shrugging into his tuxedo jacket, Xavier turned to the full-length mirror and grimaced again. A Tom Ford tux could make any man look good. It fit him like it was made for him— which it had been—and was actually comfortable. Problem was, he was not a tuxedo guy. Give him a pair of ragged jeans, a soft T-shirt, his favorite pair of beaten-up boots, and his bike, and he was in his element.

Tonight's mission called for elegance, and as much as he disliked the role, he could play it for the op. Especially when he got to sit across from the most fascinating woman he'd ever known.

With that, Xavier opened his bedroom door and then stopped in his tracks. Of all those words he'd used to describe Jazz, he'd left one word out. And that word? *Stunning.*

Dressed in a shimmering black, off-the-shoulder dress that fell about three inches above her knees and hugged every delicate curve of her body, Jasmine McAlister was breathtakingly beautiful.

Seemingly unaware that his silence was related to his inability to breathe, she smiled beatifically and said, "You clean up nice, Quinn."

Finally able to articulate some words, he managed to rasp out a gruff, "Ditto, McAlister."

Yeah, a poet he was not.

Holding up a silver and black necklace, she said, "Can you help me here? The clasp is giving me fits."

He made his way over without taking his eyes from her. In

an uncomplicated world where he didn't have to explain his actions or justify them, he'd pull her into his arms and kiss those luscious, smiling lips. But when they came up for air, he'd have to speak, and oh hell, would she have questions.

So he did what he'd been doing for years and ignored his own desires. Taking the necklace from her, he turned her toward the mirror and draped the necklace around her slender neck.

In four-inch heels, she still came barely to his shoulders. Jazz was petite and small-boned, but she more than made up for that with attitude and grit.

Willing his fingers to obey him instead of doing what they were aching to do, he hooked the clasp and then stepped back. He felt a sense of relief that he'd been able to do the small task without venturing into forbidden territory. But he made a fatal mistake when he looked at her in the mirror.

"Jazz," he groaned.

She jerked her head up and met his eyes. There was no way he could mask what he was feeling. The desire, the need, the incredible ache that consumed him.

"Xavier?" she whispered.

Going on instinct, Xavier held her shoulders in his hands and slowly turned her to face him. Her eyes were wide and glittering with a heat he'd always longed to see. He'd been so careful to hide his feelings for her. When they'd met, he'd felt an instant attraction but had squelched it, knowing a romantic relationship with a coworker could be difficult. Then, when Ash had partnered them together, he'd forced those feelings back even further. When she'd been injured and had almost died, he'd cursed himself for not telling her how he felt. Her long road to recovery had made him hold back again.

Most people who knew him would say that *caution* wasn't even in his vocabulary. But with Jazz, he had never wanted to scare her or make her uncomfortable. No, she wasn't a fragile flower, but her heart had been broken too many times in her young life. No way would he risk hurting her.

But to see his feelings reflected in her eyes was more than he could resist. Carefully, in case he was misreading her, he gently cupped her face and whispered softly, "You take my breath away, McAlister."

A soft smile curved her full lips, and a teasing glint entered her eyes. "Ditto, Quinn."

Chuckling at her repeat of his earlier response, he shook his head. "Words have never been my forte."

"Oh yeah? Then what would you say your forte is?"

Hoping like hell he wasn't reading this wrong, he lowered his head and growled against her lips, "This."

Her lips were soft, luscious, sweeter than he ever could have imagined. He could spend an eternity kissing her and still not get enough. When she opened for him, he slid his tongue inside and groaned. She tasted luscious, like strawberry-flavored cotton candy.

Not wanting to take more than she was comfortable with giving, Xavier pulled slightly away. He stopped immediately when Jazz's arms wrapped around his shoulders, pulling him deeper into the kiss. Taking that as a sign, Xavier let himself go. Drawing her closer, he explored her mouth like a starving man at a buffet.

When Jazz moaned beneath his mouth and pressed her body against his, he forgot everything. Nothing mattered but the here and now. He wanted to devour her, take his time with her, let her teach him how she wanted to be touched. Exploring Jazz would be the gift of a lifetime.

A distant beep, beep, beep was an irritating sound, and he ignored it. Jazz was the one who pulled back and whispered, "That's the alarm on your watch. I think it's time to go."

Blowing out a ragged sigh, Xavier took a step back. Not once in his adult life had he forgotten himself like that. They were on an op, had a mission to accomplish. Forgetting where he was and his purpose was unprecedented.

Unable to let this progress go without marking the time in some way, he growled softly, "Pick this up later?"

He held his breath as he waited for her answer, almost afraid she'd say it had been a mistake.

The heat in her gaze told him her thoughts before she said softly, "Sounds like a plan."

CHAPTER FOUR

The elegant restaurant was at capacity, though no one would know it. The tables were positioned to give each diner the idea that they were in a world of their own. It was an optical illusion that worked. Pristine white tablecloths, dark hardwood floors, rugged brick walls, and brilliantly shimmering chandeliers gave off an ambience that screamed wealth, privilege, and exclusivity.

LuLu's was one of the trendiest and most popular Italian restaurants in the city. With a waiting list of up to a year to get a reservation, it was no wonder the prices weren't even listed on the menu. The saying *if you have to ask how much something is, then you can't afford it* fit this place to a T.

Her game face on, Jazz sat across from Xavier and played the role of a young ingénue with a penchant for wealthy, good-looking guys. Their identities weren't especially important to this job. No one needed to know their names. The deed she was here to perform was the key to the mission.

Anyone looking at her right now would never be able to tell what was going on inside her head. During training years ago, she'd had an acting coach tell her she had a natural talent, and if she wanted, she could likely make a career in show business. That had never entered her mind. This was her dream job, and the man across from her was her dream for everything else.

And that was why she was glad she had major acting skills, because behind the calm, cool facade of a coolly sophisticated woman was a giddy, lovesick woman who was silently screaming, *Xavier kissed me!*

Yep, if she were alone right now, she'd be dancing a little jig and shouting, "Hallelujah," to the heavens above. Finally, after all this time, he had kissed her!

Xavier Quinn had fascinated her from the moment she'd met him. Yes, he was gorgeous, with thick, inky black hair that just touched his collar and a neatly trimmed mustache and beard that she had discovered during their kiss were actually soft and felt wonderful against her skin. And his eyes. Xavier had the most mesmerizingly beautiful silver-gray eyes. She could spend hours gazing into their depths.

And tonight, for the first time, she had seen something in those eyes that she had been longing to see. There had been heat, attraction…desire. She had almost given up that he would ever see her as anything other than his friend and partner.

When they'd first met, she had been as green as a new blade of grass. She'd been fully trained, but she'd only had a few soft ops under her belt, so he, along with all the other OZ operatives, had been protective of her as if she were a fragile flower. It hadn't helped that she was small-boned, petite, and looked about ten years younger than her actual age. For over a year, she had busted her butt to show them that she was just as tough and lethal as they were. She had earned their respect and admiration, which had given her even more confidence.

Then, a couple years ago, she had been injured during an

op. She had almost died. After a brutally long recovery, she was once again fully operational. Everyone else had accepted her complete return. Everyone except Xavier. He still treated her as if she would break if he did or said the wrong thing.

That was another reason tonight's revelation had been so significant. Not only was Xavier admitting his attraction, he wasn't treating her as if she would bruise if he touched her.

Things were definitely looking up!

Admittedly, relationships were not her forte. Without spending thousands of dollars on therapy, she knew there was something broken inside her. She'd lost her entire family, and knowing how easy it was to lose someone usually stopped her from allowing people into her life.

She cut her eyes over to Xavier and fought a grin, noting that he was fully embracing the sleazy side of his cover. A smarmy smirk played around his mouth, and his eyes glinted with what one could describe only as lasciviousness. She knew he hated this particular cover, but she had to admit he played it to perfection.

The mission sounded easier than it likely would be. In about ten minutes or so, a man and his entourage would be entering the restaurant. The man, Franco Bass, was her target. Her job was to get close enough to him to plant a microscopic tracker on his skin. The tiny flesh-colored device would be absorbed into his skin, unnoticed by anyone. It would give them the ability to know Bass's location for up to a week. Where he went and with whom he did business were vitally important to their investigation. If they were successful, they would be closer to an elite member of the Wren Project than they'd ever been.

But how to get to the man?

What they knew about the real Franco Bass could fill a thimble. Plenty of media had covered the man, but most of what was reported was fiction. Making someone look better or worse than they were was a popular ploy these days. Though they didn't know much about him, they knew the type of women he liked. Joy Monroe, aka Jazz McAlister, was just his type. Which should, hopefully, make it easier for her to get close to him at some point during the night.

"Your food good, baby?" Xavier asked in his best oil-slick voice.

Jazz glanced down at the mushroom risotto that she had apparently eaten half of without registering the taste. Even though Xavier had sounded as slippery as a greased eel, Jazz couldn't control the shiver up her spine when he'd called her *baby*. Yes, he was playing a part, but still…

Since their OZ teammates were monitoring them, she forced herself to stay focused on the job. "Everything's good… baby." She was gratified to see his pupils dilate slightly at the suggestive way she'd spoken. At least she knew she wasn't the only one still feeling the heat from their kiss.

She lowered her voice and said, "Just trying to figure out our best strategy."

Keeping his voice to a murmur, Xavier said, "Yeah. We'll know more once he arrives."

They'd discussed several options, but not knowing where the man would be seated, how many people would be with him, and how close a stranger could get to him, no matter how attractive, had inhibited a solid plan. The last few weeks, Bass had been one of the most high-profile people in the media and, by all accounts, was very approachable. Tonight, they would see just how true that was.

"He's late," Xavier growled under his breath.

Jazz snorted. "With all the press he's been getting lately, the guy probably has an elephant-sized ego. He likely sets his own time schedule and expects the rest of the world to adhere to it. Still can't believe he walks around as if he's an ordinary person."

"He likely thinks he's untouchable, but that's about to end."

Jazz agreed with his assessment. Wouldn't be today, or even next week, but Bass and all the evil people associated with the Wren organization would be exposed and destroyed. Option Zero would see to that.

Hawke's gravelly voice sounded in her earbud. "Just got word. Bass is eight minutes out."

"Roger that," Xavier replied. "We'll be ready."

She took a bite of her risotto, took a sip of wine, and glanced around at the other patrons. Would they be surprised when Bass arrived? His itinerary wasn't exactly public knowledge, but somehow various members of the press and paparazzi always seemed able to find him.

"Jazz," Xavier said quietly.

She jerked her attention back to her partner, surprised that not only had he used her name, but an odd, surprisingly serious expression had also come over his face.

"What's wrong?" she asked softly.

Instead of answering, he shocked her further by clicking off his earbud. He then nodded toward her, indicating she should do the same. Cutting off communication in the middle of an op went against protocol. But she trusted her partner, so Jazz followed his lead and switched off her earbud. She leaned forward and whispered, "What's going on?"

THIS WAS either the worst idea of his life, or the best. The next few minutes would tell. Going off-comms during an op was a major breach of operational protocol, and he was sure to get an earful from Ash when this was over. He'd take the reprimand and deserve it. But in this limited space and time, he had a captive audience. He intended to make the most of it.

Keeping his voice low, he said, "Can I ask you a question?"

"Of course," Jazz said. "You can ask me anything."

Yeah, he knew he could, but getting a straight answer from her on this particular topic wasn't always a surety.

"Why don't you want OZ involved in finding your brother?"

He watched her reaction carefully, waiting for the explosion. As was Jazz's way, it didn't take long.

"What are you talking about?" she snapped. "OZ has been looking for Brody since the moment I came on board. You know that."

"Yeah, I know that Serena's run a few searches, and we've run down some leads. That's about the same thing a half-assed PI would do. You know we have the resources to drill deeper than an oil rig. Yet you've never asked Ash for more. Why is that?"

Beautiful brown eyes widened with shock, and then the fire flared. He knew she wouldn't go full-on explosion inside the restaurant, which was one of the reasons he'd chosen this moment. Calling attention to them would cause all sorts of issues they wanted to avoid. However, Jazz was crafty. Her eyes and face were so expressive, she could communicate fury and displeasure without saying a word. Still, she would give him an earful.

"How dare you say that?" Her whisper-soft voice trembled with anger. "You know that I would do anything to find my brother."

"Do I? Convince me. Let's get the whole team involved instead of piecemealing it out." He leaned forward. "It's way past time to either find him or let him go."

A sheen of moisture appeared in her eyes, and Xavier felt like he'd been kicked in the gut with a steel boot. The last thing he wanted to do was hurt this beautiful woman. From the day he'd met her, she had fascinated him, enthralled him, and challenged him. She was the most maddening, intriguing, and complicated creature he'd ever known. He'd rather cut off his hand than cause her pain. That didn't mean that he wouldn't tell her the truth.

"You picked a hell of a time to confront me about this."

"I call it perfect timing. If we weren't stuck here, you would've snapped at me and walked out by now."

"No, I would've punched you in the face."

He struggled to keep from smiling because he knew she was right. She would've tried to slug him, and he might've let her. He knew she wanted to find her brother, but there was something keeping her from going full tilt to find him, and he wanted to know why.

"Yeah. So answer my question."

"I've said as much as I'm going to say."

"Want to know what I think?"

"Would saying no keep you from giving your opinion?"

Ignoring her sarcasm, he continued, "You're too proud to ask for help."

"What? That's ridiculous."

Jazz McAlister was one of the most independent people he'd ever met. She'd basically been on her own for more than half her life. Asking for anything—even for something she wanted as badly as finding her brother—went against that concrete code she had of never needing anyone.

"Oh yeah? Well, tell me this, then. Who helped you move from your old apartment to your new one?"

"A moving company. You've heard of those. Right?" she asked dryly.

She had come to headquarters one morning with her arm in a sling. Turned out she'd fallen down the stairs while single-handedly carrying an oversized chair that was twice as big as she was. Jazz was in excellent shape, and she had muscles many people would envy, but she was in no way strong enough to lift and move heavy furniture by herself.

Ignoring her sarcasm, he continued to make his point.

"When you were injured—almost died, mind you—you hired an Uber to bring you home from the hospital."

"That again?" She blew out a controlled, explosive breath. "I've told you numerous times that I didn't want to pull any of you away from an op."

"Is it because I held back the intel from you?"

"No. I knew why you did that."

Not long after she'd been injured, he'd learned some disturbing news about her brother. He and Ash had made the decision to hold off on telling her until she had recovered. When he'd finally told her that Brody hadn't left Indianapolis until years after she'd already fled, she had surprised him with her lack of emotion. It was almost as if she'd already known.

"When I told you, you didn't seem that surprised. Why?"

"Seriously? We're going to continue this conversation during the middle of one of our most important operations?"

"Answer the question and I'll turn the comms back on."

"Fine," she snapped. "No, I wasn't surprised that Brody hadn't left Indianapolis. It made no sense for him to go somewhere else."

"But it made sense for him to abandon you?"

"I never said that. Something happened to him. I don't know what, and I'll find out when I…we…find him. He had a good reason. I know he did."

Xavier didn't know if she was trying to convince him or herself. Either way, his opinion of Brody McAlister was about as low as it could go. The bastard had abandoned his fourteen-year-old sister, leaving her brokenhearted and alone. It was amazing she had survived.

He glanced at his watch. He was running out of time. Going for broke, he leaned forward and growled, "Then let's put the full force of OZ behind finding him. Trust us, Jazz. Trust me."

He locked his eyes with hers, doing his best to communicate everything he wouldn't allow himself to say. Whether she saw those things was up to her. Either way, Xavier was done with hiding.

Myriad emotions crossed her face, and it took every bit of his fortitude not to reach out for her. Jazz had been through so much hurt and abandonment in her life.

Just when he was certain she wouldn't respond and he'd have to turn the comms back on without any resolution, she blew out another explosive breath and said, "All right. Fine. As soon as we're back home, I'll meet with Ash and ask him to get everyone on board."

Feeling like he'd just won a major battle, Xavier gave her a nod of approval and clicked his earbud back to active. Jazz followed suit.

"Nice of you to rejoin us, you two," Ash said. The lethal quietness in his tone told Xavier he might get his ass kicked instead of an earful from his boss, but that was okay. He had accomplished what he'd set out to do.

"How long now?" Jazz asked.

"Thirty seconds," Serena answered. "His limo is stopping in front of the restaurant."

"Okay, everyone," Ash said. "Eyes open. Jazz, you know what to do."

Both back in operational mode, they observed the last-minute prep of the restaurant staff. Everyone from the coat check girl to the maître d' were standing straighter, their expressions ranging from excitement to extreme nervousness. A few months ago, only a handful of people had ever heard of Franco Bass, and now his celebrity status was on par with Elon Musk and Mark Zuckerberg.

The entourage entered the restaurant as if they were arriving royalty. A hush spread through the restaurant, and it seemed everyone held their breath as the man himself walked in.

Xavier had to give the man props. At a distance, Bass was an impressive-looking man. He had an old-Hollywood magnetism, steel-gray hair, lightly tanned skin, and broad shoulders. Yeah, he looked successful and powerful. But seeing the man up close revealed the snake behind the mask. Sometimes, evil couldn't be hidden, no matter how thick the facade.

Every eye in the restaurant followed Bass to a balcony where a large, cloth-covered table had been set for him and his guests. He would be stupidly front and center so everyone could see him.

The maître d' pulled out a chair for him, and Bass plopped himself into the seat with all the pompousness of royalty. The rest of his party then seated themselves. A smug smile played around the guy's mouth, and Xavier almost burst out laughing. The obnoxious prig was so full of himself, he had no idea how he was being used.

If the people behind the Wren Project had one thing going for them, it was their ability to find the right puppets. There seemed to be an unlimited number of schmucks willing to sell their souls for wealth and fame. Little did they know—or hell, maybe they just didn't care—it was a temporary gig. Once they'd served their purpose, the joyride ended. Often abruptly and, more often than not, in death.

"He's thoroughly enjoying his fifteen minutes of fame," Jazz murmured. "Wonder how long it will last?"

Jazz's words were still hanging in the air when her question was answered. A familiar whistling noise sounded, and then a tiny, neat hole appeared in the middle of Bass's forehead. The man slumped forward.

A STARK, breathless silence enveloped the entire restaurant. It was like everyone held in a collective gasp. A second later, chaos erupted. One of the women at Bass's table shrieked, another followed, and havoc ensued. People screamed, over-turning tables as they ran en masse toward the exit.

The instant the bullet hit, Jazz and Xavier were on their feet. She grabbed her gun from her purse while Xavier took his from his ankle holster. Jazz's gaze swept the room, and out of the corner of her eye, she noted the swinging door that led to the kitchen. She glimpsed a large, booted foot before the door swung shut.

"Xavier," Jazz said.

Seeing what she'd seen at the same time, Xavier said, "Let's go."

They fought through the crowd, some of whom were on their phones, recording the melee. She reached the door and looked back for her partner. Xavier was pushing people away from a woman who'd been trampled. He glanced up at Jazz and said, "Go!"

Jazz eased the door open and peered inside. Three of the kitchen staff were huddled in a corner. When they saw her, all three pointed to another door. One whispered, "He went through there."

Thanking them with a nod, she ran toward the door that had an Exit sign above it. The guy was likely headed to the alley behind the restaurant.

Weapon in hand, she eased the door open. The alleyway was surprisingly well lit, giving her a good view of the area. To the right, two dumpsters took up a large part of the area. Jazz heard a noise to her left. A man dressed in black, with a skullcap covering his head, was running down the alley toward a black SUV. Though he was covered from head to toe, she quickly assessed him at about six five, two forty, and muscular.

Jazz took off in pursuit.

The man reached the SUV and swung the door open. Before jumping into the vehicle, he glanced back.

Jazz froze, and all the breath left her body. She knew those unusual green eyes. She saw them in her dreams and her nightmares.

The man before her—the assassin who'd killed Franco Bass —was Brody.

CHAPTER FIVE

OZ Safe House
Seattle

They sat around the small living room to review the events of the evening. As ops went, this one was to have been a low-key, noneventful mission. Instead, it had turned into a shitstorm, and they were still trying to unravel the who and the why.

For Jazz, it was a million times stormier. Had she been mistaken? Had her heated discussion with Xavier somehow transported Brody's physical characteristics onto the shooter? It had been over fifteen years since she'd seen her brother. He had to have changed significantly since then. Always big for his age, Brody had seemed larger than life to her. He had been her protector, defender, and caretaker. He had been her everything.

He'd also been one of the kindest, most thoughtful people she'd ever met. How could he have changed so much that he was now a cold-blooded killer?

It just wasn't possible. It had to be a mistake. In her mind's eye, she reviewed every minute detail. Yes, the assassin had been around Brody's height and build. Yes, she'd spotted a strand of hair the same color as Brody's—golden blond—sticking out of the cap. And yes, when he'd moved to open the door to the SUV, the light from the street lamp had been bright enough that she'd seen a scar on his wrist in the exact place she knew her brother had one. She'd been there when he'd gotten it. All of that could be explained…right?

The eyes though…that had been the most telling. They had given his identity away as if he'd shouted out his name. Brody's eyes were a distinctive, almost-eerie light green. Just like the eyes of the killer.

Had she imagined the recognition in them when he'd turned to look at her? Had his body jerked slightly, as if in shock? Or was all of this just projection because she was feeling overemotional?

She hadn't said anything to Xavier or anyone else on the team. When Xavier had finally made it out to the alley, she had described the SUV and the size of the suspected killer. She'd explained he'd been covered from head to toe so he couldn't be identified. She had said nothing about her suspicions. What could she say? *Oh, and by the way, I think my brother is the assassin. So, if you find him, please don't hurt him.*

No, she needed to think about this. About what she should do versus what she was obligated to do. If she told them, what would happen? They would continue to look for him, and when they found him, they'd want to know who hired him. And while OZ wasn't known for torturing or abusing people for intel, what would happen if Brody resisted? What if there was a shootout? What if a member of her team was hurt? What if someone shot Brody?

The wild imaginings just wouldn't stop.

What could have happened to Brody? When he had disappeared, she had made all sorts of excuses for him. She'd come up with a dozen different scenarios for why he had abandoned her. Becoming a killer hadn't been one of them.

"Jazz, what about you?"

Thankful for her ability to shift gears in midstream, Jazz said, "Nothing seemed out of the ordinary. Bass was in his element, and the people around him seemed enamored. It was exactly as we thought it would be."

"And I think that's the exact reason they chose such a public arena to take him out," Ash said.

"To verify," Gideon said, "this 'they' you speak of is the Wren Project?"

"Yes," Serena answered. "Without a doubt, it's them. He was no longer useful to them."

"But why do it in such a public way?" Jazz asked. "Why not just slip him some undetectable poison? They could've done this in secret, and no one would have been the wiser."

"It likely served as a good reminder to all their other puppets. No matter who you are, if you don't toe the line, you'll pay."

Leaning back in his chair, Xavier huffed out a frustrated growl. "It's becoming like Whac-A-Mole. One goes down, and another pops up."

"That's why we've got to concentrate on the head of the snake," Ash said. "We need to find someone who's willing to talk. Someone, somewhere out there, knows who and where he, she, or they are."

"And until we find them, we keep digging," Eve said.

"Exactly," Ash said.

That someone could be her brother, Jazz thought. He could be the key to all of this.

She took in the expressions of her teammates. They wouldn't stop until this shadow organization, the Wren Project, that had destroyed so many lives was demolished. She wanted that, too. They were evil and needed to be ended.

"We'll head back home and continue the digging," Ash said. "In the meantime, Jazz and Xavier, I'd like you both to stay here and monitor the situation. Interview as many witnesses as you can. See if you can dig up any intel we may have missed."

If there was ever a time for her to speak up, this was it. But she remained silent, only nodding her head in agreement to Ash's assignment.

She told herself to wait…she needed to think. They had come here straight from the restaurant. She hadn't had a chance to consider her options.

Options? A voice inside her head screamed the word. What options did she have other than to tell the truth? She had taken an oath when she'd joined Option Zero. There were to be no secrets, no hidden agendas within the team. To have complete faith and trust in each other, full disclosure had to be made.

Over the years, it had become obvious that secrets had been kept. And hadn't she judged others for that? Hadn't she been angry when she'd learned that Jules, Ash's wife, had lied about her identity? Or when she'd learned that Hawke was still alive and Ash had known? Even Eve's secret about her family had caused a minor tug of betrayal. She had questioned why Eve would have kept such a secret.

And yet, here she was, keeping her own, very serious secret. One that had major implications for their current operation. That her brother was possibly involved with the Wren Project was monumental. She owed them the truth.

But what about Brody? Didn't she owe him her allegiance, too? He had taken care of her, protected her. He had been her hero.

But he had left her to fend for herself. No fourteen-year-old with zero experience or street savviness should be abandoned. For two years, until Kate Walker had found her, she had survived on the streets of Chicago. The fear and dread of that time still sometimes woke her up at night with terrifying nightmares that were all too real.

How did she weigh her love and devotion to her brother against his abandonment? OZ was her new family, her only family. How could she not tell them? But what if she did tell them and they found him? What if he hurt one of them? She couldn't take that risk. She had to find him first. There was no other way.

"Jazz, you okay?"

Jerked out of her thoughts, she glanced around at her teammates, who were all looking at her as though she'd lost her mind. And with good reason. Without being conscious of it, she had stood and moved several feet away from the table where'd they'd all gathered. She didn't know if she'd been trying to flee or make an announcement. All she knew was her team was looking for an explanation for her odd behavior, and this was the moment of truth.

Placing her hand on her stomach, she whispered hoarsely, "Sorry. Stomach issues." Feeling like a total coward and traitor, she took off down the hallway toward the bathroom.

BOTH SERENA and Eve stood to go after her. Xavier held up his hand to stop them. "I don't think it's her stomach. I said something to upset her earlier, and she's dealing with it."

"What are you talking about?" Eve said. "What did you do?"

"I'd like to know that as well." The heat in Ash's glare could start a forest fire. Fortunately, Xavier was strong enough to withstand the intensity. Did he regret cornering Jazz and forcing a conversation she hadn't wanted? No, he didn't. Did he wish it hadn't been necessary? Yeah, definitely.

"I confronted her about finding her brother."

Gideon groaned and shook his head.

Ash cursed softly and then snarled, "We talked about this and agreed to let her face it in her own time."

"Wait," Hawke said. "What am I missing here? I thought the team had been looking for Jazz's brother since she came on board. What's changed?"

"Nothing's changed, and that's the problem," Xavier said. "She won't ask for a full-on OZ investigation."

Eve's forehead furrowed with concern. "Why's that, do you think?"

"We've always known that Jazz has trust issues," Serena said. "Which, considering what she's been through, is understandable."

Xavier shifted in his chair. Even though he was the one who'd started this conversation, he was feeling damn uncomfortable talking about his partner without her in the room.

"Maybe we need to do some kind of intervention," Eve said. Turning her gaze toward Xavier, she added, "Gently and respectfully."

Yeah, he got the message.

"Not tonight. I've already upset her. Having that conversation now will only make her feel like we're ganging up on her."

"Which we would be," Eve replied dryly. "Why don't you let Serena and me take a shot at it?" She raised her hand and added, "Soon. Not now."

"Agreed," Ash said. "Just do it in a way that shows she has our total support, not like she's being interrogated with no way out."

Okay, yeah, that was another poke at him again. Ash was pissed and likely wouldn't let it lie until they had a one-on-one. Xavier didn't necessarily disagree with his boss's assessment. Didn't mean he hadn't done the right thing. He'd learned a long time ago that sometimes you had to do what you hated to get the results you needed.

CHAPTER SIX

Seattle

His steps controlled and precise, the assassin opened the door and walked into the hotel room. Outwardly, there was no indication of the chaos erupting inside him.

He grabbed a burner out of his stash and dropped into a chair. The only sign of any kind of turmoil was the heavy sigh he gave before pressing a series of numbers.

The call was answered before the first ring ended. "Identification?" the female voice said.

"0025413."

The instant he finished reciting the numbers, he heard a soft hitch, and then her voice gentled as she said, "Hold, please."

He didn't know who she was, knew nothing about her... didn't even know her first name. What he did know was she was the only pleasant thing in his life. They'd never had a real conversation, but for some reason, he felt closer to her than anyone else in this cursed life he lived.

She could be an octogenarian with ten great-grandchildren, but in his mind's eye, she was perfect—wavy blond hair, camellia complexion, and a smile as soft as a rose petal. The Southern drawl was almost undetectable, but when she said *please*, he heard a trace of the South, and it always soothed him.

The good feeling lasted only a second, because the next voice was as pleasant as a bullfrog. "Report."

With the same emotionless voice he used each time, he snapped, "Target down."

"Excellent. Any problems?"

"Negative."

"The funds have been transferred."

He listened carefully for any inflection or hesitation in the emotionless, almost-robotic tone. Did they know anything? There was only a slight easing of tension in his body when he detected nothing.

"We will be in touch." On that abrupt note, the call ended.

With practiced efficiency, he quickly disassembled the burner and broke the SIM card in half. Taking another burner from the stash, he made another call.

The instant the call was answered, he growled, "Jazz was there."

Shocked silence followed and then, "Did she see you?"

"Yes."

"And she recognized you." It wasn't a question. Of course Jazz had recognized him. She hadn't seen his face, but that didn't matter. He had seen the recognition in her expression. In a flicker of seconds, he'd also seen all the other emotions, like pain, fear, and deep disappointment. Each one had pierced his soul.

"What do you want to do?"

What could he do? Nothing, absolutely nothing.

"I need OZ to back off."

More silence, this time followed by a sigh. "The team makes those decisions."

"You owe me."

Okay, yeah, that might be a bit of a stretch. It had been a mutually beneficial relationship, but in this, they shared a common goal.

"I'll see what I can do."

The line went dead.

By rote, he disassembled the burner and put it with the other one. Rising, he stuffed his toiletries into his duffel, grabbed the phone parts, and exited the room. He'd been here for two days. Way too long.

It was time to move on.

CHAPTER SEVEN

Jazz stared numbly at the stack of pancakes in front of her. Why had she thought she could eat? She had gone to bed last night with rocks in her stomach that now felt like boulders. She'd gotten almost no sleep, with nightmares waking her every few moments. Though the nightmares had changed up each time, they all consisted of the same horror—OZ and Brody in a deadly shootout. In some, a member of her OZ family was shot. In some, Brody was killed. In one, Xavier made a daring maneuver to capture Brody and was shot point-blank…by her brother.

In the last nightmare, everyone was dead, and she was walking through a yard strewn with the dead bodies of her OZ family and Brody. Too afraid to close her eyes again, she had gotten out of bed after that one.

When Xavier had knocked on her door to see if she wanted to go down for breakfast, she had already been dressed and had eagerly agreed. Getting out of the hotel room had seemed vitally important.

Last night, after the meeting with the team, they'd barely spoken to each other. The moment they'd gotten back to their

49

hotel, without a word to Xavier other than a muttered, "Good night," she had gone straight to her room and locked her door. Maybe it had been cowardly of her, but she had needed to be alone.

Allowing herself to think about the way she had hoped their evening would end had been too painful to even contemplate. Their kiss before they'd left for the restaurant had been what she had hoped was the beginning of something bright and beautiful. But that dream was gone, dead like so many other dreams she'd once had. There was no way she and Xavier could ever have more than what they had now. And if she kept going down this secretive path, even that would be destroyed.

She had never kept a secret from him. Or the team. Yes, she had prevaricated a time or two when she'd been questioned about her past and what she had endured. The darkness that came with those memories was best buried deep in an abyss. She never wanted them to see the light of day again. But this was completely different. This secret involved an ongoing OZ mission. Keeping such significant intel to herself went against everything she believed in.

And still, when she'd had the opportunity to reveal all, she had kept quiet.

Brody, her gentle, caring, overprotective brother, was a killer. She simply could not wrap her head around that fact. What could have happened to completely transform his personality? People didn't just change like that.

Was this why he had disappeared? Had he been kidnapped and brainwashed? That might seem like a ridiculous premise, but it was no more unbelievable than the idea that her gentle, loving brother was a paid assassin. It just didn't seem possible.

Did this go all the way back to Arthur and his search for them? She hadn't thought about that creep in years, but had he had something to do with Brody's disappearance? If so, why?

What could the man have gotten from either of them? It made no sense.

A large male hand appeared in her line of vision, touching her wrist gently. "I'm sorry, Jazz. I had no idea what I said to you last night at the restaurant would have this kind of effect on you."

Dragging her attention back to the present, she stared at the man across from her. If anyone would understand what she was going through, it would be Xavier. Her partner might be a badass undercover operative with eight-pack abs and muscles for days, but he somehow got her. The moment they'd met, she'd felt a connection with him, as if they'd known each other in a different life.

That connection had saved their lives numerous times, but when it came to Brody, that connection failed them. She knew he understood her love for her brother and her need to find him, but there was always a tension between them when they talked about Brody. Xavier had never hidden how he felt. It angered him that her brother had left her…that he had abandoned her. But he hadn't known Brody, didn't know how caring and protective he had been.

Last night, when Xavier had confronted her about not asking the entire OZ team to search for him had been the first time he'd pushed her. She and Xavier were often blunt to the point of pain with each other. They were both strong-willed, opinionated people, and that had always worked well for them. The subject of her brother was one line Xavier refused to change his mind on.

"I don't think I've ever hated your brother as much as I do right now."

Her head snapped up. "What?"

"Well, at least that got you to look at me."

"What gives you the right to hate him? You don't know him."

51

"He abandoned you. That's all I need to know."

"You don't know what happened to him. He never would have left if he'd had a choice."

"And you're sure of this?"

No.

And that had been the crux of her reluctance to bring the entire OZ team in on finding him, the seed of doubt that he had left her willingly. What if she had been a liability to Brody in more ways than one? As much as she wanted to believe he hadn't voluntarily abandoned her, she feared that he'd wanted to wash his hands of a responsibility that never should have been his in the first place. They weren't related by blood. Just because his dad married her mom shouldn't have forced him to feel responsible for her. Maybe he'd realized that and decided to cut out on his own.

Even as she had the thought, she felt guilty for even going there. No brother had ever been more loyal or caring than Brody. And now, knowing that he had assassinated Bass, she knew her original fears were real—something awful must have happened to change him so completely.

What would happen if she told Xavier that Brody had been the shooter? OZ would go after him. While he needed to be found, what could happen once he was found was what terrified her. Those nightmares she'd had might become all too real.

No. She had to find him on her own. Once she did, she would persuade him to go with her to OZ so they could work this out together. The only way to make sure everyone stayed safe was if she found him first.

"I'm going to take a leave of absence from OZ."

His expression was a mixture of shock and regret. "What? Why? Because of what I said? Jazz...sweetheart—"

"No...not really. But it did get me to thinking that time off would be good for me. Give me some distance. Some perspective."

"You're going to do that now? While we're in the middle of an op?"

"The op got redirected last night because of…" She swallowed hard and continued, "Because of the shooting. All we're doing now is running down leads. Hawke can easily come back and help you out."

"Jazz…no." He took her hand in his and squeezed gently. "Sweetheart, don't do this. Let's work this out together."

The tenderness in his touch, in his eyes, his soft words were almost her undoing. Keeping her emotions in check was the only way she was going to get through this. Xavier meant more to her than anyone in the world, and she trusted him with her life. Unfortunately, she couldn't trust him with her brother's life. Not now.

She gave a brief squeeze to his hand and then pulled away. Getting to her feet, she leaned forward and kissed his cheek. "I'll be in touch."

She turned and sped away, knowing if she didn't move fast, she'd spill her guts.

EVERY FIBER of his being urged Xavier to stop her. His heart slammed heavily against his chest, and his muscles ached from the force of staying seated. This was all on him. He'd pushed her too hard last night. Brody was a hot-button issue for them. And he freely admitted that he wasn't good at hiding how he felt about her deadbeat brother.

She had practically run out of the restaurant, making it more than clear that she wanted to get away from him.

Maybe this time off would be good for her. After she'd almost died in that op in Zambia, everyone had urged her to stay off for a few more weeks, but she had refused. He and Ash had both agreed that while Jazz hadn't been fully healed, she needed to work. Everyone at OZ had demons they fought on a daily basis. Staying focused on a case helped keep those demons at bay. He'd been there, done that. Scar tissue from a thousand hurts had toughened him up, and he'd learned to deal. Working helped Jazz deal, too.

Guilt ate at him because he knew he was the biggest reason she needed time away. He stood, threw down enough money to pay the bill along with a generous tip, and strode out the door. Five seconds later, his phone buzzed, and he didn't even have to check the screen to know the identity of the caller.

"Hawke will be there by midnight."

The grimness in Ash's voice told him everything he needed to know. His boss was pissed.

"It was her decision, Ash."

"Yeah, and you didn't help the situation, did you?"

He already felt like a shithead. Having his boss confirm his thoughts didn't help.

"No, I didn't," Xavier admitted. "What'd she tell you?"

"Just that she needs time off. You know Jazz. She's not one to share more than the bare minimum."

And that was the heart of the problem. He probably knew more about Jazz than anyone at OZ, and still he felt as though he'd yet to scratch the surface. She kept so much of her thoughts and feelings to herself.

"Maybe this time away will give her the impetus to finally go after him for real."

"Yeah, maybe," Ash said. "We just need to give her what she needs. Whatever that is, without judgment." Before Xavier could delve too deeply into those stinging words, Ash switched gears and said, "Serena pulled the camera footage around the restaurant."

"Let me guess. It shows nothing."

"Yeah. Inside and out. Feed cut off for about ten minutes."

"How far of an area did she go out?"

"Five blocks. Did find an ATM camera that got a brief shot of the SUV Jazz described. Windows were tinted. Couldn't see a thing. Not able to see a license plate."

"Okay. I'll head over to the restaurant and start the interviews. The police have anything?"

"Guess you haven't looked at your OZ alerts."

Xavier cursed silently as he clicked the link. He'd heard a notification at the restaurant, but it had come in the middle of Jazz's announcement, and he had ignored it. He was definitely off his game.

Xavier quickly read the alert.

Shootout in Cedar Park, about an hour outside Seattle. The man suspected of killing Franco Bass was shot and killed by the FBI.

Shaking his head in disgust, Xavier held the phone to his ear. "That was quick."

"Yeah. They're saying he was a disgruntled former employee, always a good ploy."

"Happens so often nobody gives it a second look."

"All tied up with a pretty bow."

"Okay. I'll start digging."

It'd been a while since he'd done an investigation without Jazz. He already missed her intelligent wit and dry sense of humor. He'd give her a week and then reach out to her. Whether she wanted to admit it or not, she needed her OZ family. She needed him.

And yes, he definitely needed her.

CHAPTER EIGHT

Chicago, Illinois

Kevin Doyle forced himself to ignore the buzz of the restaurant two floors below and concentrate on the massive amount of work he needed to do. Usually, he could drown out the noise, but a wedding party had rented out the large private room, and the majority of the attendees were apparently already three sheets to the wind.

He didn't have to be here. He, in fact, had an entire floor of offices twelve blocks away where he could have all the quiet and privacy he needed. But this restaurant had belonged to his family for decades. It had seen them through many hardships, and for sentimental reasons, he did the bulk of his work here. Plus, it was an excellent cover for his other not-so-legal activities.

Pulling out a lower desk drawer, he lifted the false bottom and withdrew the ledger. His family laughed at him for not putting his accounts online like a twenty-first-century businessman, but he didn't trust technology. Prisons were filled with people who'd been careless and trusted their life's work to cyberspace, where hackers were just waiting to dig into your business either to steal from you or ruin you. No, thank you very much. Pen and paper had been good enough for his ancestors. They were good enough for him.

Burying himself in the numbers and shipments of his warehouse imports, he successfully drowned out the drunken noise below.

An hour later, the pounding on the door was a welcome distraction. The familiar knock—two hard, one soft— made him roll his eyes and sigh. The man was so predictable. "Come in, Oscar."

The chunky man stomped inside. He was huffing and puffing, and that was likely because he'd walked up only nine steps to get here. The man was in pisspoor physical shape, but he was loyal, and he was family, so Kevin gave him a pass he might not give to someone else.

"You busy?" Oscar wheezed.

"I'm always busy. What do you need?"

"I got something I think you're going to want to see. May be nothing, or it may be something. Something big."

Oscar had a way of delivering news. It was occasionally entertaining, but most of the time it was beyond irritating.

"All right. What is it?"

"You heard about that rich guy getting his head blown off last night?"

"Franco Bass? Yes." The assassination had been all over the news ad nauseam. Twenty-four-seven news cycles made sure everyone, including the family pets, had heard the story at least a dozen times. The killing hadn't been a surprise. Everyone in the criminal world had known Bass had been living on borrowed time. The man himself, however, had apparently never gotten that memo.

"Somebody filmed the whole thing."

"Yes, I've seen the footage." Watching someone get killed held no mystery or interest to him. He'd seen that dozens of times and had been the perpetrator for most of them.

"Well, somebody filmed the audience, not the actual kill."

Trust Oscar to call witnesses to a shooting *the audience*. "And?"

"There's something you need to see." With that, Oscar pulled his phone from his pocket, swiped his finger over the screen a few times, and then handed it to him.

Despite his irritation at Oscar's penchant for drama, Kevin found himself intrigued. The gleam in his brother-in-law's eyes told him something monumental was about to be revealed.

Kevin watched the scene unfold on the phone's screen. So far, it was just overdressed men and women sitting at various tables. Some were eating, some were talking, a few were laughing. Upscale elevator music played in the background. There was an indistinct buzzing that, based on his experience, resulted from dozens of muted conversations joined together in a cacophony of sound.

The camera feed covered most of the restaurant. There was a slight pause in sound, as if everyone stopped talking at once. Then Franco Bass appeared within the view of the camera as he walked into the restaurant. Interestingly enough, the camera didn't stay on Bass, but once again panned the room, perhaps to give the viewer the opportunity to see the impact the man's appearance had on the patrons. In the background, Kevin noticed the buzzing noise increase, indicating the excited chatter. The camera continued panning the restaurant.

Kevin was about to growl his frustration at not seeing whatever Oscar wanted him to see when the camera swept past a couple seated at a small table in the corner. It was only a flash before the camera moved on, but Kevin immediately spotted exactly what Oscar was so excited about.

His heart pounding, he snapped, "Rewind it. Let me see it again."

Oscar grabbed the phone, swiped a few times, and handed it back to Kevin.

The feed had been stopped, freezing on an attractive young couple. His pounding heart stopped, and his breath left his body.

"Looks just like her, doesn't it?" Oscar whispered. "And she's about the right age, too. That's got to be her, don't you think?"

Mesmerized, Kevin shut out Oscar's yammering and focused on the woman. Hair the color of midnight, glowing skin the shade of a light pink rose, a pointed, dainty chin, a heart-shaped face, and dark brown eyes with a hint of gold in their depths. Small, petite, and delicate looking. Sheer perfection.

Admittedly, he had seen and enjoyed many beautiful women in his fifty-five years, some just as lovely as this woman. Beauty was fleeting—it would fade and dry up. But blood? That was what mattered. And it was her blood that he wanted. This beauty could bring him to heights he'd only ever dreamed to reach.

"Too bad Ryan is married," Oscar said. "She'd be perfect for him."

Ryan? Kevin held back a huff. His straight-as-an-arrow son wouldn't know what to do with this gift. Despite all of Kevin's urgings and occasional beatings, Ryan had turned away from his legacy. He didn't deserve to reap the reward this beauty would bring.

Ideas and scenarios raced through his head. He had a lot to

think about, a lot to do. His first order of business would be to ensure that she didn't get away. Not this time.

"Guess she isn't dead after all," Oscar continued to prattle. "We looked high and low for her, though."

Of course she hadn't been dead. No one had believed that. But that had been during one of the darkest times in their organization's history. They had been too busy trying to survive to concern themselves with one little girl, no matter how valuable she was to them. They were now on stable ground, but they were still fractured—the cohesiveness they'd once enjoyed had been demolished. This one woman could change all of that. She could change everything. She could reunite them all and bring about a revolution.

A revolution that he would lead.

Not taking his eyes away from her face, Kevin asked, "Do we know where she is?"

"Not yet. Still in Seattle, hopefully. I've already dispatched Miles and Kip. They're like bloodhounds. They'll find her."

Yes, they would. In the meantime, he had a lot of things to work out.

"What do you want them to do about the big guy?" Oscar asked.

"What big guy?"

"The man with her. They seem pretty familiar with each other. The way he's looking at her, I figure he's sweet on her."

Hmm. He'd been so focused on the woman, he'd shut everything else out, including the man at the table with her.

He handed the phone back to Oscar. "Play it again."

Oscar backed up the footage and shoved the phone back beneath Kevin's gaze. When his eyes rested on the man, he saw something familiar—not because he knew the man. No, this was an instinctive awareness. Like recognized like. This man might be dressed in expensive togs, but he was no pretty boy.

Whoever this guy was, he was dangerous. Meaning he wouldn't give up easily. If they snatched the girl, the man wouldn't rest until he'd found her.

"Get rid of him."

"You want 'em to go ahead and grab the girl, too?"

"Absolutely. That's the first order of business. We can't risk losing her."

"She's a little older than Malcolm's son, but stuff like that don't matter much anymore. I hear he's got a girlfriend, but I'm sure he'd come around. She'll be a welcome addition to the family."

Marrying the girl off to a distant relative was not going to happen. This was too big of an opportunity to pass off to someone who wouldn't appreciate what they had.

Oscar was fishing, and as much as Kevin appreciated this being brought to his attention, there was no way in hell he was going to share with anyone his plans for the girl. Especially not his brother-in-law. No one could know until it was fait accompli.

Placing a friendly arm around Oscar's shoulders, Kevin led him to the door. "You did good, man. There will be a little extra something in your bank account this month."

"Thanks, Kev. Glad I could help. Let me know if there's anything else you need me to do."

"Let me know the instant you secure her. I'll have a place ready."

"Sure thing."

"Oh, and, Oscar? She may not come willingly, but tell them she's not to sustain one bruise. Understand?"

"Sure thing. These guys are professionals." He grinned and added, "Besides, how much trouble can a little thing like her cause?"

The door had barely closed before Kevin was back at his desk. He was a meticulous and organized man who planned his actions ahead of time. Taking a new notepad and pen from his top drawer, he began to jot down a list of things he needed to accomplish. He stared at the third item on the list, drew in a breath, and flipped the page. That one would require a list of its own. At the top of the blank page, he gave the new list a title: *Get Rid of Current Wife*.

CHAPTER NINE

J azz walked into her motel room and threw the keys to her rental car on the desk. She'd seen the OZ alert about the man in the next town over who had been fingered as the shooter. The "killer" had made it too easy for them. Ranting like an idiot on social media about how much you hated someone was never a good look, but when that person ended up murdered? A few planted clues, some doctored video, a quiet whisper to federal law enforcement, and voilà, a murderer was found.

Police had surrounded his home. Cornered and probably seeing no way out, the guy had reacted exactly how they'd likely predicted. The shootout had been massive and deadly. The supposed perpetrator was now dead, and as far as the world was concerned, Franco Bass's homicide case was closed.

Option Zero knew better, and they were still on the case. Jazz knew better, too. Whoever the guy had been, he had not been the one to fire the bullet that killed Bass. She knew without a doubt that that man was Brody McAlister.

Since the case was closed, investigating under the radar would take a bit more stealth than usual. Especially since

Xavier and Hawke would be asking the same questions. The last thing she wanted was to run into them. Explaining why she was still on the case would be impossible.

Her first order of business after grabbing her stuff from the suite she and Xavier had been sharing had been to rent a car and drive in the direction Brody had taken after the shooting. Though it seemed like a lame first step, she had wanted to get it out of the way. The thinking time had been good for her. She now had a plan of action.

A couple of hours ago, she had been fortunate to find a friendly, extremely chatty sous-chef named Hannah, who happened to be walking out LuLu's back door seconds after Jazz had parked in the alley. The girl had been more than happy to sit down with a cup of coffee and a slice of pie at a nearby diner and share what she knew. Jazz got the impression the shooting was the most exciting event that had ever happened to Hannah.

In the midst of the conversation, she'd told Jazz that a member of their kitchen staff, a man who'd been working there for over two months, had disappeared right after the shooting, and the phone number he'd given was no longer working. Hannah was concerned that the shooting had traumatized him. After the vague description she gave of the man, named Brian Mitchell, it was obvious that Hannah would never hear from him again—and it confirmed to Jazz that the kitchen aide had indeed been her brother.

The fact that he'd worked at the restaurant for two months prior to Bass's assassination was interesting but not that much of a surprise. The people behind the killing were definitely long-range planners. The minute Bass had signed up with the Wren Project, he'd had an expiration date.

She took a long breath and let her eyes roam the cheap, nondescript room. The motel was a no-frills and low-profile establishment, which was what she needed. It was also located across town from the restaurant, so there was no way she would run into anyone from OZ.

Earlier, she had scoured the internet for footage of the shooting. Thanks to modern technology and the age of social media, there were numerous videos of the event. She'd even found one with a three-second blip of her and Xavier at their table. She had sent Serena a text to let her know so it could be taken down. Serena had responded that she was already working on it.

Even though she and Xavier weren't in hiding, it was never a good idea for any OZ member to appear on social media. Option Zero operated best under a cloak of anonymity, with all their operatives staying as low-key as possible.

Now, after her preliminary finding, she knew one thing for sure. She couldn't do this alone. Brody, who had managed to stay off the radar all this time, now had more incentive than ever to stay hidden. He had to know she was looking for him, and based on the look he'd given her, he would not want her to find him.

She had only one choice. There was one person outside OZ who could give her the access she needed. The woman who'd saved her all those years ago and brought her into this life of intrigue.

Dropping into the chair by the window, Jazz grabbed one of her burner phones and punched in a series of numbers. Despite her wealth and influence, Kate Walker was all about secrecy and staying off the grid as much as possible.

"Jazz. It's wonderful to hear from you." Kate's warm and welcoming voice always gave her heart a lift.

"How are you, Kate?"

"I'm good. Little project keeping me busy."

That *little project* was the one they'd all been working on for over three years now. Kate was right in the thick of gathering intel on the Wren Project, the übersecretive organization they'd discovered almost by accident. It was the biggest operation OZ had ever taken on, and thankfully Kate, with her connections and wealth, was able to provide an enormous amount of assistance.

"Any progress?"

"Some. Not enough."

That was all Kate was likely to give her. Talking about the Wren Project on an unsecure line was not a good idea.

"So what's up with you?" Kate asked. "Talked to your boss, and he told me you saw an interesting event occur."

Interesting in more ways than one.

"As a matter of fact, that's why I'm calling, but I need you to keep this on the down-low. Will you do that for me?"

Jazz had never asked anyone to keep a secret. She had, in fact, deeply resented any secrets that had been kept from her by her OZ team members. And here she was doing it herself. But this couldn't be helped. She couldn't do what she needed without Kate's assistance, and she couldn't share this with the team. Not yet. Once she found Brody and was able to talk with him, then she would tell them everything. She could only pray they would understand.

"How low are we talking?" Kate asked.

Grimacing, Jazz said softly, "All the way."

The pause that followed was justified. It was a big ask. Kate was not only a good friend to everyone at OZ, she was godmother to Jules and Ash's son.

Jazz already owed Kate so much. She had no idea where she would be if not for Kate, or even if she would still be alive. Kate had found her on the street, fed, clothed, educated, and trained her. But Kate also knew that Jazz would never ask this of her without good reason.

Her tone businesslike and solemn, Kate said, "Call me back on my other line."

"Understood."

Ending the call, Jazz grabbed another burner and punched in the digits she'd memorized long ago.

Kate answered before the first ring ended. "What the hell, Jazz?"

"I know I'm asking a lot."

"Yes, you are. What do you need?"

"The camera footage inside and outside the restaurant."

There was only the slightest pause before Kate answered, "I can get you the footage that's been posted on social media, but the cameras inside and outside the restaurant were disabled."

That was a disappointment but not a surprise. With a professional hit like this, disabling the cameras was to be expected.

"Okay, any footage you can send me would be good. How about traffic cams?"

"Disabled for a three-block perimeter surrounding the restaurant."

Also not a surprise.

"Can you send me camera footage outside that blockage? Maybe about five blocks?"

"Yes. Should I ask why?"

"It's best if you don't."

She was already violating protocol by going to Kate directly for intel, and she refused to add to her sins by telling Kate about Brody being the shooter. This was her secret to keep for now.

"All right. What else do you need?"

"That's it for right now."

"Jazz, you know you can trust your team."

"I know that, Kate. I just…" She shook her head, unable to explain without giving more information than she could. "I just need to do this on my own for right now."

"All right. I've said my piece. I'll send it to you within the hour. Let me know if you need anything else."

Unable to continue the conversation because of the developing lump of emotion in her throat, Jazz said thickly, "Thank you, Kate." She quickly ended the call before she did something stupid, like spill her guts.

Her stomach churning with acid, Jazz stared at the bland walls of the room, her mind racing with questions. What had changed Brody so much? Years ago, he'd been the most protective, loving, compassionate person anyone could imagine. He'd taken such good care of her.

She vividly remembered one particular event. She'd been thirteen years old and had gotten her first period. They were living above the strip joint by then, thankfully having escaped Arthur and his sleazy friends. It had been far from a good environment for two teenagers, but they had been safe from Arthur, and that had been their goal.

Telling Brody about her first menstrual period hadn't been something she'd been prepared to do. She had put it off for as long as she could. But Brody had made it so easy for her once she'd worked up the courage to tell him. There had been the briefest moment of panic on his face, and then he'd covered it with his usual calm attitude and said in his matter-of-fact way, "No problem, Jazzy. What do you need?"

She had stumblingly told him what she thought she needed. Since she'd never purchased feminine hygiene products before, she had been mostly guessing. His face filled with purpose, he'd left. Within the hour he'd returned with pads, Midol, a heating pad she knew they couldn't afford, and a little book that described the process. He confessed he'd found a sympathetic pharmacist who'd assisted him in getting her what she needed.

That was the brother Jazz knew and loved. Whatever she'd needed, he had provided. Even when they'd had almost no money and little hope for anything getting better, Brody had made sure she knew she could depend on him for anything.

And now, apparently, he was not only an assassin, but he also worked for the Wren Project.

She knew she'd set herself up for a monumental task. And even when she found her brother, he might not even be receptive to seeing her. That wouldn't stop her from trying, though. She owed him this chance.

But first she had to find him.

Grabbing her laptop, she opened it and got to work. Two hours later, she had combed every inch of video footage Kate had sent her. It had been a bust. She thought she saw a shadow of a dark SUV about four blocks from the restaurant, but it had apparently been just a blip in the recording, because she could find it nowhere else.

She was rapidly learning how much she relied on Serena providing the intel she needed to do her job. She and Xavier were good investigators, but they worked with more intel than a half-thimble full, and that was exactly what she had.

Simultaneous hits of weariness and hopelessness almost swamped her. She hadn't slept more than a few hours since she'd seen Brody. And though her nerves made her queasy, she knew she needed food to keep her going.

With more determination than energy, she grabbed her keys and wallet. She'd find an all-night diner and get some sustenance. Even if she ate only a few bites, getting out of this room would give her a new perspective.

On the way to the door, she glanced in the mirror where a petite, pale girl with big brown eyes, short, black hair, and a smattering of freckles stared back at her. No one would recognize her as the sophisticated woman from two nights ago. She enjoyed dressing up as much as the next girl, and wearing designer clothing that cost more than a year's worth of groceries was always fun, but it wasn't her. She usually dressed in jeans, a T-shirt, and her favorite sneakers. For years, she'd had almost nothing, and though she could now have just about anything one could buy, material things still didn't mean much to her. She still lived simply, and when it came to clothes, comfort was key.

An unusual flash of insecurity hit her. She had been attracted to Xavier for years, but he'd never given her any idea he'd thought of her as anything other than his OZ partner and a good friend. Though she had often ached to tell him how she felt, she'd known it would not only change their partnership forever, but if he didn't reciprocate the attraction, it would likely destroy their friendship. So she had never tried to pursue anything and had gone to great pains to hide her feelings. Until the other night.

When he'd appeared, looking like a bearded and sexier version of Henry Cavill, she had almost swooned. Hiding her thoughts had been nearly impossible. But then she'd seen the gleam of attraction in his eyes and totally forgotten about caution. But now she was questioning that. Had his attraction been because of how she'd looked that night? How she'd been dressed so glamorously? Xavier wasn't a shallow, superficial man, but he had never acted that way with her before.

She scrunched her nose at her plain reflection. Maybe she should start taking more pains with her appearance.

At that thought, she rolled her eyes. She had a thousand and one things on her mind. Being concerned with how attractive she looked should be the least of her worries.

Giving herself one last glance, she opened the door and stepped out onto the pavement. Uneasiness hit her in a flash. With her hand still on the door, she swiped her keycard to return to her room. A rush of air blew across her skin, and she knew she was too late.

Ready to meet the danger head on, she whirled around. The four large men standing before her gave her pause.

She was in major trouble.

CHAPTER TEN

A gony drummed throughout Jazz's body. What was going on? Was she sick, or had she been involved in an accident? Her head felt overlarge and pounded like a jackhammer.

She tried to remember what had happened, but her mind was a complete blank. With the greatest effort, she managed to squint her eyelids open. Though her vision was blurred, she could make out a large bedroom. From what she was able to see, it was beautifully and expensively decorated, which meant she was neither in the small, ratty motel room she'd been staying in, nor was she at her apartment in Montana.

Where was she? And what on earth had happened?

Swallowing past a sudden wave of nausea, she closed her eyes and forced herself to focus on what she could remember.

She had been in Seattle, trying to find a lead on Brody. She had run out of ideas and decided she needed a meal to keep going. She had opened her motel room door and sensed immediate danger. She'd been about to go back into the room when she'd felt someone behind her. She had turned—and faced four large men.

Things got even blurrier after that.

She knew she had fought like hell, like she'd been taught. She knew she had caused some damage. Remembered the sounds of broken bones, busted noses, and violent curses each time she'd hit her mark. But as hard as she had fought, she had lost. As much as she hated to make excuses, four against one was unfair.

She remembered her head slamming against a wall, which had momentarily stunned her. They had taken advantage of that, because she also remembered a sting in her neck. Had she been drugged?

She lightly touched the back of her head and winced, feeling the goose egg. Yeah, there it was, and it hurt.

Requiring more effort than she liked, she gingerly sat up on the bed. The room whirled around her, and she swallowed hard to beat down the nausea. She had never had a concussion, but the signs were all there. So were the symptoms of being drugged. She had a feeling it was a double whammy. Underneath the nausea and pain, a fury of epic proportions was boiling within her. Whoever had done this was going to suffer monumental regret before this was over. This she swore.

Pulling in a breath to center herself and suppress the ill feeling, she searched for clues about where she was. The room was quite beautiful, easily the size of her entire apartment. The bed was the largest one she'd ever seen—extra king-sized maybe? The floor was a dark hardwood, the walls were creamy eggshell, the crown molding a slightly darker shade, and the artwork was exquisite. Whoever had taken her was apparently very wealthy.

And now for the two billion-dollar questions: Who had taken her and why?

She took another breath and allowed her training to squash her anxiety. Compartmentalizing her circumstances would help her focus. She started with the positive. She was alive. She was still wearing her clothes, so no sexual assault. Judging by the appearance of the room, her captor wanted her to be comfortable, at least for now. She also noted several bottles of water and a plate covered with a dome, so she wasn't to be starved either.

Now for the negative. She had been taken by an unknown person, or persons. The men who had abducted her hadn't been reluctant to hurt her. Which meant what? That if she didn't comply or obey, she would be punished or killed?

Moving on from that speculation, she continued her mental list and grimaced as the absolute worst negative moved to the forefront. No one knew where she was. Removing her tracking chip had made sense at the time, and she had not done it lightly. As an OZ operative, she was required to have one. She had even soundly criticized other OZ members for removing theirs, thinking how irresponsible they'd been. But she had known that if she was going to find Brody without anyone knowing, she'd had no choice but to hide her whereabouts. And now, because of that, she was on her own.

A noise outside the door jerked her out of her self-flagellation. Setting her jaw, she braced for whatever she would face as the door opened.

A tall, slender man with thinning brown hair and a smarmy smile entered. Jazz had no idea who he was, but the guy gave off a chilling, evil vibe. Considering he was followed by two of the four goons who'd attacked her, she could only surmise he was the one who gave the orders.

She didn't rise from the bed. As much as she would like to show strength by being on her feet and facing these monsters, throwing up or passing out—both of which were real possibilities—would not help her cause. Compromising, she sat up and settled her expression in a stone-cold glare.

The two goons bore the injuries she'd dealt them, and

despite her circumstances, Jazz felt a burst of pride that she'd been able to do that. One man sported a taped, swollen nose, and she vividly remembered the satisfying crunch she'd delivered. The other man had his arm in a sling and multiple bruises on his face. Where were the other two? She didn't remember killing any of them, but perhaps they weren't able to walk. It lifted her spirits to think she might have incapacitated them.

"Hello, my dear, how are you?" The older man's voice had an abrupt clip to it, as if he was impatient to get the words out.

She didn't answer his ridiculous, mundane question. She had been knocked out and abducted—likely on his orders. He didn't care about her. Besides, giving him anything, even that little bit of information, wasn't going to happen. It had taken her years to learn that silence made people uncomfortable, and they would naturally fill the empty air with chatter. In that chatter, one could learn a wealth of knowledge. Not only that, she knew her voice would be shaky and breathless. Not the strong front she wanted to give off. Her head pounded, and every part of her felt as limp as wilted lettuce. She needed information, and then she would figure out what needed to be done.

He tilted his head as if slightly puzzled that she hadn't answered. "My apologies for the injuries you sustained. That was not supposed to happen. The two men who caused your injuries were local hires and have been severely disciplined."

He sent a look to one of the men, who gave him an abrupt nod and a growling, "Yes, sir."

The older man continued, "These two have assured me they caused you no damage, but they are here to offer you their apologies for hiring such inconsiderate buffoons."

Her memory might be fuzzy, but she clearly remembered these two men were the ones who'd caused her the most pain. The other two might've bruised her up, but the men in front of her had hurt her the most. The one with the busted nose had slammed her head into the wall. She hoped his nose was extremely painful.

Busted-Nose Guy stepped forward. Mean eyes met hers, and the warning within them was clear. Say anything, and he'd get her back. She kept her counsel. Speaking now went against her current plan, but she might play this card later at some point.

"What do you have to say for yourselves, gentlemen?" their boss said.

Both men mumbled, "We're sorry," in unison.

The older man snapped, "Leave."

The goons moved much faster than when they'd walked into the room. Within seconds, they were gone, and she was left with the creepy old guy, who was still smiling at her as if he knew her. He was acting friendly, but his light brown eyes were cold and emotionless.

"You still look quite pale, but I want to assure you that you're going to be fine," he said. "The doctor thought you might have a slight concussion. That, along with the drugs my men were forced to give you, is causing your sickness. For your own good, you'll be confined to this room for the next few days until you recover."

Forced to give her drugs? Confined for her own good?

This guy apparently just liked to hear himself speak, because there was no way she was buying this crap.

When she still didn't respond, a flash of anger crossed his face. "I must say, your refusal to talk is quite troubling. Obedience will be the cornerstone of our relationship. However, as you are likely still in pain, I will forgive the slight for right now."

She couldn't argue with that since her head felt as though someone were hammering on her brain. Until she felt better, there was no point in attempting escape. When she did try, she knew she'd get only one chance. She had to make the most of it. Since it didn't appear he meant her any immediate harm, she would lie low and play the obedient patient.

"You were quite adept at defending yourself. Wherever did you learn those skills?"

When she continued to just stare at him, the smile disappeared, and his face matched the coldness in his eyes. "I was also told you had weapons on you. A gun and a knife. That's quite impressive for a little girl. Do you know how to use them?"

If she hadn't felt so awful, she might've laughed. The guy knew she wasn't going to answer, but he kept on asking questions as if one of them would spark her interest.

The man huffed out a breath, all pretense of politeness gone. "I will return soon, my dear, and you will be required to speak. Until then, rest up."

He stopped at the door and then turned, giving her that smarmy smile again. "I look forward to talking with you soon, Jasmine. Or do you still prefer Jazz?"

She couldn't prevent her gasp, and triumph gleamed in his eyes. He gave her a small, satisfied nod and walked out the door. The clicking of the lock barely registered as she absorbed the information he'd purposely revealed.

He knew her real name.

How? She never carried her real identification with her on a job.

The reason she'd been taken became an even more bizarre mystery.

Covering her face with her hands, Jazz drew in a shaky breath. She was in trouble. Because she'd taken a leave of absence, no one knew she had been taken.

Kate had once told her that her independence and recklessness would one day come back to bite her. Apparently, that day was today.

Jazz forced herself to her feet. She had to get out of this bed and get more intel. There was no telling how much time she had before someone came back. Not knowing her location left her at a huge disadvantage. She needed to know as much as possible, as quickly as possible.

Her head pounded with every step, and nausea swirled within her, bringing bile to her throat. She swallowed and, grinding her teeth, forced herself to the large window across the room. The first glimpse of the view outside gave her a location. She knew the skyline well. She was in Chicago.

Letting that knowledge rattle around in her brain for a moment, Jazz shuffled to the bathroom to take care of her immediate needs.

She splashed her face with water, feeling somewhat more awake. She drew in shaky breaths and took in her appearance. A large bruise covered half her right jaw, and another one bloomed on her chin. She remembered both hits well. The swelling on the back of her head was sore, and her fingers came away with a bit of blood when she gingerly touched the knot.

The rest of her body felt achy and sore, but nothing was broken or sprained. All in all, other than the monstrous headache, nausea, and severe weakness, she'd gotten off fairly lightly.

Jazz returned to the bedroom and peered out the window again. There would be no escape from here. She was easily on the tenth floor, if not higher.

Who were these people, and what did they want with her?

He knew her real name, so this was no random abduction. She had been taken for a specific purpose.

Even though she'd been working secret ops for several years now, none of them would have put a target on Jasmine McAlister. She never used her real name with anyone other than her OZ family.

Her thoughts were fuzzy and too vague to focus.

Stumbling back to the bed, she sat and rubbed her head. This made no sense. She was no one…not really. She had no value to anyone other than her friends. Why would anyone want her?

Could this somehow be related to Brody? Had he gotten involved in something, and her captor was going to use her as leverage?

Her head now felt like it was splitting open. Unable to form another coherent thought, Jazz fell back onto the bed. Her last thought was that there was one man who would tear the world apart to find her. The only problem was, Xavier had no idea she was missing.

CHAPTER ELEVEN

Seattle

Letting go a frustrated sigh, Xavier shoved his fingers through his hair. He shot a look at Hawke, who looked as though he could eat nails. Even though this was largely part of the job, neither he nor Hawke enjoyed interrogation. It was often uninformative and useless. People's memories of events could be so different, little could be learned.

This time, though, they did have a few useful nuggets of information. They knew that the shooter had been a kitchen assistant who'd worked there for almost two months. Going by the name Brian Mitchell, the man was described as a tall, muscular guy. The descriptions after that were varied. Some said he had dark blond hair, piercing green eyes, and a scar on the left side of his face that extended from his brow down to his neck. Others said his hair was more brown than blond, the scar was small and only on his cheek, and was on the right side, not the left. A couple said he walked with a limp. One woman said he had an accent, but she wasn't sure if it was Southern or British.

They all agreed that Mitchell had been soft-spoken, prompt, and reliable. He had also been a loner, rarely talking to his coworkers beyond what was necessary. No one had anything negative to say about him.

The fact that the guy, in plain sight, could change up his appearance in that many ways without anyone really noticing told them what they already knew. He was a professional.

His plan had been a good one. Get hired on a couple of months before his target was scheduled to appear. Establish himself as a loyal, competent employee, and then wait for his mark to show up.

How the assassin knew Bass would be coming to the restaurant on that particular night wasn't hard to figure out. WP had an agenda and connections everywhere. Steering Bass toward the restaurant on a particular day would have been easy. And the poor, clueless devil had taken the bait.

This was their typical method of ridding themselves of the people they either no longer wanted to use or who'd angered them in some way. Who knew which one Bass had been? One would think that, at some point, people would pick up on the fact that there was often an expiration date on their usefulness.

"Who's next?" Hawke asked.

Xavier glanced down at the list and couldn't help but grin. "Red Green."

"Seriously?"

"Yeah. Colorful, eh?"

Hawke's lip moved slightly upward. "Something like that. Let's bring him in."

Going to the door, Xavier called out, "Mr. Green?"

The name of the man who walked through the door was made even more ironic by his almost colorless personality. Youngish, with a shiny bald head, pale blue eyes, and a pasty complexion, he answered in monosyllabic murmurs. Giving more than a one-word answer or a shrug was apparently too much for him.

After interviewing twenty-three members of the kitchen staff, neither Xavier nor Hawke expected any new information about the shooter. This guy could barely get out more than a complete sentence. Xavier decided to send him on his way.

"All right, Mr. Green, thank you for—"

"You do know that they caught the guy who did this, don't you?"

How about that? Mr. Red Green actually could verbalize an entire sentence.

"We're aware, but follow-up is important for a case like this."

The man shrugged his thin shoulders, making Xavier think he was back to one-word answers and shrugs. But then, in a surprise twist, he uttered another coherent statement. "Yeah… whatever. At least that chick I talked to the other day was good to look at."

"Tell us more about this 'chick,'" Hawke said. "Who was she working for?"

"Don't know. She just basically asked the same questions you guys did."

"What did she look like?" Xavier asked.

"Good-looking. Short and kind of skinny. Had short, black hair, dark brown eyes. Classy but kinda hot, too."

Xavier shot a look at Hawke, who was apparently thinking the same thing. Why the hell would Jazz be investigating the shooting on her own? She was supposed to be taking time for herself, not working the op.

Xavier abruptly went to his feet, causing Green to show the first real sign of emotion, which was terror. Xavier knew that his size and scruffy look often intimidated people, and he didn't mind using them to his advantage.

"Thanks for your time, Mr. Green."

Looking more than a little relieved to be released, the man showed a surprising amount of energy as he scooted out of the office. The door had barely clicked shut when Hawke said, "Why would Jazz be running her own investigation? I thought she wanted some time off."

"I have no idea," Xavier said. His self-imposed time limit to contact her wasn't up yet, but that didn't matter now. "But I'm going to find out." Grabbing his phone, he punched in Jazz's number. He wasn't surprised that it went straight to voice mail.

Not bothering to leave a message, he ended the call and immediately called Serena.

"Hey," Serena said. "You guys get something?"

"Maybe. Not sure. Can you do me a favor and find out where Jazz is?"

The chip embedded inside each team member ensured that their location could be identified in seconds.

"Sure. Hold just a sec. Okay…hmm." The silence after that was deafening.

Xavier could sense immediately something was very wrong. "Serena?"

"Let me call you back." In a very un-Serena-like way, she ended the call.

"What's going on?" Hawke asked.

Xavier shook his head as an ominous feeling hit him. "No idea, but it's something. Let's get out of here and find Jazz."

Hawke gave him a curious look. "Have you talked to her since our last meeting?"

"No. I was giving her some space." Which he was now thoroughly regretting.

Xavier followed Hawke out the door, his mind whirling. When she'd said she wanted time off, he had known in his gut that rest and relaxation weren't part of her agenda. He had assumed she'd head back to her apartment in Bozeman. But instead, she was working this case by herself. That made no sense whatsoever.

The sun was a round ball of fire in the sky, and Xavier squinted as he put on his sunglasses. They'd parked at the end of the alley, behind the restaurant. The place had already reopened, and according to several of the employees, they were busier than ever. Seemed Bass's murder had caused a sensation, and everyone wanted to get a glimpse of where the murder had taken place. No doubt about it, people were odd.

He took a step and spotted a penny on the pavement in front of him. A wave of emotions swept through him at the sight. Whenever he saw a penny, his mind always went to his mother.

Sofia Quinn had never left a penny unclaimed. When he was a kid, he'd thought it was because they were so poor and needed every penny to survive. He'd asked her about it one day, and she had quickly disavowed him of that belief. She had told him that every time you see a penny, it meant that God was looking out for you, that He was reminding you to trust Him. She'd shown him the inscription: *In God We Trust*.

Xavier's faith had taken some hard hits over the years. After seeing war in all its bloody horror—the injustice and sheer depravity of what humans could do to one another—he'd been left with the shakiest of beliefs.

Losing his mother suddenly while he was on his second deployment had brought him to his knees, literally. The only person who'd loved him unconditionally had died alone, without the son who adored her at her side. She hadn't told him she was sick. The last time he'd seen her, he'd noticed she'd lost weight and had mentioned it to her. She had shushed him and told him she'd finally found a diet that worked. He had let her change the subject and cursed himself later when he'd realized that the diet she'd praised hadn't existed. It had been the cancer inside her, destroying her.

She had sacrificed so much for him. Working two jobs, as a waitress and a maid, to keep them going. She had also put up with all his stupid-assed teenage crap. Getting in with the wrong crowd in his early teens, he could have easily stayed on the dark side. But when he'd seen the tears rolling down her face because of his stupidity, he had finally cleaned up his act. He'd never felt more like shit than at that moment, and he'd vowed to never cause her another moment of sorrow. Even now, years after her death, he still strove every day to make her proud.

And not once had he passed by a penny and not picked it up. The reminder that he was always being watched over eased him. That thought in his mind, he bent down for the coin.

A loud ping sounded. The brick wall a few feet away exploded.

"Get down!" Xavier shouted. Hitting the ground, he rolled beneath the vehicle in front of him. Another ping sounded. Twisting his head, he searched for Hawke and felt his heart stutter. Hawke lay only half a yard away, blood pouring from a neck wound and already forming a dark pool around his head. Their eyes met.

Xavier heard his friend whisper, "Livvy."

He then watched his eyes dull as they closed.

Scrambling toward him, Xavier shouted, "No!" just as another shot was fired.

CHAPTER TWELVE

UW Medical Center
Seattle

Xavier sat with his head bowed, staring at his hands that were stained with his friend's blood. When he'd dragged Hawke beneath the car with him, he had believed his friend was already gone, but he had refused to let him lie there in the open. Thankfully, Hawke wasn't dead, but he'd been losing blood at a horrific rate. While staunching the blood flow, he'd managed a call to Serena. OZ's contacts were worldwide and vast. Never had Xavier been more grateful for them. Though it seemed like it took a lifetime, it had been only a couple of minutes before help had arrived.

The medics had taken control, and Hawke had been transported to a hospital. Even though he wanted to go after the shooter, Xavier knew the sniper was long gone. When he was sure that Hawke would pull through, he'd go back to the scene. For now, his focus was on his friend.

Blood had been spurting from Hawke's neck like a geyser. Could someone survive that much blood loss?

Olivia was on her way. He could only imagine what was going through her mind. She had just gotten her husband back. Their little girl, Nikki, wasn't even a year old yet. Hawke had confided in him last night that they were trying to get pregnant again so Nikki and her sibling would be close in age. They had a good, beautiful life at last. And now, it could all go away. In the blink of an eye, they could lose everything.

The OZ team was also on their way. They had already lost Hawke once. They wouldn't survive losing him again.

Raising his head, Xavier glared around the empty room. It was starkly, chillingly quiet. Too quiet. Where was everyone? He'd been in multiple hospitals over the years, but this was the emptiest one he'd ever seen. Solitude didn't normally bother him, but at this moment, he'd welcome a mass of people. Instead, he had nothing but his thoughts to torture him.

Every movement he'd made over the last few days replayed with fierce clarity. If he hadn't pushed Jazz about her brother, she wouldn't have taken off on her own. But then what? It could've been her in an operating room, fighting for her life.

That scenario sent an ice-cold chill through him, and he swiftly demolished the image in his mind. No, he could not go there.

Instead, he tried to review what had happened and why. No way was this the same guy who'd killed Bass. The guy should be long gone. Paid assassins didn't hang around and watch the investigation of their crime. They were either far away and holed up somewhere until the dust settled, or they were already focused on their next target.

It had to have been the Wren Project. That much was a given. They'd been after those bastards for several years now, and every step forward they made, they were never close enough. The people behind the Wren Project knew OZ was on to them and that it was just a matter of time before they went down.

Even though his and Jazz's original mission had been a bust, they had witnessed the murder of one of WP's own people. If they could just get their hands on the shooter, they would get an inroad they'd never had before.

And where was Jazz? Why would she be running her own investigation? Had she just felt guilty for leaving abruptly and decided to try to get some intel? That made no sense. She had to know that he and Hawke would be getting the same information.

He pulled out his phone and checked to make sure he hadn't missed any calls from her. There was nothing. Breathing out a frustrated sigh, he tapped out another text, letting her know about Hawke's injury. He'd already left so many voice mails—each one more demanding than the last— that her mailbox was full. Yeah, she'd be pissed at his autocratic demand, but that was fine. Even if she called just to yell at him, at least he'd know she was okay.

A distant, obscure noise brought his head up. When it grew louder, he went to his feet and stared at the double doors leading to the surgical unit. Was this it? Was this the moment he'd been dreading? Was he about to find out that his friend hadn't made it?

When he realized the sound was coming from the other end of the hallway, he blew out a relieved breath. Seconds later, Olivia was striding toward him, her daughter, Nikki, held tight in her arms. Behind her were four people—two men and two women—Xavier didn't recognize.

Olivia's expression was one he'd seen many times through the years. She appeared serene and in control, but the slight wobble of her mouth and the bright sheen in her eyes revealed her inner turmoil and fear. She was holding on to her composure for her daughter, but the terror was there.

She came toward him with unhurried steps, but he knew if Nikki weren't there, she'd be running. A minute before she reached him, Xavier opened his arms. She ran into them, and he held her and her daughter close. He loved her like a sister, and it was breaking his heart to see her hurting.

"How is he?" she whispered.

"Still in surgery."

She pulled back and smiled down at Nikki, who was looking like she might cry any moment. "See, pumpkin? I told you Daddy is fine." She bit her lip and breathed in a shaky breath. Then, clearing her throat, she whispered under her breath, "He's still here. Still with us."

"Yes."

She straightened her shoulders, took another breath, and said, "Xavier, I'd like you to meet my friends. This is Dylan and Jamie Savage. And Cole and Keeley Mathison."

He'd never met any of Olivia's Last Chance Rescue team members, but he recognized Dylan's and Cole's names. Olivia always spoke highly of them. They were both large, tough-looking men. Jamie was a petite, delicate-looking blonde, and Keeley was a tall, curvy brunette.

"Can you tell me what happened?" Olivia said. "Hawke told me last night you guys were basically just interviewing people about the shooting. It didn't sound dangerous."

"It shouldn't have been." He pointed to the seats. "Let's go sit down."

Before they could move, Jamie said, "Liv, why don't you give Nikki to me? Keeley and I will find a vending machine and see if there's anything the munchkin might like."

Gifting her friend a smile, Olivia kissed her daughter on top of her head and said, "Aunt Jamie and Aunt Keeley are going to take you to get a snack."

Grinning her excitement, Nikki held out her arms to Jamie.

The second the women disappeared, Xavier described in detail what had happened.

"You weren't hurt, so were they aiming at Hawke?" Olivia asked.

"I'd bent down to pick something up," Xavier said, "and their first shot missed. The brick wall exploded where my head would've been."

"Thank God you did that."

The thought that his mother had been the one responsible for saving his life wasn't lost on him. He'd take that out and dwell on it later.

"Would it be a problem if we checked out the scene for you?" Mathison asked.

Xavier was territorial by nature, and this was an Option Zero operation. Having operatives from another organization investigating felt weird to him. Recognizing his hesitancy, Cole added, "We won't touch anything. We'll just take photos. Get a feel for how it went down. It might help."

The sooner someone assessed the scene, the better the chances of getting anything useful.

He gave the men a grateful smile. "Much appreciated."

Once he gave them the location, they were gone.

Olivia took a breath and said, "Now, tell me what you're keeping from me."

"Liv…I don't—"

"No, Xavier. I know you're trying to protect me, but the more I know, the better prepared I'll be."

Knowing she was right, he said, "He lost a lot of blood, Liv. More than I've ever seen anyone lose."

"Where did the bullet hit him?"

"Neck."

She closed her eyes, and a tear rolled down her face.

She was hanging on by a thread, and all Xavier could do was squeeze her hand and reassure her with words. "He's a tough SOB, Liv. Toughest I know."

"I know he is. And he's stubborn. So very stubborn."

Xavier swallowed hard and added, "He said your name... just before he lost consciousness."

Though more tears filled her eyes, the beautiful smile she gave him made him glad he'd told her.

They sat in silence, holding vigil and barely breathing as Hawke fought for his life.

CHAPTER THIRTEEN

The waiting room that had once been empty was now filled with more people than it could comfortably hold. The OZ team had arrived. After introductions to Olivia's teammates were made, Ash herded the OZ team into a corner.

A few minutes earlier, a nurse had come by and announced that Hawke was still in surgery and was holding his own. Knowing he was still alive and fighting gave everyone a moment of ease.

Now, Ash wanted answers, and Xavier was ready to focus on finding the bastard who'd tried to kill them.

"Tell us everything," Ash said.

"We were at the restaurant. Since we'd pinpointed that the shooter had worked in the kitchen, we wanted to get more specifics. We were just about to end the last interview when the guy mentioned that a woman had been there earlier, asking the same questions. Described Jazz to a T."

"Jazz?" Gideon's brow furrowed, and he sent a look at both Xavier and Ash. "I thought she took some time off."

"Yeah," Xavier growled. "So did I."

"Okay, let's get back to Jazz in a minute," Ash said. "What happened next?"

"We walked out the door, headed to our vehicle. We'd parked in the alley behind the restaurant. I was about three yards from the car when I heard the shot. Bullet hit the brick wall in front of me."

"So the shooter missed you?" Eve asked. "Seems odd for a professional hit."

As a trained sniper, Eve would know.

"If I hadn't bent down to pick something up, he would've made a good shot to the back of my head."

"What'd you pick up?" Serena asked.

"A penny."

Any other time, he might've been slightly embarrassed to explain to the team what had been a sentimental move. But since it had saved his life, he had no problem saying what had made him bend down. *Thanks, Mom,* he whispered in his head.

"And that's when you heard the first shot?" Gideon verified.

"Yeah. I heard another as I dropped to the ground and rolled beneath the car."

"Where was Hawke?" Eve asked.

"Slightly behind me and to my right. The instant I was under the car, I turned to see that he'd been hit. I grabbed him and pulled him under the car with me."

"So there was another shot while you were getting under the car?" Eve said.

Frowning, Xavier closed his eyes and forced himself to relive those brutal seconds. Opening his eyes, he nodded and said, "Two, then I turned. Then one while I was grabbing him. Another one after we were both beneath the SUV."

"And Hawke was only hit once?"

"Yes."

"So either the shooter wasn't very good or..." Eve said.

"Or what?" Xavier asked.

"Or you were the target and not Hawke."

"Hawke was already down, so the shooter likely wanted to focus on me. Maybe he didn't—"

A sound behind them had a dozen eyes focused on the door that had just opened and the weary-looking woman dressed in scrubs who appeared.

"Mr. Hawthorne's family?" she said.

Olivia quickly stepped forward. "Yes?"

The woman gave a tired smile. "He lost a lot of blood and had to have multiple transfusions, but he should make a full recovery."

A collective sigh of relief swept through the room.

"And the bullet," Olivia said, "left no lasting damage?"

Her brow furrowing, the surgeon shook her head. "He wasn't shot. A projectile—likely a shard of brick— was embedded in his carotid artery. It took hours to remove all the pieces and repair the damage."

So the shooter hadn't gotten even one bullet into either of them. That made no sense.

After reassuring Olivia that she would be able to see her husband as soon as he was moved to a private room, the doctor left. The room exploded with cheers, and a flood of relief rushed throughout Xavier's body. Though he was not usually a pessimist, a huge part of him had believed he had lost his friend.

The celebration lasted for about five minutes, and then Olivia called out to get everyone's attention. "Thank you all. Hawke, Nikki, and I are blessed to have so many people care about us. You're all family to me, and I love you all. But now, please go and find the people who almost killed my husband. I'd like to have a talk with them."

Every adult in the room gave her a nod of approval. They

were family, they loved fiercely, and part of that ferocity was bringing justice to the wicked.

The OZ team went back into operations mode. Earlier, Olivia's coworkers, Dylan Savage and Cole Mathison, had returned from the scene of the shooting with photographs of where Xavier and Hawke had been attacked and where they believed the shooter had been positioned.

Now, Ash gave Dylan and Cole a searching look. "You guys mind going back to the scene with us?"

"Not at all," Cole said.

"We're here to help," Dylan said. "Put us to work with whatever you need."

Thanking them with a nod, Ash swept his gaze over Xavier, Gideon, and Eve. "Let's get to the scene and see what we can see." He then turned to Serena, "I need you to—"

"Find Jazz," she finished for him.

"Yes."

"That might be a problem."

"Why?"

"I can't track her anymore."

Ash blew out an explosive curse. "She removed her tracker?"

Her expression one of worry, she nodded. "So it would seem."

Xavier pushed aside the questions of why she would do something so out of character and said, "What about her phone? Can you track it?"

"The last ping shows it was in a motel here in Seattle."

So she had checked out of the hotel and gone to another place in the city? None of this was making sense.

"You know the motel's location?" Xavier asked.

"I'll text it to you. But that's where things begin to get weird."

Hell, they were already off-the-charts weird. "Why?"

"Her phone hasn't moved in days."

Yeah, that was odd. Jazz wouldn't leave without her phone, and she wasn't one to sit still. Of course, since he had no idea why she had stayed in the city, maybe it wasn't that weird.

"Also, she disabled the GPS on her phone."

"Since she removed her personal tracker, that's not that big of a surprise." He frowned in confusion. "So how are you tracking her phone?"

"When everyone started taking out their personal tracking chips, I wrote a program specifically for our phones. I added a fail-safe so I can track you guys even if the GPS has been disabled or the phone's turned off."

Xavier remembered when Serena had asked to see his phone a few months back because she'd needed to update something. "You didn't tell us that."

"No." She grimaced an apology to the group. "Sorry, I figured I would only have to use it under dire circumstances."

Xavier nodded, not one bit resentful. "This could well be one of those times."

He sent Ash a look, already knowing what the man was thinking before his boss said, "You and Gideon head to the motel. Find out what the hell Jazz is up to."

He headed to the door, aware that Gideon was giving Eve a brief kiss before following. They were going to get a straight-up explanation. If not, then he and Jazz were going to have a no-holds-barred argument.

Either way, he was going to get some answers.

CHAPTER FOURTEEN

Chicago

Rubbing his chin contemplatively, Kevin reviewed the list of things he still needed to do. Getting the girl to talk wasn't even on the list, but he needed it to happen. And soon.

Sure, he could've forced her to talk that first day. She'd been weak and sick. And it wasn't like he didn't have experience in extracting information. He'd grown up watching his old man torture and maim numerous people before he'd practiced the art himself. He knew how to get intel. She would have been easy to torture. But he had been kind. Given her a bedroom fit for a queen—in his home, no less. And how had she repaid him? With cold silence.

The doctor who'd examined her had cautioned that the drug dosage his people had used had been for a much larger person. She could have died from an overdose, and he never would have gotten this chance. His men would pay for their carelessness, but that would have to wait. He had an agenda, and he would stick to it.

What would he do if her silence continued? He had a plan for that, too. His tactics would change drastically. Blatant disrespect would not be tolerated. She would learn her place and her purpose, and she would severely regret her lack of cooperation.

Her silence wasn't the only thing that bothered him. There was too much mystery surrounding the girl. Why was she going by a fake name? Had she been in hiding all this time? Why did she have weapons on her? Both weapons, a Smith & Wesson CSX handgun and a small, wicked-looking knife were professional grade and extremely pricey. How did a girl who dressed in bargain-store clothes own such weapons? And how did a tiny woman fight and almost win against four men twice her size?

Who was this girl *really*? He knew her real name, but she had been missing for years. Where had she been? What had she been doing?

Nothing was going like he'd planned. Not only was the girl uncooperative, his own wife was giving him misery. The last time they'd talked, she'd asked weird questions, as if she suspected something. He was going to have to figure out a quick way to get rid of her, because if his son realized he planned to off his mama, things were going to get bad fast. She had mollycoddled the boy all his life, and he was totally devoted to her.

The relationship he and his son had was adversarial at best. That used to piss him off, but not anymore. With the boy's insistence on walking the straight and narrow, he'd turned his back on his legacy. As far as Kevin was concerned, he didn't have a son.

The girl could change all that. She could give him so much, including a new family. As young as she was, she could provide him with several sons. And she'd never get the chance to spoil them. He'd made a mistake with his first one and had learned his lesson. He'd create his own dynasty and have everything he'd ever dreamed.

He just needed to stick to the plan.

The door opened, and Oscar walked in, wearing an unusual worried frown.

"What?" Kevin barked.

"That fellow that was with her at the restaurant. He's still alive."

Shit, was anything going to go right?

"I thought you hired a pro."

"I did. He missed. He hit another man that was with him, but missed his target."

Being surrounded by incompetence was both infuriating and exhausting.

"Our man followed them to the hospital but couldn't finish the job because of cameras. Said the guy is now surrounded by a dozen or so people."

"Tell your hired man to get his ass out of the city. The target is no longer important. He has no idea how to find the girl, or he'd have found her by now. She's all ours. He doesn't matter."

Oscar nodded. "All right. What's next?"

Even though Kevin had no doubt about her identity, he'd ordered a DNA test. He would need absolute proof to show the others. As she was almost identical to her beautiful mother, her physical appearance was compelling, but he would need more than that. However, there was no doubt in his mind, especially after he'd called her by her name. She hadn't been able to hide her shock. She was definitely Jasmine McAlister.

"The DNA results will be available soon. Until then, she'll stay here. Then we'll see."

Apparently hearing something in his tone, Oscar said, "What happened?"

"She won't speak."

"Maybe she's scared."

That wasn't the impression he got. Even though she'd been in pain and was suffering from the effects of being drugged, he'd seen the fire in her eyes. Admittedly, people could hide behind a facade. He did it every day. But his instincts were usually on the mark. This girl was keeping secrets, and he intended to get to them all. He couldn't let her spoil his plan. She would give him everything he'd ever dreamed of having, or she would die. Those were the only two options she would be allowed.

He settled on a solid plan. "Once we get the results and confirm her identity, I'll have another talk with her. If she's still stubborn…" He shrugged. "Perhaps I'll let her see what happens to people who don't cooperate with us."

And he had just the location in mind.

CHAPTER FIFTEEN

Seattle

Xavier stood in front of the motel where Jazz was staying. Though it was a far cry from the ritzy hotel they'd stayed at during the op, this one wasn't bad. It was one travelers looking for a less expensive overnight stay might choose. Nothing fancy but serviceable. He could understand why Jazz chose it. Still, why she'd stayed in the city in the first place was still a mystery.

"Any idea why she'd come here?" Gideon asked.

Xavier shook his head. "None." He scanned the parking lot, noting two cars that not only looked like rentals but were also facing outward, the way Jazz would park.

Turning to the door, he knocked rapidly and called out, "Jazz, it's me. Open up." Greeted with silence, Xavier had no compunction in using the key he'd bribed from the desk clerk. The man had claimed Jazz hadn't checked out, but something was definitely wrong.

On instinct, he and Gideon both pulled their weapons as

they entered the room. At first glance, he saw no luggage or any indication that Jazz, or anyone, had even been here.

"It almost looks like it's been wiped down," Gideon said. "You smell that?"

Xavier took in a breath, and his gut clenched, but not with worry. "That's likely Jazz's doing."

"What do you mean?"

"She travels with antibacterial wipes." His mouth twisted in a fond smile. "She wipes everything down, from doorknobs to the bathroom sink."

"I didn't know she was such a clean freak."

"I think it goes back to her childhood." He had asked her about it when they first became partners, and she had flushed a bright pink as she explained that she'd stayed in some shitty places in her life and didn't mind doing that now. However, since she could now afford antibacterial wipes, she'd said it helped her feel like it was her choice—that she hadn't been forced to do it.

"Front desk said Housekeeping hasn't touched the room," Gideon said.

"Then it's definitely Jazz's doing." He glanced around the room, noting there was nothing left of hers here. He slid open the closet. No clothes or luggage. So she had left without informing the front desk. Not all that unusual, but something still didn't fit.

Getting an uneasy feeling, he looked over his shoulder at Gideon. "Check with Serena about the two cars parked outside that are facing outward. See if either of them was rented under one of Jazz's aliases."

"Will do. After that, I'm going to go talk to the front-desk guy again. Seemed a little squirrely to me."

The instant the door closed, Xavier dropped down on the edge of the bed, closed his eyes, and whispered, "What are you doing, Jazz? What's going through your mind? Where the hell are you?"

He played back what had happened over the last week. When they'd arrived in Seattle, there had been nothing to indicate she wasn't totally committed to the mission. Everything they did prior to going to the restaurant had been status quo. Except for one thing. They'd shared that surprising and very hot kiss. That had never happened before, but he hadn't gotten the idea that she hadn't wanted it. She had, in fact, mentioned that she looked forward to coming back to their room and continuing that kiss.

He shook his head. No. It hadn't been that.

When they were seated at the restaurant, he'd done something dumb. He admitted that now. He should never have brought up her brother. She'd had no way out. Even though he'd done it for that exact reason, his plan had backfired. Yeah, he'd gotten her to agree to make a formal request to Ash to put the OZ team on finding Brody, but it had been done under duress.

Still, she hadn't seemed angry—maybe just a little sad or resigned?

When Bass had arrived, they'd both been in operational mode. She'd been as professional as ever, and he'd detected nothing off. Then the assassination had occurred. They'd gone into action. He'd gotten delayed, and she had gone off on her own. Not unusual. They were both professionals, and she could take care of herself. He hadn't worried.

But when he'd found her, she had just been standing there, looking at the empty alley. She'd given him a description of the shooter and the SUV. Looking back, he could say that she'd looked pale, maybe a little lost. But that could've just been the frustration of not catching the guy.

Then, after they'd joined the rest of the team at the safe house, she'd been uncharacteristically quiet. So quiet that several of the team had asked her if she was all right. She'd claimed to have a stomach issue and disappeared into the bathroom. She'd been very subdued when they'd returned to the hotel suite. Neither of them had mentioned what they had once planned. Returning to the intimacy of before had seemed out of place.

The next morning, when they were sitting at breakfast, she had told him she was taking time off. And then she'd just left. She had claimed it had nothing to do with what they'd talked about the night before, but what else could it have been?

And, instead of leaving the city, she'd gone to another place to stay and apparently then questioned the staff at the restaurant. Why the hell would she still be working the case?

None of this made sense.

The more he thought about it, the more his concern grew. The room was empty of her stuff, but that didn't mean there weren't clues.

Standing, he started a more thorough search, meticulously looking through each drawer. She had left nothing behind, which was no surprise. Jazz traveled light and often didn't unpack unless she intended to stay awhile.

He went into the bathroom and looked around. It was almost pristine. He took a step back and then stopped, spotting something at the corner of the mirror. Using his phone's flashlight, he peered closer, and his heart stalled. Blood. There were several smears of blood. It looked like someone had worked hard to wipe it away, but they'd left some behind.

He told himself it could have been left by someone else. Maybe the cleaning people had missed it, but it didn't look old. And Jazz wouldn't have missed it when she'd done her usual pre-stay cleaning. He'd seen how meticulous she was with those wipes.

He gave one more look around and walked out of the room. The empty closet caught his attention. Or rather, what was at the back of the closet. A safe. He didn't question why he would open it. Even though it was obvious Jazz had left, something told him to check.

Squatting, he keyed in a number he knew well. When they'd started their partnership, they'd agreed to use each other's birthdays for their safe combination. That way, they would always have access to each other's safes. This was the first time he'd ever had to do this. The instant the door swung open and he saw the contents, his heart dropped to his feet. *Oh hell no.*

Taking his phone, he punched in Serena's number. When she answered, he rasped out, "Get a forensics team to the motel. I think Jazz has been taken."

CHAPTER SIXTEEN

Chicago

She'd been here three days and still knew nothing. The man responsible for her abduction had been a no-show since that first day. Meals had been delivered by a silent, older woman who refused to look directly at Jazz. When she asked questions, the woman ignored her. If she were feeling stronger, she was sure she could have overpowered the woman and escaped. But today was the first day she'd woken clearheaded. Between the severe headache and bouts of nausea, she had been useless. When she hadn't been moaning in pain or vomiting, she had slept like the dead. The concussion, along with whatever drug they'd used, had totally incapacitated her.

She had finally been able to eat a substantial meal for the first time since her arrival. Though she had worried the food or drink could be drugged, she knew she had to take the chance. She needed nourishment if she was going to get out of here. Besides, if they had wanted to do anything to her, she would have been an easy mark. She wouldn't have been able to fight them, so drugging her wouldn't have been necessary.

Now, however, she was ready to deal with these people and get the hell out of here.

Her luggage from her Seattle motel room had been delivered to her the first day. Unless they'd been able to open the safe in the motel room, she'd had nothing that revealed her identity. If they'd looked inside the safe, she was sure they would be having a different conversation. As it stood now, they knew nothing. Sure, they had her real name, but they knew nothing more than that.

Having felt well enough to shower and wash her hair, she was pleased to be able to put on her own clothes. That went a long way to making her better prepared to handle whatever was coming her way.

As she exited the bathroom, the bedroom door clicked and swung open. Since it wasn't time for a meal, she knew whatever was coming her way had arrived. She had briefly wondered if there were hidden cameras in the bedroom and became even more suspicious.

Refusing to wait for whatever they had planned, Jazz strode determinedly to the middle of the room. The older man from the first day entered. The anger she had felt at being beaten, drugged, and abducted was now back in full force. Today, she was going to get answers, and then she was going to leave. There was no other option.

"So good to see you're feeling better, Jasmine. I've been worried about you."

"Who are you?" Jazz snapped. "Why am I here?"

A delighted smile spread across his face. "So you can speak. Now we're getting somewhere."

"You didn't answer my questions."

"And that's the way it will remain until you answer some of

mine. If you hadn't noticed, you're in my territory, and I have the advantage."

"Fine," she bit out. "What do you want to know?"

"Well, first, I want to know how you're feeling. How are the headache and nausea?"

"Better. Now, tell me who you are."

"Again, it's my show." The smile was still in place, but she could tell it was teetering on disappearing. "Let's start with something simple. Why are you going by an alias? Are you in hiding?"

"Why would I need to be in hiding?"

"Answering my questions with questions of your own will not get you anywhere."

"Very well. No, I am not in hiding. My name is Joy Monroe. I'm twenty-three years old. I live in Seattle, where I am a receptionist at a doctor's office. Is that enough for you?"

The man shook his head slowly and sighed. "I'm deeply disappointed in you, Jasmine. None of the things you've told me are correct, and I am not a man of patience. So here's what we're going to do. For every lie you tell me from here on out, it will be a strike. Three strikes will result in a severe penalty."

She'd had enough. Fury fueling her steps, she stalked up to the man and stared him down. "Listen here, you freak, you had me beaten, drugged, and abducted. I will not stand for this. I want out, and I want out now!"

The punch to her face came faster than she'd anticipated. Thankfully, her reflexes were excellent, and she managed to dodge a direct hit, with only a slice of pain across her jaw. If she weren't so infuriated, she was sure it would have hurt worse. Not giving him time for another hit, she returned the jab with a punch to his jaw, making an excellent connection. Just as she was about to deliver a roundhouse kick to his gut, she halted in midstrike as he pressed a gun to her forehead.

"I don't believe I will give you a chance for those three strikes after all. It's clear there's some humbling that needs to take place." Though he kept his tone low, his voice shook with fury.

"Go ahead, asshole. Shoot me. I dare you," she sneered. Yes, she was poking a rabid bear, but she knew enough to realize that this man had gone to too much trouble to just kill her off. He wanted her alive. A bullet to her head was not part of his plan.

Taking two steps back, he yelled, "Gentlemen!"

The two men who'd helped abduct her walked into the room.

"Please take Jasmine to her new location."

No way in hell was she going anywhere with them. Being small and fast were two qualities that had gotten her out of many sticky situations. She feigned going left and then went right instead. All three men went to grab her, and she scooted around them and ran out the door.

Two long hallways, one on each side of the door, were her choices. Having no idea which way was the best, she took a right and zoomed down the hallway like her life depended upon it, knowing that it did.

Spotting a stairway, she put on the speed and raced to it. Halfway there, a bolt of electricity seared through her body, and she crashed to the floor. Her body spasming with agony from a taser, she glared up at the three men who stood over her. The one in the middle, the bastard responsible for all of this, was grinning down at her like a self-satisfied loon.

Before she could recover a semblance of control over her body, the other two men went to work on restraining her. One of them grabbed her wrists and zip-tied them together. She didn't protest too much. She knew how to break zip ties. The other man did the same to her ankles. That was no cause for alarm either. She'd learned early how to get out of these kinds of bonds.

"You have your instructions."

"Yes, sir," one of the men said.

The bastard responsible for her current misery smiled down at her. "Now, Jasmine, when you are ready to admit who you are, we will have a more enlightening conversation. Until then, enjoy your new accommodations."

Before she could respond, another bolt of lightning struck her, and all coherent thought disappeared beneath the scorching, electrified agony. Unable to maintain consciousness, Jazz had no choice but to let the darkness take her.

HEARING A FAMILIAR MOANING, Jazz willed her eyes open. Memory came quicker this time, as did coherency. She moved slightly and was relieved to find that not only were her legs and hands free, she was also still wearing her clothes. That might seem insignificant, considering she was still a hostage, but she would take all the wins she could get.

Gingerly, she sat up, looked around, and released a shaky sigh. She was indeed in new accommodations, and they weren't nearly as nice as the others had been. In fact, if she didn't know better, she would say she was in a prison cell. But this small enclosure wasn't as clean or as comfortable as what a prisoner might be given.

Getting to her knees, she was pleased that though her entire body was sore and weak, she had no nausea or headache. Another win. Yes, she knew she was stretching the optimism.

Standing, she looked around at the new location. The room was concrete, about eight by ten. In one corner, she spotted a bucket, which she assumed was to be her toilet. In the other corner was a blanket and small pillow. And on top of that pillow was a clear plastic bag with a toothbrush, toothpaste, and floss. How nice that dental hygiene was important to the bastard.

Other than those things, the room was empty. However, she also noted a long, narrow drain on the other side of the room. She didn't need to wonder what it was for. She looked up and saw stars and a midnight-dark sky through the open bars above.

Several years ago, before she'd met Kate and had her life turned around, she had worked at a dog kennel. Few legit businesses wanted to pay cash under the table, but she'd been a hard worker and agreed to less than minimum wage. The kennel's owner hadn't minded taking advantage of her circumstances, but that had been okay with her. The money had not only bought her food and the occasional cheap motel room, she'd been able to spend as much time as she wanted with the dogs and cats being housed there.

She'd never had a pet. Just before her parents were killed, they'd mentioned the possibility of a kitten or puppy as an early birthday present. She'd always been grateful they hadn't had the opportunity to get her one, as that would have been one more loss and would have broken her heart even further.

Her job at the kennel had lasted only about four months, but it was one of the more pleasant experiences of her teenage years. Which was why she knew without a doubt that she was in a dog kennel run. Not the kennel itself, as she would have a roof over her head. This type of enclosure allowed dogs to get fresh air while still being penned.

There were no noises. No barking, no sounds whatsoever. And no animal smells, which told her this place was no longer in business. So, she was locked in an abandoned kennel, and as she shook the cage door, she knew without a doubt there was no way out.

Refusing to panic, she walked every inch of the small enclosure, looking for a weakness. She came to the gritty conclusion that the only way out was through the locked cage door. Even though bars made up the top of the cage, revealing the open sky, she didn't have a way to climb up there. Even if she could, the bars were too close together to fit her body through them.

She was here until someone showed up to let her out.

CHAPTER SEVENTEEN

Xavier took a long swallow of his now cold coffee, ignoring the churning of his gut telling him he'd had enough. Coffee didn't usually faze him, but since he'd been living on it for the past couple of days, his stomach said, *Enough.*

The OZ team sat at the conference table on their private jet. It was a much smaller gathering than usual. Hawke was still in the hospital and would be there at least a week before he'd be allowed to go home. The biggest issue had been blood loss, but once his strength returned, the doctors anticipated a full recovery.

Liam would have been here, but Aubrey was now giving birth to their baby girl. Xavier had talked to him last night, and he'd been torn up because he couldn't help out. Even though Liam would cut off his right hand if someone tried to pull him away from Aubrey and the birth of his child, Xavier knew he was conflicted. Liam loved Jazz, just like they all did.

Xavier mentally shook his head. No, that wasn't the case, because while all the OZ team loved Jazz like family, Xavier knew his own feelings for her were different and stronger. Would he ever get the chance to tell her?

Shutting down those negative feelings, he glanced at the small group again. Sean was still MIA also, and from what Xavier knew, no one had any idea where the asshole was. As soon as they did, Xavier knew there would be several pissed-off OZ operatives on his doorstep, demanding an explanation.

"Okay," Ash said, "let's go over what we know."

Giving a nod, Serena started, "Forensics pulled a half-dozen prints from Jazz's room. We should be getting some matches soon. Also, they were able to get enough blood off the bathroom mirror for a DNA test."

"Any intel on who might've take her or when?" Gideon asked.

"Maybe," she said. Clicking something on her keyboard, she turned and pointed to a photo on a big screen on the wall. "This is from a pawnshop camera across the street from the motel. It doesn't show the door to Jazz's room, but I've reviewed all the footage for the last three days. Nothing strange happened except for this."

Xavier squinted at the screen. "Dark blue van?"

"Yes," Serena answered. "Four days ago, it entered the parking lot at 1:38 AM and exited at 1:52."

"Okay," he said. "But why—" He caught his breath when he saw the guy in the passenger seat. The van was leaving the parking lot, and though it was just a brief glimpse, he could see that the man had his head leaned back, and a cloth covered part of his face. It's what someone would do if they'd been punched in the nose. Was that where the blood had come from? Had Jazz busted the nose of one of her abductors? Had he gone to the bathroom and tried to clean up, leaving the blood evidence behind?

"I know it's not much," Serena said, "but I checked the front-desk registry. None of their guests registered with a dark blue van, and if you'll notice…" She enlarged a photo of the van as it was exiting the parking lot. "No tags."

"That's a good lead, Serena," Ash said. "We got anything else?"

"Yes. Since the van seemed like the likeliest, I've tapped into traffic cam recordings throughout the city. I managed to follow the vehicle all the way to Highway 405. They got off on an exit that leads to an industrial area. Lots of factories and businesses. I sent out a drone to explore the area, but nothing helpful has come back yet."

"And once we get fingerprint matches or DNA on the blood, we'll have a better idea of where else we need to look," Ash said.

"Yes. It shouldn't take long. I've got our best people on this."

"Okay. Good work. Anything else?"

"Yes," Serena said. "Xavier was right about the rental car. The white Toyota Camry was rented by Joy Monroe, Jazz's alias for this op."

Yeah, he'd figured one of the cars had belonged to her.

Ash turned to Xavier. "While we wait for more intel, let's review Jazz's last few known movements."

Drawing in a breath, Xavier said, "Jazz told me she was taking time off. She never said anything, but I thought she would go back to her apartment. When Hawke and I were at the restaurant, doing a final follow-up, one of the employees mentioned a young woman who'd been asking questions. He described Jazz to a T. That was my first clue that she was still in Seattle."

"So instead of taking off like she said she was, she continued to investigate but on her own?" Eve said. "That's so out of character for Jazz."

Xavier agreed wholeheartedly. Jazz was the ultimate team

player and had a tendency to get pissed if one of them did something without involving the entire team.

"And you have no idea why she would do this?" Ash said.

"No."

"Okay. Let's take a look at what she left in the safe."

Grabbing the bag he'd put beside his chair, he opened it and spread the contents across the table. There were no real clues here—at least nothing that would tell them what might have happened. However, what she had left behind was beyond significant and had confirmed to Xavier that she had left the motel against her will.

The items in front of them consisted of Jazz's OZ-issued cellphone, two burner phones, two passports, and driver's licenses for two different aliases. There was also more than twenty-four hundred dollars in cash, as well as Jazz's back-up gun, which she usually wore either strapped to her ankle or in a thigh holster. All these things were consistent with what any OZ operative would have with them on an op. One never knew when another alias might be required. The cash amount was fairly standard, if a little low.

If she had checked out of the motel voluntarily, she would never have left those things behind. But those items weren't what had solidified his belief that Jazz had been taken. Two other objects stood out conspicuously. First was the tiny vial containing the GPS skin patch they had planned to use to tag Franco Bass. She had likely forgotten to return it after the op, but there was no way she would willingly leave behind such expensive and rare tech. It would have been the height of unprofessional, and that was not Jazz.

But the number one item that he knew she would never have left behind lay before him like a lone teardrop. A sterling silver heart-shaped locket, which held the only photo she had left of her family. Though she never wore it on a mission, not wanting anyone during an op to ever see a glimpse of the real

Jazz McAlister, everyone at OZ knew that she carried the
locket with her at all times.

Xavier didn't need to look at the photo to see it in his
mind. She'd told him that her mother and stepfather had given
her the locket when she was eight years old. The picture was
of the four of them—her mother, stepfather, stepbrother, and
Jazz. In the photo, Jazz was seven years old—a tiny little girl
with a big grin, a missing front tooth, and twinkling dark
brown eyes. Her stepfather was a tall, blond man who towered
over his small wife and stepdaughter. Jazz's mother had long,
black hair and was slender. With the exception of her eye
color and hair length, she was a replica of how her daughter
looked today.

Brody, only eleven years old at the time of the photo, was
already almost as tall as his father, with golden-brown hair,
vivid green eyes, and an oddly serious look for one so young.

The locket was Jazz's most cherished possession. It was all
she had left of her family, and unless the devil himself swept
her away, she would not leave the locket behind. And that was
Xavier's biggest fear. Some devil had taken Jazz.

A soft hand landed on his arm, and he glanced over at Eve.
"She's tough as nails, Xavier. She will figure out a way out or a
way to contact us."

Xavier nodded, praying with everything within him that
she was right. Yes, Jazz was tough as nails. He remembered the
first time he'd seen her. OZ had been in business for about a
year by then, but they'd desperately needed more operatives.
Times were getting more dangerous, and the number of
people they could trust seemed to be shrinking at an alarming
rate.

Kate had invited them to the training camp she co-owned
with a fellow former FBI agent. Ash, along with Xavier, Sean,
Liam, Gideon, and Eve, had gone to observe and hopefully
pinpoint a new recruit. They had evaluated five potential

operatives that day. None of them had known they were being observed. They had believed they were going through a regular training session. Three men and two women had competed in a series of trials while the six of them had watched.

The moment Jazz had entered his field of vision, Xavier had been mesmerized. It hadn't been her looks, which he had to admit were stunning. It hadn't been her skills, which though impressive, were just as good or even somewhat subpar to a couple of the other recruits. It hadn't even been her smile, which could light up the room like a blazing fire. No, what had fascinated him had been her courage and grit. He had never seen anyone with more sheer determination and drive to succeed. She just never quit. No matter how many times she got knocked down.

Skills could be learned, honed, perfected, but the kind of fire and drive Jazz McAlister possessed was inherent in her DNA.

The vote had been unanimous that day. Not one of them had considered hiring anyone other than Jazz.

Yes, she looked fragile. Jazz was small-boned and, as she liked to put it, length-challenged. There wasn't a man or woman on the OZ team who didn't secretly want to protect her because she looked so breakable. But there wasn't a one who didn't think that she couldn't handle the job just as well as any of them. She might have to go about it in a different way, but no one, after working with her for even an hour, would ever question her capabilities.

So yes, Jazz was tough, and she would do everything within her power to escape or let them know how to find her. But she was as human as anyone, and he knew to the depths of his soul that she was in serious trouble.

"She never would have left that locket," Serena said softly.

"No, she wouldn't."

The silence as they all stared at the locket was explosive with tension. If any of them had had any doubts that Jazz had been abducted, they no longer existed.

Finally, Ash spoke, his voice slightly gruff. "Okay, while we're waiting for more intel on her abductors, let's talk about the why."

"I know we're not big on assumptions," Eve said, "but don't we have to look at WP as the likeliest suspects? They know OZ is hot on their trail. They might not be able to easily identify us, but with you guys asking questions about the shooting, maybe somebody put it together. Doesn't that make the most sense?"

"Does it, though?" Gideon asked. "We all saw the location of the shooter who tried to take out Xavier and Hawke. Any half-assed amateur could've made the kill shot. Seems like if WP wanted to get rid of them, they would have hired someone who wouldn't miss."

"Unless he was trying to miss," Eve said.

"Then why do it at all?"

"Maybe a warning?" Serena offered. "'We know you're on to us, so back off'?"

"I don't see that happening," Xavier said. "These people aren't shy about killing for all different kinds of reasons. I think if they meant to kill Hawke and me, they would've hired an expert marksman to do the deed. The assassin who took out Bass was an obvious pro. No reason not to hire him, or someone like him, to take us out, too."

Eve nodded slowly. "All right, then, if that's the case, maybe we need to look at Jazz's abduction and the attempt on Xavier as the same party."

"Other than OZ and a few of our closest associates, who would know that Jazz and I even know each other?"

"They could have seen you together at the restaurant." Serena clicked several keys on her keyboard, and a shot of Jazz and Xavier sitting at the table at the restaurant appeared on the screen.

A punch to the gut couldn't have had more impact on Xavier than seeing Jazz looking so beautiful and vibrant. His throat closed up with emotion at the sight. Would he ever see her like that again?

"This was just a three-second shot. In fact, Jazz herself called me about it. I was already working on getting it taken down, but I'm sure thousands of people saw the clip before I was able to get to it."

"A video caused all of this?" Gideon stood and began pacing up and down the small aisle of the plane. Everyone was used to his way of working things out. "That seems like a big-assed leap, guys. Somebody sees Jazz, decides he wants her, hunts her down, takes her, and tries to take out Xavier, who he thinks is his competition?"

Xavier had to admit—and everyone else's expressions showed they thought the same—it was indeed a big-assed leap.

"Could this be related to Jazz's past?" Eve asked. "I know she doesn't talk about it much, but her mother and stepfather died under mysterious circumstances, despite what the official records show. And her brother disappeared. Maybe someone is targeting her family and saw her."

"After all this time?" Gideon said.

"Could Kate give us some insight, Ash?"

"Maybe. I've put off calling her until we could get more intel. She's going to want answers, and I—"

Ash cut off his words when an alert sounded on Serena's phone.

"Fingerprint match came in," Serena said. All eyes watched as she clicked several keys on her keyboard. The face of a large, rough-looking man appeared on the big screen. "It matches this guy—Alton Nix. Here's his record."

Beside the photo of Nix, a list as long as Xavier's arm

showed up. The man's record included everything from shoplifting to animal abuse to assault with a deadly weapon. The guy was barely forty and looked like he'd been in trouble for more than half his life.

Another man's face appeared on the screen, only slightly smaller but even rougher looking with a long, filthy-looking beard and mean, beady eyes. "This guy, Joey Holms, is Nix's best friend. They met in prison when they were both twenty and have been partners in crime since then. They've lived in Seattle for the past eight years."

Xavier reviewed their vital statistics. Even though the photo of the two men in the van had been slightly grainy, he could definitely see a resemblance between the driver and Nix and the passenger and Holms.

"So why would two thugs have any interest in Jazz?" Eve asked.

"Hired goons," Xavier said. "Or, as slimy as these two are, maybe they saw her and decided to take her."

"No," Eve said, "that doesn't match up with the shot taken at you."

"I agree," Ash said. "Serena, find out whom they've worked for in the past—any other known associates. Dig into their bank accounts and anything else you can find about them."

Her brow wrinkled in concentration, Serena was already clicking away as she said, "On it."

Grabbing the phone on the table in front of him, Ash punched in a number, and Kate answered immediately.

"Hey, Ash, good to hear from you. Are you back home with Jules and Josh yet?"

"No. We've had a development."

"Okay." In an instant, her voice went from easygoing to serious. "What's wrong?"

"Jazz has been abducted. We don't know who or—"

Before he could say anything else, Kate snapped, "Call you back." The line went dead.

Everyone stared at the phone in Ash's hand as if it would give them answers.

"What the hell?" Eve asked. "Did Kate just hang up on you?"

His face morphing from confusion into a severe thundercloud, he growled, "So it would seem."

Distracting them from their confusion at Kate's unexpected reaction to the news about Jazz, another alert sounded on Serena's phone. When her face paled, Xavier felt his heart plummet.

"What?" he barked.

"A dark blue van was found in the parking lot of an industrial landfill. Two men with bullets in their heads were found in the front seat. They've been identified as Alton Nix and Joey Holms."

So the two leads they'd had were already gone, leaving them with nothing other than the knowledge that Jazz had been taken by someone who didn't mind killing to cover up the crime.

Where the hell was she?

CHAPTER EIGHTEEN

Chicago

She had been here for five days, and she wanted out. Now! The first night she had barely slept, dozing only intermittently. Every odd sound woke her. She wasn't usually afraid of the dark, but she had discovered that there was darkness, and then there was the total absence of light. An overcast sky had obscured even the moon that night, and she'd had only the sounds of crickets and the distant howls of coyotes to keep her company.

At about noon the next day, someone had shown up. She hadn't had water or food in over twenty-four hours and had felt like a ravenous beast. When he'd shoved a paper bag filled with a cold hamburger, fries, and a melted milkshake at her, she had grabbed it and devoured the food like a starving animal. She hadn't cared if he reported back to the asshole that she'd appeared desperate. Keeping up her strength was her only way to get out of here, and she would do what she had to do to make that happen.

The smug bastard had left without a word, and she'd been alone again. That day might have been the longest, because she had no idea when he would be coming back.

The meal had given her a needed boost, but she had been desperate for more. The asshole had made sure he'd furnished her with a toothbrush and toothpaste, but brushing her teeth without water was almost impossible. Especially when her mouth had felt like a desert.

In the middle of the night, an unexpected rainstorm had arrived. Using the cup that had held the shake, she captured enough to fill it twice, finally satisfying her desperate thirst for water and giving her the opportunity to use the toothpaste and brush the creep had so thoughtfully provided.

And since she was feeling decidedly grubby from sweating in the summer heat, she had removed her clothes and taken a shower in the rain. It wasn't the first time she'd had a rain bath. When she'd lived on the streets, it had sometimes been all the cleanliness she'd had for weeks at a time. Occasionally, she could sneak into the bathrooms at the Y and grab a quick shower before anyone noticed her. Even though there were several homeless shelters in Chicago, she had avoided them. If any responsible adult saw a kid alone, without parental supervision, they would have had to call child services. Getting into the system was the last thing she had wanted.

The rain bath had perked up her spirits, and she had slept much better once the rain had stopped.

The next day, no one had shown up. She had saved a cup of water from the rain and had sipped on it when her stomach grumbled. In those minutes, she had actually found herself laughing. These people had no idea who they were dealing with. She had lived on the streets of Chicago for two years. She had known hunger, thirst, and a filth so deep, she'd doubted even the occasional shower she'd managed to sneak in had done more than clean the surface dirt. It had been hellish, brutal, and often humiliating, but she had learned lessons that would last her a lifetime.

These bastards could not and would not defeat Jasmine McAlister.

The next day, the same man arrived and, without a word, handed her another burger, fries, and a shake. Apparently realizing she needed water to live, a small bottle of spring water was also in the bag. She had savored each bite and sip, knowing that this might be her only meal for a while.

Sitting by herself, without any distractions, gave her plenty of thinking time. When she wasn't trying to figure out who and why she'd been kidnapped, she thought about Brody and what might have made him become an assassin.

And she thought a lot about Xavier.

What was he doing now? Were he and Hawke still in Seattle working the case, or had they already gone back to OZ headquarters? Did he have any inkling that she was in trouble? If he did know, he, along with the entire OZ team, would be working to find her. Of that she had no doubt.

But how could he know? She had deliberately hidden herself and her movements so no one could find her. Had stupidly removed the tracker in her arm. Jazz knew she'd done some foolish things in her life, but this one might be the most costly.

Why hadn't she trusted Xavier enough to tell him about Brody? Even though she knew he wasn't her brother's biggest fan, he would have done everything he could to help her find him. She had panicked, and she never panicked.

Unable to sit in the corner any longer, Jazz willed herself to move around. She'd tried doing her regular workout of pushups and crunches, but the heat and humidity had zapped her strength. The last thing she needed to do was get dehydrated. One tiny bottle of water wasn't going to sustain her, and she couldn't depend on having a rainstorm every night.

Pacing the tiny enclosure, Jazz focused on what she would do once she escaped. First, she would find the bastard who'd done this to her, get some answers, and then she would do some damage to his smirking face. He would pay for putting her through this torture.

Then she would find Brody. And to do that, she would involve Xavier and the rest of the team. Confessing that she hadn't trusted them enough to tell them the truth would be difficult, but she knew they would forgive her. That was what family did. They loved and they forgave.

Before she did any of that, though, she would do what she had been putting off for what seemed like forever. She would tell Xavier how she really felt about him. Hiding it any longer made no sense. She'd been in love with him since the first month they'd started working together. She was good at hiding her feelings, so she didn't think he'd ever suspected. Being afraid wasn't usually her thing—she'd seen too much in her life to let fear guide her actions. But she had to admit when it came to Xavier and her love for him, she had been terrified. The last thing she had wanted to do was ruin their partnership by spilling her guts.

Now she looked back and realized how much she might have missed by not being truthful. No, she didn't know how Xavier felt, but the kiss they'd shared had shown her that he felt something. She could build on that.

But first, she had to get out of here. To do that, she was going to have to do something she hated, even if it was necessary. She despised the thought of anyone looking at her as a victim. It made her feel weak and not in control of her life. However, she could act the part. She was an excellent actress, and these bozos would see an Oscar-winning performance of a scared, hurt, and hungry little girl. Then, when she had them where she wanted them, she would show them exactly what Jazz McAlister was made of. The freaks wouldn't know what hit them until it was too late.

JAZZ WOKE to the sound of a cage door opening. Her eyes popped open, and she sat up, scooting into a corner. This was it…her moment to shine. She had to make every second count and sell the poor-pitiful-me victim persona.

"Time for your feeding, bitch."

The man had gotten increasingly meaner with each visit. He had never been respectful or kind, but she could tell he resented having to bring her food. Or maybe his boss had told him to treat her like a nonhuman. Who knew? Either way, she would be more than happy to give him an attitude adjustment.

Whistling like he was calling an animal, he grinned, waiting for her reaction. In the past, she hadn't minded revealing how much she reviled him. But it was time to reverse course.

She went to her feet slowly, almost falling a couple of times before she could stand up straight. Not all of it was an act. She was weak and dizzy. The small bottle of water and occasional meal weren't near enough to sustain her.

"Get over here, or I'm going to drop it on the ground and let you try to lick it up like the bitch you are."

Wow, forget about disrespectful—the guy had gone full-on psycho.

Ignoring his taunts, she wobbled toward him. Once she reached the bars, she stuck her arm through the opening, reaching for the bag of food and shake in his hand. Instead of giving her the meal like he usually did, he backed away with a smirk on his face.

"What…" she began.

He shook his head and nodded at the floor. "Get on your knees. Beg for it."

Okay, this guy was going to be in a world of hurt when she got through with him.

Here we go.

Scrunching her face, her mouth trembling with grief, she forced tears from her eyes. "I can't do this anymore," she sobbed. "I'll talk…" She gulped, swallowed hard, and sobbed some more. "I'll tell him everything. Just please…let me out of here. I can't take…" Sobbing hysterically, she covered her face with her hands.

The silence that followed her outburst was promising. As tempting as it was to peek through her fingers to see what kind of impression she had made, Jazz continued her sobbing.

A full minute later, she heard him say, "Aw, shit." There was some shuffling and then, "Boss, it's Kip. She says she's ready to talk."

She couldn't hear what the voice on the other end of the call said, but Kip's response was encouraging. "Yes, sir. She's crying like a little girl. Looks kinda weak and pale."

Two more "yes, sirs," and then, "Got it."

"Okay, bitch. Look at me."

She lowered her hands and gazed hopefully at him, her face filled with as much sorrow and sadness as she could muster. When he snapped several photos with his phone, she ground her teeth together to keep from snarling and growling like an abused animal. She had felt hate in her heart before but that emotion was mild to what she was feeling now. Something untamed and feral rose up inside her and she knew if she was set free, she would attack without mercy.

"Boss says that's a good start. Wants to give you a few more days to think about it."

What?

"And since I gotta go and you didn't do what I said, I figure

I can still make you get on your knees, even if I won't be here to see it."

With that, he put the paper bag and shake on the floor several inches from the cell door and out of her reach.

Giving her an arrogant, smug smile, he said, "Bon appétit." Turning his back on her, he walked out the door.

CHAPTER NINETEEN

Bozeman, Montana

Xavier turned the key and pushed open the door to Jazz's apartment. He felt like an intruder, and though he knew he wouldn't likely find any clues to what had happened to her, he had to make sure.

Having all agreed that Jazz was no longer in Seattle, the team had returned to headquarters. The two men who'd abducted Jazz were dead, which meant someone else had been responsible. Getting rid of the hirelings and then getting her out of town made sense. Without any clear leads, they were going on the assumption that the man or men responsible had seen her in the video from the restaurant, hired local thugs to help with the kidnapping, and then killed the men to keep them quiet.

While Serena was digging into every known associate of the two thugs and tracking their actions over the last few months, Eve and Gideon were investigating those leads along with putting out fires in other ongoing cases.

Ash had gone to North Carolina for a face-to-face with Kate. After hanging up on him when he'd called her about Jazz's abduction, she had called back half an hour later and requested a meeting. It was obvious she had some intel, but why wouldn't she blurt it out if it would help find Jazz?

Kate Walker keeping secrets from OZ was bizarre on its own merits. She had been their biggest supporter from the beginning. They wouldn't have accomplished nearly what they had been able to do without her assistance. So why the hell would she be reluctant to share what she could to help find Jazz? It made no sense.

So everyone had an assignment, and this was his. He hated invading her space. This was Jazz's sanctuary—where she lived her real life, away from the role she played as an OZ operative. As much as Jazz loved her OZ family, when it came to her personal life, she could be very private. He got that. Independence and self-sufficiency were of utmost importance to her. And he felt like the biggest slug alive for invading her privacy. But he was desperate. She had disappeared eight days ago, and they still had no inkling who had taken her or why.

Jazz lived simply and was a minimalist almost to the point of deprivation. There wasn't a lot of color in her décor, which suited her personality. The living room held a comfortable-looking faux suede sofa with numerous colorful throw pillows and an old rocking chair by the window where he imagined she liked to sit and look at the mountains in the distance. A television hung on the wall, and an old forty-five record player sat in the corner. He remembered that Jazz had told him about that purchase—she had been excited to find some-thing rare and old that still worked.

There were a few framed photographs on the walls, not of people but of landscapes. They were black-and-white and, though stark, seemed to fit the overall theme of simplicity.

The kitchen was utilitarian with just a coffeemaker and toaster on the counter. He spotted a mug beside the sink and smiled at the picture of a large orange cat with the name Scaredy beneath the photo. He knew Jazz was an animal lover, but she had always claimed she couldn't get a pet because of her work schedule. While he agreed they were out of town a lot, he wasn't sure that was the biggest reason. She had lost so much in her life. Sometimes, it was easier to go without than to take a chance on losing it. He understood that philosophy all too well.

Shaking himself out of his psychoanalyzing mode, he quickly went through her cabinets. He didn't expect to find any insightful information, but he was too thorough to not look. Other than an inordinate supply of Jiffy peanut butter and several cans of SpaghettiOs, her shelves were almost bare.

The fridge held even less—a gallon of milk, butter, eggs, yogurt, and cheese.

He went to her bedroom and felt his heart lift at the scent that hit his nose. Jazz had a preference for jasmine. She'd told him since it was her name, how could it not be her signature fragrance?

Her bedroom was no more elaborate than the rest of her apartment. A regular-sized bed with a simple white coverlet, a nightstand holding a candle, flashlight, and a worn-looking paperback of *Little Women*. The surface of the eight-drawered dresser across from the bed was empty. Grinding his teeth and feeling like a voyeur, Xavier opened each drawer and searched through her things. Jeans, T-shirts, and underwear were stacked neatly in each one.

He was about to close the last one, her sock drawer, when his fingertip happened to tap the bottom. A hollow sound caught his attention. Removing the socks, he tapped harder and realized it was a false bottom. Taking his knife from his pocket, he pried open the cover and found a small wooden box. The guilt in his gut didn't prevent him from opening and rifling through the contents. He'd apologize after he found her.

All he found was an envelope addressed to Brody McAlister in Indianapolis. He opened it and felt a lump develop in his throat as he read the simple, heart-wrenching note from a heartbroken little girl.

Dear Brody, you left to buy groceries, but you never came home.

Jazz had actually told him about the letter. When she'd first explained about her background and how her brother had disappeared, she'd told him how she had written and mailed him a letter. She'd said she had remembered her mother filling out a change-of-address form when they'd moved to Atlanta with her new stepfather and stepbrother. Her mother had told her that if anyone wanted to get in touch with them, the mail would be forwarded from their old address to their new one. She had thought that perhaps Brody had left her and might have a new address.

She had given a small, self-deprecating laugh as she described how the innocent little girl who'd had no idea what to do to find her brother had done the only thing she knew to do. Xavier thought that might have been the beginning of his hatred for Brody McAlister.

Being a nosy asshole was anathema for him, but as he read the letter, his anger against her brother grew with each line he read. Desperation and loneliness filled the short note. Xavier folded the letter and returned it to its envelope. He really hoped he got the chance to put his fist in Brody McAlister's face one day.

He returned the box to its hiding place and closed the drawer. He would have to tell her he'd read it. He just hoped he got the chance to do that.

Not seeing anything that would lead him to finding Jazz,

he left the bedroom and did a cursory search of the bathroom. Feeling even more helpless than he had when he'd entered the apartment, he quickly headed to the front door. His phone buzzed just before he put his hand on the doorknob.

He saw a number on the screen that he didn't recognize, and his heart leaped. He prayed that Jazz had somehow found a way to call him. He quickly answered, "Jazz?"

"Z, that you?"

Xavier held his breath to keep from letting out a huge sigh of disappointment. There was only one person who called him Z.

"Cotton? How are you, man? Haven't heard from you in a while. Everything okay?"

He'd gone through basic training with Clayton Cotton, and their friendship, such as it was, had lasted for over a decade. He only heard from him every few years now, but he always tried to be available when the man called. Some people just needed an extra shoulder to lean on during tough times, and Cotton was one of those people.

The first time Xavier had seen the man, he had been lying on the ground. Blood had covered his face, and the asshole beating him hadn't been stopping. Xavier hadn't cared what had started the fight, but watching a kid who obviously had no fighting skills get beaten to a pulp pissed him off mightily. He'd jerked the guy off Cotton and kicked the bully's ass. That day, he'd made a friend. Xavier had long forgotten the bully's name, but Cotton had stayed in touch with him.

Last time he'd heard, the man was tending bar somewhere up north. He'd left the military a few years after Xavier, and though they'd never served together in the same places, they'd somehow stayed in touch.

When Cotton didn't immediately answer, Xavier knew something was up. "What's wrong, Cotton? You in trouble?"

"Sort of. I just…I need to tell you something."

Xavier settled his back against Jazz's door. Cotton didn't have family or many friends he could go to in times of trouble. Xavier always tried to be there for him. Even though his mind was screaming at him to go out and find Jazz, he forced himself to give his friend his attention. "Okay. What is it?"

"Remember last year when Alfredo Lopez was almost killed in that restaurant blast in Puerto Rico?"

Xavier straightened his shoulders, now completely focused on Cotton's words. "How did you know about that?"

"It was me. I set the charge."

"What? What the hell, Cotton?"

"I'm sorry, Z. I took the job but didn't know you'd be there…that you were working an op. When I saw you in the kitchen that day, I knew if I pulled out of the job, they'd find someone else. So I protected you. I made it a small blast. The old geezer was about a thousand years old. I figured he'd die from fright even if the explosion didn't kill him."

He and Jazz had been working undercover in the restaurant, keeping eyes on Lopez, a cartel leader who was there to meet someone. If the plan had been to kill Lopez, they'd always wondered why there had been only one charge.

Afterward, he and Jazz had stayed in Puerto Rico for several days, trying to get answers. Even though they'd gotten answers, who'd actually set the charge had remained a mystery.

"Why were you trying to kill a cartel leader?"

"It was my job. I'm a gun for hire."

Xavier closed his eyes. Cotton didn't always make good decisions. A shitty childhood had messed with him in a big way. But now he was a paid assassin?

"How…why…"

"Listen, I can't really explain other than I kind of got lost after I left the service. Didn't know what direction to take. I needed money, and some of the things I'm trained for… Well, there's not much call for them in the regular world. You know?"

Yeah, he couldn't argue with that. When you'd been trained to do certain things and you were in a normal world, things weren't always black and white. If not for Option Zero, the same thing might've been his fate.

"Anyway, I needed the money, so I took the job. Guess you know it was his nephew who hired the hit."

"Yeah." Cartels were often good at solving their own crimes. Alfredo's nephew had gotten tired of waiting for his uncle to die so he could take over. Thought he'd help things along. Instead, his uncle hadn't died, and the nephew had paid for his betrayal with his life. Justice, especially in the criminal world, could be quick and brutal.

"So anyway, my reputation took a major hit when I didn't make the kill. I decided that life wasn't for me."

"That's good, Cotton. You made the right decision."

"Yeah, I know. But the other day, I caught wind of another hit. And I… Well…"

His heart dropped. "Cotton?"

"I got a text from a friend. Said a man out of Chicago was looking for some local talent. My friend knew I stay around that area, so he went ahead and sent me the name and photo. It was a different name, but when I saw the photo, I knew I had to do something. The photo was of you, Z."

Closing his eyes, Xavier breathed out gruffly, "You were the shooter in Seattle."

"Yeah. But you gotta know I missed on purpose. I'm a good shot, Z. You know that for a fact."

Yes, he did know that. And Eve had been right when she'd suggested that the shooter had been trying to miss.

"Why, Cotton?"

"Client wanted it done ASAP. I knew if I didn't take the contract, someone else would. Thought I'd give you a few warning shots, you'd get out of town, and that would be that. Since they didn't have your real name, I thought you'd be safe." He swallowed hard and said hoarsely, "I didn't mean for the guy with you to get hurt."

Xavier closed his eyes again, seeing Hawke's lifeless body, blood pouring from his neck. That was an image he'd never get out of his head. To know this man—his friend—had caused it was both infuriating and gut-wrenching.

"Z?"

Pulling in the anger, Xavier said, "I know you didn't, Cotton." Out of all the thoughts whirling in his brain, that was one thing he knew for a fact. Cotton didn't have a killer instinct. The man wasn't evil—he was just lost.

"Who's the client? Who put out the hit?"

"Don't know. Just some guy out of Chicago. Funds were transferred from a bank in Barbados."

Thinking Serena could trace the money, he said, "Can you text me the bank info and tracking number?"

"Sure thing, Z. Anything I can do to help."

"How much for the job?"

"Twenty thousand. Ten up front. Ten when the job was done."

As hits went, that wasn't a lot. It made him wonder how motivated these people were to get rid of him.

"And I was the only target?"

"Yes. The photo showed you at some fancy restaurant. Looked like you were with someone, but your face was the only one shown."

That was one bit of good news—maybe. At least there hadn't been a hit out on Jazz, too. At least as far as he knew. But her abduction and this contract on his life had to be related. Had some creep seen them together at the restaurant, decided he wanted Jazz for himself, and thought getting rid of Xavier would cut out his competition? That was an insane premise, but crazy things happened every damn day.

Rubbing his forehead where a headache was setting up camp, Xavier tried to see past the confusion and figure out what the hell was going on. Who was this person, and what did he want with Jazz? There was still so much they didn't know.

Chicago, though. That was something they could work with. Without ending his call with Cotton, Xavier texted Rose. *Get me on a flight to Chicago. ASAP.*

"Z, you there?"

"Yeah, I'm here. Just trying to get my head wrapped around this."

"Is he… Is that guy… He going to be okay?"

"Yes. He lost a lot of blood, but he'll be fine."

"I didn't mean… Shit. I'm just real sorry, Z."

"I know you are, Cotton. So what now? Where do you go from here?"

"I gotta get out of the country. I took half the money, so I figure they're going to be looking for me to get it back."

Reminding himself that OZ hadn't been created only to bring the wicked to justice but to give second chances to those who'd lost their way, Xavier said, "Listen, I can help. A woman named Rose is going to call you and give you what you need. She'll get you a new name, new everything. You can start all over again."

"You don't have to do that, Z. I can take care of myself. I just wanted you to know."

"Listen, Cotton. They'll probably be looking for you. Ten thousand is nothing to sneeze at. This is a chance to start over. Find yourself. Take the chance, man. Get a clean start."

"You're a good friend, Z. The best."

"Just take care of yourself. Get a place to live, a regular job. Find a girlfriend. Have a good life. You deserve it. Okay?"

"Yeah… Thanks again, Z. Take care."

The instant the call ended, he punched in Ash's number.

"Xavier?"

"Yeah, I got a lead."

"Me, too," Ash said.

They spoke simultaneously. "Chicago."

His heart rate kicked into high gear. "Kate told you something?"

"She did. Not everything, though."

"She's still holding back on you? Why would she do that?"

The thought that Kate Walker would hold on to information that could help them find Jazz was bizarre.

"I don't know. She swears the things she's keeping to herself aren't related to this. Says there are bigger things afoot."

"Bigger than saving Jazz's life?"

"That's the thing. She said she doesn't believe Jazz's life is in jeopardy."

"What the hell does that mean?"

"Hell if I know. It was like I was trying to solve a puzzle while the pieces were in the mouth of a tiger. She promised me that she doesn't know who took Jazz but said to look into the Byrne family out of Chicago."

"Byrne? Who are they?"

"Not sure yet. I've got Serena running intel as we speak."

"What are you going to do about Kate?"

"I'll have to face that when this is over. We can't work this way. People holding back intel won't work. But for now, my focus is on finding Jazz."

"I've asked Rose to get me on the next flight out," Xavier said.

"Good. I'm headed there, too. Eve and Gideon are still a few hours away from home. Once they get there, they'll grab

Serena and take the chopper to Chicago. Everyone will be just a few hours behind you."

"Sounds good. See you there."

Xavier pocketed his phone and took one last glance around Jazz's apartment. They had leads—a name and a city. It was significant. He would keep digging, do whatever he had to do to find her. And once he did? Yeah, he already knew the answer to that, too—he was never letting her go again.

CHAPTER TWENTY

Chicago

S he was still here. Barely.

It had taken her over two hours to get the food the guard had dropped outside her cage. She'd had to create a pole and a hook using the wire from her bucket, her toothbrush, and one of the old milkshake cups. It hadn't been pretty, and she'd been worn out and sweating a river by the time she'd gotten the bag within grasp of her fingers. She'd tried to get the shake but had ended up spilling most of it on the floor before she could retrieve it. All in all, it had been an infuriating and humbling experience, and if the guard had stayed to watch, he would have thoroughly enjoyed the show.

Had she messed up? Had he not bought her act? Even now, looking back on it, she couldn't see where she got it wrong. So what if he'd called the old man and told him she wanted to talk—he hadn't relented. At least not yet.

She wasn't giving up, though.

The burger, fries, and shake hadn't come in a couple of days. Thankfully, it had rained last night, so she'd been able to stay hydrated. It was the lack of food that was starting to wear her down.

She didn't believe death was their plan for her, so at some point, they would return. This whole experience was to humble her, and while she had no choice but to play their game, she thoroughly intended to reverse the situation.

Noises sounded, and she winced because, like Pavlov's dog, her stomach started making horrific growling sounds. She moved as far away from the cage door as possible, placing herself in a corner. This time, she'd give them another performance—this one would put the other one to shame. This time, there would be no doubt in their minds that she had learned her lesson. They would be in awe of how powerful they'd been to break her will. She would do what she had to do to convince them that she'd spill every secret and give anything to get out of here.

Even as hungry as she was, the thought of eating another burger and fries held little appeal. Not that it mattered. She would accept it with gratitude and show absolute humility. They would see her as a broken, pitiful doll and let her out of here. Then…then she would reveal to them who Jasmine McAlister really was. They wouldn't know what hit them.

"Okay, little girl. Here's how this is going to go."

Instead of one man today, there were two. The same two who had abducted her. And instead of a meal for her, each held a bucket filled with water.

"Boss wants to see how much you've learned, but he wants you clean first." Kip, as she'd learned from his call last time, grinned that evil grin she couldn't wait to wipe off his face. "And we get to be your cleaners."

Oh hell no. These creeps were not going to touch a hair on her head…or anywhere else, for that matter.

Standing, she maintained her look of humility and fear as they opened the cage and headed toward her. Bracing her hands on the wall, she allowed them to come closer. And then she attacked. She went for the biggest one first, who was Kip. Moving with swift precision, she double-kicked, hitting his crotch both times. The bucket dropped to the floor, water gushed everywhere, and Kip fell to his knees, screaming bloody murder.

The other man reacted quickly, but instead of dropping his water, he threw the entire bucket at her. Any other time, she might have appreciated being drenched with clean water, but not when she was fighting for her life.

Refusing to let it stop her, she barreled toward him, screeching like a banshee at the top of her lungs. When she'd lived on the streets, she had learned that a well-timed screech could throw someone off their game. The startled expression on his face told her she'd freaked him out. Taking advantage, she struck quickly, jamming one fist into his nose and the other to the side of his jaw. His howl almost made her wince. This was the same guy whose nose she'd broken not too long ago.

Knowing he was addled, she grabbed the gun out of the holster at his waist. The open door beckoned, and sweet freedom was only a few steps away.

"Come back here, bitch!" one of the men roared.

Not looking back, Jazz practically flew through the door. She heard shots and felt stings on her hip, thigh, and leg but refused to let that slow her down. Getting out was her only priority, and if it took breathing her last breath to escape, then that's what she would do.

A bullet slammed into the wall, six inches from her head.

"The next one goes through your skull," he snarled. "Now put the gun down and get on your knees."

No way was she doing any such thing. Dropping into a squat, Jazz whirled around and took her own shot. The bullet landed exactly where she wanted it—right in the middle of his forehead. Kip's face registered extreme shock a second before he fell onto the concrete floor.

She turned the gun on the other man, who held up one hand, while covering his nose with the other one. Blood continued to poor from his damaged nose, but he managed to mumble, "Don't shoot. I'm unarmed."

"Do what I say, and you'll live. Using your left hand, slide your phone toward me."

"Okay. Give me a sec."

"Clock's ticking, asshole. I've got no problem shooting you and taking the phone for myself. I'm giving you one chance."

She watched as he slowly pulled a phone from his pocket and slid it forward. When it barely went a foot, she knew he was still planning on trying to stop her.

Pain in her hip and leg were becoming problematic, so she was thankful for the adrenaline that continued to surge through her. Pain she could handle.

Stumbling only slightly, she made her way forward, the gun trained directly on the man's chest. She didn't want to have to kill him, because she needed answers. Having no idea where the man responsible for all this lived, she was counting on getting what she needed from this guy.

Moving faster than she could have anticipated, the man went for his ankle. Jazz had only a second to see the bulge of his backup weapon before it was in his hand. She fired, hitting the man in the chest.

The minute he went down, all strength left Jazz's body. Her legs went wobbly, and she crumpled to the floor. The two dead men were only a few feet away from her, but for some reason they seemed to be moving farther and farther away. She blinked rapidly, realizing she was about to pass out. That could not happen.

Getting to her knees, Jazz gritted her teeth as she crawled toward the phone. She knew it was only a couple of feet from her, but it seemed like a mile. The pain was becoming excruciating, and she knew if she looked over her shoulder, she'd see a trail of blood.

With one last gasp of energy, Jazz grabbed the phone and swiped it on. She was thankful when she saw that the man had enabled facial recognition rather than a PIN to unlock his phone. Another adrenaline rush went through her. She was so close to getting help. She just needed to hang on for a few more seconds. Scooting closer to the man, she held the phone in front of his face. When the screen changed, her heart almost exploded in her chest.

Telling herself she could do it, Jazz stood and stumbled out of the enclosure. No way was she staying in this hellhole any longer. When she spotted the front door, she hobbled forward and, with one last surge of energy, practically threw herself through the opening.

She landed on the pavement on her side, several feet from the building. Her strength now completely demolished, Jazz lay on her uninjured side and tapped the phone icon on the screen. Her fingers shaking, her mind blurring, she managed to tap the nine digits that would get her to the one person who would tear the world apart to get to her.

She prayed he would answer.

CHAPTER TWENTY-ONE

Chicago

Kevin Doyle was on top of the world. Everything was working out just as he'd planned. It amazed him at the amount of items he'd been able to check off his list. If nothing else, what he had accomplished clearly proved that he was meant to be king of Chicago.

Admittedly, things got off to a rocky start. What with the girl being so uncooperative and then the hit on her companion from the restaurant going awry, he had been concerned that he had miscalculated. However, once he'd adjusted his expectations, things had gone swimmingly.

The ten thousand dollars he'd lost on the failed hit was infuriating, but it was a measly amount compared to what awaited him in the future. Whoever the man was who had been with the girl no longer mattered. As far as he knew, no one cared about her. But even if someone did, no one knew where the girl was or who had taken her. She was at his disposal, to be used at his discretion. And, oh, did he have plans for her.

For right now, his little prize was exactly where she needed to be. When he'd purchased that old veterinarian's office a couple years back, he'd had in his mind that some of their products could be stored there until they were ready for transport. He'd discarded that idea later, as the building wasn't nearly as ideal as he'd thought. It had just been sitting there, languishing. Putting the girl there had been a stroke of genius.

The photo Kip had sent was one of the most fascinating things he'd ever seen. In just a few days, she had become broken and compliant—the total opposite of what she'd been before. The girl had seen the dark side of how her life could be, and it had barely taken a week. Now she was a mess. Ready to come crawling and begging for mercy.

He'd ordered that she be fed but not so much that she took it for granted. Apparently, the girl needed a lot of calories, because she looked like she'd lost a few pounds. She would need to put on some weight before he introduced her to his world, but they had plenty of time to make that happen.

He'd instructed his men to clean her up and bring her to her new home. She would stay there, learning the things she needed to know for her new role.

His second task, which had been more difficult but equally important, had taken less time than he had anticipated. Getting rid of his current wife hadn't been pleasant. He was fortunate that she had had some health issues already. The woman hadn't taken care of herself. No matter how many times he had told her to lose weight and exercise, she'd ignored all his warnings.

He hadn't wanted her to suffer. After all, she had done her duty and given him a son. The fact that his son was a huge disappointment was another matter. And other than having a sour disposition and losing her looks, she hadn't been a bad wife. But it was time for him to move on to younger, greener pastures. The little needle prick at her hairline while she'd been asleep had been both compassionate and expeditious. Within two minutes, she'd been gasping for breath, and in less than five minutes, she was gone. It wasn't the first time he'd killed, but he had to admit it had been one of the easiest.

Things had moved quickly after that. Calling the ambulance, having her declared dead, and then getting the coroner to doctor his report had been done as speedily as possible. Two days after she was gone, cremation had occurred. His son had been furious with him. Admittedly, foregoing the wake, mass, and burial had gone against tradition. In his family, saying goodbye to a loved one could take days, sometimes a week. He didn't have time for all that malarkey. Cremation was not only strongly discouraged, but to his immediate family, it was a sacrilege. However, when he'd shown his son the notarized statement from his mother insisting on cremation, he had backed down. Of course, she'd signed no such thing, but a little money under the table to a paralegal at a law firm had fixed that.

Now that the small matter of his first marriage was taken care of, he could concentrate on his upcoming nuptials. It couldn't be for a while yet. No way would anyone believe he had just happened to find Jasmine McAlister and fallen immediately in love with her. These things took time. And during this waiting period, the girl would learn who she was and exactly what was expected of her.

A couple of his most trusted people had dug deep into the identity she'd been using, and what he had learned had set his mind at ease. The girl was a nobody. She'd been living an aimless, pointless existence with no goals or hope for the future. From what he could tell, she had zero ambition. Considering what she came from, that had been a surprise. However, when one wasn't taught correctly, one likely didn't know to reach for more. A classic case of nature versus nurture. The girl just didn't know any better. But he would educate her, and she would soon learn her place.

At this very moment, his men were attending to her needs. His instructions had been clear. Clean the girl up well enough for transport and get her to the new location. It was much nicer than where she currently resided. The kennel had been a humbling experience for her and had gotten the desired results.

Her new location would be like heaven compared to the kennel. He'd rented a nice house outside the city. The girl would have good food to eat, a clean bed to sleep in, and access to as many showers and baths as she wanted. There would be no restrictions placed on her inside the house. She even had a pool to frolic in, if she so desired.

Clothing would be provided for her, as well as books and music to her heart's content. Obviously, there would be no Internet or phones, but he'd provided over a thousand DVDs that would keep her entertained.

She was going to be treated like the queen she was, and when she took her crown, she would give him all the credit.

Of course, she would be reminded that if she misbehaved, her circumstances would change in a heartbeat. But after seeing how broken she was, he had no doubt that the mere mention of the kennels would bring her to heel.

While he waited for the appropriate time to introduce her and claim his queen, she would learn how to behave. Though the girl was comely enough, her hair brought to mind a teenage boy. She was small and fine-boned, like a pretty little bird, but she was going to have to look the part for her new role. She would learn how to act and speak in the manner befitting her position. Her clothing would be chosen for her, and she would learn how to look regal at all times.

And when he introduced her, no one would question who she was or why she would become his bride. Sure, his son would rebel, but his opinion no longer mattered. Kevin had given him a chance to join the family business, and he had refused. As far as Kevin was concerned, he was now childless. He would remain that way until he remarried and started a new family, this time one that would be loyal to him.

Kevin shook his head, a smile spreading across his face as he considered all the riches and rewards that would be coming his way. He wasn't usually one to pat himself on the back, but he had to admit that, in this, he was a genius.

Nothing would stop him from claiming what should have been his long ago.

CHAPTER TWENTY-TWO

Xavier wove in and out of the heavy Chicago traffic, his mind running as fast as his bike. Twenty-four hours here, and he was no closer to finding Jazz than he had been in Seattle. Kate had told Ash to look at the Byrne family out of Chicago. There were over two thousand Byrnes in the city. Needle meet big-assed haystack.

He'd investigated over fifty of them so far. He'd found Realtors, doctors, restaurant owners, teachers, grocery store owners, mechanics, and a dry cleaners. Not one of them looked remotely suspicious.

As soon as his plane had touched down, he'd taken a taxi to the closest BMW motorcycle store. For getting in and out of traffic quickly and going places other vehicles couldn't go, nothing beat a motorcycle, and in his opinion, nothing beat a BMW for speed and quality. He had one back home, and now he owned another one. Jazz had mentioned that she'd like to go riding with him sometime, and he wanted to make that happen.

He just had to find her.

Ash and the rest of the team had arrived a few hours ago.

They were at the hotel setting up, but he hadn't been able to sit still. While every Byrne he'd checked into looked clean, not knowing why Jazz had been taken made it a lot harder to figure out what to consider as suspicious.

Kate's reticence about giving them intel to help find Jazz was infuriating. Xavier didn't care that she'd sworn that what she was withholding wouldn't help find her. She was keeping something from them that pertained to Jazz, and that wasn't right.

When this was over and Jazz was safe, they were going to have to confront Kate. She might not be an official OZ operative, but for years they had relied on each other to provide intel and assistance as necessary. Not being able to trust Kate Walker hit at the very heart of who Option Zero was and what they fought for every day.

An unusual feeling of helplessness washed over him. Jazz had been taken almost two weeks ago, and other than a name and a city, they had absolutely nothing to go on. Two of the men who'd abducted her were dead, which showed whoever was responsible didn't have a problem with killing.

Why she'd been taken, who had taken her, what, if anything, was being done to her were all still mysteries. Option Zero was one of the most powerful covert ops organizations in the world. They had taken down terrorists, prevented wars, and destroyed dictators. And yet, one of their own had been taken, and it was as if they were fumbling around in the dark, having no idea which direction to head.

Jazz was counting on them to find her. He knew she was strong and resilient. If she could get away, she would. Her size and beauty took nothing away from her strength and courage. She'd had his back more times than he could count, and he trusted her with his life.

And she trusted him with hers. That was one of the most

frustrating things. Jazz needed him, was depending on him to find her, and he had no idea how to do that.

He thought about all the missed opportunities he'd had to tell her how he felt about her. He'd let fear of rejection hold him back. If he'd told her he was falling for her, and she hadn't felt the same way, he had known their partnership would be ruined. All that fear was gone now. The moment he found her, she would have no doubts about where he stood. If she didn't feel the same way? Then he'd do his very best to convince her otherwise.

The vibration of the phone in his pocket jerked his attention away from his worry. Serena was supposed to call with a whole new list of Byrnes to check out. Quickly turning into the parking lot of a convenience store, he turned off his engine and grabbed his phone. Not looking at the screen, he clicked the answer icon and growled, "What've you got?"

A weak, whispering voice said, "Xavier?"

Every cell in his body stiffened as his heart stalled in his chest. "Jazz?" he whispered. "Is that you?"

"Xavier…I need help."

"Where are you?"

"Not sure. Close to Chicago…I think."

"Okay. Hang on, baby. I'll trace the call." Quickly putting Jazz on hold, he punched in Serena's number. The second she answered, he said, "I've got Jazz on the phone. Can you trace the call?"

"Yes! I'm on it."

Returning to Jazz, he said, "Jazz…you there?" When there was no answer, his heart fell. Had she passed out? "Jazz! Can you hear me?"

"Xavier…I need…"

"We're on the way, baby. Just hang on."

"It hurts…"

Hearing those words almost broke him. "I'm on the way, Jazz. Are you safe?"

"Yes…think so… Please hurry."

His phone pinged with a text from Serena with an address and a map of Jazz's location. Another text followed: *We're jumping on the chopper and will be right behind you.*

Needing no more encouragement, Xavier hit the starter on his bike and took off. He was grateful he'd packed his helmet since he was able to turn on the Bluetooth and continue talking to Jazz.

"Hey, you there?" he asked.

"Yes," she whispered. "Feeling woozy."

Since he needed to keep her awake and talking, he asked, "Can you tell me what happened?"

"Not sure. Some men grabbed me in Seattle. Brought me to Chicago."

Weaving around a slow-moving van, Xavier asked, "Do you know who they worked for?"

No answer.

"Jazz!" he shouted. "Stay awake!"

"Sorry…I…so sleepy."

"I know you are, baby, but you've got to stay awake. Can you do that?"

"I'll…try."

In the five minutes or so they'd been talking, her voice had gotten progressively more faint. He had to keep her awake.

"Concentrate, Jazz. Tell me what happened."

"Okay…okay… Um… I woke up in a bedroom in Chicago. A creepy old man came in. Never told me his name."

"Okay. Did he say what he wanted?"

"No. But he knew me…my real name."

Then this had to be related to her life before she'd joined Option Zero. No one outside the OZ family knew their real names. They used aliases on every mission.

"Can you describe the guy? What he looked like?" When she didn't answer, Xavier feared the worst. "Jazz!"

Still no answer. Had she lost consciousness? Was she even alive?

He checked the GPS screen. He was still eight minutes out at least. The highway was filled with midday lunch traffic, and while his bike could dodge and weave, and he could drive like a bat out of hell, that wasn't going to get him there right this minute.

Hoping that some part of her was still aware and could hear him, Xavier did the only thing he knew to do.

"Jazz," he whispered, "I don't know if you can still hear me, but I need to tell you this. You're the most important person in my life. Just…hang on, baby. Please, hang on."

Hearing a thump-thumping roar, he looked up and spotted the OZ chopper. It would get to her faster, and he felt a swell of relief. Gideon was on the helicopter. Though they all had some emergency medical training, Gideon was their go-to guy for anything more complicated. He would get to Jazz first and be able to help her.

As he watched the chopper fly over him and continue toward their destination, he prayed with all the hope and passion in his heart that they would get there in time.

THE MINUTE Xavier skidded into the parking lot of an abandoned-looking building, any hope that Jazz would be in less serious condition than he feared disappeared the minute he saw Serena on her knees beside Jazz's head, talking to her while Gideon was on the other side, hooking her up to an IV. It was hard to believe that the small, huddled figure lying on the ground was his partner. Blood pooled around her body, and even before he got close enough to see her face, he could tell she was hideously pale.

Jumping off his bike, he ran forward, shouting, "How is she?"

Gideon shook his head. "She's lost a lot of blood. She was conscious when we arrived but passed out seconds later."

"Why is she bleeding?"

"Three gunshot wounds."

His legs no longer able to support him, he fell to his knees beside her. Some bastard had shot her three times? How the hell was she even still alive?

"Quinn?"

He turned to see Ash, who was standing close to the building where Xavier assumed Jazz had been held. The rage on his boss's face was telling. Whatever he'd seen had infuriated him.

"Go with Gideon and Serena to the hospital," he said. "Eve and I will finish up here and meet you there."

Though he had a thousand questions about what Ash and Eve had seen, Xavier knew his first priority was Jazz.

"Okay," Gideon said, "we can't wait any longer. Xavier, you lift her. Be careful of the wounds—right hip, right thigh, and right calf. Serena, you hold on to the IV."

His heart pounding with anguish and fury, Xavier gently lifted Jazz into his arms. He had carried her once before when she'd been injured a couple of years ago and remembered how light she'd been. That was nothing to how she felt now. Not only had the bastards shot her repeatedly, it looked like they'd starved her, too.

Serena got on the chopper first and held the IV steady while Xavier climbed into the open space and carefully placed Jazz onto a blanket someone had already laid out.

Gideon jumped into the cockpit, and they were airborne in

less than a minute. As he looked down at Jazz's pale, still face, Xavier made a silent promise that he would find who had done this to her, and he would end them.

CHAPTER TWENTY-THREE

On the edge of consciousness, Jazz's first impression was the feeling of safety. Though full awareness hadn't kicked in yet, she somehow knew that she no longer needed to be afraid.

Soft, feminine whispers around her brought her closer to the surface. She took in a shallow breath, working toward coherency. That's when she felt it. Pain was everywhere...even though it was on the outer edge—more like a distant threat—she recognized that something bad had happened. That something was causing her to hurt. Her mind was still too foggy to comprehend details. Waking up seemed suddenly imperative. Where was she? Why were people whispering?

"There she is." The soft whisper made her smile. She recognized Serena's low, quiet tone, almost lyrical in its sweetness.

"Yes, she's definitely waking up."

Her smile grew wider. That husky, feminine voice was none other than Eve's.

Two of her closest friends were with her. She really was safe.

"She's smiling."

Aw, she'd know that gruff, masculine voice anywhere. Gideon was also here. Even though she was ready to open her eyes, she waited for the voice she wanted to hear the most. He had to be here. No way would he not be close by when she woke up.

She pushed aside for now the questions about why she'd been unconscious and why she was hurting. Having the reassurance that her friends were close by was enough. Knowing Xavier was here, too, would be the ultimate reassurance. But why hadn't she heard him?

Unable to wait any longer, Jazz forced her eyes open. Though her vision was slightly blurry, she made out the faces of some of her favorite people. Serena stood on one side. Eve was on the other. Gideon was at the end of the bed.

She shied away from the knowledge that she was in a bed —most likely a hospital bed. She'd think about that later.

There was no one else in the room, and the surge of disappointment caused her mouth to tremble. Why wasn't Xavier here?

"Jazz?" Serena said softly.

She tried to speak and realized her mouth was so dry, she couldn't get past a raspy groan. A glass of water with a bent straw appeared before her, and she took a short sip, thinking that nothing had ever tasted sweeter than the deliciously cool, clean water.

Swallowing down the liquid, she tried again. "Where's Xavier?"

Eve and Serena exchanged a look, and fear flooded her body, increasing the pain she'd refused to acknowledge. Her voice trembling, she whispered, "Is he okay?"

"He's fine," Gideon said. "He and Ash had to leave for a few hours. They'll both be back soon."

Serena punched in something on her phone as she said,

"He told us to call as soon as you woke up." Holding the phone to Jazz's ear, she said, "Here he is."

"Serena?" Xavier said.

Just hearing his voice calmed her. "Hey, it's me," Jazz whispered.

"Jazz…baby. It's so good to hear your voice again. How are you feeling?"

"A little woozy."

"Are you hurting anywhere? If so, they can give you—"

"No." The last thing she wanted was to be drugged and miss whatever was going on. "I'm okay. Where are you? Where's Ash?"

"We're trying to get some answers for you. Hold on. Ash wants to talk to you."

Despite herself, Jazz tensed. She respected Ash so much, and she knew she'd screwed up by going off grid. Just removing the tracker in her arm was grounds for dismissal, not to mention all the other things she'd done to violate protocol.

"Jazz, thank God you're okay," Ash said. "How are you feeling?"

"Not too bad, considering. I'm sorry, Ash. I shouldn't have—"

"Don't worry about that now. We'll talk when you're better."

"Okay… I—"

"Here's Xavier again."

"Jazz, sweetheart. Rest and get better. We'll be back soon." Before she could say anything else, the call ended.

She shook her head, more confused now than when she'd first woken. First, things had definitely changed between her and Xavier. Not only had he called her *baby* and *sweetheart*, his voice had been warm and tender. She hadn't necessarily expected explosive anger—that wasn't Xavier's way. But she'd never expected to hear the raw emotion he'd revealed in their short conversation. Had they finally turned a corner?

Second, he and Ash were going somewhere to get answers. About her abduction? Did they know who'd taken her and why?

Handing the phone back to Serena, she looked at the three people in front of her. "Somebody want to tell me what's going on?"

~

NORTH CAROLINA

Sitting in the passenger seat as Ash drove them toward Kate Walker's estate, Xavier blew out a relieved, shaky breath. Jazz really was going to be okay. There had been a part of him that hadn't believed that. She had looked so broken, so lifeless. Thankfully, the bullets hadn't hit any organs or done any major damage. Even though she was suffering from dehydration and, based on her weight loss, had apparently been almost starved to death, the doctors were optimistic that she would be up and back to work within six to eight weeks, maybe less. But until he'd heard her voice, he hadn't allowed himself to truly believe she would be all right.

When Ash and Eve had arrived at the hospital, Jazz had been in surgery. He, along with Gideon and Serena, had been pacing in the waiting room. The description of what they'd found had left him stunned and enraged. They'd taken photos of the cage where she'd been held. He had seen the evidence of the inhumanity and brutality of what she had endured. And he'd seen the body of the man she'd killed. Besides the dead body, there had been additional blood as well, which made him wonder if a third person had been there and possibly escaped.

Knowing what she had been through, how she'd been

abused, it took every bit of his willpower not to tear the whole city down to find everyone who was involved in her abduction and torture and do the same thing to them that had been done to her.

Ash had been of the same mind, but he'd had a cooler head and a plan. Kate Walker knew more than what she'd shared. Why she wasn't telling them everything was a mystery they needed to explore. Getting in her face as soon as possible was imperative. When Ash said he'd go alone, suggesting Xavier should stay with Jazz, he'd balked. Serena, Eve, and Gideon would stay with Jazz, keeping her safe. The only way Xavier knew to make sure she stayed one hundred percent safe was to find the danger and extinguish the threat. To do that, he wanted information, and he wanted it yesterday.

He shot Ash a glance. "You think she'll tell us everything?"

"Hard to say. If you'd told me before this happened that Kate would keep any intel from us that might save Jazz's life, I'd have punched you in the face. Now? I just don't know. Kate's been in this game longer than I have. She's involved in more than just Option Zero missions. But the intel she's provided us, along with the assistance from her people, have saved numerous lives. I'll never discount what she's done for us."

"And she's your son's godmother."

Ash ran his fingers through his hair and sighed. "Yeah, there's that. Plus, if not for her, Jules might not be alive. And I certainly would never have met her without Kate's assistance."

"According to all that Jazz has told me, Kate saved her life, too. They have a close relationship. Makes no sense that she wouldn't tell us if she knows who took her."

"I agree. But she's keeping things from us for sure. If we can't trust her, then Option Zero might need to cut ties with her."

Xavier hoped that didn't happen. Kate Walker had aided

them in numerous ways. Without her, some of them might be dead. To think she was working against them seemed almost impossible. But Ash was right. If she was keeping secrets that involved who'd taken Jazz, then all bets were off.

The car slowed as Ash braked and then turned into the private drive that led up to Kate's home. The first time Xavier had seen the compound, he'd been awed, not only by its vastness, but also the grandeur of the structure. Lars, Kate's late husband, had been from England and had built a home that brought to mind an old English castle, including turrets and a stone bridge that separated several buildings from the main structure.

As they pulled onto the circular drive, Xavier paid little attention to the magnificence and grace. His only priority was obtaining the answers they needed.

Kate met them in the drive. Ash hadn't informed her he was coming, but Kate had access to intel some countries would probably envy. She likely had known the moment their plane had landed at the airport.

Dressed in a pair of black pants and a multicolored blouse, her dark hair falling around her in a casual way, Kate Walker looked both elegant and relaxed. At about five feet seven, with a slender build and the rigid posture of her former law enforcement background, she was a force to be reckoned with. The confident air she exuded had always been something he had admired. Today, he felt none of those things.

The minute they stepped out of the car, she said, "I understand you found Jazz."

Of course she knew this. Xavier didn't even bother to wonder how she'd gotten intel that only a handful of people knew. His priority was getting the information he needed.

"Kate," Ash said calmly, "we need to talk."

"Of course we do. Follow me." With that, she turned and walked through the front door.

Following her, Xavier ran through a litany of things he wanted to ask. And even though she didn't seem worried, he'd noted a slight furrowing of her brow, as well as a clenching of her jaw. She wasn't nearly as calm as she wanted them to think.

They followed her into a large room filled with several sofas, along with some low tables and a few overstuffed chairs. She led them to a raised area with a table and four chairs. Coffee mugs and a carafe awaited them, along with a plate of sandwiches and a small cake. She had definitely been expecting them.

"Have a seat, gentlemen."

Playing along, Ash sat, poured himself a cup of coffee, took a couple of swallows, and then said, "Tea time's over, Kate. Time to tell us what the hell's going on."

"Always to the point, Ash." A softness entered her eyes as she said, "How's Jazz?"

"Why don't you tell us, Kate?" Xavier snapped. "Seems like you know a helluva lot."

"I know less than you might think, Xavier. But I would like to know how Jazz is doing."

"She was shot three times. Did you also know that?"

"Yes, but fortunately they were non-life-threatening injuries."

"She was kept in a fucking kennel like an animal," Xavier snarled. "Almost starved to death. You act like it's no big deal."

"On the contrary, I'm infuriated that she was hurt. You may not believe this, but I'm extremely fond of Jazz."

Holding up his hand and giving Xavier a telling look, Ash turned to Kate. "We know you are, Kate. And that's why you're going to tell us everything you know about the people who took her."

"I've already told you that I—"

"You told us to go to Chicago and look at people with the name Byrne. Why?"

"Did you ask Jazz what she knows about who took her?"

Xavier ground his teeth. He wasn't sure he'd ever been more disappointed in anyone. It was obvious that Kate was holding out on them.

"Jazz was unconscious when we found her," Ash answered. "She had to undergo surgery to have three bullets removed. She's suffering from blood loss, dehydration, and exposure. So no, Kate, we didn't ask her for intel. We were waiting to see if she was going to live."

Though Ash never raised his voice, it was more than obvious that the man was teetering on the edge of losing his famous cool. And that was just fine with Xavier. He was seconds away from pulling his gun and making threats. It would likely get him shot—he was sure Kate had more than one weapon on her—but he was willing to take the risk.

A flicker of distress traveled across her face, and then she sighed. "Ash, there are things at play here that are bigger than me, bigger than you, and bigger than Jazz."

"Don't give me that. We've known each other a long time. We've kept secrets that would make the devil himself tremble if he knew them. There is nothing you can tell me that would be detrimental to you or anyone else."

"What I can tell you is that I believe Jazz's abduction is related to her past—her childhood." Twisting round, she pulled a folder from a nearby credenza. Sliding it across the table, she gave them both a determined look. "Here is every-thing I know about Jazz and the people who might have abducted her. That's all I can give you."

Ash opened the folder, then pushed it toward Xavier so they could both read the brief, short sentences within and see that Kate was very likely telling the truth.

"How much of this does Jazz know?"

Just for an instant, Kate showed a momentary guilt as she said softly, "She knows absolutely nothing."

THE MINUTE ASH and Xavier walked out of the room, Kate let loose a long, shaky breath. That hadn't gone well, but she really hadn't expected that it would.

All her energy had been focused on not thinking about what Jazz had gone through. If she had known exactly who'd taken her, she would have rescued her without a qualm. She wasn't heartless. Jazz meant the world to her, but that didn't mean she could distract key players from the bigger picture.

But now, not only was her relationship with the entire Option Zero team in jeopardy, she needed to make another phone call. One she had put off for too long.

Retrieving her satphone, she punched in a series of numbers. The instant the call went through, she said, "Before I tell you what's happened, I'll say up front that Jazz is safe."

"What does that mean?"

As she explained what had happened, she could feel the explosive anger all the way across two continents. If he were here in front of her, she had serious doubts that she would survive his wrath. She wasn't afraid of this man, but she did respect his skills.

"And the reason I wasn't told?" he growled.

"There wasn't anything you could do. The team was working the case. I had no real intel on who was responsible. It could have been one of a hundred or more. You know that."

"That wasn't your call to make."

They could argue that point, but she wasn't going to even try. They had more than enough on their plate as it was.

"She's going to want some answers soon," Kate said. "When she's well enough."

"I don't want her involved."

"She's already involved. She's a valuable member of the most elite black ops team in the world. She's tough as nails."

There was a long silence, and she knew he was thinking long and hard about where this needed to go. Finally, he gave her the words she knew he despised saying. "When she's well enough, I'll give her what I can."

Before she could feel a modicum of relief, he added, "And, Ms. Walker, if you keep anything like this from me again, no agreements or obligations will keep me from coming after you."

The line went dead before she could respond to his threat. She didn't work for him. He didn't work for her. And even though they were on the same side, they were adversaries in many ways.

Her shoulders drooping with the weight of her world, she placed the phone on the table in front of her and said softly, "I know you're disappointed in me, my darling. And out of everyone who's angry with me in this, the idea of disappointing you rips at me more than anything."

Turning, she looked up at the portrait of the man she had adored…still adored. They'd had only a few short years together, and she would give everything she owned just to have one extra day.

"But hear me now, my love. They will pay for what they did. I will not rest until it's done. No matter who stands in my way, I will end them."

XAVIER AND ASH were halfway to the airport before they spoke. The intel Kate had given them was minuscule in some ways, but in light of what had happened to Jazz, it was earth-shattering.

"When do we tell her?" Ash asked.

Xavier appreciated that his boss was asking for his input. Telling Jazz was going to be a delicate matter, to say the least. Not only was she in for some major surprises and heartache, there were still gigantic holes in the information Kate had provided. She would have questions and would want answers immediately.

"She's not going to be in any condition to hear any of this for a while. Because once she does…"

Ash nodded. "Once she does, she's going to want to get to work."

"Yeah."

"Okay. We'll wait."

Xavier didn't ask for how long. This might be a one-day-at-a-time thing until they both thought she was ready. Yeah, she'd take a giant bite out of his ass if she knew his thinking, but this was going to have to be the way until it wasn't. He wasn't going to take the chance of losing her again.

"And Kate?" Xavier said.

"She's holding on to a boatload of intel. Until we can figure out what's going on, or until she's willing to spill, we keep her out of our circle."

"What she gave us is a good starting place," Xavier said. "She wasn't lying about that."

"No. I don't think she's lied about anything. She just knows a lot more than she's willing to share. For now, we'll focus on who grabbed Jazz and why. Based on the little intel she gave us, we know the major player in this massive cover-up is dead, as is his family. But someone wanted Jazz for what she could do for them. We find out what that is, then we might pinpoint who took her."

Nodding his agreement, Xavier took in the scenery as they sped down the highway. The Blue Ridge Mountains were a beautiful, impressive sight, but he missed Montana's massive peaks and snow-covered vistas. When Jazz was well enough to be moved, he wanted to take her to his cabin. He would care for her and make sure she regained her health. In the meantime, he and the team would dig deep to find out who'd had the audacity to capture and torture one of their own.

And when she was ready, he would tell her everything, including what was in his heart.

CHAPTER TWENTY-FOUR

Chicago

O scar Sullivan glared at the dead coroner lying on the floor. Dead men told no tales, and that was something his good-for-nothing scum of a brother-in-law had forgotten. Guilt lay heavy on Oscar's shoulders, but it had nothing to do with killing this crap of a dead doctor. This had all started because Oscar had found the girl in the first place. Going to Kevin had been a mistake.

If only he'd just taken the girl for himself and used her for what she was meant for, none of this would have happened. He knew a part of him still had that old-school mentality. In the old days, Kevin had been of a higher rank, and Oscar had followed that odd kind of protocol. And now his beloved sister was dead.

The coroner had been easy enough to break. For a nice chunk of change, the doctor had skewed the autopsy findings to show an aneurysm had killed his sister and not the poison Kevin had injected into her scalp. And that was why the coroner would never be able to draw another breath. He might not have done the actual deed, but he had covered it up, and that made him guilty in Oscar's book.

He still had no idea how his sister's will had come to indicate that cremation was her preference instead of a traditional Irish funeral. He'd known his sister—obviously better than her husband had—because there was no way she would have chosen such a thing. Not only would she have considered it a sacrilege, she had once told him that she was terrified of cremation. She wouldn't have changed her mind. So either Kevin had forged that document, or he'd somehow coerced her into agreeing to it. Either way, he knew without a doubt that the man was responsible.

A deep, dark sadness swept over him. He had acknowledged his role in how this played out, and he would regret to his dying day his part in making this happen. The only way to make amends for the wrongs done to his sister was to destroy the person responsible.

Once that was done, he'd find the girl again. Just because she had escaped didn't mean he didn't still need her. She was the key to everything. But once he had her, he'd do it right this time. Just because the girl was the key didn't mean she needed to survive. He just needed her for a few statements and signatures. Having her breathing after that would be more of a problem than he'd want to handle.

But first things first. Some retribution needed to take place.

Pulling his phone from his pocket, he placed a call to get everything started.

HIS HAND SHAKING, Kevin poured himself another three fingers of Scotch. The first two glasses had eased the pangs of disappointment, but what was left was a rage beyond anything he'd ever felt before. He had to get ahold of himself to handle the fallout. He had to figure what to do and where to go from here.

Obviously, he had underestimated the little witch. She had looked so tiny and harmless. No one that small, especially a woman, should have been able to take down two of his men. They might not have been the smartest, but what they'd lacked in intelligence, they'd more than made up in bulk. They'd certainly known how to subdue a hundred-pound woman. So what the hell had happened?

He'd never gotten any answers from her. Where had she gotten her self-defense training? She'd had two professional-grade weapons on her when she had been taken, and she had never told him why or how she'd come by them. Had she known how to use them?

The video feed he'd seen of her whimpering and crying for mercy had been faked. That much he knew. She had been playacting this whole time, pretending she'd learned her lesson and was ready to comply with his demands.

He'd thought limiting her food and water intake and treating her like an animal with absolutely no comfort items other than the blanket and pillow would have broken her. And while he'd allowed her a toothbrush and toothpaste, that had been more for him than for her. The last thing he'd wanted was a wife with rotting teeth.

But those items were minuscule compared to what he would have given her if she had just done what he wanted.

When his men hadn't brought her to the house like he'd ordered, he'd pulled up the feed from outside the kennel. The live feed had given him nothing. Just an empty parking lot. Then he'd pulled up a recording from two hours prior, and his whole world had shifted.

He'd watched Miles and Kip go into the building. He now regretted not adding cameras to the inside, but since he hadn't planned for the girl to stay longer than a few days, he hadn't wanted the added expense. What had gone on inside he could only guess, but fifteen minutes after the men had entered, the girl came stumbling out. Alone.

The angle of the camera had been off, so he couldn't see her all that well, but from the way she walked, he knew she'd been injured. She'd barely made it outside the door before she'd stumbled and fallen. As she lay there, he had held his breath, figuring at least one of the men would follow her out. He'd watched as she made a call from a cellphone. It had to have belonged to one of the men. So not only had she disabled the men, she had managed to get a phone to call for help.

The call lasted only a couple of minutes, but he could tell the girl was on her last dregs of consciousness. Then, to his surprise and delight, Miles had come staggering out of the building, holding a hand against his shoulder. He'd glared down at the girl, and though Kevin couldn't hear any words, he knew the man was furious. When he'd spat on the girl and kicked dirt into her face, she hadn't reacted, which made him wonder if she was even alive.

Still, he had assumed the man would pick her up and bring her to the house, dead or alive. But no, that hadn't happened. Instead, Miles had taken the phone out of her hand, spat on her again, and then gotten into his truck and driven away.

Kevin had sat there for the longest time, watching the girl and waiting for something else to happen. He thought maybe Kip, his other man, might come out. Or even that Miles would return to get her. But that hadn't happened. He'd called Miles to demand an explanation. So far, the man hadn't returned his call.

Then, what had occurred after that was so far-fetched, even now he questioned if he'd actually witnessed the events.

A large helicopter had appeared out of nowhere and landed in the parking lot. Two men and two women had emerged from the chopper and run toward the fallen girl. All four of them were armed. The men were large and looked fierce. The women were small but appeared just as dangerous.

While one of the men and one of the women attended the girl, the other man and woman went inside the facility. Seconds later, a man on a motorcycle skidded into view. The man jumped off the cycle and ran to the girl. They apparently knew him, because they talked to him as they continued to work on the girl. Even though Kevin got only a side view, he was almost certain that the motorcycle man was the one he'd seen with the girl at the restaurant. And now he, along with some others, had rescued the girl and erased all of Kevin's hard work.

They'd administered first aid and then taken her away, no doubt to a hospital. Two of them had stayed behind, apparently trying to figure out what had gone on inside the building.

Kevin tried to find anything positive in all this, but there was absolutely nothing there. True, the fact that they likely didn't know who'd taken the girl was a definite plus. He didn't know what her injuries were—didn't care. But he didn't want her dead. She was of no use to him dead. Unfortunately, it was now going to be even harder to get to her. Especially since he didn't know where she was or what name she might be using. He knew only what was in her bloodline, and that was the most important thing of all.

Going to the kennel and checking it out for himself was out of the question. He was sure someone would be keeping an eye on it for some time to come. The body of Kip had already been carried out by some cleaners. He assumed they belonged to the same group who'd rescued the girl.

Thankfully, Kip had no relationship to him or his family. He performed grunt work for various families throughout the city. Tying him to just the Doyle family would be impossible.

True, he and Miles had likely worked for him more lately, but since that development had been a recent happening, no one should be the wiser.

The kennel couldn't be traced back to him either. He'd paid the guy under the table for the building, so there was no paperwork to be found. The man he'd bought it from had died a few months later—not his doing. He'd just been old.

So Kevin knew he was in the clear in that respect. Now he just had to figure out how to get the girl back.

As he downed the last of his Scotch, he decided that things weren't really all that bad. For one, he knew the girl existed. That was huge, because before, there had just been conjecture.

He would hire private investigators to find her again. Good ones this time. Yeah, it would be expensive, but once he found the girl, all his money problems would be over. He'd have plenty of cash to take care of any expenses he incurred.

Although he was a little concerned that Oscar suspected him of doing something to his wife. They hadn't really talked since the memorial service, but he thought he'd caught his brother-in-law giving him the stink eye a few times. But that could just be his imagination—he'd been under a lot of stress, having just lost his wife and all.

There was no way to prove he'd had anything to do with her death. The coroner had been well paid to skew the results of the autopsy. He wouldn't snitch since his ass was on the line, too.

He poured himself just a smidgen more Scotch to take that final edge off. Everything was just fine. Just fine.

A noise outside in the parking lot caught his attention. Sounded like a car door slamming. He frowned because it was well past midnight. The restaurant downstairs had closed a few hours ago. There would be no reason for anyone to be here.

Staggering to the window, he looked down into the empty

lot, and his heart almost stopped. The glass fell from his hand, and he stumbled back. His son was headed to the back entrance. The streetlight had given him a good view of his expression. He'd never seen that look on his face before—he had, in fact, tried to teach him that look to no avail. Everything he knew about torture and killing he'd learned from Kevin, but Kevin hadn't believed it had ever taken. But now, seeing that expression, Kevin thought he might have succeeded all too well.

Whirling around, he desperately searched for a way out. He was here for him—of that he had no doubt. In a moment of clarity, Kevin knew what had happened. Oscar had double-crossed him. Probably told Ryan that Kevin had killed his mama. The kid had been a mama's boy, through and through. No matter how many times he'd beat him till he was broken and bloody, determined to destroy any tender feelings and make him a man he could be proud of, Ryan had never gotten over his affection for her.

The thud of footsteps on the stairway sounded like thunder. His heart pounded so hard against his chest, he could barely think straight. Ryan wouldn't kill him outright. He'd torture him first, just like he'd been taught.

Dashing to his desk, he now cursed the Scotch he'd consumed. His stomach roiling with acid and bile, he pulled open a drawer and withdrew his nine millimeter. He'd shoot him. Once he got the girl back, he'd get another son—maybe two or three. This time, he'd raise them right. They wouldn't be weak mama's boys like this one.

Leaning against the desk, he pointed his gun at the door. The footsteps were close now. In seconds, Ryan would burst through the door. Even drunk, Kevin was smart and aware enough to know that his aim would be off. He'd have only one chance.

A ping on his phone behind him caught his attention. His

hand shaking, he clicked without even thinking about the threat he was about to face. When he saw the text and the photo, he knew he was done for.

A harsh sob escaped him. None of this had worked out the way he'd planned. And it was all the girl's fault.

Closing his eyes, cursing the girl for destroying his dreams, he turned the gun, pressed the barrel against his temple, and pulled the trigger.

CHAPTER TWENTY-FIVE

Her first moment of awareness was the feel of a large, warm hand holding hers. Jazz blinked sleepily and then smiled at the sight before her. Xavier sat in the chair beside the bed. He looked like he'd been there awhile. He was slightly slumped over, his eyes were closed, and he was softly snoring. His beard was more straggly than usual, his face was pale, and the shadows beneath his eyes were a testament to his worry and loss of sleep.

Those beautiful eyes blinked open, and when he looked at her, she felt as if her whole world had been set right again.

"Hey, you," he said gruffly.

"Are you okay?"

Confusion flickered across his face. "I think that's what I should be asking you."

"You look…" She'd never been one for diplomacy, often speaking bluntly. This was no exception. "You look like hell."

"That's what happens when the most important person in your life disappears."

Everything within Jazz stilled. Seeing her brother again, realizing he was a killer, being abducted, tortured, and starved… None of those things had brought her to tears. But Xavier admitting how he felt about her brought up a well of emotion she could not quell.

Saying her name softly, Xavier surged up from his chair and gathered her gently in his arms. Burying her face against his chest, Jazz finally let go of the fear and outrage that had consumed her for the last two weeks. She was here, with Xavier. This man—this honorable, courageous, wonderful man—meant the world to her. All that she had suffered and endured was smothered by the comfort of his arms.

"I was so worried about you, baby," Xavier whispered against her hair.

"I'm so sorry," she whispered.

"No. You have nothing to be sorry for. What those bastards did to you was not your fault."

Maybe not, but if she had just been honest and forthright with him, none of this likely would have happened. Even though she still didn't know why she'd been taken, she knew she'd put herself in a vulnerable position, and that was on her.

"I kept praying that you would find me."

Neither of them mentioned how much easier it would have been to find her if she hadn't removed her tracker. She knew that explanation would have to be given soon.

He held her a while longer, letting her cling to him as long as she needed. For most of her adult life, Jazz had hidden her deepest emotions behind a facade of bravado. It was how she'd learned to cope with all the emotional pain she'd endured. With Xavier, that never seemed necessary. It was as if he had an insight into her mind that defied basic physics. Xavier saw *her*—not who she pretended to be.

"Think you can talk about it?" he asked gently.

Jazz drew in a breath, inhaling bergamot and ginger, two fragrances she associated with Xavier, and then nodded. "I think so."

Drawing away from her, he pressed a soft kiss on her forehead and then a quick, but firmer kiss on her mouth. When he pulled away, a slight, satisfied smile curved his lips.

"What?" she asked.

"Kissing you could become my favorite pastime."

Feeling suddenly shy, she said softly, "Mine, too."

Gifting her with one more quick kiss, Xavier settled her back against the pillows and returned to his chair. He picked up her hand again. "Ready?"

She nodded. She had told Serena, Eve, and Gideon a little when she'd first woken, but she had been so out of it, she didn't really remember if she'd told them anything useful. Today was the first day she felt clear-minded enough to give significant details.

"I don't know who took me."

"Start from the beginning."

She wiggled slightly in the bed to find the most comfortable spot. The doctor had told her the day before that her wounds were healing nicely, and though she felt much better than she had two days ago, there were still twinges of pain.

Apparently seeing her wince, Xavier said, "Want some pain meds?"

"No. Maybe later. I want to be awake enough to give you everything I can."

"Okay. Let me know if you change your mind."

Settling deeper into the bed, she began to describe her ordeal. "It was late...maybe around one in the morning. I couldn't sleep and thought I'd find a diner and get something to eat. I opened the door, and four men attacked me. I got in a few good hits, but they overpowered me. I woke up in a bedroom."

She closed her eyes and described the room in detail. She knew most of what she said was unimportant, but she'd learned that detailing as much as possible often brought to mind items she might have missed otherwise.

"I was sick…nauseated and had a horrific headache. I had a knot on the back of my head and thought it was likely a concussion. I later learned I'd been drugged, too. I don't know what with."

Xavier squeezed her hand. "The doctors ran a blood panel. Since you were given the drug so long ago, there's no evidence left in your blood. They didn't see any anomalies, though, and don't believe there'll be any lasting effects."

"Good. Thank you."

"Go on," he encouraged.

"This older man came in. In his late fifties or early sixties, iron-gray hair, a little thin on top. Light brown eyes, pale complexion. About five eleven, on the slender side, maybe about a hundred fifty pounds. Sophisticated clothes, cultured voice. Looked like he came from money.

"He didn't introduce himself and apologized for how I'd been banged up. Made two of the guys who'd taken me apologize. Said the other two had been disciplined."

"They were," Xavier said abruptly. "Their bodies were found in Seattle at a dump site. We figured they were local hires."

She didn't question how he'd known who they were. She'd get the details later but figured that Serena had likely worked her magic.

"What did the man say to you? Did he tell you what he wanted?"

"Not really. He started out by wanting to know why I was going by another name. Where I'd gotten my weapons and self-defense training. When I was taken, I only had my fake ID with me, a burner phone—which had nothing on it—plus my gun and knife."

She gasped as a thought suddenly hit her. "Oh no. The safe in my motel room. It's got—"

Xavier shook his head. "Already taken care of. We got everything—your OZ phone, your other weapons, and the tracker you were supposed to place on Bass."

She grimaced. "Sorry, I should have returned that before I took off."

Again, there was no mention of the reason for that, and she wasn't about to bring it up now.

"Also, I have this."

Pulling something from his pocket, he placed it on her palm he'd been holding. She looked down to see the chain and the locket that held the only photo she had of her family. Emotions swamped her, and it was all she could do not to give in and cry again. Swallowing past a lump in her throat, she said huskily, "Thank you."

"You're welcome."

Knowing she needed to continue, she said, "I didn't tell him anything…actually didn't speak, figuring the less I said, the more he might reveal. He didn't appreciate my silence. Told me he'd give me a few days to recover, and then he'd come back for another conversation. Right before he left, he called me Jasmine and then asked if I still went by Jazz."

"So he knew exactly who you are."

"Yeah."

"And then what happened?"

"Nothing for about three days. I was sick—really kind of out of it. Nausea and major headache. Food and water appeared three times a day. Usually delivered by a woman who wouldn't speak to me. On the third day, I finally felt halfway human and was able to eat a full meal for the first time. I took a shower and dressed in my clothes. The instant I was dressed, the man showed up again."

"He had cameras in the room."

She shrugged. "That was my guess, but I never saw them."

"What happened when he came back?"

"I went on the offensive—demanded to know who he was, why I had been taken. He didn't appreciate my attitude. Told me he was in charge. Started drilling me about my weapons, my training, and why I was using an alias. He called his goons back in. I ended up slugging him and running out of the room. The place—wherever I was—was quite large. I ran down a hallway and spotted a stairway. Before I could get to it, I was tased. I went down. And then I woke up in the kennel."

The flare of anger in his eyes told her exactly how he felt about that.

"I was told until I answered his questions honestly, I wouldn't be released. Every few days, one of the men would drop off a burger, fries, milkshake, and small bottle of water."

She didn't bother to tell him about the heat, the powerful thunderstorms, or the desolation she'd felt. This was a fact-finding interrogation, not a pity party.

"Around the fifth day, I decided to change strategies. When the burger guy arrived, I told him I was ready to talk. I pretended to break down and cry. He recorded me, took some photos. I didn't think my act worked, because the jerk basically told me it was a good start and then left.

"A few days later, the two men who'd taken me showed up with buckets of water. They said they were going to clean me up and take me back. Maybe I should have waited and let them take me back to him so I could get some intel, but I'd had enough. The minute I could, I attacked."

"You did the right thing."

She was happy to hear he agreed. It had felt good to be able to take back control. "I disabled and disarmed one guy. The other guy got to me before I could get away. He shot at me, and I turned around and killed him. I ended up killing both of them. Then I grabbed his phone and called you. I don't remember much after that."

"There was only one dead man."

Jazz shook her head. She had been weak and out of it, but she knew for a fact that she'd shot two men. "I shot one man in the head and the other in the chest."

"We found the one with the head shot. The other one apparently managed to get himself out of there. There was no vehicle there and no phone on you. So he must've taken it from you and left."

Before she could say anything else, Xavier said, "I'll get Serena to check with local hospitals to see if a gunshot victim has shown up in the last couple days."

Jazz nodded. Wherever the man was, he would either be dead or in severe pain if he hadn't gotten medical treatment. She couldn't feel the least bit of sympathy for him.

"Any identity on the dead man in the kennel?" she asked.

"Yeah. His name was Kip Warring. Small-time criminal. No known association with any particular group. We're still digging, though."

"Finding the man who took me is going to be difficult, isn't it?"

Xavier wanted to say no, that they'd be able to find him quickly and mete out justice for her. But she was smart enough to know that wasn't the case. Without having any real idea why she had been taken, they were still dealing with a large pool of suspects.

Hearing Jazz talk so dispassionately about her ordeal only reinforced his belief that she was one of the strongest people he'd ever known. She had stuck to the facts, which meant she hadn't mentioned how alone and terrified she must have been. The starvation and lack of water alone would have broken most people. But Jazz had had to fight for her life multiple times, and she had always come out on top.

He hadn't asked her why she had stayed in the city or the reasons she was investigating Bass's murder on her own. Now was not the time. Their priority was uncovering the identity of the scumbag responsible for hurting her. That meant getting as much intel as possible. There would be plenty of time for other questions later.

"Serena will be here in a few minutes to get your description of the man. He sounds like he knew what he was doing, which means hopefully he's got a record. If so, we'll use facial identification to find him."

"It's definitely a face I won't soon forget."

"There's something you need to know." He had specifically requested the team not mention what had happened to Hawke. He'd wanted to be the one to tell her. And while it would definitely upset her, he was already keeping things from her until she was stronger. If he waited any longer, she would see him not telling her sooner about Hawke as one more betrayal. He wouldn't do that to her.

A flicker of alarm crossed her face, and he wondered what she thought he was going to say. Deciding he'd take that out later and examine it, he said, "Before we learned you were taken, Hawke and I were at the restaurant, following up on some final questions. When we were leaving, someone took a shot at me."

"Who? Why?"

He would tell her about his friend Cotton later. The identity of the shooter was much less important than the man who'd paid for the hit.

"We're fairly sure the same man responsible for abducting you was the one who hired someone to kill me."

"That's insane! I thought my abduction might have something to do with my past, since he knew my real name, but if he's after you, too, there's something else going on. Is this related to one of our ops?"

"No. We've ruled that out. It's a long story, for a different day, but I know the man who took the contract. He called me after the fact and told me what had happened. He actually missed on purpose."

The confusion in her expression was battling with the fatigue he knew she was feeling. Wanting to get this said and let her rest, he continued, "Again, that's a story for another day. Thing is, even though he missed on purpose, a shard from a brick wall caught Hawke in the neck."

Gasping, Jazz sat up, horror in eyes. "What? Is he okay?"

"Yes, he's fine now. It was touch and go for a few hours because of where the piece hit and the loss of blood, but he's going to make a full recovery."

Pressing her head back against the pillow, she whispered, "Thank God for that. Liv must have been terrified."

"She was. But he's already been released from the hospital and is home with Liv and Nikki. It'll take him a few weeks to get his strength back."

Surprising him, she grabbed his hand and brought it to her mouth for a soft kiss. "I hate that Hawke was hurt, but I'm so happy you're okay."

"Yeah, me, too. We need to find this bastard and get some answers."

"And you really think it's all related? My kidnapping and someone trying to kill you?"

"Yes. But that's something we can talk about after you get some rest."

"I'd like to argue with you, but I'm not sure I can stay awake for the argument."

He laughed, and damn, did it feel good to be able to do that. He hadn't felt the slightest amusement in over two weeks —not since she'd walked away from him.

"I'll be back in a few hours. Get some rest." Standing, he leaned over and kissed her again. This time, he let his lips linger, softly caressing her mouth. She moaned beneath him, and he thought it was the sexiest, most beautiful sound in the world. He wanted to hear more of those moans.

He stopped at the door and turned to see she'd already closed her eyes, but what caught his breath in his chest was the little satisfied smile playing around her lips. Two days ago, he hadn't been sure he'd ever see her again, and now, not only did he have her back, they were both finally on the same page. He'd dreamed about this forever. And he would kill anyone who tried to take her away from him again.

CHAPTER TWENTY-SIX

Montana

S itting on the back porch of Xavier's cabin, Jazz drew in a breath of crisp fresh air, relishing its perfection. Before moving to Montana to work for Option Zero, she had always been a beach person. Mountains were pretty to look at, but you couldn't swim in them like the ocean or walk barefoot through them, the way you could on a sandy beach. After she'd lived in the state for less than a month, her attitude had undergone a drastic change. There was nothing more beautiful than a snow-capped mountain, the sweet music of a meadowlark, or the sun reflecting on a golden aspen leaf.

She was relieved to be out of the hospital and a thousand miles away from Chicago. The doctors hadn't been thrilled about her leaving, but after agreeing to follow every medical instruction and Xavier's solemn vow that he would take the very best care of her, they had relented.

Funnily enough, their greatest concerns weren't her gunshot wounds. Only one bullet had entered her, and it was actually still there. The other two had thankfully created only deep creases in her skin. She'd required stitches and antibiotics, but all in all, she'd been extremely fortunate. It had been the other things that had caused them concern—mainly her dehydration, exposure, and weight loss. Staying above one hundred ten pounds was always her goal. Most times, she didn't make it, but she normally had a healthy appetite and tried to consume enough calories. Having been deprived of food and water for almost two weeks had dropped her weight much more drastically than she'd thought. She was now hovering just below a hundred pounds.

Fortunately, her appetite was returning, so with the additional promise to eat full, healthy meals and get plenty of sleep, she had been released.

"You need anything?"

Her heart performed a double flip at the gruff, sexy voice behind her. She looked over her shoulder and inwardly sighed. Xavier had been nothing but gentle and solicitous since she'd been here, treating her as if she were made of the most fragile of porcelain. She couldn't say she hated it, because it felt so good to be cared for with such detail and determination. When Xavier Quinn set his mind to something, he was like a bulldozer, knocking down anything that might get in the way of his goal. And it was obvious that his goal was to make sure she fully recovered.

Such total focus from her sexy, handsome partner was a double-edged sword, though. On one hand, she appreciated everything he was doing for her. On the other hand, being seen as an invalid or weak was not how she wanted him to view her. Jazz thrived on her independence. And Xavier, bless him, was so vigilant that she was surprised he even allowed her to feed herself.

Realizing he was waiting for an answer, she shook her head. "I'm good."

"Are you warm enough?"

It was the middle of summer, and though they were at a high altitude, it certainly wasn't cold. However, he'd insisted on covering her with a blanket when she'd come out to sit on the porch.

"It feels good out here. Why don't you sit with me?" She scooted over on the bench. "You've been working your ass off ever since we got here."

"Just want to make sure you're taken care of."

"I know that...and I appreciate it, but you can take some time and relax with me. Okay?"

For just a second, he hesitated, and then he dropped down beside her. Then, before she could say anything, he lifted the blanket gathered on her lap and gently tucked it over her shoulders.

"Enough," she said dryly. "I'm not your grandmother."

In a tone even drier than hers, he said, "Trust me, I know that."

Twisting around to face him, she said, "Listen. I know I was in rough shape, but I'm much better now. You can relax. Okay?"

"I won't relax until we catch the bastard responsible."

"Anything new on that?"

"Not really. Serena sent out the sketch she created from your description of the guy to all our contacts in Chicago, but so far, no hits."

"I wish I could have talked to him one more time."

"Hopefully, you'll get to when we take him down." Surprising her, he threw his arm around her shoulders and pulled her closer. "But for now, you need to rest."

Since arguing would do no good and being held so close to him was a dream come true, Jazz nestled her head against his shoulder and closed her eyes. Despite everything she had gone through, she couldn't deny that she was exactly where she wanted to be.

XAVIER ALLOWED the peace to surround him. When he'd had this cabin built a couple years ago, he had imagined having Jazz here with him. Looking like a gentle breeze could knock her over hadn't been part of that vision. No matter how much she protested that she was better, she still looked as though she were from a war-torn third-world country. He wanted her stronger, healthier.

Telling her what he and Ash had learned from Kate had to be put on the back burner until she was stronger. She would have a ton of questions, and so far, he had no answers. He and Ash were digging, trying to find what they could, but the intel was almost three decades old. It was harder to find, but he was determined to get what he could before he blew her world apart.

He hadn't even talked to her about why she'd taken off and tried to work the case in Seattle on her own. There had to be specific reasons, but until she showed him she was strong enough to take some emotional turmoil, he'd keep it light and easy for her. No questions, no pressure. Just rest and good food.

Good food? He grimaced. That was one thing he hadn't considered. He wasn't a good cook. When he was home, not on an op, he usually threw a couple of sandwiches together and called it a meal. When he and Jazz were on an op, they either ate out or picked something up. But now that they were here, he wanted her to get some well-rounded healthy meals— and that was why, in between digging for intel, he'd been perusing cookbooks. So far, his efforts had been less than impressive.

The vibration in his pocket alerted him to a call. Easing

Jazz off his shoulder, he gently tilted her head to settle against the cushion behind her. She slept so deeply, she never noticed. His heart literally broke to see how pale and emaciated she looked.

Standing, he walked back into the house quickly and grabbed his phone. "Quinn."

"Hey, how's it going?" Ash asked.

"About the same. She's sleeping, eating. That's about the extent of it."

"Is she well enough to—"

"No, not yet. She needs at least another week before she faces this."

"I won't argue, but she'll need to know soon. If this intel is related to her abduction—which I feel sure it is—things are in the works we need to address."

"I know." Xavier swiped his hand down his face. Oh hell, did he know. Every moment he held off telling her, the less likely she would forgive him when he did reveal what they'd learned. He'd have to take that hit when it came, because he refused to put this on her until she was healthier.

"Serena called in and said she's running down a thread that she thinks will lead to something. She didn't go into detail."

"Is she not in town?"

"No. Her grandfather fell and broke his leg."

Xavier knew what that meant. Most of Serena's family lived in Wisconsin, and she was extremely close to them. If they needed her, she was there in a heartbeat. But what he found remarkable was her ability to continue to work on her OZ projects as well as be there for her family.

Since Sean, her husband, had pulled his disappearing act, Xavier knew she was staying extra busy to counteract the heartbreak. Some people used all sorts of crutches to deal with grief, and Serena's was her work. When he'd asked her a few weeks ago how she was doing, she'd told him that staying busy by focusing on what had to be done was the only way she'd been able to deal with Sean's defection.

Xavier had no idea where Sean had gone or why he was behaving like such an ass. All he knew was when he did turn back up, he'd have a lot to answer for. Serena meant the world to everyone at Option Zero, and they were all infuriated on her behalf.

"Jazz mention to you yet why she tried to investigate Bass's shooting on her own?"

"Not yet." They'd literally had zero conversations about work or anything remotely related to any hot-button issue. All of that was going to have to wait. "Anything come up on his killing?"

When Jazz had disappeared, all efforts to find Bass's killer had been put aside.

"No, not really. Serena put together a sketch based on the descriptions of the kitchen workers, but there were so many contradictions about them, she doesn't feel comfortable with it."

That wasn't a surprise. Even though the guy had worked at the restaurant for almost two months, the descriptions given to them by the people who'd worked side by side with the killer had been blurry at best. He'd somehow subtly changed his appearance numerous times, but not so much that those alterations had been glaringly obvious. Xavier wasn't one to admire a cold-blooded killer, but he had to give this guy props for being so crafty.

"Yeah," Xavier said, "even his height and weight fluctuated. That's a helluva talent."

"Indeed. The man's a professional. Finding him might even be harder than getting to the root of Wren itself."

The sound of a timer going off caught his attention. "Gotta go. My bread is done."

"You're baking bread?"

"Yeah…maybe."

"What does that mean?"

"It means I don't know what the hell I'm doing."

The call clicked off on Ash's guffaw of laughter. Grumbling to himself, Xavier raced to the kitchen to see just how bad this evening's meal was going to be.

CHAPTER TWENTY-SEVEN

Being as discreet as possible, Jazz spit the burnt piece of food into her napkin. She wasn't quite sure what it had been, but it no longer resembled anything edible. She knew there were bad cooks in this world—she was one of them. Xavier Quinn had taken it to a new level.

"Sorry, I think I overcooked the roast beef."

So that's what it was supposed to be.

"You told me once that you weren't much of a cook."

A chagrined expression appeared on his face. "Yeah...sorry. That hasn't changed."

"I'm not much of one either, but maybe, between the two of us, we can work together and see what happens."

"What do you mean?"

"Let's learn how to cook together."

Humor gleamed in his eyes. "I promise I'll get better. You're supposed to be resting."

"I have rested. I'm feeling tons better."

"It's only been a few days. Give it a few more, and then we'll see."

"But—"

"Seriously, Jazz. You're recovering from three bullet wounds, dehydration, and food deprivation. Not to mention the psychological trauma you went through. I'm not letting you work until you've regained some of your strength."

"You're not *letting* me? As far as I know, you're not my boss."

"No, I'm not your boss. I'm your partner and someone who cares about you a helluva lot more than you seem to care about yourself."

"I know what my strengths are and my limits."

"Oh yeah?" Standing, he dropped his napkin on the table and said, "Follow me."

Jazz did what he'd said. A part of her was already wishing that she'd just kept her mouth shut. Yes, she was bored. And yes, she absolutely hated being treated like a victim, but a part of her that was still rational told her he wasn't treating her like a victim. If he had been hurt, she would have been just as protective of him.

Knowing she'd set herself up for whatever he had planned, she followed him toward a door she hadn't even noticed. It was built to blend in with the rest of the wall, but when he pressed against it, the door opened. Inside was a veritable array of gym equipment, including a treadmill, rowing machine, boxing bag, and a ton of free weights.

Before she could comment, he turned to her and said, "Go a quarter mile on the treadmill. You make it that far without passing out, I'll give you an assignment."

She glared at his bossiness. "You don't have to be such an ass."

"I'm not being an ass. I'm proving a point."

With a growling huff, Jazz went to the treadmill and stepped up on it. Her usual, comfortable running speed was just under a seven-minute mile. Since she knew that wasn't remotely possible, she began a slow, measured pace.

"No running. Just walk."

She threw a shocked look over her shoulder. "Walk? That's it?"

"That's it. A fourth of a mile, as slow as you want."

"Fine," she snapped. Turning back to the controls, she punched what she considered a sedate speed and began to move. Thirty steps later, barely a fraction of the way through, she was breathing like an asthmatic eighty-year-old. Determined to finish, no matter what, she ground her teeth together and continued on.

A giant, masculine hand punched the controls, stopping her progress. "You beautiful, stubborn woman," Xavier growled. Before she could catch her breath and yell at him for stopping her, he gently lifted her and carried her out of the room.

"Wait…I can—"

"You absolutely cannot. I was stupid for challenging you."

Unable to respond without looking more childish than she already had, she allowed him to carry her into her bedroom and lay her on the bed.

Hovering over her, his beautiful eyes gleaming with both exasperation and affectionate warmth, he said softly, "No one thinks you're weak, and you are as far from a victim as anyone I've ever known. However, other than showering, eating, and sleeping, you will not do anything more strenuous for the next week."

He pressed a quick kiss on her forehead, gave her a heated look that made it clear he'd like to do more but wouldn't, and then walked out of the room.

Finally having caught her breath, Jazz allowed her body to sink into the luxurious mattress. She'd overplayed her hand. She had known she was still weak, but he'd been treating her like she was a weakling. And then what had he done? He'd proven that she was. Instead of gloating, which she wouldn't have blamed him if he had, considering how childish she'd acted, he'd treated her with tenderness.

Since they'd been here, Xavier had yet to say anything about the kisses they'd shared or his statement that she was the most important person in the world to him. Had she imagined he'd said that because she wanted it to be true?

A wave of exhaustion fogged her mind. After her nap, she'd think on those things. For right now, she had to recover from the embarrassing display of almost collapsing after walking an eighth of a mile.

ON THE WAY DOWNSTAIRS, he placed a quick call to Serena. "Hey there," she said. "How's Jazz?"

"Already going crazy with nothing to do."

"Boredom's a good sign. It means she's recovering."

"She is, which means she needs to keep busy. Can you send the photos you've compiled of the shooter?"

"Sure. You think she might be able to identify him? She said before that she didn't get close enough to really see him. Since all the descriptions you and Hawke got were so vague, I've got well over a thousand possibilities."

"Ha. That should keep her busy for a while."

"Yeah, if it doesn't blind her first."

Serious now, he said, "She needs to feel useful."

"I understand," Serena said softly. "I'll send them over. Give her my love."

"Will do."

Ending the call, Xavier went to the kitchen and began the cleanup. If he didn't get better at cooking, there was no way Jazz was going to recover her strength. Her offer to help him cook had been sweet, but he didn't want her to do anything even remotely strenuous for a least a few more days. Even though it had proved his point, her very brief struggle on the treadmill had torn at his gut. She wasn't strong enough to do much more than eat and sleep right now. Which made him doubly glad that he hadn't told her what he and Ash had learned from Kate. There would be plenty of time for that when she was better.

She'd waited this long to know the truth. What would a few more days matter?

CHAPTER TWENTY-EIGHT

J azz hid a yawn behind her hand and blinked to keep her eyes opened. Ever since that embarrassingly short walk on the treadmill, revealing her lack of strength, her body had decided to show her exactly how right Xavier was. Other than sleeping, eating a bit, and then sleeping some more, she'd done absolutely nothing. She would be infuriated if she'd had the energy to feel that much emotion.

For some reason, Xavier had been staying out of her way the last couple of days. Other than sitting down with her at mealtimes, he'd been surprisingly absent. Which, considering the cabin wasn't all that large, was quite a feat.

She knew she needed to talk to him about Bass's shooting…about Brody and what she'd seen. The longer she waited, the angrier he was going to be when she finally told him.

"You getting bored?"

She started, somehow surprised he'd come up behind her without her hearing. She shouldn't be. As large as Xavier was, he could be as quiet as a jungle cat when he wanted. "A little." That was an understatement, but he wasn't here to entertain her.

"Serena sent some photos the other day. You feel like going through them?"

Her shoulders straightened. Okay, now he was talking. She'd be able to pinpoint the bastard the moment she saw him. "Yes. That sketch she did was fairly accurate, so there shouldn't be that many people who resemble him. I'll know him in an instant."

"No, not of the guy who abducted you. Bass's shooter. You're the only one who got a halfway decent look at him."

Her limbs stiffened, and her mouth went dry. "But I thought he worked at the restaurant. Did you not get a good description of him from the employees?"

"Nope. The guy apparently changed his appearance almost daily. No one could agree on even the most basic of physical characteristics."

That didn't really surprise her. During just the few interviews she'd done with the kitchen staff, each person had seemed to remember something different that often contradicted what another person had said. Even the young girl she'd taken out for coffee couldn't seem to pinpoint his exact description. Brody must be a master of disguises to be able to make so many changes. Skills like that took years to develop.

A wave of sadness swept through her at the thought. *What happened to you, Brody?*

Realizing Xavier was waiting for her to dive into this assignment with both feet, she gave him a doubtful look. "I don't know that I saw him well enough to get a good description either."

"Maybe not, but you might see something that'll spark your memory."

Now would be the time to tell him that she could easily identify the shooter. Had she not lambasted herself while she'd been stuck in that cage about how she should have trusted him with the truth? That she should have come clean with him and the team from the beginning? So why couldn't she speak up and say, *Hey, I've already identified the shooter. He's my brother.*

When had telling the truth become so hard?

Instead of doing the thing she knew she needed to do, like a zombie with no knowledge of right and wrong, she took the laptop he held out to her and walked out of the room.

Settling into the thickly padded chair next to the window that looked out over the vast mountain range, Jazz pulled up the file that Serena had sent. Guilt was a complex emotion. She was as human as the rest of humanity and had suffered that feeling for a variety of different things she'd done. Things she'd said that had hurt people unintentionally, bad thoughts about people when she'd later realized she'd been judgmental without cause. And many more things. But this? This was not only blatant and wrong, it went against everything Option Zero stood for. How many times had she judged other team members for ignoring their duties and going off on their own agendas? This was no different. In fact, it was worse because it was a willful intent to deceive.

Without much interest, Jazz went through the photographs. There were some good likenesses, but none was Brody. She closed her eyes and thought back to that day, to those seconds when their gazes had met. *Had* she made a mistake? Could that man have only resembled her brother and not been him after all? She had told the truth about that. It had truly been seconds. A short blip in time like that could create all sorts of wild errors. Moments before Bass's shooting, she and Xavier had argued about her search for her brother. Could she have subconsciously combined those two events and come up with a wild scenario that really hadn't existed at all?

What had she seen, really? A large, muscular man. He had been covered from head to toe. The skullcap he'd been wearing had exposed nothing of his face. So what if she had spotted a dark gold strand of hair sticking out from the bottom of the cap? Lots of people had that hair color. And so what if when he'd opened the door to his SUV, the shirt sleeve on his right arm had moved up just a few inches, exposing a scar on his wrist? Lots of people had scars. She definitely had more than her share.

But the damning part, the part that she could not talk herself out of, no matter what excuse she came up with, had been the eyes that had stared at her. Light green eyes.

Yes, Brody had dark, golden-blond hair. And yes, Brody had a scar on his right wrist.

About a year after her mother married Connor McAlister, he and Brody had been working on a wood project for a school assignment. Brody had moved too quickly with the saw he'd been using, and it had sliced his wrist to the bone. She remembered crying when she'd seen the blood, and even though they'd gotten him to the hospital and he'd received the stitches he needed, she'd never forgotten the terror of seeing him hurt. The stitches had come out a week or so later, but the injury had left an impressive scar. But Brody couldn't be the only man on the planet with that kind of scar in that location.

The eyes weren't so easily explained. Brody's eyes had come from his mother's side of the family—startling green, so vibrant and penetrating that they could mesmerize. Her mama had described them as bottle green. And she clearly remembered how the older girls in school had sighed over him whenever he'd come to one of her school events.

The shooter's eyes had, without a doubt, been Brody's.

Slamming the laptop closed, Jazz jumped to her feet. She was in the den, walking toward Xavier before she knew it. She still had no idea what she was going to say, but she could no longer live with this on her conscience.

She opened her mouth, about to call out his name, and then came to an abrupt halt. He was asleep. A book lay open on his chest. A smile lifted her lips at how relaxed he looked. Whenever Xavier was awake, the fierceness of his personality always made her think of a predatory animal, like a tiger on the prowl, ready to strike at any moment. But now, he looked peaceful and calm.

Taking a step closer, she tried to see what he'd been reading that had apparently been boring enough to put him to sleep. When she saw the title, her heart melted. He had told her he was trying to improve his cooking skills, and she had to admit the last few meals had been much more edible. And now she knew why. In between taking care of her and digging for intel on who had abducted her, he'd been reading cookbooks.

How could she not trust this man with her secrets? He had done nothing since she'd known him to make her believe he'd be anything but supportive, no matter what she told him.

Vowing that the instant he woke, she would spill the secret she'd been keeping, she took a step back, not wanting to disturb him. The floor creaked beneath her foot, and in an instant, Xavier's eyes popped open.

Instantly alert, he sat up and said, "Jazz? Everything okay?"

"I…" She swallowed past her now sandpaper-dry throat and tried again. "I have something I need to tell you."

"Okay." His eyes went to the laptop in her hand. "Did you find something?"

"No, it's not that. Well, it is that…but not really."

Confusion furrowing his brow, he said, "Okaaay."

Sometimes not having a filter worked to her advantage because if she had to think about what she was going to say, she might never get it out. Instead, like a pressurized water spout, the words spewed forth. "I know who the shooter is."

"You do? Who?"

"Brody. My brother. He's the one who killed Franco Bass."

CHAPTER TWENTY-NINE

O f all the things he'd thought he'd hear Jazz say, her telling him that Franco Bass's assassin was her brother had not been on his radar.

Examining her face, he saw resolve, fear, and a whole lot of guilt. What he didn't see was doubt.

"Sit down and tell me."

Still gripping the laptop, Jazz perched on the edge of the chair across from him. "I know it's him... I'm sorry I didn't tell you before... I just..." She took a shaky breath. "I'm sorry."

"Slow down and start from the beginning."

As if a dam had burst, she explained how she'd followed the shooter out the door of the restaurant and what she'd seen. She described the features that had given her the notion that the shooter was her brother. She explained how and why she'd chosen to conduct her own investigation. Her abduction in the middle of that investigation had, of course, halted everything.

He now knew why she'd taken off on her own. Why she'd removed the tracker. And why she'd been investigating the case by herself. Before he could get his head wrapped around the possibility that Brody McAlister really was the assassin who'd taken out one of the Wren Project's major players, he had to know one thing.

"Why the hell would you not tell us, Jazz? Why wouldn't you tell me?"

If guilt had had a face, it was Jazz's. "I panicked. I thought if I could find him first, I could convince him to come in on his own and work with us."

"Do you think your abduction had anything to do with him?"

"What?" Horror replaced the guilt. "Of course not. Brody would never have anything to do with me being hurt."

"If the assassin truly is your brother, do you really know him anymore? Would you ever have considered that he would become a paid assassin?"

All the air left her body as she slumped down into her chair. Maybe she hadn't considered that, and he didn't want to hurt her any more, but it was something they needed to pursue. If—and it was a big if—the shooter actually was Brody.

"Okay, let's go over it again. Tell me specifically why you think he's your brother. Leave nothing out."

With meticulous detail, which was one of her greatest gifts, Jazz described every aspect of the event, from the time the bullet had left the chamber of the gun that had killed Bass. He'd been there for the first part of it, but still he listened carefully, knowing that she often saw things he didn't.

When she finished, he said carefully, not wanting her to shut down, "Jazz, do you not trust me?"

"Yes, of course I do."

"Then why didn't you tell me?"

He hated seeing the pain in her face. She had been getting her color back and light back into her eyes. Now she looked defeated and so incredibly sad.

"I'm sorry. I just…" She closed her eyes and blew out a long sigh. "I kept envisioning scenarios where the team and Brody, or you and Brody, got into a confrontation. No matter what happened in it, someone I loved got hurt. I thought if I could take care of the matter myself, I could protect everybody."

Holding out his hand, he said, "Come here, baby."

She took his hand, and he pulled her gently to him and then into his lap. Wrapping his arms around her, he said gruffly, "You're not only important to me, you're important to the entire team. There's nothing we wouldn't do for you."

"I know I should have trusted you. But we'd just had that argument about Brody, and I—" She shrugged and added, "I just didn't know how you'd handle it."

He pressed a kiss to her forehead and just held her close while a multitude of emotions battled within him. Yeah, he was hurt that she hadn't trusted him, but in a way, he could see her point. He hadn't exactly been quiet about his opinion of her brother. And now it looked like he had one more reason to not like the guy.

"So what happens now?" Jazz asked.

"You know the answer to that. You have to tell Ash."

"I know," she said softly. "You think he'll fire me?"

He jerked at the thought. "Hell no. We've all screwed up, even Ash."

"But I held back intel on an ongoing op."

"I'm not saying he isn't going to be pissed, but he'll get past it. Promise me something."

"What?"

Shifting her so he could see her face, he let the anger show. "Don't ever keep anything from me again. We're partners. We trust each other and tell each other the truth, even when it hurts."

"I promise."

Even though he knew they needed to make the call to Ash,

Xavier couldn't resist the luxury of just holding her in his arms for a little longer. When Jazz was healthy and on her game, she could sometimes be as prickly as a cactus. And while he'd never want to see her hurt or weak again, he couldn't help but enjoy this needy, vulnerable Jazz.

So he held her, relishing that she was in his arms, that she had finally told him the truth, and that things between them, while not perfect, were finally headed in the right direction.

JAZZ OPENED her eyes and looked around, vaguely surprised that she was in her bedroom at the cabin. Her body felt relaxed and worry-free, and for the first time since she'd been abducted, she felt no pain anywhere.

As events from earlier came back to her, she tensed. She had finally told Xavier the truth. It hadn't been fun. Though there had been hurt and anger, she'd also seen understanding and forgiveness. Other than a few initial questions, he hadn't even really questioned the validity of her belief that the shooter was Brody. That was trust and true partnership. He had given that to her, and from now on, no matter what, she would do the same.

After that, she'd been exhausted. She vaguely remembered him carrying her to bed, and the instant her head hit the pillow, she'd been out like a light. She also remembered getting up in the middle of the night to use the bathroom and brush her teeth. When she'd come back to bed, she had been surprised because she hadn't noticed that the place beside her on the bed had been occupied. Xavier had lain down beside her when he'd brought her in and never left.

He'd been sitting on the bed, apparently ready to leave her alone when she had returned from the bathroom. She had whispered, "Stay," and he'd given her a smile she'd felt all the way to her soul.

"Let me lock up, and I'll be back."

True to his word, he'd returned ten minutes later and pulled her into his arms. They had slept like that all night.

Suddenly, achingly aware of the big body lying beside her, Jazz rolled over and let her eager gaze roam over him. When he was awake, Xavier had the alert awareness of a jungle cat. Asleep, his appearance was no less dangerous, but at least with his eyes closed, he didn't look as though he could see her every thought.

She had never told him that the first time she'd seen him, he had terrified her with that searing look. When she'd gotten to know him, the terror had shifted. Wary respect had moved to admiration and then to genuine affection. Those feelings morphed over time, and then one day, without even realizing when it had happened, she knew she loved him. Not just love in a friendship way, but love in the deepest sense of wanting to spend every moment of every day with him for the rest of her life.

Fantasizing about kissing him, making love with him, had taken up more time than even she would admit. Then there were the days that she had dreamed he felt the same way, too. She had never considered herself a romantic. She'd fought too hard most of her life to not see things in a rational and logical manner, but the emotions Xavier invoked in her made her feel both vulnerable and ultrafeminine.

"Good morning," Xavier said in a sleep-husky voice.

Startled, she looked at his face, feeling a blush start from the tips of her toes and travel rapidly throughout her body. She couldn't hide the fact that she had been ogling him like some kind of salivating idiot.

"Morning," she said softly. "Sleep well?"

"Better than I have in a long time."

Unable to lie beside him and not touch, Jazz raised a tentative hand and lightly traced the curve of his mouth as it tilted up in a smile. She had dreamed of kissing those lips so often that she had thought she would know their taste, their texture. But when he'd kissed her the first time, it had been better than she could have ever believed possible. She wanted to taste them again.

"What do you want, Jazz?"

"You, Xavier," she whispered. "Just you."

In a swift, graceful move, Xavier rose up and hovered over her. Straddling her hips, he braced himself with his hands on either side of her shoulders. Eyes glittering with need, sensual mouth still turned up, he looked like a beautiful pirate assessing his bounty. From the gleam in his eyes, he liked what he saw.

Apparently seeing the acceptance in her expression, he sat up slightly and tugged his T-shirt over his head. Jazz's breath caught in her throat. She'd seen him shirtless numerous times, but she'd never had the opportunity to reach out and touch the granite-hard muscles. His skin was naturally bronze from his mother's side of the family, and the instant she touched him, her stomach did a double dip. He was like warm, hard silk that her fingers longed to explore. Before she got farther than the eight-pack abs, Xavier took her hands, kissed each one, and then raised them over her head. Then he pulled her T-shirt over her head.

Jazz wasn't ashamed of her body. She was naturally small and not especially curvaceous, but with her weight loss, she wasn't particularly fond of how she looked right now. The expression on Xavier's face told her he didn't agree. Along with a ravenous need that made her feel gloriously feminine and desirable, his heated gaze filled with awe and wonder as it roamed over her body.

"You're beautiful, Jazz." The husky gravel in his voice sent fire throughout her bloodstream.

Before she could consider a response, Xavier bent down and proceeded to show her exactly how much he wanted her. With his mouth, his hands, his words, every caress, every kiss, and every growling word, he created a maelstrom of desire she'd never experienced. Need grew and expanded until she was solely a sentient being, glorying and reveling in everything he gave her.

By the time he slid into her, Jazz was not much more than a whirlpool of heated desire, wanting only to reach that exquisite peak, but almost afraid to arrive because she never wanted the pleasure to stop. With every ebb and flow of Xavier's body into hers, she gained a new understanding of giving and receiving physical gratification. She felt treasured, desired, and, most of all, adored.

Almost at the pinnacle, nanoseconds away from the ultimate ecstasy, Xavier growled into her ear, "Come with me, baby."

Jazz wrapped her arms around Xavier's shoulders, her legs around his waist, and welcomed the pleasure she'd only ever experienced in this man's arms.

CHAPTER THIRTY

Dressed in a ragged pair of shorts and nothing else, Xavier sat on the back porch and slugged down his second cup of coffee. Even though he wanted nothing more than to go back and hold Jazz, he needed to get his head back on straight. Being around her right now seriously screwed with that.

He hadn't planned what had happened. When she'd asked him to stay with her, he'd intended to hold her if she needed his reassurance. Or, if she'd had another nightmare, he wanted to be close enough to wake her before it got too bad. Instead, she'd told him she wanted him, and without a second thought, that's what she'd gotten.

No, he hadn't forced her, and yes, she'd been responsive and eager, but had it been too soon? He'd done his best not to hurt her. She was still weak and recovering from her ordeal, so he hadn't exactly ravaged her like a wild animal, but still, he felt like he'd taken advantage of her in some way.

Even before he'd fallen for her, he'd always felt protective of Jazz. Yes, she was fine-boned and delicate-looking, and next to her, he felt like a giant. But that wasn't the biggest reason. Not only had Jazz been hurt a lot in her life, she had a charming, unaffected kind of innocence that made him want to fix everything for her. She often called him out on his actions for being so solicitous with her, and he did his best not to go overboard, but it was hard. He would fight demons to keep her from being harmed.

And now another challenge to keep her from being hurt had been presented. She believed her brother was an assassin who had taken out Franco Bass. If it had been anyone else, he might've questioned whether she'd really seen her brother or just someone who'd resembled him. Identifying someone in a matter of seconds with adrenaline pumping through you could be difficult, if not impossible. And considering the emotions that were involved, doubting her might seem reasonable. But this was Jazz. Her recall was second to none. Even if her emotions were all over the place, he trusted that the man she saw was indeed Brody McAlister.

So what did that mean? Did McAlister work for the Wren Project? He could see why she'd be worried about OZ going after him. Xavier didn't condone that she'd gone off on her own to try to find him, but he could definitely understand where she'd been coming from.

She needed to tell Ash about this, and it needed to be soon. She'd fallen back asleep after they'd made love, but when she woke and after she'd had some breakfast, he was going to encourage her to call him and get it over with. Not only did Ash need to know because this was an ongoing investigation, having it hanging over her head was only going to make her feel worse.

The phone on the table beside him buzzed, and without looking at the screen, he already knew it was his boss, as if he and Ash were mentally connected.

"Hey, Ash. Anything new?"

"Not sure yet. Serena is following a lead that might give us something. I'll let you know if it does. I'm just checking in to see how Jazz is doing."

"She's getting stronger."

"But...?"

He wouldn't reveal to Ash what Jazz had told him. That was her story to tell. However, he knew Ash was asking about something else. Jazz might've had her secrets, but Xavier had one, too. A secret that would create even more questions and worry for her. He'd put off giving her the intel until she was stronger. After last night's confession, he knew he was living on borrowed time.

"Soon, Ash. I'll tell her soon. But before I do, Jazz has something she needs to talk to you about."

"So she told you why she went off on her own?"

"Yes."

"You can't give it to me?"

"No, this is her story, but I do want to say one thing."

"What's that?"

"If you upset her, I'll bust your face open."

"Threatening your boss?"

Thankfully, he heard a tinge of amusement in Ash's tone. Threatening friends was not his style, but if Ash let loose on her, Xavier would be pissed. Advising him beforehand to prevent it from happening had seemed appropriate.

"Respectfully," Xavier added.

Ash barked out a laugh. "Never heard of a respectful threat, but okay. And you know I'm not going to go off on her."

"Yeah, I know. Just wanted to make sure."

"So is she around?"

"She's still asleep. I can—"

"Is that Ash?"

Xavier whirled to see Jazz standing in the doorway. Her hair tousled around her face, she was dressed in the T-shirt he'd worn to bed, which reached past her knees, and a pair of yoga pants, and she looked both sexy and adorable.

"Yeah," Xavier said. "He's just calling in to see how you're doing."

"Did you say anything about—"

"No," he cut in quickly. "That's for you to explain."

OKAY, this was it. Taking a bracing breath, Jazz went to Xavier and held out her hand for the phone. Pushing her hair back, she pressed the phone to her ear. "Ash?"

"Hey, Jazz. You feeling better?"

"Yes, getting stronger every minute."

"Good."

"Listen, there's something I need to say, and I want to do it face-to-face. Can you arrange that?"

"Yes. Give me about five minutes to set up a secure line, and I'll call you back."

"Okay, thanks."

She handed Xavier's phone back to him with a slight grimace. "He's calling back in a few minutes."

"Have you had coffee?"

"No, not yet."

"I'll get you some." The instant he stood, he pulled her into his arms and spoke into her ear. "Everything will be okay."

Before she could answer, he pressed a kiss to her cheek and walked away.

Wrapping her arms around herself, Jazz looked out over the mountain range. For some reason, she hadn't been nearly as anxious last night when she'd told Xavier the truth. Confessing it to Ash gave her the heebie-jeebies. He could fire her on the spot. She didn't think he would, but she also knew he'd be justified. She'd broken a multitude of OZ rules, and he had every right to come down hard on her.

"Here," Xavier said behind her, "take a few fortifying sips. You'll feel better."

"Thanks." She took several swallows of the scalding, bracing brew, appreciating that the cream-to-sugar ratio was just the way she liked it. With each sip, she did feel slightly stronger.

"He's not going to tear into you, Jazz. Or fire you."

"He'd be justified."

"Perhaps. But if he did that to every OZ operative who's screwed up, there would be no OZ."

That was true. And she knew that Ash was a fair man. Maybe one of the biggest reasons she dreaded telling him was the disappointment she knew she'd cause him. But she had learned her lesson, and she would take her medicine, no matter how bitter the pill.

The phone in her pocket jingled. Ash was calling on her phone. She answered and saw his handsome face on the screen. He had strong features and steely eyes, but they'd only ever looked at her with kindness. Today was no different.

"Jazz, you're looking better. There's color in your face."

"I'm getting stronger, Ash. Xavier is taking good care of me." Remembering what had happened a couple hours ago brought an unexpected heat to her cheeks. If Ash looked closely, he'd see the deep red blush she wasn't able to hide. She glanced over at Xavier, and the grin on his face made her blush even more. The man was enjoying her embarrassment.

"That's good. Now, you have something you need to tell me?"

Settling into the chair Xavier had been sitting in earlier, Jazz started with the shooting. What she had seen, what she had done, and why—all the way up to when she'd been abducted. Ash didn't speak or ask questions. He just let her get it out. Once she finished, she held her breath, waiting for his judgment.

"Did he recognize you?" Ash asked.

"I think so…maybe. It's hard to say. He looked at me for a second, but that doesn't mean anything really."

"This definitely gives us another avenue to pursue."

"Yeah," she said softly. She knew that avenue had been delayed by weeks because of her.

"Jazz, let me ask you something. What did you think would happen if you had told us what you saw?"

"I didn't know, Ash. I…I panicked. The last thing I wanted was for Brody and the team to get into a shootout. I thought if I found him first, I could talk him into coming in on his own."

"That was damn dangerous, Jazz. But you already know that."

"I know…and I'm very sorry. I broke a ton of OZ rules."

"Rules that are there to protect you."

"Yes."

"Don't do it again, Jazz. You need to remember that blood doesn't define family. It's people who love and protect you and always have your back, no matter what. That's what you've got in Option Zero."

"I know that, Ash. Again, I'm sorry."

"Let's move past this. Feel better soon so you can get back to work and we can all figure this out together."

"Thanks, boss. I will."

The screen went blank, and Jazz let loose a huge breath, unaware until then that she'd been holding it in.

"See? That wasn't so bad."

"Still, I'd rather face down a pack of hyenas than do that again."

Laughing, he held out his hand. "You against a pack of hyenas? My money's on you."

Taking his hand, she allowed him to pull her into his arms. And when his mouth touched hers, she forgot everything except the joy of being here with him.

Raising his head, he captured her gaze. "About this morning…"

There was that dratted blush again. She'd blushed more in the last few hours than she had in ten years.

Instead of laughing at her embarrassment, Xavier gave her a look of serious concern. "Are you okay? I didn't hurt you?"

She didn't have a lot of experience, but she did know that she'd never had someone treat her as if she were not only desirable but also precious and valuable.

"No," she said softly. "You didn't hurt me."

"And your wounds? I tried to be careful, but—"

Taking one of his hands, she held it against her heart, marveling that a hand so large that could be so gentle with her could also knock a giant down with one blow. She'd seen him do it.

"We didn't use protection, Jazz."

It was standard procedure for all female OZ operatives to receive a birth control shot, but that was likely one detail of Option Zero health care Xavier might not know.

"I'm protected. Don't worry."

"Good. I wasn't sure… I don't… I mean, we've never really talked…"

It suddenly occurred to her that he was just as uncertain about this new step in their relationship as she was. Xavier exuded confidence in every other aspect, but when it came to romance, it was good to see that he could be just as awkward as the next person.

Hoping she wasn't moving faster than he wanted, but wanting to reassure him, she said, "I like where we're going."

A confident gleam returned to his eyes as he said, "Good, because we've only gotten started."

"TELL ME ABOUT YOUR MOM," Jazz said. "You don't talk about her very much."

After breakfast, Xavier had suggested a short walk. Even though he knew Jazz wasn't up to doing much more than a half mile at the most, building up her stamina was paramount to her recovery.

They were walking at a leisurely pace, and it felt good to just be with each other, forgetting all the other stuff they'd soon have to face.

"My mom was the best. She worked so hard to give us a good life."

"And your dad. He was killed when you were just a baby. Right?"

"Yeah, I don't remember him. I was barely two when he died."

"You don't have any other family, then?"

Familiar anger surged through him. "Oh, I've got plenty of relatives—but I don't consider them family. Grandparents, aunts, uncles, cousins. A whole hoard of them."

She stumbled slightly, but Xavier caught her before she could fall. "Really?" she gasped. "You've never mentioned them."

"That's because I don't know them. I just know they exist."

"What do you mean?"

Realizing she was breathing heavier than before, he slowed their pace. "My mom came from an upper-middle-class but very strict Italian family. She was the youngest daughter of a family of six. Their plans for her didn't include getting herself hitched to a young mechanic with no pedigree or money."

"How did they meet?"

"She was on her way home from shopping and had a flat. My dad stopped to change her tire. They hit it off and started dating. She took a chance and took him home for one of their big family dinners. It didn't go well."

"That's awful. So they kicked her out of the family?"

"Literally. She walked out with the clothes she was wearing and never went back. She told me more than once that it was the best decision she'd ever made. She and my dad were married about six months later. I came along a couple years after that."

"And then your dad died a couple years after that."

"Yeah. My mom never stopped grieving."

"And you lost her when you were in the Army?"

He nodded, a lump growing in his throat when he thought about that time. "She never even told me she was sick. I remember her hugging me before I boarded the plane. It was my second deployment, and I knew I wouldn't see her for a while." He swallowed hard as he recalled how tightly her arms had been around him and how she'd whispered how proud she was of him. "She knew she was sick then, but she didn't want me to know."

"That's so sad." She squeezed his hand in sympathy. "And you never heard from anyone from her family?"

"An uncle—one of my mom's brothers—called about a month after she passed. Left a voice mail wanting us to meet. I never called him back."

"You didn't want to at least give them a chance?"

"For over two decades, they ignored her. Pretended she didn't exist. I wasn't about to give them a second of my time."

When he'd lost his mom, the pain had been all-consuming. But Jazz had been through so much more. Not only had she lost both parents, she'd lost the brother she adored. She rarely talked about what had happened to her after Brody had disappeared, and he wasn't going to bring it up now, but Xavier knew she'd had it rough until she'd met Kate Walker.

And that was a conversation for another day, too.

They came to his favorite place on the property—one of the biggest reasons he'd wanted to build up here.

"Oh, Xavier," Jazz breathed, "it's beautiful."

Smiling proudly, as if he'd had anything to do with the view, he pointed to a bench a few feet away. "Come sit."

Dragging her eyes away from the magnificence of the snow-capped mountain range, she glanced to where he was pointing.

"Did you put that there?"

"Yeah. While the cabin was being built, I worked on this."

She jerked her head around, surprise on her face. "You built this? How did I not know that you're a talented carpenter?"

"I'd say there are a lot of things we don't know about each other."

Nodding, she dropped onto the bench with a sigh. "True. When we're on missions, our focus has to be on the job."

Settling down beside her, Xavier inhaled deeply, the combination of some of the purest air on the planet and Jazz's sweet fragrance was a heady mixture. How many times had he envisioned sitting beside her on this bench and sharing this view with her?

"Can I ask a favor?" she asked softly.

"Of course."

"Can we take the next few days just for us?"

Turning to face her, he asked, "What do you mean?"

"It's just what you said. There's still so much we don't know about each other. Maybe that seems selfish, since there're people out there who are literally looking to kill us, but—"

Xavier pressed a finger to her lips to stop her. "That's an

excellent idea. You and me…we don't take vacations like a lot of people. There's no reason we can't take a few days off and just be together."

"So that sounds okay to you?"

Pulling her closer, he wrapped an arm around her shoulders and whispered against her hair, "I can't think of anything I'd rather do."

CHAPTER THIRTY-ONE

Chicago

Rubbing his chin thoughtfully, Oscar considered all the tasks he still needed to do. Just because things had worked out well so far didn't mean he could rest on his laurels. There were miles to go before he slept—or something like that.

Now that Kevin was out of the picture, he could move forward at the pace he preferred. At the thought of his nemesis, he let a smirk twist his mouth. The idiot had never known how much he'd hated him. Playing the lackey for years had been infuriating, but also amusing because he'd known he was ten times smarter than his stupid-assed brother-in-law. The man had never had a clue. Kevin Doyle had gotten what he deserved, but Oscar had never thought Kevin's demise would come at the man's own hand. That had been just too perfect to consider.

When he'd told Ryan, his nephew, what his father had done, the boy hadn't believed him at first. Why would he? Ryan hadn't known about the McAlister girl or what his father had planned. Learning that his father had killed his mother had come out of the blue. Not that Ryan had any kind of affection for the old bastard. Kevin Doyle had been a shitty father.

But Ryan, despite his upbringing and who his father had been, had naïvely believed the coroner's report that an aneurysm had taken his mother's life. He had grieved like any good son who'd adored his mama. Though Ryan had been furious at the way his father had handled her burial service, Oscar knew Ryan hadn't considered that his father had had anything to do with her death.

Oscar wasn't one for regrets. They never did a damn bit of good. But in this situation, he did feel an unfamiliar tinge. If he'd had any inkling what his brother-in-law had had up his sleeve, he could have prevented his sister's death. The idea that Kevin would want the girl for himself had never once crossed his mind. Why would it? Not only had the slimy slug been almost thirty years older than the girl, he'd been married to a wonderful woman. Bridget had given Doyle a good strong son, overseen his household, and supported her husband in every way a good Irish wife was supposed to. The very idea that the man hadn't appreciated her went against everything Oscar believed in.

Susan, his own dear wife, God rest her soul, had died in childbirth. Even though she'd managed only to give him a sickly daughter who'd died when she was still an infant, he'd never held that against her. She'd done her best. And while he'd had plenty of women to warm his bed over the years, he'd never replaced her. To him, marriage was a sacred oath.

Kevin Doyle had broken that oath and thrown it to the wind as if it were chaff. He'd gotten what he deserved.

Oscar let the scenario play out in his head of what had likely gone down the night Ryan had gone to confront his father. When his nephew had finally accepted the truth of what his father had done, he'd said he was just going to talk with him. He hadn't acknowledged it at the time, but Oscar knew that Ryan had left with vengeance in his heart. He believed the intent had been to torture and maim his father until he gave him the truth.

He imagined Kevin sitting at his desk, pulling his hair out because the girl had gotten away. Then he'd likely heard his son coming up the stairs for him. At three o'clock in the morning, he wouldn't have had any doubts of why Ryan was coming to see him. Especially when Oscar had done his own little bit of torture and sent him a photo of the bloody coroner with a prediction: *You're a dead man.*

Kevin had no doubt been thinking about how it had all gone wrong right before he'd put a bullet through his head. Picturing that scenario brought a smile to Oscar's face.

Ryan still didn't know about the girl, and Oscar had no intention of telling him. Not only was Ryan not interested in the darker side of the business world, this was Oscar's game now, and no one else would be invited to play.

Of course, the game couldn't continue until he got the girl back. He had no idea where she was now. When he'd learned she had escaped, he'd been just as shocked as Kevin likely had been. The brief glimpse he'd gotten of her before Kevin had shipped her off to the kennel had been unimpressive. She was pretty enough, with her short, silky, black hair and ivory skin, but she also looked like a feather could knock her down. After days of starvation, how she'd escaped remained a stunning mystery.

The fact that she had somehow taken down both Kip and Miles had been an astonishing and frankly unbelievable bit of news. He knew that Kip was dead. His body had mysteriously shown up at a morgue with a bullet between his eyes. As far as he knew, no one had been fingered for the crime.

Miles had been another matter. He had called Oscar, ranting about the girl and how she'd killed Kip and had shot him. He had actually had the audacity to ask for help, and Oscar, being the compassionate man that he was, promised to bring him medical aid.

A smile twitched at Oscar's mouth when he remembered the expression on Miles's face when it had just been Oscar to show up with another bullet for him. After messing up so spectacularly, the idiot had actually believed he deserved help. Miles was now rotting at the bottom of Lake Michigan. He had gotten exactly what he deserved.

So he was now the captain of this ship and he was going to sail it as he saw fit. Once he found the girl again—and he would find her—he would do things right. First, he had no romantic or sexual interest in the girl. She was a means to an end. Second, he had absolutely no sentimental attachment to her bloodline. The old days were over and done with, never to return. Third, and finally, once she'd performed the tasks he set before her and done what he needed her to do, he would do away with her. She would be a liability and a loose end.

Oscar sat back in the chair and contemplated the future. A future that included all the things he'd been deprived of all his life. Playing second fiddle hadn't been easy. Having people think of him as slow or dumb had often worked to his advantage, but that didn't mean he'd enjoyed it. But now he would reap the benefits of all his hard work.

But first, he had calls to make, deals to offer, and an elusive butterfly to catch.

CHAPTER THIRTY-TWO

Montana

"You've got to be kidding me," Xavier said.

"Nope. You picked last night's movie. It's my turn."

"But it's a musical. People bursting into song. You really want to see that happen?"

"Yep. And what's even better," she announced smugly, "I'm going to burst into song with them."

"But you can't sing."

She let loose an evil laugh. "I know! That's the whole point."

"You're just trying to get back at me for making you watch the entire Godfather saga in one day."

"You bet your sweet bippy, Mr. Quinn."

"What the hell is a bippy?"

"I have no idea. Serena says it sometimes, and it seemed appropriate."

"All right, Miss McAlister. I will suffer through *The Phantom of the Opera*, with your foghorn voice singing along, but only because you're so damned cute."

Grinning like a maniac, Jazz did a little celebratory dance in the middle of the kitchen floor.

"And just for that little display of smugness, all the Milk Duds belong to me."

Snatching the box out of his hand, she took off running, shouting over her shoulder, "We'll see about that!"

Sprinting into the den and knowing he would be behind her in seconds, Jazz quickly grabbed the remote and keyed in the movie. If she didn't go ahead and get it on the screen, he would try to seduce her into forgetting about it. Two days ago, when she'd wanted to watch a rom-com, he'd kissed her until she was a mass of jelly in his arms. By the time he was through, she'd weakly nodded at his suggestion of some Western. When she'd finally come to her senses, the movie was already in progress, and he'd been smirking. If he hadn't looked so smug and sexy, she would have been mad, but she had instead sat back and watched the movie with him. Letting him win wasn't all that bad.

But today, she would watch one of her favorite movies and make him listen to her caterwauling. That was his penance.

"All right, McAlister, get the wretched thing going," Xavier grumbled.

"Ahh, poor baby. Come over here and snuggle with me."

"Fine. But can you give me notice before you start singing?"

Lying through her teeth, she said, "But of course," and then gave him her most innocent grin.

The twinkle in his eyes told her he knew she was lying but that he didn't mind. When he settled onto the sofa with her, she clicked the play button and snuggled against him.

As the opening music started, she reflected that, oddly enough, this was the happiest she'd ever been. Even though she was still healing from three gunshot wounds, her brother was an assassin, and someone out there still wanted to torture and possibly kill her for some unknown reason, these last few days with Xavier had been the best of her life.

Their days had been filled with laughter, eating, and lots of lovemaking. Each day, she seemed to fall further in love with him, and she hadn't even believed that was possible. Perhaps it was because Xavier seemed to feel the same way about her. Even though she'd been through hell to get here, she wouldn't trade the last few days for anything. They had been magical.

She had learned so much more about him, things she'd never even considered. On top of not knowing he was a talented carpenter, he was also a skilled architect—something she'd discovered when she'd found the plans for the cabin on his desk and realized he'd been the one to draw them.

They'd shared more these last few days with each other than she'd ever shared with anyone. She knew this cocoon of peace and happiness would soon come to an end, but until that day, she was going to enjoy every second.

Xavier nudged her shoulder with his. "So who are you rooting for here, the Phantom or the long-haired guy?"

"Actually, neither one."

"Seriously? Why?"

"Because they both want to control her. The Phantom adores her because of her talent, not because he really loves her." She grinned up at him and added, "If she sang like me, she'd never stand a chance."

Surprisingly, he didn't come back with an insult or agreement. He looked genuinely curious about why she didn't like either of Christine Daaé's choices.

"And the viscount? He seems to love her."

"Maybe so, but he treats her like a child. Her opinions don't matter to him. He thinks he knows best."

A slow smile curved the mouth she loved to kiss. "Your independence is showing."

She shrugged. "This was written during a time when men

saw women as weak creatures, lesser beings. Thankfully, men have wised up since then."

"Then why do you like the movie so much?"

"What's not to love? Beautiful music, a gorgeous setting, danger, intrigue, laughter, tears, and two gorgeous men. It's got everything."

"You're a complicated woman, Jasmine McAlister."

"And yet, you love me anyway."

The minute the words were out of her mouth, she wanted to call them back. Not since he'd told her she was the most important person in the world to him had he indicated he might love her. Even though every touch and every look told her that he did, she didn't want to push him too far.

Instead of looking embarrassed or denying it, he planted a kiss on her lips and said, "With all my heart." He then grabbed the Milk Duds box out of her hand, dumped the entire contents into his mouth, and turned back to the movie.

She couldn't care less about the candy. Xavier Quinn loved her. It didn't get better than that.

CHAPTER THIRTY-THREE

Xavier knew he was running out of time. The last few days had been perfect, but they couldn't last forever. Jazz had come a long way in her recovery, and while she wasn't completely healed, she was close. A few more weeks and she should be one hundred percent. He knew he needed to talk with her about the intel he and Ash had gotten from Kate. He also knew what would happen when he did. She'd want answers immediately, and since he had none to give her, she would want to leave to find them out for herself.

Kate Walker likely had those answers, and without a doubt, Jazz would want to confront her. He wouldn't blame her, but that didn't mean she should forge ahead without caution. She wasn't fully recovered, and she was still in danger, whether she wanted to acknowledge either of those things or not.

While he and Jazz had taken these days for themselves, Ash and the team had been hard at work, trying to find the bastard responsible for her abduction. So far, they'd come up with a thousand possibilities and no real leads.

"Xavier...earth to Xavier."

He looked over his shoulder to find Jazz standing at the door of his office, grinning. "What? Did you say something?"

"I've been calling your name for the past five minutes."

He quirked a brow. "Five minutes?"

"Well, okay, not that long. But at least a minute. Where's your mind?"

"Just thinking about some things."

The light in her eyes dimmed. "Something happened? You got new intel?"

"No, and that's the problem. This guy in Chicago. He shouldn't be that hard to find."

"What about the prints at the kennel?"

"Serena said most of them were too smudged to come up with anything decent. Her people are still working on them, but she's not optimistic."

"Nothing else on the dead guy?"

That had been one of the easier questions to answer. Kip Warring had been a local thug who'd hired himself out to various people, many associated with the Irish mob. But from what they could find, he hadn't attached himself to any group full time. The other man Jazz had shot was still a mystery. No unknown dead bodies had turned up with a chest wound. No one had checked into a nearby ER for treatment. Whatever had happened to him, he was either lying low, or he was dead and hadn't been discovered yet.

"The camera feed? She wasn't able to trace it?"

"No, it got cut off, and the line was corrupted."

"The good thing is that even though the main guy is still out there, there's no way he can figure out where I am now."

"True, but we need to find him. He can't get away with what he did. Plus, he's never going to stop looking."

"I've been thinking about why he would want me. He knew my name. I don't use my real name for anything. Even my car is registered under an alias."

Even though he was glad she was feeling stronger and was ready to fully discuss why she'd been taken, Xavier didn't know if he was ready. What lay ahead was going to hurt Jazz, and he'd do anything to keep that from happening.

"My apartment, credit cards, driver's licenses, passports— they're all in different names and can't be traced back to Jasmine McAlister. And when the old guy said my name, he was very smug, as if he knew I'd be shocked that he knew it." She frowned and shook her head. "Unless this goes back to when Brody and I ran away from Arthur. But that was two decades ago. He can't still be alive."

"Arthur Kelly is dead. Serena tracked him down a while ago. He's been gone for years."

She froze in front of him as awareness entered her eyes. Instead of asking questions about the man who'd abused both her and her brother when they were kids, she honed in on one thing only. "You've been keeping things from me."

"You didn't need to—"

She held up her hand to stop him. "I can't believe what an idiot I've been. I knew everyone was working on this back at OZ, but how stupid of me not to consider that you would keep any leads or intel from me." Her fingers went up in air quotes as she added sarcastically, *"For my own good."* Her eyes narrowed accusingly. "Did you take that responsibility on yourself? Keeping things from me? Or is everyone in on it?"

Xavier snorted. "It's not a conspiracy, Jazz. If I thought there was anything I could tell you that would help identify the bastard who did this, I would have told you. You needed this time to recover."

She took a few more seconds to just glare at him, likely hoping to guilt him into spilling his guts. When that didn't work, she crossed her arms in front of her in a move he knew all too well. Jazz in her most stubborn, most defiant pose.

"Very well. I have recovered. It's time to tell me what you know."

Well, hell.

JAZZ GROUND her teeth to keep from spewing more anger at Xavier. She knew his protection came from a good place. Arrogance? Yes, without a doubt, but also from his heart. He cared about her and wanted to keep her from harm. However, that should never, ever include not telling her the things she needed, and deserved, to know.

"This no-secrets things we agreed to—I didn't know it was one-sided."

"Dammit, Jazz. It's—"

"Trust is a hard thing for me, Xavier. You know that better than anyone."

"I do, baby. But your health was, and is, my priority." Surging up from his chair, he wrapped his hands around her upper arms and stared down at her. "You almost died, sweetheart."

"How would you feel if the roles were reversed? Would you be okay if I kept information from you for your own good?"

Letting go of her arms, he turned away and shoved his fingers through his hair. She knew the answer to her own question. He would be infuriated. It was the same old excuse that had been used before. She was too young, too fragile-looking, too innocent.

"If you don't see me as an equal, Xavier, how can we keep on working together? How can you trust me to watch your back if you don't think I can handle it?"

"That's an absurd example," he snapped. "Of course I trust you to watch my back. I've trusted you on every op, every step of the way." He strode toward her again, grabbed both her shoulders and shook her lightly. "You. Almost. Died. Do you get that? I couldn't find you. I had no idea who'd taken you."

His throat worked as he swallowed, and then he said hoarsely, "I almost lost you, Jazz. I never want to go through that again."

Instead of growling at him like she should, she found herself patting his forearms, trying to soothe him. "I know that, and a big part of the reason it happened was because I made the stupid mistake of going off on my own. I'm not going to do that again. But we've got to get back on even ground, or our partnership isn't going to survive."

"You're right." Backing away, he gestured toward the sofa. "Sit down, and I'll tell you what I know."

Since Xavier's expression looked almost as dour as it had after they'd found her in Chicago, Jazz braced herself. Whatever it was, she could handle it. She was no weak-kneed Nelly. Whatever they'd discovered, she'd deal.

"Before I get started, tell me—have you talked to Kate?"

Startled at the question, Jazz shook her head. "Just briefly when I was in the hospital. We've texted back and forth since then but mostly with her checking to see how I'm doing. What's Kate got to do with what you found out?"

"When you disappeared, Ash called Kate to see if she could offer some kind of intel."

"Wait." Jazz held up her hand. "Something I should have mentioned before. I don't want to get Kate in trouble, but when I went off-grid to look for Brody, I asked Kate to pull traffic cam footage around the restaurant. I didn't tell her why, and bless her, she didn't ask. I know that's not likely related to what we're talking about, but I thought I should mention it. I don't want her to get in trouble on my account."

When Xavier's eyes narrowed and his mouth tightened, Jazz wondered if it did have something to do with that after all. Still, she waited, hoping he'd get on with whatever he had to tell her.

"Kate never mentioned that you'd called her. But that's not why I asked. Ash went to see her. When he'd called her about your disappearance, he could tell she was holding back information, so he went to confront her. She's the one who told us to go to Chicago. She also told us to check into the Byrne family."

"Byrne? Who are they?"

Instead of answering, he said, "What do you know about your birth father, Jazz?"

If Xavier had pulled a rabbit out of his ear, he couldn't have surprised her more. "My birth father? Not much."

Her mother had never shied away from telling her how Jazz had come to be. The love Eliza had had for her daughter had been more than enough for two parents. And then when Connor McAlister had appeared in their lives, bringing Brody with him, their family had been perfect and complete.

"My mom told me his name was Stan Hensley, although she later learned that was a lie. She said she met him when she was out with friends one night. They started seeing each other and had a brief, passionate affair. He told her he was in town on business. Then one day, he just stopped calling. She went to where he'd told her he was staying, and they had no record of a man by that name. She found out a few weeks later that she was pregnant with me. She never heard from him again."

She remembered how her mother had talked about her surprise pregnancy, saying her biggest mistake had turned into her greatest blessing.

"He likely told your mother that lie because he didn't want her to know he had a wife and son in Chicago."

Her heart dropped. She didn't know why. Nothing really had changed. She was still Jazz McAlister, but she hated that her precious mother had been betrayed and lied to so cruelly.

"So who was he?"

"Ronan Byrne. Head of the Chicago Irish mob."

She was glad she was sitting, because she was sure her legs would have just given out. Her real father was a mobster? That would be laughable if it wasn't so tragic. He was a liar, a cheater, and a criminal.

"Does he still live in Chicago? Did he have something to do with my abduction?"

"No, he's dead. He, his wife, and son were killed in a car crash more than twenty years ago."

Wow, so she'd had a father who was a mobster and a half brother she hadn't known about. And they were both dead. Nothing about this felt right or good.

"Okay." She shook her head quickly to clear it from information overload. "So how does this relate to my abduction? Did the old guy have a problem with Byrne? Did he want revenge or something?"

"We're not sure. Since we still don't know who took you, it's hard to say. But the fact that he knew your name and was from the same city seems too coincidental to not be related in some way."

That was a lot to process in such a short amount of time. And even though the information was surprising, it still didn't really answer any questions.

"I need to see Kate," she said. "She's got to have more information."

"I agree."

"Why wouldn't she tell me about this? And how does she even know this stuff?"

"I don't know. She won't tell Ash either. Says all of this is bigger than what we think it is."

"What's bigger?"

"I don't know, Jazz."

Rising from the sofa, Jazz headed out the door.

"Where are you going?"

"I'm going to pack. I want answers, and she's going to give them to me."

"Jazz, wait."

Turning back to him, Jazz shivered as she watched Xavier turn from the gentle, understanding man he'd been for the last few weeks into the grim-faced OZ operative. She recognized that expression well and had always appreciated how fierce and immovable he'd looked against their enemies. This was the first time he'd looked at her with that unflinching resolve.

Refusing to buckle under the obvious intimidation tactic, she snarled, "What?"

"Your leave isn't over."

Crossing her arms in front of her, she glared at him. "Excuse the childish rebuttal, but you're not the boss of me. I damn well come and go as I please."

"No, I'm not your boss, but I am the one who has the keys to the only vehicle out of here. It's a twenty-mile hike down the mountain, babe. I don't think you have it in you to get down there on foot."

She could feel the fury begin from the bottom of her feet as it surged upward toward her head. Of all the arrogant, self-aggrandizing, smug jerks!

"Is this how you want to play this, Xavier? We go from being lovers to being enemies?"

Though his expression never thawed, his eyes dulled with sadness. "No, Jazz, that isn't what I want at all. You're the one who decided to change course. You agreed to six weeks off. It's barely been three weeks, and you're ready to fly out of here without a single thought to your well-being."

"I'm not going to take off again, but I deserve answers. After all I've been through, I deserve the truth."

"Yes, you do. And you'll get the truth, but there's not a

thing out there that can't wait until you're physically able to handle it."

All the air went out of her body. Yes, she was still weak, still recovering, but her brain was fine. Xavier wasn't going to relent, though. She knew him well. When it came to setting his mind on something, he didn't back down, no matter how tough it got.

"Fine," she snapped. "But it's time I stopped sitting around and wasting time. I need to get into the gym and get stronger."

"Fine," he snapped back.

Huffing out her displeasure, Jazz whirled and stomped toward the bedroom. She pulled out a pair of workout shorts and a T-shirt. She would do her workout and pretend that her heart wasn't breaking.

HIS FISTS POUNDING into the leather, Xavier went after the boxing bag like it was his number one enemy. Every bit of ire, fury, and frustration was let loose on the innocuous gym equipment. In his mind, he named the people he held responsible for the shitshow that had just taken place in his den. His first target was Kate Walker. She knew things—things that threatened Jazz's safety. He didn't care how much she had helped OZ over the years. She had no right to hold on to intel that could put Jazz's life in jeopardy.

The second person was the man who'd abducted her. For reasons they still didn't know—although it was looking that, more than likely, it had something to do with her birth father.

And that was the third person on his list. The man who'd lied to a vulnerable young woman, leaving her alone and pregnant. Even though Eliza McAlister had raised an amazing young woman, that didn't negate the damage a lying, piece-of-crap adulterer had done to them both.

Though the bag was getting crowded with the faces of people he wanted to punish, he added one more to the list. And that was Xavier himself.

It didn't matter that he'd kept the truth from Jazz to keep from hurting her. No one, especially someone as independent as Jazz, appreciated being lied to for their own good. It went against every thing he believed about her. She was strong, resilient, and well-adjusted enough to handle anything anyone dished out to her. She'd just survived almost two weeks of torture and abuse. Hell yes, she could handle the truth.

He just hadn't wanted to give it to her and see the light die in her eyes.

A slight draft of air alerted him that she'd come into the room. He knew why she was there. She was going to get stronger and be ready for the last day of her "imprisonment."

At that thought, Xavier delivered one last agonizingly hard punch to the bag in front of him. Jazz had accused him of keeping her prisoner. After what she'd already gone through, how the hell could he do that?

He turned, ready to apologize. He'd get down on his knees if he had to. He'd help her pack and give her the SUV keys. If she really wanted to go, he wouldn't stop her. The instant he saw what she was trying to do, his mind instantly shut that down. Hell, she couldn't even lift a twenty-five-pound weight. This wasn't about making sure she didn't get hurt. This was about making sure she didn't get killed, or get anyone else killed. OZ operatives didn't go out into the field unless they were one hundred percent. She was barely forty, if that.

As if aware that he was staring at her, she dropped the weight on the floor and said, "I called my doctor to see what I need to do. He sent me a list of rehab exercises."

He took a step toward her. "Good. I can help you—"

"No." Turning to face him, she lifted her chin and glared at him. "I agree I'm not strong enough yet, and I won't fight you to leave. But that doesn't mean I forgive you. For weeks, you've known something deeply personal about me, and you hid it."

He was not going to let her get away with that.

"And you've never kept anything from me? Like not telling me that the shooter was Brody?"

She had the grace to flush, and even as frustrated and angry as he was, he felt his heart turn over and a pebble of guilt gnaw at his conscience. He knew why she hadn't told him, and he'd forgiven her. To use that against her felt wrong. But not nearly as wrong as letting her go out while she was weak and unprepared to fight.

"Fine. We've both lied to each other," she said. "It's fairly obvious we don't trust each other like we should. Maybe it's best if we end this."

The anger he'd managed to slightly quash furled back up at an astounding rate.

"End what exactly?"

"Us. Maybe…"

Before she could finish that sentence, he was on her. He would never raise a hand to her in anger, but that didn't mean he wasn't going to make sure she knew how infuriated he was.

"Listen to me, Jazz McAlister, and listen good. What we have is more than not telling each other information. It's more than an argument, a disagreement, or a damned OZ mission. You don't get to back away when things get rough and uncomfortable. You fight. Don't start being a coward now."

As their eyes locked in a battle of emotions and anger, Xavier held his breath to see which road she would take. He was not about to give up on her. He loved her, and he knew, even if she hadn't said it, that she loved him, too. What they had was too special to let angry words destroy it.

Disappointing him, she backed away and said, "I need to

work out." Turning her back to him, she picked up a smaller dumbbell and began lifting.

He knew he could continue their argument. And he might even persuade her to make a concession, but it wouldn't be permanent. Jazz had to work this out herself.

He just hoped that when she did, she remembered how great these past few days had been and what they could have.

CHAPTER THIRTY-FOUR

Two weeks later
Bozeman, Montana

Shaking off another nightmare featuring OZ and Brody, Jazz sat up in her bed. She was finally home. Against Xavier's wishes, against doctor's recommendations, against everyone who had an opinion about her health and well-being. Also against the voice inside her head that asked her time and again just what she thought she was going to accomplish. She didn't know. What she did know was she could no longer hide away and pretend things would somehow work out. She had to do something.

When Xavier had dropped her off yesterday, he had silently, without asking permission or telling her what he was doing, spent hours adding more locks to her door, as well as enhancing her security system. She hadn't protested or complained. She knew he'd done it because he cared. The odds that whoever was after her knew where she lived were slim. However, being cautious would hurt nothing.

Right before he'd walked out the door, he had taken her by

her shoulders and stared into her eyes. "I know you're hurting and confused. And I know that independent spirit of yours is telling you to get out there and find out as much as you can. But know this—I will never, no matter what happens, abandon you again. I will watch your back, not just because you're my partner or my friend. I will watch your back because you are a part of me, Jazz McAlister. I will not give up on us. No matter what."

Then, with a hard kiss to her lips, he'd walked out the door. She hadn't seen him since.

The distance that had grown between them had still been there. She had felt it, and so had he. Some of that was her fault —okay, most of it was her fault. Xavier had gone out of his way several times to try to mend what was fractured between them, but she had cut him off each time.

For the last two weeks, since she'd learned what he'd been holding back from her, she had focused solely on regaining her strength and getting back into fighting shape. When she wasn't working out or sleeping, she was doing her own research, not only to find the man who had abducted her, but to also find what she could on Ronan Byrne, the man who'd apparently been her birth father.

It was stupid to think of Byrne as anything other than a sperm donor. In every way that counted, the only father she'd ever had was Connor McAlister. He had been the epitome of what every father should be. She shared nothing with Ronan Byrne other than some DNA.

For the most part, Xavier had left her alone to do what she wanted. Though he'd continued to cook and feed them both, the fun days of taking long walks, watching movies, and making love had been over. In their place had been a coolness and emptiness that tore at her heart.

She told herself they could mend the fracture, but for now, she was home, and she wanted to get to work.

She took stock of her bedroom, the familiar surroundings easing her mind. Admittedly, it wasn't much. A bed and nightstand, a chair in the corner where she read, and a dresser. Other people might describe it as sparse, but to Jazz, it represented what she didn't mind losing. She had learned the hard way that material possessions were just objects and could be left behind. She'd been there, done that multiple times. Now she kept only what could be carried in a backpack. All the rest was worthless. Attaching sentimental value to an inanimate object hurt when you eventually lost it.

With people, the pain of loss was infinitely greater.

Feeling that familiar heaviness, Jazz put her feet on the floor and took in a deep breath. Onward and upward, as her mama had often said. Today was the day she'd been anticipating. She would learn as much as she could at OZ, and then she would go to the one person who seemed to know it all.

Kate Walker, mentor, teacher, friend, and advocate, had been keeping secrets from her. For how long, she didn't know. The one conversation Jazz had had with her, after learning about her parentage, had been frustrating and hurtful. Kate had been short with her, giving her no real answers.

Allowing anxiety and uncertainty to fuel her, Jazz readied herself for the day ahead. She took a shower, washed her hair, which surprisingly was almost to her shoulders since she hadn't bothered to have it cut and styled in a while. She lathered herself with her favorite fragrant lotion of jasmine and orange and then spent a surprising amount of time on her makeup. Usually, she made do with mascara and a bit of blush, but needing a little extra confidence, she focused on making herself look a bit more put together and mature.

Returning to her bedroom, she pulled out the outfit that had been sent over at her request. Thanks to Rose Wilson, OZ's majordomo extraordinaire, she could dress in designer clothes and look like a million bucks. Material things might not mean a lot to her, but that didn't mean she didn't appreciate them. She had zero fashion sense and was more comfortable in khakis and T-shirts for work and yoga pants and T-shirts for leisure. However, today of all days, she needed to exude confidence and professionalism. Today, Jazz McAlister would prove to everyone that she could handle anything, even the hard stuff.

It was time for her OZ family to again see her as a full-fledged, capable operative. Admittedly the last year or so, they'd had reason to worry about her. The injury on the op in Zambia had almost taken her life. For weeks, she had barely been aware of her surroundings, and recovery had been long and arduous. When she'd returned to work, her team had shielded and protected her as if she were fragile. She'd just been getting back into the groove and feeling on her game again when she'd been abducted and for a second time found herself at death's door. Almost dying again hadn't exactly inspired confidence with her team.

Before she did anything else, though, she needed to apologize to them for going off on her own. She hadn't trusted them, and that was on her. But she'd learned her lesson—the hard way.

It was time to move on. Her agenda was set. She would meet with her team, discuss whatever intel they had, and then she would go to Kate and demand answers. The knowledge that her friend and mentor had betrayed her was almost too difficult to comprehend. There had to be a rational and reasonable explanation for why Kate was withholding intel. Whatever it was, Jazz intended to get it out of her.

Difficult tasks? Absolutely. Impossible? No. Especially when you had the backing of the best covert ops organization in the business.

Standing in front of her full-length mirror, Jazz gave her appearance a once-over. The black Hugo Boss pantsuit was simple, businesslike, and fit her as if it were designed for her. The stark white, long-sleeved shirt she wore beneath the jacket was just as basic. She had learned long ago that when it came to her body size and youthful looks, simple and plain worked much better. Being five three and fine-boned, with a pixielike face, she was still occasionally mistaken for a child. Sometimes, her size came in handy for her job. But today was not the day to look small, weak, or young. She was a kick-ass OZ operative. She needed to look the part.

She tugged on a lock of her hair that just touched her collar. Maybe it was time to consider growing it longer. At one time, her hair had reached the middle of her back. It had been her favorite feature, in part because it reminded her so much of her mother. Eliza McAlister had had gloriously long and thick ebony hair. For years, Jazz had kept her hair long as a loving reminder of her beautiful mother. Until that day when it had almost gotten her killed. She'd cut it off that day and had kept her hair short ever since.

She shook her head, forcing her thoughts away from her looks and to the day ahead. Meeting her eyes in the mirror, she promised that whatever she learned today, she would remain professional and focus on what lay ahead. Nothing would stop her from achieving her goals.

Knowledge was power, and she was tired of being weak. From this day forward, no matter what, Jazz McAlister could handle anything that came her way.

CHAPTER THIRTY-FIVE

Zooming down the road that led to OZ headquarters, Xavier tried to push the worry aside and enjoy his ride. The motorcycle he'd purchased in Chicago had arrived while he'd been away with Jazz, and this was his first time riding it since his return home. There was almost nothing that soothed him like an exhilarating bike ride through the winding, mountainous terrain of Montana—the wind on his face, the vibration of the powerful motor beneath him, and the excitement that came with the challenge of handling such a beautiful piece of machinery at breakneck speed. Today, he felt none of those things. He was headed to a meeting that might well end in disaster for Jazz.

The last two weeks with her had been some of the most frustrating of his life. She had made it clear that she wanted space. And since he'd been the prick who'd told her she wasn't allowed to leave the cabin, he'd figured giving in to that request was the least he could do. Hadn't made it easy or enjoyable, though. Especially since any closeness they'd shared before had also seemingly ended.

Increasing the bike's speed, Xavier ground his teeth in both frustration and denial. No way had it ended. He had backed away to give her some space, and yes, he'd give her time, but they were not over. He'd made that clear when he'd walked out of her apartment. What they had together was genuine and solid. She might try to deny what she felt, but he knew the truth. They were forever, even if forever was going to take a little more time than he liked.

He pulled into the parking lot of OZ headquarters, noting vehicles belonging to Ash, Serena, Liam, Eve, and Gideon were already here. Jazz's gray BMW was nowhere in sight. His mouth tilted slightly as he remembered how excited she'd been when she'd purchased the little SUV, extolling all the gadgets and features as if it were an exotic spaceship and not a four-year-old used vehicle with over eighty thousand miles. It had been new to her and had replaced her fifteen-year-old Toyota.

The fact that Jazz could afford a new vehicle every year if she wanted had been lost on no one. However, not one person had mentioned that to her. Jazz was Jazz, and that was all right with them.

He parked and jumped off his bike, debating whether he should wait in the parking lot for her arrival. He wanted to talk to her, see how she was doing. Tell her he was there for her if she needed him.

At that thought, he shook his head. No, she knew he had her back and how he felt about her. He needed to treat her as she'd requested. She was a member of the team, and he would treat her as one. Their personal relationship was just that— personal. When they were on the job, they were partners and teammates, nothing more.

When he stepped into the conference room and took in everyone's expressions, he saw the same emotion he was feeling. None of them knew what the next few hours would mean for Jazz, but they would all be ready to help her, come what may.

Jazz took a deep breath and then walked into the conference room. Everyone was waiting for her. On most days when OZ had team meetings, everyone was milling around, drinking coffee, and chatting about odds and ends. That wasn't the environment she walked into today. Every operative sat at the conference table and, from the look of things, were barely speaking to one another. The instant she entered, though, light entered their eyes, and every one of them smiled at her.

The last thing she wanted to do was get emotional. She was here to get answers and give answers, but seeing their delight in her recovery was almost more than she could handle. A lump developed in her throat, and she was only able to manage a husky, "It's good to see everyone," before she shut up and sat down.

Xavier sat at the end of the table, close to Ash. When his eyes met hers, the heat in them skyrocketed her already jittery nerves. That look said so many things, and deciphering them all was beyond her at the moment. Then, as if he knew exactly how she felt, he gave her a gentle, encouraging smile, and suddenly she felt stronger than ever. How did he do that?

"Jazz," Ash said, "it's good to see you looking so fit."

Jerking her attention back to the entire room, she cleared her throat and said, "Thank you, Ash. And thanks to all of you for saving me. I did something dumb and almost died. I'm truly grateful to all of you."

"We're just relieved you look so well," Serena said.

"Thank you. I'm feeling great and ready to get to work."

"That's good to hear, but I think you wanted to say something before we get started?" Ash said.

This was their signal. She'd sent a text to her boss this

morning to let him know she wanted to make a formal apology and explanation to the team. He'd replied with, *Sounds good*.

"I feel the need to explain in detail why I did what I did. When Bass was shot, I took off after the shooter. Xavier got caught up in saving a woman from being trampled, so I went on ahead. When I ran out to the alley, I saw the shooter getting into a black SUV. The description I gave you was mostly accurate. His height and weight were accurate. What I didn't mention was that a strand of golden-blond hair was sticking out from beneath his skullcap. Also, when he went to open the car door, I saw a glimpse of his wrist and noticed a thick scar. Additionally, our eyes met for a second or two before he got inside the vehicle. His eyes were an unusual shade of green, a blend of aquamarine and jade. They were vivid and unlike any color I've ever seen, except for one person."

"Your brother," Ash said solemnly.

"Yes," she answered softly.

Thankful there were no interruptions, Jazz continued, wanting to get everything out in the open. "I panicked. I couldn't get my head wrapped around the fact that my loving, kindhearted brother was a killer. I thought if I could find him first, I could talk to him and bring him in.

"I had nightmares of OZ finding him and there being some kind of shootout that didn't end well for anyone." She glanced around the room again, wanting to make sure they understood her sincerity. "I messed up, and I'm incredibly sorry."

"I'd like to suggest that we move on from here," Eve said. "Jazz, yes, you screwed up and didn't trust the team. But there's not one of us who hasn't screwed up in some way. We're human, and we make mistakes."

"I agree," Liam said. He sent Jazz a grim look. "I'm sorry I wasn't there to help you, Jazz, but Aubrey and I were over-joyed with relief when you were found."

"Thank you, Liam. And even though I sent you a text, I want to say in person, congratulations on your baby girl. I cannot wait to meet Lily."

Grinning like only a proud father could, he said, "And she can't wait to meet you."

"All right, then," Ash said. "Are we agreed that we need to move on? Jazz has owned up to her mistakes, and we've got a lot on our agenda. However…" Pausing for effect, he sent each of his operatives a warning glare. "This better be the last time any of you remove your trackers. They're there to protect you, not inhibit you. Understand?"

Jazz nodded along with everyone else. It had been an insane thing to do, and its absence had almost gotten her killed.

"Next up, let's talk about Jazz's abductor." He looked at Serena and said, "I understand you have some interesting intel to share."

"Yes." Serena sent an apologetic grimace to Jazz. "Sorry. If I'd searched the correct parameters earlier, I would have found him sooner."

Jazz sat up straight in her chair. "You found him?"

"I believe so." She clicked a couple of keys on her laptop, and the photo of a well- dressed older man with thinning hair and a sallow complexion appeared on the large wall screen. Jazz knew the face well, as it continued to appear in her nightmares.

"That's him," Jazz whispered.

Serena sent her another quick, apologetic smile. "His name is Kevin Doyle, once a high-ranking soldier for the Byrne crime family in Chicago. When Byrne and his family were killed, the organization fractured into various factions. Doyle took a piece of it with him, but he never could gain the support to grow beyond a small-time gangster."

"But why did he take me?" Jazz asked. "I knew nothing about Ronan Byrne and want nothing to do with him."

"Maybe so," Ash answered, "but you're the daughter of the man they looked upon as a king."

"So they wanted to use me…for what?"

"That's a question we all want answered," Gideon said.

Her mind whirling in a thousand different directions, Jazz let the intel sink into her brain. She was aware that her teammates continued to make remarks and give their opinions, but she heard the comments only in her periphery. That was, until Liam said, "Serena, you said if you'd used the right parameters, you would have found him sooner. What did you mean?"

"I should have broadened my search to include the deceased."

Jazz's attention jerked back with a vengeance. But it was Xavier who growled, "What? Doyle is dead? How?"

"He died two days after we found Jazz. There was no obituary, nothing online. The only way I discovered it was one of my people found a two-line statement that the owner of Archie's, a restaurant in the Loop, was now Ryan Doyle, the son of the late Kevin Doyle. I did a deep dive and found a death certificate. It had been altered, but I was able to root around till I found the original. He died of a self-inflicted gunshot wound."

"He killed himself?" Jazz whispered to no one in particular. "But why?"

"Not sure," Serena said, "but I also found a death certificate for his wife, who died of a brain aneurysm the week before."

"Jazz," Ash said, "Eve, Gideon, and I are headed to Chicago in a few hours. We'll be meeting with Doyle's son to see if he knows what his father's intent was and why."

"Aren't we opening ourselves up—exposing Jazz even more by meeting with him?" Liam asked.

"We're going in undercover as an investment group interested in buying into one of Ryan Doyle's businesses. I want to get the lay of the land before we show any of our cards."

Jazz tried to get her head wrapped around this new intel. All the time she'd been hating on the guy responsible for kidnapping and torturing her, he'd been dead. And though there were some clues about why he'd taken her, it was all too fuzzy and murky to see anything solid.

She sent a look to Xavier and wasn't surprised to see his eyes were on her. Any other time, they'd be sitting together and discussing the findings and what they meant. Even though she could see love and warmth in his gaze, she still felt a huge disconnect from him that she didn't know how to overcome. No matter which way she turned, confusion reigned.

"Damn," Ash said softly.

"What's wrong?" Serena said.

All eyes went to Ash, who was looking at something on his phone with a grim set to his mouth.

"Looks like we're about to have company," he said.

"Who?" Liam asked.

Ash stood and headed to the door, but before he walked out, he looked at Jazz. "Kate is on her way here. She said she has the answers you're looking for. And it's about damn time."

CHAPTER THIRTY-SIX

His phone to his ear, Ash pushed the front door open and stomped down the steps. The minute his wife answered his call, he said, "Kate's here."

Jules's heartfelt sigh told him she hadn't known of Kate's plans. Then she confirmed it with, "I haven't talked to her in a couple of days, Ash. I didn't know she was coming."

He and Jules had been arguing about Kate for weeks. Nothing had been resolved. While his wife agreed that Kate keeping back intel that would greatly increase their chances of finding the people who'd taken Jazz was insanely wrong, she was torn. Kate was her mentor and friend, the godmother to their son. They had both trusted her with their lives. But while Ash had become skeptical of Kate's loyalty over the last few months, Jules's opinion of her friend had never wavered.

Against Jules's wishes, Ash had barred Kate from Option Zero grounds. Before, she had enjoyed the freedom to come and go just like any other OZ employee. But now, she required an escort. He hadn't told her, of course, and when she'd texted that she couldn't get through the gate because her code wouldn't work, he'd read between the lines of her terse state-ment. She was pissed.

Well, so was he. And until she came clean with everything, she would remain on his "watch list."

He drove the two miles to the OZ entrance, a well-hidden drive that no one would see unless they were looking directly at it. Kate's car was idling, and her face through the wind-shield clearly showed her temper. What he didn't like was seeing the hurt in her eyes. Kate had been his friend for a long time, and she had done some remarkable work to make the world a safer place. But secrets within the OZ community could not be allowed. They'd learned the hard way that when things were hidden, everyone suffered for it.

Ash got out of his vehicle, walked to the gate pad, and keyed in an access number. When the gate went up, he gave her a stiff nod and returned to his car.

Just as he reached the parking lot, another notification came through. Another car had arrived at the gate, and this person had clearance. Jules was going to join them.

WHILE THEY WAITED for Ash to return with Kate, it was all Xavier could do not to grab Jazz and run out the door. She had walked into the conference room earlier with all the confidence and cockiness he was used to seeing in her. And now, not half an hour into the meeting, she was looking pale and worn out.

Whatever Kate was bringing to the meeting was bound to have an even more devastating impact on her. He wanted to shut it down, but there was no way around it. She would resent his intrusion, and as much as he didn't want her hurt, he agreed with her that she needed to know the truth. Whatever the hell it was.

The hard, set expression on Ash's face when he'd walked out the door was a reflection of Xavier's own ire. Kate hadn't been invited to the meeting. She had, in fact, lost her security clearance to even come onto the property without an armed escort. That's how pissed Ash was, and Xavier joined him in his feelings.

Unable to sit and wait without at least touching Jazz, Xavier stood and rolled his chair over to where she sat. She'd been doodling on the pad in front of her, but he knew her mind was running a thousand miles an hour.

"You okay?" he asked.

Without looking up, she said, "Oh yeah, peachy."

"Have you talked to Kate since you've been back?"

"No. I sent her a text and told her I needed to talk to her. She responded with an obscure 'I know,' and that was that."

"I don't know if he told you, but Ash barred her from OZ unless she has an escort."

Her head popped up, a startled, concerned expression on her face. "That's insane. Does he think she's working against us?"

Xavier shrugged. "She's not been forthcoming, Jazz. She's holding back intel."

"Well, so did I."

"Yes, but you gave an explanation for it—one everyone understood. Kate's only excuse is that things are in play that are bigger than us."

"That doesn't mean she's working against us."

"Maybe not, but I do know that her intel to find you came much later than it should have."

"Kate wouldn't hold back intel if she thought my life was in danger. She just wouldn't."

He didn't know who she was trying to convince, him or herself, but Xavier didn't respond to her statement. Whatever

Kate was bringing today would be upsetting enough without him adding to it.

Looking for a safer topic, he said, "Probably felt good being in your own bed the last two nights."

"I missed you," she said quietly.

Now it was his turn to jerk his head around and stare at her. This was the first time in over two weeks that she'd given any indication that she missed the intimacy they'd shared. After their argument, she had moved into a different bedroom, and they hadn't even kissed since then, much less shared a bed.

"I miss you, too, baby."

A sexy smile curved her mouth. "I love when you call me baby."

"I'll call you that every night if you let me."

"I'd—"

"Hello, everyone."

All eyes went to the door. Kate stood there, the defiant glint in her eyes telling them she was not only infuriated at their treatment of her, but she also wasn't the least bit remorseful for causing their distrust.

Yeah, things were about to get even rockier.

HER NERVES ON EDGE, Jazz resisted the impulse to go to Kate and pull her into a hug. This woman had done so much for her. To think that she might have held back information that could have ended her imprisonment sooner—or even prevented it in the first place—caused her stomach to roil.

"Jazz, it's so good to see you looking so well." Kate's voice was both soothing and sincere.

Her stiff limbs loosening, Jazz breathed out a relieved sigh. There was no way this woman had anything but good intentions inside her. The tension between OZ and Kate had been distorted and blown out of proportion.

Her chin jutted out. She wanted to make sure everyone knew Kate had her full support, so she said with all the affection in the world, "It's good to see you, too, Kate. I'm so happy you're here to clear up the miscommunication and confusion."

"Thank you, Jazz. That means a lot," Kate said in her calm, cool voice. "But I'd like to talk to you in private."

As much as she trusted Kate and wanted everyone to know it, she was tired of the secrets. "If you don't mind, I'd like for our conversation to stay out in the open. There've been too many secrets. Whatever you have to say, I don't mind my OZ family hearing about it."

For the first time since Kate had arrived, Jazz spotted a flicker of guilt before she was able to mask it. Tensing once more, she waited for whatever Kate was about to reveal.

"Very well." Seating herself at the table, Kate nodded to Ash, who sat next to Jules a few feet away. "I know that all of you believe I have information that could have saved Jazz earlier, but I promise you I gave you everything I had."

"All right," Ash said. "Then let's move on to the other intel you're keeping from us."

Kate's throat worked as she swallowed, and Jazz saw the nerves behind the cool mask. Hating seeing her friend like this, she said, "Kate, you saved my life years ago. I don't know where I would be, or what I would be, if you hadn't found me and helped me. You have my love, my gratitude, and my allegiance. The people here are my family as much as you are. Whatever you have to say, they should hear it, too."

"Thank you, Jazz. I hope you still feel the same way after this is over."

A cold chill swept up Jazz's spine, and before she could question exactly what that meant, Kate went on, "What do you know about your father?"

Oddly relieved, since all this was apparently related to Ronan Byrne, Jazz said quickly, "Just that he was apparently a mob boss in Chicago and that he's dead."

Kate shook her head, her mouth tight with irritation. "I'm sorry. It's hard for me to think of Byrne as your father. I was referring to Connor McAlister."

As all breath suddenly left her body, she had no air to respond to Kate's question. She managed a headshake and a shrug.

Apparently understanding her lack of response, Kate sent her a tight smile and continued, "When I first met Connor, he was investigating the Byrne crime family. He was one of the finest men I've ever known."

As bombshells went, it was a big one, and all Jazz could manage was, "You knew Papa Mac?"

"At the time that we met, Connor had been with the FBI for over a decade. I was a new recruit and was in awe of him. He was my friend and mentor. I joined the investigation late, mostly doing grunt work and behind-the-scenes tasks, but Connor always had a kind or encouraging word for me. He took me under his wing and allowed me in on all the meetings related to the case.

"When we learned that Byrne had fathered a child with Eliza Whitmore, the bureau wanted to bring her in and interrogate her. Connor didn't like that approach. He chose to go undercover, get to know your mother, and see if she knew anything that could be helpful in bringing him down."

Jazz didn't know when it had happened, but at some point in the midst of this misery, Xavier had taken her hand in his. She appreciated it because her hand was the only thing she could feel. Every other part of her body was frozen in shock, horror, and abject grief. Papa Mac had used her mother for information? Had the only decent family life she'd had been a lie?

"It took him all of a week to learn that Eliza hadn't even known who Byrne was. She was no help to the investigation, and Connor was ordered to cut her loose." Kate shook her head and smiled. "It was already too late. Connor was over the moon for your mother. So much so that when he realized that not only would the FBI not be interested in Eliza, but at some point, they might use the information that she had a child by Byrne for their own agenda, he wanted to cut all ties with them."

Finally finding her voice, Jazz rasped out a stuttering, "Did my mother... Did she know?"

"Connor told her on their second date who he was and why he'd set up the meeting. By then, Eliza was already in love with him, too."

Their love had happened fast, that much Jazz had always known. She remembered hearing a conversation between her mama and a friend a few days after her mother had told her that she was going to marry Papa Mac. Her mother's friend had admonished Eliza for being so reckless as to fall so fast for a man she hardly knew. Her mother had laughed and said that if one was going to do something reckless, then it should be for love.

Kate continued, "So Connor chose to leave the FBI and move the family to Georgia, far away from Byrne and anything to do with the investigation of him."

Every question that was answered was replaced by ten more. Even as much as Jazz wanted to speak, to demand all the answers, she could only remain seated and take each hit as it came. And oh, did they keep on coming.

"The investigation against Byrne went on, but with a new team leader. I heard from Connor from time to time. As you know, he had an accounting degree, and he put it to use working for one of the larger accounting firms in Atlanta. Maybe things would have continued on without a hitch if

Ronan Byrne and his family hadn't been killed in a car accident a few years later."

"Was it a hit?" Eve asked.

Jazz had been so lost in all the information being thrown at her, she'd completely forgotten that her team was sitting there with her. And maybe she was crazy, but she was glad they were hearing this at the same time she was. It made her feel less alone.

"No, it wasn't a hit," Kate replied. "It was clear at the accident site that Byrne had lost control on the icy road and gone over an embankment. He, his wife, and his fourteen-year-old son were killed on impact."

Jazz once again thought about the half brother she'd only recently discovered she had. Had he planned to follow in his father's footsteps? Would he have become the head of the crime family?

"So when Byrne was killed, there was no one to take over?" Gideon said.

"Correct. There were lots who tried, but none of them inspired loyalty the way Byrne could. The organization fractured after that. There were lots of killings and disappearances and absolutely no cohesiveness. So much so that our task force dropped from a dozen people working the case to just two. I went on to another case. And then, somehow, someway, it was discovered that Byrne had another child."

Oh sweet heavens. Jazz was glad she was sitting down, because even before Kate said the words, she knew what was coming.

"They tracked Connor and your family to Atlanta."

"The explosion?" Jazz whispered, her mouth desert-dry.

"Yes. Getting rid of your parents was the first part of their plan. And then, before the FBI could get to you, someone showed up and took you and Brody away."

She remembered the harsh-looking woman who had

introduced herself as a social worker. She had claimed that Arthur Kelly was a distant cousin of Eliza and was the only one willing to take both her and Brody together.

"Who is this 'they' you keep mentioning?" Xavier asked.

Something flickered in Kate's expression before she said, "That is something no one has been able to figure out. Could have been one of the old guard or someone new."

"Why didn't they do away with Jazz's brother?" Liam asked. He sent her an apologetic look, but she was actually wondering the same thing.

"They knew they'd have a tougher time with Jazz by herself. They figured they could use Brody to control her."

And they had. How many times had Arthur made threats against Brody to keep her in line? How many times had Brody been abused because of something she should have been punished for?

"It worked," Jazz said softly. "They knew exactly what they were doing."

"The FBI was looking for you, but Arthur Kelly was not even a blip on their radar. Then, one day, Brody overheard Arthur bragging about how his ship would finally come in when you were eighteen and could be used for what you were intended."

"What?" Jazz's mouth felt so dry, she wondered if anyone had even heard her.

A bottle of water appeared in her line of sight, and Xavier leaned forward and whispered, "Take a sip, baby."

She did as she was told, taking several fortifying swallows before she was able to say in a surprisingly calm and coherent voice, "Kate, how do you know what Brody overheard?"

As if her words weren't going to cause a massive hemorrhage in their relationship the minute she uttered them, Kate said quietly, "Because your brother has been working with me for over a decade."

CHAPTER THIRTY-SEVEN

Jazz distantly heard Xavier curse, and she thought Serena might've gasped. There was a roaring in her ears, though, so hearing anything substantial was out of the question. She even knew that Kate's lips continued to move, but Jazz had completely zoned out.

Brody had been working with Kate for ten years? Brody had known where she was all along? Kate had known how badly she wanted to find her brother and had never told her?

Trust had never been one of Jazz's strong points, and right now, she was sure it no longer existed in any form.

"Breathe, Jazz," Xavier said beside her.

A gasping sob burst from her lungs, making her realize she had been holding her breath for who knew how long.

"I know you're hurting, Jazz, and I'm so sorry for your pain," Kate said. "But this was what he wanted."

"Maybe you should back up a bit, Kate," Ash said. "I don't think she heard your last few sentences."

Kate sent a grateful look at Ash and then turned back to Jazz. "A few years back, I was in Chicago, and I saw a man who looked almost identical to Connor coming out of a restaurant. I knew he had to be Brody. He didn't see me, but I followed him to an apartment building. He went inside, and so did I. When I knocked on his door, I don't know what I was expecting, but it wasn't the hard-faced, soulless-looking man who answered the door.

"I introduced myself, and he allowed me to come inside. What he told me I've never told another soul. I know for a fact Brody wouldn't appreciate me telling you now, but if you're feeling what I think you're feeling, then you need to know all the facts."

Kate paused and took a breath. "When you were living in Indianapolis, the Irish mob found Brody and wanted him to reveal your location. He refused. Even though he knew he was abandoning you, he couldn't allow them to find you and use you." She gave Jazz a telling look as she added, "They weren't kind.

"Instead of killing him, they forced him to work for them, but he had no freedom. He was their prisoner, doing what they told him to do, but he had absolutely no autonomy. He managed to sneak away from them one day and went to the apartment, hoping you'd still be there. You had been long gone by then, and the place was cleaned out. He had no clue what had happened to you.

"We had a long talk, and I gave him a chance to escape the mob. His only request was that I find you and give you a home. It took over a year before someone spotted you on the streets in Chicago."

Jazz remembered that day well. It had been snowing, and she had spent an uncomfortable night in an alleyway, beneath a large rug she'd found in the dumpster. She had been living on the streets for two years by then. Going to homeless shelters or churches had been out of the question. She had still been a minor, and they would have been obligated to report her to the authorities. It had been rough, scary as hell, and often humiliating, but she had survived. Whenever she thought about those days, that's what she reminded herself: She had survived.

Kate had walked up to her on the sidewalk and introduced herself. To this day, Jazz didn't know if she'd trusted Kate because she had been so hungry and cold, or if she had recognized that the woman truly did want to help her. Either way, Kate had walked to a car, and Jazz had silently followed her like Kate was the Pied Piper. From that moment on, she had never wanted for anything.

Jazz cleared her throat and managed a raspy, "So the same people who took Brody...they're the ones who tried to kidnap me in Indianapolis?"

"I imagine there were lots of people looking for you," Kate said. "Those goons likely got tipped off by the kid in the market and saw some easy cash."

She could only imagine what her life would have been like if they had caught her. And Brody...sweet heavens, what had they done to her brother?

"Did you order Brody to kill Franco Bass?"

The question surprised everyone, not just because it was a major subject change, but also because it had come from Jules, who was looking at Kate as if she'd never seen her before.

"No. I don't give orders to Brody."

"Then who does?" Ash asked.

"I don't know."

"Bullshit, Kate."

"I'm telling the truth, Ash. Brody and I are not a team. And I am most definitely not his boss or handler. He's done some favors for me. I've done several for him. But he's got his own contacts, his own agenda."

"Does he work for the Wren Project?" Ash asked.

"No, I don't believe so. From what I can tell, he's working against them, but again, he doesn't report to me, nor does he confide in me. We have a semicordial relationship, mostly because I kept my promise and found Jazz."

"Why doesn't he want to see me?" Jazz asked.

Compassion wasn't something Kate was known for, but Jazz saw it in her eyes when she said, "Because he isn't the same man he was when he was just your big brother."

"That shouldn't be his decision to make. I should get the choice of whether or not I want him in my life."

"I agree, Jazz, and that's what I told him." She opened her purse and retrieved a burner phone that she slid across the table to her. "His phone number is the only one on this. He's expecting your call."

She would finally hear her brother's voice after all these years. Jazz didn't hesitate. She grabbed the phone and stood. "Excuse me."

She practically ran out of the room but stopped in the hallway and took a shaky breath. Her heart was pounding as if she'd run a marathon, and she feared she wouldn't be able to hear Brody over the noise it made.

"Jazz," Xavier said behind her.

Turning, she stared up at him with tear-glazed eyes. "I know it's crazy but I'm scared."

With a soft curse, he pulled her to him and wrapped his arms tight around her. The comfort in his embrace was everything. A huge part of her wanted to just let go and sob out all the pain and sorrow. But that steel core within her told her to straighten her spine and get the job done. She'd been hoping and praying for an opportunity like this for over a decade. She wasn't going to back away now just because it was hard.

She took a few more seconds to draw strength from his

embrace, breathed in the familiar male fragrance that she so loved, and then drew away. "I'll be fine."

"I know you will, Jazz. You're so strong. You want me to stay?"

"No. That's okay. I think I need to do this alone."

"Very well. I'll be in the conference room. Let me know if you need me."

"Okay." Before he could walk out of her sight, she said, "Xavier?"

He turned back quickly and said, "Yes?"

"Thank you."

WALKING AWAY from her was one of the hardest things he'd ever done in his life. She had received blow after blow today. And now she might possibly get one more—possibly the biggest one of all—by talking to her brother who could hurt her even more.

Fury fueled every step back to the conference room. He didn't know who he was angrier with, Kate or Brody McAlister. Both of them had lied to and deceived Jazz for years. And though he knew his rage should be tempered by the knowledge that they'd both done what they could to take care of her, that didn't negate the lies. No wonder Jazz had trust issues. The people she loved continued to lie and keep things from her. And yes, he silently admitted, he knew he was one of those people.

That stopped now. He could do nothing about the past, but he could damn well make sure it didn't happen in the future.

He stopped at the conference room door, where Jules and Kate were in a whispered conversation while Ash sat a few feet away with a fierce scowl on his face. Eve and Gideon were talking in low tones to each other. Liam was on his phone, and the smile on his face told him the man was likely talking to his wife. Serena had positioned herself in a corner and was frowning as she typed away on her laptop.

Even though they were all seemingly occupied, he knew they were well aware of what was going on only a few yards away from them. And while his heart told him to turn around and check on Jazz, he forced himself to stay put. She had asked for privacy, and he would honor her wishes, no matter how difficult. That didn't mean he couldn't get more answers. His gut told him Kate was still holding back.

"Why did Kevin Doyle take Jazz?" Xavier asked as he walked in.

Kate glanced up, and while he noted she looked as though she'd aged a decade since she had arrived, he refused to relent. If she was holding back intel that could keep Jazz safe, then he had absolutely no sympathy for her.

Pushing her hair back with her fingers, Kate blew out a heavy, weary-filled sigh. "I imagine for the same reasons they used to justify killing her parents and giving her to Arthur Kelly to hold for them."

"Because she's Byrne's daughter? He had that much influence?"

"Yes. As far as crime families go, he was the king in Chicago."

"So they want to use her for what—some kind of archaic arranged marriage to unite the mob?"

Before Kate could answer, Serena said in the grimmest voice he'd ever heard from her, "I don't think that's the biggest reason."

"What do you mean?" Xavier asked.

"Come look."

Striding over to where she was, he stopped beside her and looked down at her laptop screen. His heart stopped, and his gut roiled. No wonder they wanted her. Jazz was in just as much danger as she had been before. In the grand scheme of things, the fact that Kevin Doyle was dead meant nothing. A dozen more just like him were likely plotting how to get their hands on Jazz.

And she had no idea.

CHAPTER THIRTY-EIGHT

The phone in her hand was going to break if she didn't stop gripping it so tightly. Nerves weren't usually a big issue for her. When you'd seen and done things that would make most people cringe, you learned to let adrenaline steel your resolve to get the job done. She told herself to do that this time, but for the life of her, she was having trouble following through with the norm. With just one push of a key, she would hear Brody on the other end of the line. Something she'd longed for with all her heart for over a decade was within her grasp, and she was hesitating. How insane was that?

Her impatience with herself at an all-time high, Jazz let loose a low growl and punched the key that would connect her with Brody.

The instant the call was answered, her throat closed up. He didn't say anything, but she knew he was there.

Swallowing hard, she rasped out, "Brody?"

"Hey, Little Mighty." Though the voice sounded gravelly and slightly husky, she had no trouble recognizing it as her brother's.

Dropping into a chair behind her, she whispered, "It's really you?"

"Yeah, it's me, Jazz."

"I can't believe I'm talking to you. It's been so long."

"I know, Jazzy. I'm sorry. I'm so damn sorry."

"I waited for you, and then I had to leave. I knew there was no way you'd be able to find me, but I didn't know what else to do."

"You did the right thing, Jazz. It was months before I could get back to the apartment. If you hadn't left, they would have found you."

"Where have you been all this time? What are you involved in? Why did you kill Franco Bass? Do you work for the Wren Project?"

"That's a lot of questions, and I don't have a lot of time. I can't stay on the phone too long. Just know that I'm so proud of you, Jazz. You've become a force to be reckoned with. But be careful, because those bastards are still looking for you. And even though Kate Walker has done a lot of good things, don't trust her. She's hiding things, and I can't tell whose side she's on."

"But, Brody, I want to see you. I—"

"No, Jazz. You go live your life. Do your thing, Little Mighty. Just know I love you, and Mom and Pop would be so damn proud of you. I know I am."

Before she could say another word, the call ended, and he was gone. Angry that he'd just hung up, she immediately called back, but an automated voice came on the line to say the number didn't exist.

She wasn't sure how long she sat there, just staring at the phone and trying to will it to ring. She told herself she should be happy. Her beloved brother was alive, and while she still had so many questions, just being able to talk to him had been a gift she'd never expected.

He wanted her to let him go—to live her life and forget about him. That wasn't going to happen. Someway, somehow, she would find him. He was her beloved big brother, and no matter what he was involved with, or what he'd done, she would never give up on him.

"Jazz?"

She looked up into Xavier's concerned eyes, and everything hit at once. Sobs tore through her chest, and an awful sound erupted from her mouth. Before she could take another breath, Xavier was pulling her into his arms. Burying her face against his neck, Jazz let go of years of grief, fear, and loneliness. Not since she was ten years old and was told that her mother and stepfather were dead had she felt this broken. Almost two decades of sorrow had finally spewed over, and she could no longer contain it.

Xavier held her as if she were something precious. He whispered soothing words that she couldn't even hear over her bellowing, but they still comforted her. His arms were solid and strong, his chest against her face was both hard and warm, and his scent enveloped her in comfort and familiarity. He was everything she needed.

How long they stayed there, she had no idea, but when she finally looked around, they were in one of the large, overstuffed chairs in the living room, and two steaming cups of what smelled like chamomile tea were sitting on a nearby table.

"Want some tea?" Xavier asked quietly.

"Yeah," she said gruffly.

It didn't surprise her when Serena suddenly appeared and prepared the tea just as she knew Jazz liked it. That was one of the many beautiful things about Serena. She knew each of them inside out and used that knowledge to love more deeply. It was one of her many gifts.

Handing Jazz the teacup, she said softly, "Come home with me, Jazz."

"To your apartment?"

"No, to Wisconsin. It's simple and easy there. You'll get the peace you need to deal with all this."

Simple and easy sounded so tempting. As much as she wanted to say she was fully recovered and one hundred percent ready to deal with everything, she knew she wasn't. And after today, the idea of peace seemed further away than ever.

"I think that's a good idea," Xavier said. "What do you think?"

"I think I'd like that. Thank you, Serena."

She took Jazz's hand and squeezed it gently. "My pleasure." She then glanced over her shoulder and said, "I think there are a few other things you need to learn before we leave."

Yes, there were, and she had a feeling Kate knew every one of them. Question was, would she tell her?

XAVIER PRESSED a kiss to the top of Jazz's head, his heart literally breaking for her. In less than an hour, the world she knew had been shattered, her heart broken, and her trust demolished.

In all the years he'd known her and all the shit he'd watched her go through, he had never seen Jazz sob like that. On occasion, he'd seen tears fill her eyes, but she rarely allowed them to fall. She'd once told him that tears came only when there was no hope left. So was that the way she felt now? Hopeless?

He refused to allow that to happen. She had been knocked down again and again, but she would get back up again. He would ensure that.

He let her sip her tea in silence, not pushing her to talk or do anything other than recover from the maelstrom of emotions. If Kate was waiting for her in the conference room, then she could damn well wait.

Finally, she whispered, "He doesn't want to see me. He told me to go live my life and that he was proud of me. But he doesn't want to see me."

Once again, the surge of anger for her brother rose within him. Okay, yeah, the guy had had a tough time. There was no telling what kind of torture the mob had put him through to try to get him to tell them where to find Jazz. He had protected her as much as he could. But it was his call to stay away from her now. He'd obviously known where she was for years and, since he'd been in touch with Kate, had to know how badly Jazz had wanted to find him, and yet, he'd done nothing to make that happen.

Unable to reassure her that she'd ever see her brother again, Xavier just held her closer, giving the only comfort he could.

A couple minutes later, as if she'd gotten a second wind, she straightened in his arms and said, "I need to talk to Kate."

"Yes, you do."

She turned her face to his. Though her eyes were bloodshot and swollen from crying, her nose was red and still a little drippy, and her mouth drooped with exhaustion and sadness, he had never loved her more. This was Jazz in her element. Determined, stubborn, and filled with resolve.

"Then let's go."

Bounding out of his lap, she took a step forward and then turned back to him. Holding out her hand, she said softly, "You and me, right?"

Engulfing her hand in his, he nodded. "You and me."

They walked into the conference room together, something he hoped they would do from now on. He wanted to spend a lifetime with her, but they had some demons to put down. And then, he swore, he would bring her brother back to her. He didn't care if he had to drag him, bloodied, half dead, or screaming, he would bring Brody back to her, no matter what.

CHAPTER THIRTY-NINE

Jazz stood at the conference room door, Xavier at her side. Her back straight, her chin jutted out in rebellion against whatever else was going to be thrown at her, she said, "All right, Kate. Why did Brody kill Franco Bass?"

"I'm afraid that's something I don't know."

"But you knew he did?"

"Yes."

"Does he work for the Wren Project?"

"No, as I said before, I don't believe so."

"And he doesn't work for you either?"

"No. We've worked together on some things, but he does not work for me. Brody goes his own way, and I truly don't know who he reports to—if anyone."

This was like pulling teeth, and Jazz was getting tired of it. Kate was going to share only what she wanted. No matter how many times Jazz asked, nothing would be revealed that Kate hadn't already planned in advance to reveal.

"All right, last question. Why did Kevin Doyle have me kidnapped? What did he want with me?"

"You're the only living heir of Ronan Byrne."

"So? What does that mean?" She let loose a derisive snort. "They want me to be some kind of crime family moll?"

"No, I don't think they considered you to be anything other than a pawn. They likely have someone they want you to marry, to bring all the fractured pieces of the organization back together."

"That's it? I'm just supposed to be some kind of superglue for them?"

"That's one way of putting it, but that's not the biggest reason they want you."

"Then what is it?"

Kate's gaze turned to Xavier. "I'm surprised you didn't tell her."

"We had other things to discuss," Xavier said.

"Very well. When Byrne died, his will was explicit and ironclad. Only his heir could inherit his fortune. You were named as his secondary heir and were supposed to get his fortune when you turned eighteen. That's why they stuck you with Arthur Kelly. But then you and Brody disappeared. Now that they've found you again, my guess is that they want to use you to claim the inheritance and build the organization back up."

"So Byrne knew he had a daughter?" Eve asked.

"Yes. I'm not sure how—maybe he kept tabs on Eliza. Regardless, he named Jazz in his will."

Jazz would examine that "kept tabs on Eliza" information later. She needed to concentrate on other things now. "So this inheritance is so immense that it's worth kidnapping and torturing me to get it?"

"It was to Kevin Doyle, and I'm sure there are a few more just like him. So yes."

"How much?" Jazz asked.

"A little over a hundred million dollars."

After a jaw-dropping second of astonishment, Jazz had no

choice but to burst out laughing. The little girl who'd once gotten excited when she'd found a half-eaten hot dog on the street that someone had thrown away was actually a multimillionaire. Jazz remembered devouring that hot dog and thinking nothing could ever taste better. And only a few miles away, a fortune had been waiting for her.

"Wait," Serena said. "When an heir isn't located within a certain number of years, the money is normally turned over to the state, isn't it?"

Kate's smile was both grim and slightly admiring. "In most cases, that's very true. However, Ronan Byrne was not your average, everyday person making out his will. He locked it in a way no one could touch it."

"But how—" Serena said.

"Byrne had more politicians, judges, and lawyers in his pocket than anyone I've ever seen. If he wanted to make it happen, it happened." Kate looked at Jazz and said quietly, "The money is yours to claim."

Jazz had had her fill. No longer wanting to even think about Ronan Byrne, Kevin Doyle, or any other freak affiliated with the Irish mob, or all the dirty money waiting for her, she sent Serena a look. "I'd like to leave now, if that's okay."

Her eyes bright with warmth and sympathy, she said, "Let's go."

Without another word to the woman who'd both saved her life but also betrayed her, Jazz walked away.

Wisconsin

The minute Jazz had stepped off the private jet that Ash had chartered for them, she felt as if she were in another world. The city of Appleton, Wisconsin, wasn't especially large —it had just a little under seventy-five thousand residents—

but it had a lovely, quaint atmosphere that made Jazz feel immediately at home.

Traveling twenty miles down the road to the much smaller community of Francine made her feel as though she'd entered a magical kingdom. Everything—trees, bushes, plants—were lush and green, animals grazed in verdant fields that seemed to stretch for miles, and beautiful, colorful farmhouses dotted the gently rolling landscape. If elves and fairies had suddenly appeared, she wasn't sure she would have been all that surprised.

"Serena, it's lovely here," Jazz said.

"It is," Serena agreed. "Every time I leave, a piece of my heart stays."

"This is where you grew up?"

"Yes." With one hand on the steering wheel, she waved her other hand in a sweeping gesture. "My great-great-grandparents owned and operated one of the biggest dairy farms in Wisconsin."

"Your family has cows?" She didn't know why, but she was excited about that. Until she'd moved to Montana, she'd lived most of her life in big cities. Farm animals were as exotic to her as a leopard or a tiger.

Laughing at her excitement, Serena nodded. "We have cows, but nothing like it used to be. We no longer have the dairy farm. Just a few milk cows, along with some chickens and a few goats. Dogs, cats, and I think my nephew got some hamsters the other day."

After the day she'd had, Jazz hadn't thought she could feel anything other than exhaustion and sadness, but she was wrong. An odd sort of calmness swept over her at the peaceful surroundings, and she felt a zing of excitement for this new adventure.

"Your mom and dad won't mind me coming for a visit?"

"I've already called them, and they're beyond thrilled to

have you. But just as a warning, it's not just my mom and dad you'll be meeting. My grandparents from both sides of the family, as well as my five brothers and their families, live there. Plus several aunts and uncles and a ton of cousins."

"Wow, like all in the same house?"

Serena snorted out a small gulp of laughter. "Good heavens, no. Just my mom and dad in the house we're going to. It's where I was raised. Everybody else has their own place. All my brothers are married and have kids.

"The dairy farm used to be about five thousand acres. The land area has been reduced over the years, but my grandparents—my dad's parents—wanted to keep as much of the family together as possible. They gave everyone some of the land to build a house. Altogether, about twenty houses make up our little community of Francine, which by the way, was my great-great-grandmother's name."

Enthralled, Jazz gazed out the window at the beauty and simplicity before her. The idea of having that much family so close by seemed overwhelming, but she couldn't help but think how incredibly comforting it must be to never be alone. To always have someone nearby who cared about you.

They turned down a paved, two-lane road, and Jazz sat up straighter, eating up the sights. Cows grazed in one pasture, sheep in another, and several horses roamed in yet another.

"You had a happy childhood, didn't you?"

Sending her a quick smile tinged with sympathy, Serena nodded. "Yeah, I did."

Passing several houses along the way, Serena waved and blew her horn as several people waved back at her.

They finally pulled into a long driveway and, after two or three turns, arrived at a large white farmhouse. Flowers were everywhere—on the porch, in little beds around the house, in giant pots, and some even hanging from the trees.

"Someone has a green thumb."

"Both my mom and dad. They compete with each other to see who can grow the prettiest flowers."

The instant the car stopped, a slender older woman with shoulder-length blond hair and a smile just like Serena's stepped off the porch. With a squeal of delight, Serena put the car into park, jumped out, and ran toward her, her arms open wide. Seconds later, a big man with iron-gray hair and a military posture opened the front door and came running down the steps as fast as his wife had, a big grin covering his face.

Jazz couldn't help but feel just the slightest tinge of envy at the enormous love she was witnessing. Just in those few seconds, it was obvious they were a close-knit family.

"Jazz," Serena called out, "come meet my mom and dad."

Pulling in a breath, Jazz got out of the car and went toward the older, smiling couple, already knowing that she was going to love them.

It didn't surprise her in the least when Serena's mom held out her arms and said, "Welcome, Jazz. We're so happy you're here."

CHAPTER FORTY

Chicago, Illinois

"Any questions about our cover before we head out?" Ash asked.

Sitting on the sofa in the hotel suite they'd booked for the week, Gideon draped his arm around Eve and shook his head. He then glanced down at his wife for confirmation. "Seems fairly straightforward to us, right, darling? We go in as investors interested in either buying or forming a relationship with Ryan Doyle."

Taking a drink of coffee, Ash swallowed and nodded. "Ryan Doyle has been putting out feelers for investors for a few months now, so it shouldn't raise any flags that we're anything other than that. I want to get the lay of the land and get a feel for the family as a whole."

"Because there's no indication that anyone in Doyle's family knew what that bastard Kevin did," Gideon said.

"Exactly."

"Both men, Kevin and Ryan, have successful, legitimate

businesses, which means they both knew how to hide behind a facade," Eve warned.

"True. I don't expect Ryan to give up any secrets, but I want to see him face-to-face before we start accusing him of anything nefarious. Serena has found no evidence that Ryan Doyle is not one hundred percent legit. From all accounts, he and his father were not close. So just because the old man was a scumbag doesn't mean the son is."

Xavier sat a few feet away from the group and listened to the plan. He was here only for observation and backup. They were going on the assumption that Kevin Doyle had found Jazz because of the social media posts about Bass's shooting, and Xavier had been with her in those videos. If Ryan Doyle was involved with what his father had done and Xavier showed up as an interested investor, Ryan might recognize him, thwarting this fact-finding mission.

Which was why this low-key mission was driving him out of his mind. Everything within him wanted to go through the city and clear out every single threat against Jazz. Problem was—they had no idea who and how many there were. Had Kevin Doyle been a lone wolf, taking it upon himself to try to grab power and money and establish himself as the leader of their newly regenerated organization? Or were others involved?

He considered himself a patient man, and he liked mysteries and puzzles. This wasn't one of those times, though. Jazz's life was in danger, and taking the slow, methodical route went against every instinct he had.

Returning his eyes to the intel lying on his lap, Xavier reviewed what Serena and her people had been able to uncover about Doyle and his family.

On paper, Kevin Doyle had been a wealthy businessman, owning several businesses, including three restaurants, two convenience stores, and a dry cleaner. They were good fronts, and as long as you didn't dig too deep, you wouldn't be able to tell that they were all excellent sources to launder a ton of money.

Fortunately, OZ knew how to dig beyond the depths most people could never reach. So beneath that sparkling-clean surface, Kevin Doyle had been a small-arms dealer and importer of designer knockoffs from Thailand, which he sold for ten times their actual value to local clothing stores.

Years ago, when Ronan Byrne had been alive, Doyle had enjoyed a high position within the Byrne crime family. Then Byrne died and everything fell apart. Doyle had likely seen Jazz as his way back to the top of the crime family, with him calling the shots.

Only it hadn't worked out that way. Doyle had had no idea what he was getting himself into when he'd captured Jazz McAlister. He had, in fact, likely never met anyone quite like Jazz. Xavier smiled at the thought, because there *was* no one quite like her anywhere.

Why Doyle had died by his own hand was a mystery. That left the hundred million dollars up for grabs for anyone willing to get their hands dirty and go after the only person who would have access to those funds. Who would that be?

Ash was right, though, that Doyle's son looked clean. Ryan was a thirty-year-old father of two sons and had a baby girl on the way. He looked like a successful man, totally devoted to his family. He'd even married his childhood sweetheart, who had absolutely no ties to the Irish mob.

The "get the lay of the land" meeting that Ash, Gideon, and Eve were getting ready to attend would hopefully give them all a better idea of what they were facing. And while he couldn't be there, Eve would be wearing a brooch with a small camera and microphone so he'd be able to hear and see everything.

For about the twentieth time in the last half hour, Xavier

checked his phone for a text. Even though it would've chimed if he'd gotten one, he couldn't help looking anyway. He knew Jazz was fine. She'd called him last night, right before she went to sleep. She'd sounded wiped out, but she'd also seemed to be at peace. Maybe going to Wisconsin and getting away from all this shit was exactly what she needed. Even though he missed her like a lost limb, he was glad to know she was safe and well.

He'd texted her this morning but hadn't heard back yet. As exhausted as she was, she'd likely slept in, so he told himself there was no reason to worry. Besides, Serena would have called him if anything had happened.

They'd barely had a moment alone to say goodbye to each other before she'd been whisked away by the private jet. Flying commercial airline had been out of the question. Who knew how many people were on the lookout for Jazz?

The brief hug and kiss they'd shared before she'd walked up the steps to the plane had been sweet but entirely unsatisfying. It didn't matter to him if the team knew they were now more than just partners, but since they hadn't discussed it, and he wasn't sure how or when she wanted to inform them, he'd kept the kiss discreet. There would be plenty of time when this was over to reveal to the others that he was crazy about her and that he planned to spend the rest of his life showing it.

"Xavier, you have any questions before we leave?"

Did he have any questions for the man who might've been involved in kidnapping and torturing the woman he loved? Hell yeah, he did. But he knew that wasn't what Ash was asking.

"No, not really. I'll let you know if I see anything off."

Ash gave him a searching look, and Xavier could only smile. His boss was likely wondering if he was going to go off the hinges and do something crazy. Barging in and threatening Ryan Doyle would be tempting, he couldn't deny that.

But he was willing to let this play out for now. Didn't mean he wouldn't change his mind later.

After thirty seconds of silence, Ash nodded and said, "Then let's get this done."

They drove to the meeting place in two separate vehicles. Ash, Eve, and Gideon arrived at their destination in a black Rolls-Royce Phantom, looking every bit like wealthy investors. They stopped in front of a large office building, and a valet eagerly rushed to the driver's side, most likely hoping for a sizable tip.

Xavier arrived a minute later in a ten-year-old van with a cracked windshield and rusty tailpipe. Even though it looked rough on the outside, the sophisticated camera equipment in the back had cost more than the Rolls.

He parked on a side street half a block away but within easy distance of getting inside fast if the meeting somehow went sour.

Opening the back compartment, Xavier climbed inside and turned on the equipment. It took only seconds for the camera to show that the trio was walking into the building and then onto an elevator. Ash pressed the button for the eighteenth floor.

Xavier sat back and waited for something to happen.

The instant the elevator door slid open, Ryan Doyle was there to meet them. His voice slightly on the gruff side, as if he had a cold, he introduced himself and welcomed them to Chicago.

There was nothing threatening about the guy and he didn't exhibit even the slightest hint of darkness. Tall, lean, and blond, with the athletic build of a swimmer and a slightly nervous grin as he shook everyone's hand, the man looked as unintimidating as apple pie. Even though some of the most-innocent-looking people could hide the evil within their soul,

Xavier had to admit his first impression of Kevin Doyle's son did not change his belief that the man was innocent.

Since snap judgments weren't his thing, he paid attention as the meeting got under way. After an hour and a half of intense questioning by all three operatives, and surprisingly frank answers from Doyle, Xavier's butt was numb, and they were no closer to getting answers to their questions.

Well, with the exception of one. If Ryan Doyle had been involved in Jazz's abduction, Xavier would eat his proverbial hat.

He watched as his three teammates ended the meeting and walked out the door. He'd wait until they gave their opinions, and then, if they agreed with him, they would starting looking in a different direction. What that direction would be, he had no idea.

A chime from his phone showed a text from Jazz. His heart leaped into his throat, but the minute he read the message, he laughed out loud.

I just finished milking a cow, and now I'm cuddling a baby goat! Wisconsin is awesome!

CHAPTER FORTY-ONE

Francine, Wisconsin

It took Jazz all of two hours to decide that the place where Serena had grown up was as close to heaven on earth as one could get.

Ed and Mallory Allen, Serena's parents, had welcomed her into their family as if she were one of their own. She had been ushered into their home and treated as if they'd been anticipating her visit for months, when she knew for a fact that Serena had called them about an hour before they arrived.

She'd been given the bedroom of one of their sons, and it still had baseball trophies and sports paraphernalia on the shelves. After a quick, delicious meal of beef stew and cornbread, Jazz had barely been able to keep her eyes open to get to her room. She hadn't expected to sleep a wink last night, sure that with all the turmoil of yesterday, her brain wouldn't shut off or her heartache wouldn't let her close her eyes. Instead, the minute her head hit the pillow, she was out. She woke ten hours later, amazed not only at how well she'd slept, but how good she felt.

Embarrassed to have slept so late, she quickly showered and headed downstairs. Following an incredible fragrance, she entered the kitchen to find Serena and her mother baking bread.

Looking up from kneading a mound of dough on the counter, Serena flashed a bright smile. "Morning, Jazz!"

Surprising herself, she laughed out loud. After yesterday, she hadn't been sure she'd ever feel joy again. But somehow, being with Serena and her family helped her to remember the sheer simplicity of family, affection, and loyalty.

"I didn't mean to sleep so long."

"You slept well?" Serena asked. She turned away from the dough, wiped her hands on a towel, and went to the coffee carafe. Grabbing a mug from the cabinet, she turned back to Jazz. "Still two creams and three sugars?"

Grinning, Jazz nodded. Xavier always teased her that she liked dessert coffee. Her heart turned over as she remembered how careful and loving he'd been with her yesterday. He hadn't wanted to be away from her, but she knew he was focused on finding what other threats were out there.

He had texted her last night, and she'd read it numerous times before she'd fallen into bed. The message had been short but had said everything she could have wanted. *I love you, Jazz. I'll talk to you soon.*

She hadn't heard from him yet today, but she knew he was in Chicago with Ash, Eve, and Gideon. If they learned anything valuable after meeting with Doyle's son, she knew they would let her know.

A thick slice of bread slathered with bright yellow butter appeared before her. "Eat this up, and then I'll show you around."

Even though her appetite had been nonexistent the last few days, her stomach made an embarrassingly ferocious growl of approval. She practically swallowed the slice whole, and then, when Serena smilingly put another slice on her empty plate, she ate it, too, albeit a little more politely.

"While you finish up, let me get this bread in the oven."

Settling back in her seat, Jazz enjoyed the gentle chatter between Serena and her mother as they worked together in the kitchen. A pang of longing hit her, one she hadn't felt in a long time. If her mom were still alive, she liked to think they would have worked together in the kitchen this way. Jazz had barely learned how to scramble an egg before she had lost her mother.

Even though she hadn't brought it up yesterday, she hoped that in the course of finding more intel on Doyle, perhaps they could also find out who was responsible for her parents' deaths. She wished she had thought to ask Brody if he knew that information, but their extremely brief conversation had prevented even the most basic questions.

Feeling sadness sweep through her again, Jazz stood and walked over to the window looking out into the backyard. Everywhere she looked, she saw beauty. From the flowers that seemed to spring up everywhere, often without any kind of pattern or symmetry, to the lush green bushes and giant ancient-looking trees.

"Your backyard is lovely, Mrs. Allen."

"Thank you, Jazz, but you call me Mallory, you hear?"

"Yes, ma'am," she said. "I'll—" She broke off and leaned forward, trying to make out what was running across the yard. Excited, she turned to Serena. "There's a goat running across the yard."

"Uh-oh. Is it black with a white face and black and white ears?"

"Yes."

"Is there a tall, slender lady with short gray hair running after it, holding a red flyswatter?"

She turned back to the window and saw the exact scene Serena had just described. "Yes. How did you know?"

"That's Henry, and the lady running after him is my aunt Jackie. It's a game they play. He eats her gladiolas, and she pretends she's mad at him, when we all know the only reason she plants them in the first place is because he loves to eat them."

"Why a red flyswatter?"

Serena shrugged. "She says it's his favorite color." Grabbing her arm, she tugged Jazz to the door. "Come on. I'll introduce you to both of them."

FIVE HOURS LATER, Jazz was sitting amid the largest family gathering she'd ever seen. Serena had explained that every Thursday evening, everyone gathered in the field just beyond the house for a family dinner.

Jazz had never met so many people at one time. She'd met all five of Serena's brothers, their wives, and children, as well as aunts, uncles, cousins, and both sets of grandparents. Considering she rarely spoke to a half-dozen people outside her OZ family in a month's time, this should have been overwhelming. She'd always considered herself an introvert and quite shy. These people had changed her mind. They had welcomed her as if she were already one of them.

Since she wasn't much of a cook, she helped set tables and ran interference for the kids who raced around the tables, almost tipping over an entire table filled with desserts. She loved that they all seemed to enjoy one another's company and that laughter was the noisiest part of the meal.

Her day had been filled with milking a cow, cuddling baby goats, feeding chickens, and petting more dogs than she could count. Now, she sat at the table with her belly full of some of the most delicious food she'd ever consumed. She could have made an entire meal of the fried cheese curds alone.

"Is all this too much for you?" Serena asked. "They're wonderful, but I know they can be a bit much at one time."

"No. It's lovely…really."

"Feel like a walk?"

After all that food, a walk sounded perfect. From the look on Serena's face, she had an ulterior motive.

Standing, Jazz followed her friend to the front of the house and onto the road. "Where are we going?"

"I need to show you something. I've not told Ash about it yet. Still feel like it's too soon, but I want you to see it. Get your take."

Getting more curious, Jazz said, "Okay."

"Have you talked to Xavier today?"

"Not yet. I texted him that I milked a cow and cuddled goats, and he sent me a laughing emoji back. Have you talked to any of them?"

"I heard briefly from Ash. He didn't have any real information other than he doesn't believe Doyle's son knew anything about your abduction. Says he's so clean looking, he should squeak when he walks."

"So it's back to square one."

"Maybe. We'll see." Serena stopped in front of a pretty gray and white cottage and took a key from her pocket. "Follow me."

Jazz went into the house behind Serena, surprised that they would just walk into someone's home, even if it did belong to a family member. It was a lovely, simply decorated home but had an empty feel to it. "Who lives here?"

"No one. It's actually the first house that was built here. My great-great-grandparents lived in it when they first married.

It's been remodeled and redone over the years. My dad fixed it up for my great-uncle Percy a couple years back. Percy stayed here a week in January and decided Wisconsin winters were too harsh for him, so he moved to Florida. We keep it for occasional guests."

Confused on why they'd come here, Jazz asked, "Is this where you want me to stay?"

"Goodness no. You're my sister. Family stays with family."

Before Jazz could respond to her sweet statement, Serena went to the back of the house. She stopped at a door and, using another key, unlocked it. Turning back to Jazz, a glint of excitement in her eyes, she explained. "My dad tore down a lot of the original house, but one thing he kept was the bunker below it."

"Bunker?"

"Yeah. My great-great-grandparents were worried about the atom bomb in the fifties. They built the bunker, thinking they might have to live in it for years. We don't really use it since all our houses have a safe room, but we do keep supplies and odds and ends here."

She switched on a light and then started down the stairs. "The last time I was here, I swept out the cobwebs and filled it with some other things."

"Like what?"

Stepping onto the concrete floor, she flipped a couple of switches on the wall and said, "Take a look."

Jazz stepped down beside Serena. The room was about the size of a small auditorium. And though she spotted some shelves at the end of the room filled with a substantial stash of canned food and bottled water, most of the space was filled with at least fifteen large, freestanding whiteboards that lined the walls. Over half of them were filled with writing.

"What is this, Serena?"

"I found him, Jazz."

"Found who?"

Turning to face her, Serena's eyes gleamed with excitement. "I found the head of the snake."

CHAPTER FORTY-TWO

S tunned, knowing exactly what Serena was talking about, Jazz whispered, "The head of the Wren Project."

"Yes."

"Who is he? What's his name?"

"Follow me. I'll show you."

They went to the closest board, and Jazz stared at the massive amount of information. Names, locations, and dates were connected with arrows. The biggest arrow led to one name.

"Lazarus? How do you know it's him?"

"Remember that game Six Degrees of Kevin Bacon?"

"Yeah. Everyone in the world is somehow connected to him via six people?"

"Something like that. Players pick an actor and then try to connect that person to Kevin Bacon via other actors in the most direct way possible. So say someone challenged you to connect Henry Cavill and Bacon. Cavill played Clark Kent in the movie *Man of Steel*, and Diane Lane played Clark's mother, Martha Kent. Diane Lane was also in the movie *My Dog Skip* with Kevin Bacon."

"Okay. So this is like that?"

"Yes, except this is more like Seven Degrees of Lazarus."

"Show me."

"Okay. Here's where I got started, since this was our first encounter with WP. You remember Nora Turner, the senator from Ohio?"

"Yes."

That name was one that no one at OZ would ever forget. Because of Turner's incredibly selfish act, many people had died. Ash had almost been one of them. He had been the lone survivor of an attack that had seen a bunch of politicians and business people load themselves onto a helicopter and abandon the men who had been protecting them, leaving them to fight an army. Ash had spent years trying to expose and bring Turner down, and in the midst of doing just that, they had learned there was a larger, more heinous group of people behind the corrupt politician.

With Serena leading her, Jazz followed the path from Nora Turner through events and people until it ended with the name Lazarus.

"Okay, but who—"

Before Jazz could finish, Serena said, "Follow me."

Trailing behind her, Jazz saw all the connections as if she were watching a movie. Aubrey, Liam's wife, had discovered the connection between her uncle and the Wren Project. The uncle and Aubrey's cousin Becca were both dead because of WP. Through all the intel she had unearthed, Serena showed Jazz the trajectory of events that led once again to Lazarus.

In each case they had worked on that involved the Wren Project, including the connection Hawke had made with the Gonzalez cartel and even Eve's family connection, Serena had uncovered the links. They were sometimes shorter than seven steps, but they all led to one person named Lazarus.

"Okay, those are four cases. What's on the other boards?"

Serena pointed to one several feet away. "Remember that man and his wife from Michigan who were in Madrid for their twenty-fifth anniversary and were found dead, supposedly by murder/suicide?"

"Yeah. I remember thinking if they were going to do something like that, why go all the way to Madrid?"

"Yes, I agree." She shrugged and gave a chagrined smile. "I keep a list of strange deaths and unusual events. Anyway, so far, I've been able to link Lazarus to at least sixty-two of them."

Jazz stared in open-mouthed wonder at her friend. "Seriously?"

"Yes. He's not doing the deeds himself, of course, but in each case, there's a link where he somehow shows up in relation to them. I believe he is the proverbial snake we've been looking for."

In awe of this amazing woman, she asked, "How on earth did you do this all by yourself?"

For the first time since they'd arrived, Serena's expression showed the heartache that continued to haunt her. "I've had some extra time on my hands."

Sean, Serena's husband, had taken off about a year ago, and no one knew where he'd gone or really why. He'd given some lame-assed explanation, but no one was buying it. There was some other reason why he'd left his wife and Option Zero.

"I can't believe Sean just up and disappeared like that, Serena. When he finally returns, he's going to get an ass-kicking he won't soon forget."

"I found him, Jazz," she said softly.

For a second, Jazz thought Serena was back to talking about Lazarus, but then she saw the tears streaming down Serena's face.

"Sean? Where is he? When is he coming home? Have you talked to him?"

"He called me a few months back."

"Why didn't you tell us? What did he say?"

"He's got some issues to work out. Some I knew about, a few I didn't. I told him I would give him time, but…" She shook her head and then said, "He asked for a divorce."

Her heart dropping, Jazz grabbed Serena's hand. "No. I can't believe he would do that. What did you say?"

"I told him that when I married him, I promised I would give him anything he asked me for, if it was within my power. I never anticipated this would be what he'd ask for, but I couldn't say no."

"I'm so sorry, Serena."

Jazz was shocked when Serena turned to look at her. Instead of the sorrow she expected, she saw only peace.

"Don't be. Sean is the love of my life." Her brow furrowed as she continued, "Have you ever been with anyone that when you were talking to him, he actually listened to you? Like, really listened? He saw you for you? He got who you were and understood you on a level no one else ever has?"

Before Xavier, she would have said absolutely not. But she knew exactly what Serena meant. A man who not only loved his woman on a physical and emotional level, but also had a deep understanding of who she was beneath the surface and appreciated her for those things was definitely something to be treasured.

Not wanting to stray into her own personal experience at this time, Jazz nodded her understanding.

"That was Sean… That *is* Sean." A glimmer of amusement lit her face. "I'll never forget the first time we met. Back then, I was a frowsy-looking blond chick with thick, dark glasses. I'd spilled half my coffee on my white blouse that morning, and I was trying to wipe it off while I was walking. I rounded a corner and slammed into Sean. He grabbed me before I could fall, and instead of telling me to watch where I was going or ignoring me, which most men did, he spent ten minutes just talking to me.

"I didn't find out until I went home that night that I had worn two different-colored shoes. I was a mess. But I'd met this handsome, gentle giant with a beautiful smile and a wicked sense of humor who actually listened when I talked and appreciated me, despite the mess I was that day. I don't think I stopped smiling that night.

"He asked me out the next time we saw each other, and from that day forward, Sean Donavan was it for me."

"You're never going to give up on him, are you?"

"No, I'm not. He has my heart forever."

"I'm glad you're not giving up on him, but I still want to kick his ass."

Laughing, Serena pulled her into a hug. "You may have to get in line. I think everyone at OZ has threatened the same thing."

Serena pulled away, drew in a shaky breath, and then gestured at the board beside them. "So what do you think?"

"I think you've done some amazing work, but I have one big question."

"Let me guess. You want to know who Lazarus is."

"Yes. Do you have any idea?"

"Yes and no. A lot of what I know is conjecture. There's chatter on the dark web, but it's obscure and vague. I believe he lives in various parts of the world. I've tracked him to Portugal, Greece, and most recently Japan. I believe he has a daughter and a son-in-law. He keeps his circle extremely small."

"Any idea what he looks like?"

"No. But I think I might be able to find him through his daughter. She lives in New York City."

"Wow, and Ash doesn't know about any of this?"

"Nope. You're the first. So what do you think?"

"I think, thanks to you, we are finally going to get to cut off the head of the snake we've been hunting for years."

CHAPTER FORTY-THREE

Montana

X avier slammed the fridge door and held the bottle of beer against his forehead for a second before he twisted off the top and downed half of its contents in one swallow. What a frustrating, mind-numbing day. His head was so full of useless information, he wished he could take a shovel and dig out the gunk.

After they'd eliminated Doyle's son as a suspect, they'd covered every known man or woman who was tied or previously tied to the Irish mob in Chicago. It had been a long list. They'd found money launderers, weapons and designer knockoff smugglers, and a surprising number of people who earned their wealth by demanding money for providing protection. Kevin Doyle had made his fortune from all those activities, but they could find no ties between those illegal activities and Jazz's abduction.

There were tons of illegal happenings tied to the mob, and more than a few of those people would likely be very interested in snatching a woman with blood ties to Ronan Byrne, as well as someone who could bring in a load of cash to sweeten the deal. But so far, not one person gave off the slightest hint of a vibe that Jasmine McAlister had been located, much less abducted.

So they were left with some possibilities, and Xavier didn't like any of them. One, Kevin Doyle, along with a few of his goons, had been working alone. Two, someone out there was manipulating the data, just waiting for OZ to give up so they could strike again. Three, everyone was lying.

His gut told him the first possibility was wrong. Doyle might've kept things close to his chest, but no way had he done this solo.

The third possibility was off, too. There were way too many people giving them the same answer. None of them were novices when it came to interrogation. Someone usually flipped or said something by mistake, leading to the guilty party. As of yet, that hadn't happened.

The second scenario seemed the most likely and was his least favorite. Data was being manipulated, intel was being buried, and someone was waiting in the wings until they let their guard down.

Chugging down the last of his beer, Xavier opened the fridge, reached for another one, and then stopped. What was he going to do? Get drunk? How was that going to help? Admittedly, he could put away more than a couple of brews before he felt a buzz, but drinking another one would be useless. Nothing was going to make this better.

Bypassing the bag of takeout he'd purchased on his way home, Xavier stripped off his clothes and headed to the bathroom. He'd had maybe five hours of sleep in the last three days. A shower, sleep, and then maybe he'd be able to get his head on straight and actually accomplish something.

The minute the water pounded down on him, he leaned his head against the cool wet tile and admitted the truth. He missed her. Heaven help him, he missed her so much. Why had he waited so long to tell her how he felt? They'd had only a few weeks together after he'd cut out his heart and handed it to her. And now, they were thousands of miles apart, and he wasn't sure when he'd be seeing her again.

He'd made a promise to himself that he would uncover the threat before he followed her to Wisconsin. So far, it had been an epic fail.

The only good thing about this, and it was a very good thing, was that she was safe, and from the calls and texts he had received, she was thoroughly enjoying her time with Serena's family.

Serena was keeping him updated as well and had reported that Jazz was sleeping well and had put on a couple of pounds. Knowing that she was recovering and getting the peace she needed kept him here, continuing to dig.

Blowing out a sigh, he finished up his shower, dried down, and brushed his teeth. Grabbing a pair of loose shorts, he slid them on and fell face-first into bed.

Two hours later, he heard the slightest of sounds and knew he wasn't alone. With swiftness born out of practice, he went for his gun on the nightstand, only to find an empty space.

"Relax," a gruff voice said in the darkness, "if I'd wanted to kill you, you would've been dead years ago."

It took half a second for him to know the man's identity.

"About time you showed up, McAlister."

"How's my sister?"

Xavier's first instinct was to bark out a furious, scathing response, lambasting him for abandoning his sister. He couldn't do that because from what Kate had told them, Brody had been abducted, tortured, and held against his will for years without ever revealing his sister's location. He had protected her the only way he could.

Xavier wasn't willing to give him a total pass, though. The

man had known Jazz's location for years and knew how much it would mean to her if he'd come back into her life. He hadn't done that, and that pissed Xavier off.

"From your silence," McAlister said, "I can only surmise that you can't decide whether you want to kill me or answer my question."

"Hurting you would hurt Jazz, so you're safe."

"So how is she?"

"She's recovering."

"Good."

"Is that why you're here? To ask about your sister?"

"That and to give you some advice."

"What's that?"

"Keep looking at the Doyle family."

"We've dug into them as deep as we can go. There's nothing there."

"What about Sullivan?"

"Doyle's brother-in-law? He came through as a wannabe gangster without any real substance. He's got no known ties to anything illegal. He seems harmless."

"Look again."

"All right, thanks for the tip. Can I ask you a question?"

"You can. I don't promise to answer."

It was worth a try. "Why'd you kill Bass?"

"You know as well as anyone that you sometimes have to do things you'd rather not. He was going to die by someone's hand. Might as well have been mine."

And whether Brody had intended it or not, he had confirmed what Xavier had been thinking all along. Brody was working an angle.

"All right. One more?"

"You can try."

"Do you know who killed Jazz's mother and your dad?"

"That's for me to take care of. You just concentrate on taking care of my sister."

Though Xavier still couldn't see him, and could barely hear his movements, he knew the other man was now standing.

Xavier went to his feet, not willing to let him go before he got more answers. Brody McAlister had other ideas. He was out the door before Xavier could get to him. Flipping the light switch, Xavier managed to see the hulking guy slip out his front door as quietly as a ghost.

Turning, he noted that Brody had left Xavier's gun on the chair he'd been sitting in, along with a piece of paper. Grabbing it, he read the cryptic one-line message. *Tell the brilliant spitfire in Wisconsin that she's on the right track but to watch her back.*

CHAPTER FORTY-FOUR

Chicago, Illinois

He couldn't find her. After spending weeks and thousands of dollars searching, not one of his investigators had unearthed the slightest clue. He knew the girl existed. He'd seen her himself, but now it was like she'd disappeared off the face of the earth.

Oscar grabbed another handful of chips and stuffed them into his mouth. He followed that with a long swallow of Pepsi and then belched. He was a stress eater—had been all his life. When frustrated, he could demolish food like a bush hog mowed down weeds. Eating helped him think, and he'd had a lot to think about over the last few weeks.

He'd even lowered himself to search his brother-in-law's office and pore over his ridiculous notepads, looking for clues. Kevin had insisted the girl had told him nothing, but he'd held her for almost ten days. Surely she had told him something, but if she had, it wasn't to be found.

Two investigators had spent a week in Seattle, since that was her location at the time of her abduction. Of course, the fact that she'd been checked into a cheap motel with zero camera footage helped not at all.

There was only one choice left. It wasn't one he wanted to make. Even though it had always been in the back of his mind that he could reach out and ask for help, the very idea of what he would have to give up to get what he wanted was, well, in a word, terrifying.

He knew people who had fallen into their trap and sincerely regretted their decision later. Some had paid by having to carry out horrendous tasks. Others had paid by doing something as simple as making an introduction to a high-powered individual. What they wanted you to do and when they wanted you to do it was never within your scope of knowledge or control. The call came, and you either obeyed, or you paid. And even sometimes, when you did exactly what they asked, if it didn't work out, you forfeited your life.

Take Franco Bass. He had done exactly what they'd asked of him, but when their plans had fallen through, they'd gotten rid of him as easily as one would wad up a piece of paper and toss it into the trash. Stupid bastard had never seen it coming.

But he reminded himself of one big difference between him and Bass—he wasn't stupid. He knew the score up front. He could control the narrative. Once he had the girl, all the power would be his.

The Wren Project—what a stupid-assed name for what they were—made it so enticing. Just one little phone call, and he'd have exactly what he needed.

Years ago, when he'd been approached by one of their minions, he hadn't been interested. The leader of his organization, Ronan Byrne, had just died, and things had been in turmoil. If he'd tried to take over then, he wouldn't have been successful. Things had been too murky and shaky. And in all honesty, he would have been too afraid. But age and life experience had taught him that if you didn't seize the moment, then someone else would.

There were tons of people waiting in the wings for this chance. He'd seen more than a few threads on the dark web of just how deep these people could reach and how insidious they could be. If he didn't take this chance within his reach, someone else with more backbone would do it, and all would be lost. He couldn't take that risk.

Pulling out a burner phone he kept ready and charged for the dirtiest of deeds, Oscar punched in the number he'd been given years ago. The instant the call was answered, he figured they knew exactly who he was and what he wanted. They were just that good.

"Number," an androgynous voice said.

"43412." Oscar winced at how shaky his voice sounded. He cleared his throat and took a calming breath. Showing these people any kind of weakness wasn't the way to start out.

The voice said, "State your request."

As succinctly as possible, Oscar explained what he wanted and how he wanted to go about getting it. He tried his best not to prattle, but when he was uncertain, the nervous habit revealed itself. When he finally finished, he held his breath, waiting for the verdict.

"One moment please," the voice stated.

It was the longest moment of his life. What if they decided not to grant his request? He was now on their radar. They could come after him without giving him anything in return. He shook his head. No, why would they bother with him? But that didn't negate the fact that he was currently engaging with the deadliest organization on the face of this earth. Their tentacles spread through every branch of government in every city and country in the world. With one nod, leaders fell, leaders succeeded, and people, no matter how high up, jumped to do their bidding. Giant organizations could be demolished with one word from the top, and thousands of lives could be destroyed. He'd seen it happen. Even while people were scratching their heads and wondering how something so awful could happen, he had known the truth.

What on earth had he been thinking? He couldn't do this. Should he just hang up? Could he pretend he had been kidding? Maybe if he told them he was someone else. Maybe…

In the midst of his threatening hysteria, the mechanical voice suddenly said, "Your request is approved. We will be in touch."

The call went dead, and Oscar practically fell out of his chair. It was done. He panted and looked wildly around his small office. What had he done? *What had he done?* Then he thought about all he could have, and his panic quickly subsided. His time had come. He had worked hard for this, and he was finally going to get what he wanted.

The money would be his. The power would be his.

Grabbing the bag of chips, he stuffed his mouth full, and a slow smile spread across his face.

CHAPTER FORTY-FIVE

Francine, Wisconsin

J azz took a long sip of her icy drink and sighed her
contentment. This had been the girliest day she'd ever
spent. After breakfast, Serena had suggested they walk to
the empty cottage they'd visited before. She had assumed they
were going to the bunker below the house to discuss Serena's
progress on finding Lazarus. She couldn't have been more
wrong.

The instant the door opened, she had been greeted with a
light floral fragrance, soft music, and three smiling women.
What had followed was nothing short of amazing. She'd had
her hair cut and styled, a massage from one of Serena's
cousins, a massage therapist in Appleton, and a facial and
makeover by one of Serena's sisters-in-law, a cosmetologist.
After the women left, she and Serena had snacked on tacos her
mother sent over. They were now painting their nails and
sipping the most delicious margaritas she'd ever tasted.

After more than two weeks of doing nothing more strenuous than long walks in the nearby woods and setting the

table for dinner, Jazz was feeling stronger and healthier than she had in a long while.

A part of her felt guilty for taking it easy when her other OZ teammates were working their butts off trying to find out if anyone other than Kevin Doyle was after her. As odd as it seemed that she could be worth a hundred million dollars to someone, the chances that Doyle had been the only one who wanted to grab her were slim.

Each night before she went to sleep and in the morning right after she woke, she and Xavier would talk. Most of their chatter revolved around all the various activities she was experiencing on the farm. He'd told her that hearing about them was the highlight of his day, so she went out of her way to describe each event in the most entertaining way possible. To her ears, there was no more beautiful sound than Xavier's laughter.

She felt like it had been a lifetime since she'd seen him, felt his arms around her, kissed him. She missed him like she would miss an appendage. He was an intrinsic part of her, heart and soul.

Her time here had to end at some point. As much as she was enjoying the peace and simplicity, she couldn't stay here forever. She had a life to get back to, a job she loved, and a man she adored.

As if Serena knew exactly what she was thinking, she said, "So what's going on with you and Xavier?"

Knowing her face was already a little flushed from the margarita she'd consumed, Jazz felt the heat hit her like a flame. And if that weren't enough, the instant Serena saw her color rise, she gave a shout of gleeful laughter. "I knew it! You guys finally admitted how you feel about each other!"

"You knew?"

"Of course I knew. Everyone knew. We've just been waiting for you two to finally figure it out."

"Did Xavier know?"

"How you felt? No. You both were so clueless. " She grinned and added, "It was adorable."

Shaking her head, Jazz laughed at Xavier being called adorable. He was many things, but being adorable wasn't one of them. Gorgeous, sexy, rugged, and manly. *And mine.*

A rush of emotion followed that thought. She had loved him for so long, and apparently he'd had feelings for her for a long time, too. And now that they had admitted it to each other, they couldn't be together because of this insanity.

"I so want this to be over," she muttered.

"I know," Serena said softly. "And it will be. You just have to be patient."

Jazz grimaced. Patience wasn't one of her strongest traits.

"Have you thought about the money you've inherited?"

"Not really. It's blood money. There's no telling how many people died or were tortured to get it. I don't want anything to do with it."

"Hmm."

"You don't agree?"

Serena gave a delicate shrug. "It's your choice, of course. I was just thinking how cool it would be to use it to do the opposite of what it was intended for."

"What do you mean?"

"Well, the people trying to get it obviously have evil intentions. But you could use it for good. Think about all the charities out there and the children and animals you could help."

She had been so angry after learning why she had been abducted, she hadn't even considered what opportunities that much money would allow her. Having been homeless herself, the very thought of being able to aid others, especially children and animals, gave her goose bumps. Her mind boggled at the good that could be done.

"Thank you, Serena. I never even considered that."

"I know some people who could help when you're ready."

Jazz let that settle within her. When this was over and if it was true that she would inherit this money, then she would definitely use it only for good. Using it for herself would go against everything she believed in—material possessions meant very little to her.

Taking another sip of her margarita, Jazz asked, "When are you going to tell Ash about Lazarus?"

Serena looked up from painting her toenails. "Soon. He knows I'm working on an angle. And it's not like I know exactly who the guy is or where he lives. I'm narrowing it down for sure, but I want to give him something concrete. If I tell him now, it's just going to frustrate him more."

Serena's phone pinged, but Jazz barely noticed the sound anymore, as the woman's phone seemed to ping 24/7 with intel from various sources all over the world. It amazed Jazz how her friend could keep up with everything and stay sane.

This time when Serena read the message, a look of delight spread across her face.

"What's that smile for?" Jazz asked.

"Aunt Jackie is getting another goat."

Out of all Serena's relatives, Aunt Jackie was one of Jazz's favorites. The woman had a delightful sense of humor and a way of looking at the world that was both unique and hilarious.

A knock on the front door surprised them. Since they had decided to spend the night here, they weren't expecting anyone.

"Would you mind getting that?" Serena asked. "My nails are still wet."

"Sure thing." Pulling herself up from the floor, Jazz took one last sip of her drink and then made her way to the door. Since she rarely drank alcohol, two margaritas would have to be her limit, as she was feeling a little loopy. Not bothering to look out the peephole, since their caller could be only a member of Serena's family, she opened the door with a big smile on her face.

"Now that's what I call a welcoming smile."

"Xavier!" Her heart soaring, she leaped into his arms.

As HIS ARMS closed around her, Xavier felt himself settle with a serenity and peace he'd never known. She was here, she was healthy, and she was his. Two long, agonizing weeks without holding her had been all he could handle.

"I've missed you so much," Jazz whispered against his neck.

Squeezing her tight, he muttered, "Not nearly as much as I missed you, baby."

Pulling her head back, she looked up at him and gave the brightest, most beautiful smile he'd ever seen. "I can't believe you're here. Did Serena know?"

"Of course she knew," Serena said from a few feet away. "And now she's going to leave you two alone."

"Thank you, Serena," Xavier said.

"Wait." Jazz dropped her arms from around Xavier's neck and turned to face Serena. "Was that text really from Aunt Jackie?"

"No. It was Xavier, letting me know he was out front. But Aunt Jackie really is getting a new goat. You can meet him tomorrow."

With a wink, she scooted past them out the door, leaving them alone.

The instant the door shut, Xavier pulled Jazz back into his arms and gave her the kiss he'd been dreaming about since the last time he'd kissed her. Her lips were even sweeter than he remembered, and it took all his control not to devour her there on the spot.

Instead, he lowered her feet to the ground and loosened his

hold, wanting to get a full assessment of how she looked. The healthy glow of her skin and the brightness in her eyes said it all. His Jazz was healthy once again.

"Come on in," she said as she took his hand. "Have you eaten? We had tacos and margaritas. I think there's some left."

Following her into the kitchen, he breathed in the spicy scent of tacos and felt his stomach rumble. "That sounds good. I haven't eaten since breakfast."

Delight danced in her eyes. "Sit down, and I'll fix you some. Serena's mom made them, and they're spectacular."

She chatted as she moved around the kitchen, reheating the meal. "Any news? Any new clues?"

"Yes, and yes."

She stopped in the middle of stirring the taco meat. "Really? What?"

"I had a visit from your brother."

She rushed over to him. "You saw Brody? How is he? What did he say?"

Since she didn't appear to realize she was animatedly waving a spoon around, he grabbed her hand to keep taco meat from flying. "I didn't actually see him."

"What do you mean?"

He explained the encounter and told her word for word what her brother had said. Keeping anything from Jazz was out of the question. Secrets were no longer part of their relationship.

A frown furrowing her brow, she returned to preparing the tacos. The pensive look in her eyes concerned him.

"What's wrong?"

She shook her head as she placed the taco fixings before him. "I just wish I could talk to him. The two-minute conversation we had wasn't nearly enough."

Downing half a taco in one bite, Xavier took a moment to

savor the delightful flavor before he said, "Your brother is definitely not one for words."

She dropped into a chair across from him and sighed. "Even when he was younger, he wasn't a big talker. I made up for it, though. Papa Mac used to say that the McAlister men let their size do their talking for them."

It lifted his heart to envision a young, energetic Jazz chatting away with her family. And he could definitely see where Brody McAlister's size would send a message to anyone without him having to use words.

"He loves you." Xavier hadn't thought he'd ever say that about her brother, but it was obvious. While he might not approve of the way the man had handled things, he would no longer deny that Brody did care about his sister.

"Of course he does."

She said it so simply, so assuredly, his heart practically jumped from his chest. The fact that she'd never lost faith in her brother, even after all this time and what she'd been through, was a testament to the character of Jazz McAlister. She was loyalty, strength, and bravery wrapped up in a beautiful, delightful package.

And showing that she was also still a keen-eyed OZ operative, she continued, "So what's the deal on this Sullivan guy he told you about? Is he after me, too?"

"Hard to say. He's Doyle's former brother-in-law, so the possibility of his involvement is strong, but his digital footprint is almost nonexistent. He's either completely innocent, or he's very, very good at covering his tracks."

"But Brody obviously thinks he's dirty."

"He does, and that's why we're focusing on him." He took her hand and said, "I couldn't stay away from you any longer, though. I've missed you so damn much."

When he tugged on her hand, she stood and walked around the table to him. Sitting on his lap, she cuddled against him and whispered, "I can't believe you're really here. This seems like a dream come true."

Xavier drew in a breath. This wasn't how he'd planned it at all, but he could no longer hold himself back.

"I love you, Jazz. You know that, right?"

Lifting her head, she gazed into his eyes and said softly, "I do. And I love you, too."

Withdrawing a small box that had been burning a hole in his pocket all the way here, he handed it to her as he asked gruffly, "Then would you make me the happiest man on earth and marry me?"

She froze in his arms, and the shocked expression on her face sent terror throughout Xavier's body. Had he jumped the gun and scared her off? He should have waited, given her a chance to talk about where she wanted to go with their relationship. Maybe his idea of love wasn't hers. They should have talked about it before he'd thrown the question out there.

Swallowing past a rapidly developing lump of dread in his throat, he rasped, "Jazz, you don't—"

Tears gleaming in her eyes, she stopped his stumbling words with her fingertips to his mouth. "Xavier Quinn, there is nothing I would love more than to be your wife."

CHAPTER FORTY-SIX

Chicago

S omeone was on to him. It was the only explanation for all the increased interest about him online. Whoever was digging into him was good, almost as good as he was. They had erased all digital footprints that would lead him to their identity, but he had trigger alarms set up to alert him of any unusual activity, and over the past few days, there had been a lot of it.

Chewing nervously on his lip, Oscar continued to click through the latest batch of worms trying to infiltrate his personal data. Every time they came close, one of his soldier worms ate the intel, and it disappeared. At any other time, he would enjoy the challenge, but this concerned him on a level he had never experienced.

Had the people who were supposed to be helping him sold him out? Were they perhaps dallying with him, mocking him, and then they planned to eliminate him? The very idea that he had worked so hard for all this for it to fall apart on him was mind-blowing. He wanted to call them and demand answers, but he also didn't want to call attention to himself again.

Couldn't they just do what he had asked them to do? Wasn't that the agreement? And if they were going to do what they'd said they would do, why hadn't they? They had spies everywhere. Surely they knew where the girl was. Were they just toying with him?

Slamming his laptop closed, he surged up from his chair and paced around his desk. What was he going to do if he was their target now? He was on their radar. Nothing would protect him if they wanted to take him out. They had thousands, perhaps millions, of people in their debt who, at a moment's notice, might be told to do away with him. And he would never see it coming—just like Bass and so many others.

How could he have been so stupid?

Oscar pulled at his hair and ground his teeth till his jaw ached. If he weren't so distraught, he would be laughing, because he suddenly wished Kevin were alive so he could get his take. He hadn't had a lot of respect for his brother-in-law, and he deserved to be dead after what he'd done, but for just a few minutes, he'd like to have the man here.

A buzzing noise sounded, and he almost jumped out of his skin. When he realized it was just his phone, a strangled laugh emerged from his dry mouth. If he jumped at every small sound, he'd likely die of a heart attack long before anyone from the Wren Project could get to him.

On shaky legs, he went back to his desk and grabbed his phone. Noting it was an unidentified caller, he felt his breath catch in his throat. Was this them? Were they calling to tell him he was a dead man?

"Hello?" he said breathlessly.

The same androgynous voice as before said, "Your target has been located. Once the package is secure, you will be notified of the pickup location."

Astounded, he tried to ramble out a thank-you, but the line was already dead. Dropping the phone, he covered his face with his hand and then let out a giant belly laugh. He'd been worried about nothing! So what if people were trying to find him? They wouldn't succeed. And when the girl arrived, he'd force her to do what he wanted, get rid of her, and then he would be set for life.

His day had finally arrived.

CHAPTER FORTY-SEVEN

Francine, Wisconsin

"Xavier, would you like more potatoes and gravy?" Mallory asked.

"Yes, ma'am, thank you."

Jazz couldn't help but smile at the meal Xavier had consumed. That was his third serving of potatoes and gravy. The first two had disappeared off his plate before she'd finished half of hers. Mallory Allen was a wonderful cook, and Jazz loved watching her man enjoy his food.

Her man. Xavier was hers. He had asked her to marry him. He was going to be her husband. She was going to be his wife. Jazz could barely comprehend the magnitude of what had occurred in the last twenty-four hours. First, she had thought it would be at least a week or two more before she would see Xavier again. When he'd shown up at the door, she'd been astounded. But then for him to propose to her? She'd gone from being absolutely blown away to…whatever level followed that one.

Gazing down at the beautiful round diamond sparkling on

her finger, Jazz could only marvel at what it signified. She, Jazz McAlister, was engaged to Xavier Quinn!

"Jazz, are you not hungry, dear?"

She jerked her head up to see everyone's eyes on her. "Sorry. Sort of in a daze."

Mallory laughed softly and sent a warm look to her husband. "I remember when Ed proposed to me. I was in a daze for weeks."

Grabbing his wife's hand, Ed brought it to his mouth for a kiss. "Best decision I ever made."

She winked at her husband and said, "Back at ya, my love."

Jazz released a happy sigh. Some people did stay in love long after they said their vows. Serena had told her that Ed and Mallory had been married for almost forty-five years, and having observed them over the past couple of weeks, she knew without a doubt they were still in love and totally devoted to each other.

As if reading her thoughts, Xavier squeezed her thigh. It had been almost twenty-four hours since he'd proposed, and with the exception of going to the bathroom and taking a shower, he had not stopped touching her. She'd never noticed what a tactile person he was, and she totally loved it.

They'd spent the day together, and she had shown him all the different delights of country living, including milking cows, feeding chickens, cuddling lambs and goats, and playing fetch with Rosco and Rusty, the Allen family dogs.

In the midst of all that, a lot of Serena's family had shown up to say hi and offer their congratulations. News traveled fast in Francine.

"Have you two talked about setting a date?" Serena asked softly beside her.

Taking a sip of the champagne Serena's parents had insisted on opening to celebrate the engagement, her nose twitching at the bubbles, Jazz shook her head. "Not yet."

She didn't know Xavier's view on engagements. As far as she was concerned, tomorrow couldn't be too soon. She felt like she'd waited a lifetime for this man and wanted to be his wife as soon as possible.

"You know," Serena continued softly, "my dad is an ordained minister."

Her eyes darted to Serena's, and she saw the gleam in her eyes. Wouldn't that be something? Would that freak Xavier out to suggest having their wedding here, before they went back home?

"I don't want to scare him off," she whispered back.

"Scare him off? Girl, that man's so crazy about you, I think he'd say 'I do' here at the table if he could."

She laughed and sent Xavier a look, trying to read whether she should bring it up. When his cellphone buzzed, she took that as a sign to keep quiet. There would be plenty of time to talk about weddings later on.

FIGURING it was an OZ team member calling to congratulate him, Xavier swallowed another mouthful of the best mashed potatoes and gravy he'd ever eaten as he answered his phone. "Quinn."

"Get Jazz to safety," a male voice barked. "You've got trouble coming your way."

He didn't bother to ask the identity of the caller. Even though he'd spoken with Brody McAlister only once, he recognized the man.

Going to his feet, he said, "How many?"

"My intel says at least ten. I'm counting on you to keep her safe, Quinn."

The line went dead.

"Xavier, what's wrong?"

Instead of answering Jazz, he looked at Serena. "We've got incoming."

Her eyes wide with alarm, Serena turned to her father. "Code red, Pops."

His face one of calm resolve, Ed surged to his feet and strode to the kitchen. In seconds, a loud whistle sounded through the house.

Serena turned to Xavier and Jazz. "That alert is set up in all the houses in the area. They're all equipped with safe rooms. The vulnerable will go there. Those who are trained will be armed and ready."

"How many are coming, and how much time do we have?" Jazz asked.

"At least ten," Xavier said. "Don't know how much time we—"

The lights went out.

"Hold on," Ed said. "Generator will kick in."

Seconds later, the lights returned, revealing Serena's parents, who both looked determined and angry.

"Mallory, grab your furbabies and get to the room."

Without missing a beat, Mallory scooped up Rosco and Rusty. Ed pressed a kiss to his wife's mouth and said, "See you soon, sweetheart."

She turned and gave everyone a worried look and said, "Be careful." Then she scooted toward the back of the house with her pets in her arms.

Xavier took Jazz by the shoulder. "Jazz—"

"No, Xavier. Don't even say it. These assholes are here because of me. No way am I going to lock myself up."

He'd known he'd be facing resistance, but he had to say it. "You're their target."

"Yes, I am. And now they're my target." She raised her chin even higher and added, "I'm staying."

"Okay, let's not waste any more time," Serena said. "Since

they took out the power at the main station, we can figure they're about seven minutes out."

"You have weapons?" Xavier asked.

"Follow me," Ed said.

Doing just that, he, Jazz, and Serena went through the family room into a small alcove. Ed removed a photo of his family from the wall, revealing a keypad. He punched in several numbers, and a part of the wall opened, revealing a large enclosure filled with enough weapons to arm a small army.

"Saddle up, boys and girls," Ed said. "We've got some business to take care of."

GRATEFUL SHE WAS DRESSED in her favorite pair of worn jeans and her sneakers, Jazz took the pistol Serena handed her, checked the magazine, and then slid it into the holster she'd wrapped around her waist. The worry for everyone here pounded into her head. If she had never come here, none of this would have happened. She should have stayed at Xavier's cabin. Whoever these people were, it was clear they wouldn't mind killing to get to her. How many people would die because of her selfishness?

"Hey, Jazz," Serena said gently. "Get that look off your face. This is not on you. Okay?"

She nodded because it would do no good to argue, but if anything happened to anyone, including any of the multitude of pets and animals in this amazing community, she would never forgive herself.

"Everyone geared up and ready?"

Ed and Xavier were both carrying AR-15s. Jazz and Serena each held a SIG Sauer MCX Rattler and had a SIG P365 holstered at their waists. They were ready for battle, but again, Jazz couldn't help but feel the heavy weight of responsibility.

By being here, she had brought trouble to these wonderful people.

"Hey, McAlister," Xavier said.

She met Xavier's gaze and knew he understood exactly what she was thinking. "It's going to be all right," he said softly. "I promise."

"You can't know that. If I hadn't—"

"Wherever you go, it's going to be like this. At least here, we're prepared to deal with it. Out in the open, there's no telling what might happen."

"How can you say that? There are women and children here that aren't prepared."

"We don't have a lot of time, young lady," Ed said, "so let me say this. The majority of our family is military. We do drills once a month. If there ever was a group of civilians prepared for this, it's this community."

Swallowing a lump of emotion, she nodded her thanks to Ed. Her eyes met Xavier's, and a surge of energy and confidence swept through her. They could do this.

A cellphone buzzed and Ed answered with, "What's going on?"

They watched as he listened to whoever was on the other end of the call, and then he said, "Let it fly."

Pocketing the phone, he said, "They sent a drone this way to scope things out. It'll be here in about a minute. Let's get in place and turn the lights out."

That was a good plan. The drone would show nothing but a dark household that looked unprepared for an attack.

The four of them marched out the door together. The instant they were on the porch, the confidence inside her tripled. At least twenty-five men and about a half-dozen women were standing in the front yard, and they, too, were heavily armed.

"Hell, Serena," Xavier said, "you've got some kind of family."

Her smile brilliant, she nodded and said, "I know."

"Okay, everybody," Ed said in a commanding voice. "We know there're only about ten of them, so we got 'em outnumbered. They're about to fly a drone over us, so take your places and stay quiet. When they arrive, we'll give 'em a chance and then see what we see. Take 'em down if you have to. If possible, we'd like a couple left alive so we can have a chat with them."

"We're ready, Ed!" one of the men shouted from the back. "Let's get rid of these suckers so we can get back to our supper."

There was a group laugh, and then Ed shouted, "Places, everyone!"

Men and women dispersed, hunkering down behind cars, bushes, and giant flowerpots. Xavier grabbed Jazz's arm and pulled her with him down the steps toward a large flower box. It would keep them hidden, as well as give them an excellent line of sight.

The entire area went dark, and everyone froze in place as they waited. A minute later, the unmistakable buzz of a drone sounded. Jazz held her breath. Even though she knew drones couldn't detect breathing, she couldn't help herself. She wanted no movement to be detected. The drone flew over the perimeter only once and took barely two minutes, but it seemed like forever before the sound faded away.

About a minute later, the unmistakable rumble of heavy vehicles heading their way broke the silence.

"Sounds like Hummers," Xavier said.

Jazz nodded. "Yeah."

"You okay?"

"I should have stayed in Montana," she mumbled. "Everyone would have been safer."

"No matter where you go, until these bastards are dealt with, you're going to be a target. And Ed's right. If ever there was a group prepared, it's this family." He touched her arm in a light caress. "It'll be okay."

She nodded, but the closer the sound of the vehicles came, the less sure Jazz was that it would work out okay. She wasn't allowed to worry long, because the first vehicle arrived. Stopping several yards from the house, the Hummer's doors flew open, and four men in tactical gear and helmets jumped to the ground and started running toward the house.

Another Hummer pulled in behind it, and six more soldiers jumped out. Like stealthy robots, they spread out. From their demeanor, it was obvious they had no idea what they might face. They had likely been given an order to collect a young female and take out anyone who got in their way. With everyone hidden and the drone revealing only a darkened household, the soldiers likely believed they were approaching unaware victims.

Nothing could have been further from the truth, which they learned when Ed Allen fired the first shot. Landing about a foot in front of a soldier, it was their only warning.

The soldiers froze in place and exchanged looks with one another. "Send out the girl, and no one gets hurt," one of them yelled.

"Not going to happen!" a man shouted back.

Jazz wasn't even sure she knew who that was. Maybe one of Serena's brothers?

Then, surprising everyone, especially the soldiers, three bright spotlights glared. Suddenly, it looked like all ten soldiers were now starring in a nightmarish play in which they were the prey.

"Drop!" one of the soldiers shouted. As one, they fell flat to the ground and began crawling for cover.

If Jazz weren't so infuriated that they had come here to

kidnap her and hurt the people she loved, she'd almost feel sorry for them. They were outgunned, outsmarted, and didn't stand a chance.

Xavier had been in many battles in his life. Having fought in some of the most violent hot spots in the world, he knew what war sounded like. This was a battle unlike any he'd ever seen. These people were farmers, businessmen, teachers, doctors, and lawyers. Yes, most of them had a military background, but what they were doing, protecting someone they barely knew, showed exactly who they were. He knew Jazz was terrified that something would happen to one of them, but it had to warm her heart to know that these people cared so much for her that they would put their lives on the line.

As quickly as the spotlights had been flicked on, they shut off, leaving inky darkness in their wake. He knew exactly what those men were seeing. The helmets they were wearing were equipped with night vision, which meant their retinas had gone haywire the instant the lights hit them. And now that they were in total darkness again, their eyes were having to adjust. He'd been there. It was discombobulating and frustrating, but a trained soldier powered through.

Xavier was beginning to think these men, no matter how lethally they were armed, weren't up to the task they'd been assigned. It almost made him laugh, because he knew they had no idea what they were facing.

Moving slowly, he eased away from Jazz and made his way to the corner of the house. "You're outmanned and outgunned," he shouted. "Give up and go home!"

A shot rang out, pinging off the side of the house. Xavier cursed.

"He's right," Ed shouted. "You're surrounded, boys. Might as well give it up."

Another shot rang out in Ed's direction.

A window shattered. And then, as if that had been some kind of signal, the soldiers let loose, apparently not caring who or what they hit.

Not another word was uttered by anyone in Serena's family before their full fury made itself known. If the soldiers had simply laid down their arms and given up, none of this would have been necessary.

"Xavier!" Jazz yelled. "Watch out!" Turning, Xavier spotted the soldier just as he flew over a bush toward him. Barely getting out of the way of the torpedo body slam, Xavier grabbed the guy in a headlock and threw him to the ground.

The guy was having none of it, and in an impressive, acrobatic move, he twisted out of the headlock and landed on his feet. Seeing that the man had lost his weapon at some point, Xavier dropped his own.

The guy went after him again. Xavier blocked the upper cut and whirled, kicking the guy in the gut and his nuts. The guy didn't drop, but forged ahead. Xavier saw the glint of a knife in his hand. A second before it could slash his face, a gunshot exploded, and the guy went down with a howl akin to the cry of an injured rabid wolf.

He turned to see Jazz standing a few feet away, holding the gun that had shot the bullet that had shattered the guy's knee.

"Thanks, baby, but I had him."

"Maybe so," his beautiful fiancée answered, "but nobody messes with my man."

Snorting at the cheesy line, he grabbed her and held her tight. "I love you, Jasmine McAlister."

CHAPTER FORTY-EIGHT

The trussed up soldier on the ground looked miserable as sweat poured down his pain-filled face. With a shattered knee and a bullet hole in his shoulder, the man was hurting. Serena's sister-in-law, Mina, a trauma surgeon, had patched him up and even given him a little something for the pain. Not too much, though, because he needed to be alert for the next part.

Xavier glanced behind him at Serena's relatives, noting that just one of the men standing there would intimidate most people. Ten of them was a little much, but that was okay with him. These people deserved to be here, to hear what this man had to tell them. He, along with nine others, had invaded their territory, caused untold property damage, and terrorized their families. The other nine were dead. This man had survived and would bear the brunt of their wrath.

No one would outright kill him, of course. That wasn't who they were, and Xavier knew the men behind him would not shoot an unarmed man. They were, however, prepared to scare and intimidate him until he gave up what he knew. Fear of torture and death was often much more effective than the acts themselves.

"Okay, I'm going to ask you some questions, and if I don't get the answers I'm looking for, I'll let my friends behind me loose. They'll be more than happy to get the answers their way."

"I don't know anything, man," the soldier said. "I'm just a hired gun."

"All right," Xavier said, "tell me what you were hired to do. Your exact orders."

Blinking from the sweat stinging his eyes, he looked up at Xavier. "Grab the girl."

"And which girl were you to grab?"

"They gave us a photo of her. It's in my shirt pocket."

Reaching into the man's pocket, Xavier pulled out a photograph of Jazz. It was a still shot from the video of when they'd been at the restaurant the night Bass was shot. This confirmed everyone's thinking that someone had recognized Jazz in that video online and set all of this into motion.

"What were you supposed to do with her?"

"Take her to a secure location."

"And that would be where?"

"I don't know."

"Wrong answer." He looked behind him, and all ten men, their weapons raised, stepped forward.

"Killing me won't help get you answers."

"Who said anything about killing? These men know exactly where to shoot to cause maximum pain without death. Not gonna lie—ten bullets, along with the holes in your shoulder and knee, are going to hurt."

Sweat flew everywhere as the soldier gave a vigorous shake of his head. "But I'm telling you the truth, man. I don't know where we were supposed to take her. After we grabbed and secured her, we were to call the guy in charge. He was going to tell us then where to take her."

"Who's the guy in charge?"

"I don't know, I swear. Only one man among us knew, and he's dead." A small smirk played at his mouth. "Guess you're screwed."

It took every bit of self-control, plus a hand wrapped around his arm, to keep Xavier from smashing the bastard's face to a pulp.

"Careful, son," Ed said. "It'd be easier on him if you killed him. That's what he wants. Don't fall for it."

Grinding his teeth, Xavier nodded, knowing the older man was right.

"You got anything else to say?" Xavier asked.

"No."

"Very well."

Turning, he looked at the men who appeared even more ravenous than before. If this guy knew anything, he'd be spitting it out soon.

"Guys, he's all yours."

"What? Wait! I told you what I know!" he screamed.

Looking over his shoulder at the horrified man, Xavier gave him a similar smirk. "I don't believe you. So I guess *you're* screwed."

Striding toward the house, he held his breath, hoping to hear something, anything that could help them find this bastard. He heard the guy scrambling back as the armed men advanced. Finally, just as Xavier's foot landed on the first porch step, the man shouted, "I know the number we were supposed to call!"

Xavier closed his eyes on a thankful prayer and strode back. "What were you supposed to say?"

"I don't know. I just saw the guy in charge call a number. I'm good at remembering, so I watched him punch it in."

They could play this out and, at the very least, get a location of where the soldiers were expected to drop her off. The OZ team could meet Xavier and Jazz there, and they could have another showdown.

Xavier stared down at the man on the ground, trying to determine if he was telling the truth or just spouting things that he hoped would save his skin.

"You do realize that if you're trying to set us up, you're going to be in a world of pain?"

"Listen, I'm just a guy who does this stuff for money. I have no agenda, no loyalty."

That was likely the truth. Xavier had seen more than his share of mercenaries who went from one high-risk job to another. Not only did these jobs often pay well, some people got off on the adrenaline rush.

Pulling an unused burner phone from his pocket, he asked, "What's the number?"

The man called out the digits.

"Any particular words you were supposed to use?"

"Not that I know of. Just that we had the package."

Hearing Jazz referred to as "the package" infuriated him, but these people were soulless.

Punching in the number, he held his breath until it was answered. "Report," a mechanical voice said.

"We have the package secured," Xavier growled into the phone.

"Excellent. The client will be notified for pickup in two days."

The line went dead.

His teeth grinding together, he went back to the soldier. "They didn't tell me a location." Pressing his gun against the man's forehead, he growled, "What is it?"

His eyes wide, his mouth trembling, he said hoarsely, "I

promise you, man. I don't know where we were supposed to take her."

Wanting to pull his hair out by the roots, Xavier walked away from the guy and holstered his weapon. If he didn't get far away from him, he would take out his frustration on him. There had to be a way to—

Striding to the house, he ran up the steps and called out to Serena, who was standing in the hallway, tapping out something on her phone. "Hey, did we collect all the phones?"

She scrunched her nose in a grimace. "Yes. They're all burner phones with nothing on them. The men carried no ID."

"Maybe facial identification will give us something."

"It might, but that could take a while. And it won't get us the drop-off location."

"We still have eyes on Oscar Sullivan. Right?"

"Yes. I have Blue Cagney's team out of Los Angeles on him."

Cagney's team was good. OZ had used them several times in the past. "Can you let them know to stick like glue to Sullivan? If he's the culprit, chances are he'll try to do the pickup himself."

"What do you want them to do with him if he's the one?"

"Just tell them to hold on to him until further notice."

"Will do."

"Where's Jazz?"

"I think she's still helping with the cleanup at the side of the house."

The sudden need to have Jazz in his arms and assure himself that she was okay almost overwhelmed him. Until this bastard was caught and dealt with, having her out of his sight for more than a few minutes wasn't something he wanted to risk.

"So you don't know where they were supposed to take me?" Jazz asked.

Sighing, Xavier pushed his fingers through his hair, his frustration obvious. "No. Apparently, one of the men who died knew the location, and the idiot didn't bother to share it with anyone else."

Even as aggravating as it was not to know where to go to face the man who'd ordered her abduction, Jazz couldn't find it within herself to feel major disappointment. No one in Serena's family had been hurt. Yes, there was massive property damage, but the instant the shooting had stopped and they'd known everyone was safe, the cleanup had begun. With dozens of people pitching in, it had taken only a few hours. Windows needed to be replaced and a few outer walls needed repairs, but by the time the sun rose, it was hard to tell there had even been a battle.

The dead men had been transported to a barn a couple miles down the road, and Serena's brothers were there now with someone from the sheriff's office. Since two of Serena's cousins were on the police force, they had the credibility needed to explain exactly what had happened, that Serena's family had defended their homes from armed intruders.

The news that Xavier hadn't been able to secure the drop-off location didn't faze Jazz nearly as much as it might have. They had been so fortunate, because if Serena's family had been any other family, untrained and unprepared, the devastation would have been brutal.

Xavier pushed a lock of hair behind her ear and gave her a tender look. "How can someone who fought in a war and has been up all night still look so damn beautiful?"

She wrapped her arms around his neck. "You tell me. You look good enough to eat."

He lowered his head, his mouth meeting hers in a kiss filled with passion.

Jazz groaned beneath his lips. She could spend a lifetime kissing this man. With that thought in mind, she pulled away from him and said, "Can I ask you a question?"

"Of course."

"Do you want a long engagement?"

"No. I've waited for years for you to be mine."

Love swamped her, and she fought to keep her voice from cracking when she said, "I feel the same way. So, how would you feel if we got married here? Today?"

"Are you sure about that? You don't want a big wedding with everyone from OZ there?"

She would miss having her OZ family in attendance, but she knew they would understand. And while she knew that a big wedding might be the dream of many women, she wasn't one of them. Besides, she had learned that life was too short to wait for the perfect time or for everything to fall in line before acting on something.

"We'll have a party when we get back home for our OZ family. But what I want more than anything is to be yours. And I'd like to make that happen as soon as possible."

"I can't think of anything that would make me happier." Pulling her into his arms, he whispered against her mouth, "Let's make it happen."

CHAPTER FORTY-NINE

J azz was convinced that Serena Allen Donavan was an
angel on earth, because no one else would have been able
to coordinate an entire wedding, including a wedding
dress for the bride and a tuxedo for the groom, along with a
giant tented wedding reception, in just a few hours.

Yet here Jazz stood, looking at herself in the full-length
mirror, and oohing and aahing over the beautiful sight before
her. The off-white sleeveless dress was perfect for her small
stature and slender body. The beaded V neckline and
princess-cut lace bodice emphasized what curves she had, and
the short train didn't overwhelm her petite frame.

Serena had shown her dozens of dresses, and this had been
the second one she'd seen. None of the others had come close.
Her shoes were the same color and gave her a couple of inches
of added height. The only jewelry besides the beautiful
diamond on her hand was the heart locket around her neck,
which looked perfect with her dress.

She'd used a minimum of makeup, just a touch of mascara
to lengthen her lashes, a hint of bronze and purple to make
her brown eyes look smoky, and a reddish coral for her lips.

Since her cheeks were flushed with excitement, added color was not needed.

"Oh, Jazz, you look spectacular."

Whirling, she grinned at Serena. "Thanks to you. I can't tell you how much I appreciate all of this."

"I'm thrilled you guys are doing this here. We haven't had a wedding in our little chapel in years."

Serena had pointed out the family chapel the first day Jazz had arrived. She'd explained that though her family preferred to worship in Appleton because of the larger congregation, when the winter weather prevented them from traveling, they worshiped at the chapel.

"I should have asked if I could help clean it or—"

"Not necessary. We take turns cleaning it each week. It's just sitting there, waiting for people to fill it."

At that thought, a hint of sadness dimmed her smile. If she had waited until later, she could have had her entire OZ family here. Even though she wanted to marry Xavier as soon as possible, she couldn't help but feel guilty that she was leaving them out.

"What's wrong?"

"I was just wishing everyone could be here."

"Nonsense. They're all thrilled for you. Like you said earlier, we'll have a big party when everyone is together again."

She knew Serena was right. When she had talked to Ash this morning, she had heard the happiness in his voice when she'd told him she and Xavier were getting married today.

"You're right." Jazz gestured to the pale peach gown Serena was wearing. "You look lovely, by the way. Thank you for being my matron of honor."

"I can't think of anything I'd rather do. You and Xavier are going to be so happy."

Tears misted Serena's eyes, and Jazz felt a tug at her heart.

As much as Serena tried to pretend everything was fine with her, Jazz knew her heart was still broken over Sean's desertion and his request for a divorce. She remembered when they'd gotten married and how incredibly happy they had both been. How could something so right turn out so wrong?

She made a vow, right then and there, that no matter what, she and Xavier would not allow that to happen to them. She didn't care if they had to hogtie each other to stay together. This was forever for both of them.

Serena glanced at her watch. "Okay, bride-to-be. We need to go. You ready?"

Ready to marry the man of her dreams? Oh yes, she most definitely was.

THE SOUND of romantic music coming from the sanctuary sent goose bumps across Jazz's skin. Serena had steered her toward this little room to wait while all the guests were seated. It melted her heart to know that Serena's entire family would be in attendance. Only hours ago, they had fought alongside them, not only to protect their families, but to protect her, too. And now, they were shifting gears and coming together for a wedding. Life really was full of surprises.

Should she have checked out the church beforehand? She'd been so busy picking out a wedding dress and getting ready for the ceremony, she hadn't even considered all the things that most people expected in a wedding. Should she have picked some flowers for a bouquet, or maybe put out some candles or something? She'd been to elaborate weddings before, as well as simple ones. From what she remembered, they'd all looked like a lot of prep work went into creating the perfect setting. Maybe she shouldn't have rushed this.

The knock on the door pulled her from her worried thoughts.

Figuring it was Serena letting her know it was time to walk down the aisle, Jazz drew in a shaky breath and called out, "Come in."

The door opened, and there stood Asher Drake, decked out in a black tuxedo.

"Ash! You're here? How?"

His eyes twinkling, Ash came toward her. "You think I'm going to let two of my best operatives get married without me being here?"

She gasped. "Does that mean…"

"That everyone is here? Of course they are. Do you know how long we've been waiting for you two to finally realize how crazy you are about each other?"

With a soft little cry, Jazz hugged her boss as hard as she could. She could not believe her OZ family had come all this way to be with her and Xavier on their wedding day.

"I was wondering if I could have the honor of walking you down the aisle."

The lump in her throat was so large, it took every bit of her breath to squeeze out the words, "That would make me so happy."

"Oh, before I forget. Serena wanted me to give this to you." He held out a bouquet of white, pink, and red roses. It was the most beautiful bouquet she'd ever seen.

Taking it from Ash's hand, she sniffed the flowers and felt a peace all the way to her soul. This day could not be any more perfect.

"I think they're ready for us," Ash said.

He held out his arm, and Jazz put her hand on it. Her heart was double-timing at the sheer excitement of what was about to happen. They walked out into a small lobby and then to the double doors that led to the sanctuary. Knowing that Xavier was inside, waiting for her, was the best feeling in the world.

Stopping at the door, as she waited for the music to begin,

Jazz looked up at the man who meant the world to her and had given her so much. "Ash, I don't think I've ever said this, but thank you for allowing me to be a part of OZ. It's been the best part of my life."

Though Asher Drake had a tendency to look stern most of the time, a rare smile brightened his face, and his eyes were filled with affection. "You're family, Jazz. We love you. You know that, right?"

She gave him a dazzling smile, and then looking around the crowded room, she gasped at the abundance of flowers everywhere—draped over the pews, sitting in baskets, hanging from the ceiling, and lining the aisle. The soft, floral fragrance permeated the room.

Serena's family filled both sides of the aisles. When she had first arrived in Francine, Jazz had worried whether she would fit in. Other than OZ, she had been alone for so long. But they had welcomed her into the fold as if she were one of their own, and she knew she couldn't look at them as just Serena's family anymore. They were her family, too.

At the front, Serena stood to the side of the altar. Also standing there, looking absolutely gorgeous in an ice-blue gown, was Eve. Beside her was Olivia, who looked lovely in a light green gown. And Jules stood to her left, beautiful in a light blue gown. Her OZ sisters were here for her.

On the other side of the altar were Gideon and Liam, both in tuxedos. And beside them…

Jazz gasped. "Hawke is here."

"Of course," Ash said. "He wouldn't miss this for the world."

She had talked to Hawke several times on the phone but hadn't seen him since before he'd been injured. He looked wonderful, and she couldn't wait to hug him.

Her eyes shifted to the front of the altar, where the hottest, most gorgeous man she'd ever known was staring directly at her as if she was his world.

Her heart filled to the brim with happiness, Jazz took the first step to her bright, beautiful future. No matter what life had in store for them, she knew without a doubt that with Xavier by her side, nothing could keep them from their happy ending.

EPILOGUE

Holding his beautiful bride, her body swaying with his while music swirled around them, Xavier wasn't sure he'd ever known a happier moment.

A swell of emotion washed over him as he looked down at the woman in his arms. Earlier, when she was walking down the aisle toward him, it was all he could do to stand still and wait for her to reach him. He had never wanted anything more in his life.

"Jasmine McAlister Quinn," he said roughly, "did I tell you that you're the most beautiful bride I've ever seen?"

Her eyes glittering like diamonds, her face flushed with love, she grinned up at him. "Yes, you did, Xavier Quinn, but I don't mind hearing it again."

The expression on her face was one he would remember forever. He didn't think he'd ever seen her like this. This was what he wanted for her—to feel happiness and excitement for the rest of her life. He would do everything he could to make that possible.

Things were in place to make that happen. He'd gotten word just before the wedding started that Oscar Sullivan had abruptly canceled all his meetings to go out of town. Cagney's team would detain him once Sullivan arrived at his destination. Xavier knew his lovely bride would like to meet the man, and Xavier looked forward to having a chat with him, too. It might be a bit of an odd beginning to their honeymoon, but not for two seasoned OZ operatives.

Once that immediate danger was out of the way, he would encourage Jazz to meet with the attorney in charge of the Byrne estate and claim her inheritance. She had described what she wanted to do with the money. He not only wholeheartedly approved, if possible, it made him love this woman even more.

As if she'd read his thoughts, she gazed up at him and whispered, "I love you, Xavier."

Shutting out the music and all the chattering around them, Xavier lowered his head and kissed his beautiful bride with all the love and tenderness he had in his heart. She had given him so much, and in return he wanted to give her the world.

When the kiss ended, her eyes were glazed, and the pink flush in her cheeks had deepened. The buzzing noise of a text arriving on the phone in his pocket pulled him from the sweetness of the moment. He was waiting to hear from Cagney's team and didn't want to miss anything, but he didn't want to let her go either.

A tap on his shoulder brought his head around. Hawke stood behind him. "Mind if I dance with your bride?"

To see his friend standing there, alive and healthy, was one of the best things Xavier had ever seen. He'd talked to him several times since he'd been injured and knew he had recovered, but to see him in person made all the difference. Xavier had told him how Clay Cotton had reached out to him with the backstory on the shooting. Even though Hawke had every reason to be angry, Xavier knew he held no ill will against

Cotton. If another shooter had taken the job, the outcome might've been much worse.

Another buzz reminded him he had a text. Before handing his bride over to Hawke, he gave her a quick kiss and whispered, "Be right back."

The delighted smile on her face as she went into Hawke's arms told him she was thrilled to be able to dance with one of her favorite people.

Xavier grabbed his phone, glancing at the text as he strode toward the door. When he saw that it wasn't from Cagney's team, he jerked to a stop. The instant he read the short, terse message, he took off running.

Jazz took another swallow of iced tea. She had danced with Hawke, Liam, Gideon, and Ash, as well as Serena's dad and all of her brothers. She was having too good of a time to be tired, but she did need a break to catch her breath.

Hearing a childish giggle, she looked up to see Nikki, Hawke and Olivia's daughter, trying to catch the attention of Josh, Jules and Ash's son. The two looked delighted to have found each other.

The fact that all of her OZ teammates were here, along with Aubrey, Liam's wife, and their new baby daughter, Lily, melted her heart.

"I can't believe everyone was able to get here so quickly."

Holding Nikki in her arms while Olivia held Josh, Eve said with a laugh, "You should have seen us. The instant Serena called and told us what was happening, we were scrambling to get dressed in the fancy clothes Rose got out for us. We looked like frantic circus monkeys."

"I can attest to that," Rose said, the twinkle in her eyes showing her amusement. "Ash and Gideon tried to get into the same pair of pants, and Eve stood in the middle of the room, laughing like crazy."

"True story," Eve said. "I only wish I'd gotten a recording of it."

"Me, too," Aubrey said. "I would have paid money to see that."

"Speaking of seeing, where did your handsome husband get to? I haven't seen him in a while."

At Rose's words, Jazz looked around for Xavier. She had been so involved in catching up with her friends, she hadn't noticed that he hadn't returned from whatever message had pulled him away from the party.

Worried now, she stood, ready to go find him. When she spotted him heading her way, relief rushed through her. Silly, she knew, but until the threat against her was over, she wanted to know where he was at all times.

The look in his eyes said he had something on his mind, but the instant their gazes met, a smile lit up his face.

Suddenly needing to be in his arms, Jazz practically ran to him. "I missed you. Where have you been?"

"Just seeing to some unfinished business. Follow me."

Intrigued, she allowed him to pull her out of the tent to the parking lot. He led her to a car and helped her inside, then got into the driver's seat. Two minutes later, they were stopping in front of the little cottage she and Xavier had been staying in since he had arrived.

Only half joking, she said, "If we're starting our honeymoon already, give me five minutes to put on the black lace lingerie Eve gave me."

"Now that's something I look forward to."

Hand in hand, they walked onto the porch, and then, giving her a thrill and a giggle, he scooped her into his arms and carried her over the threshold.

When he dropped her to her feet, she said, "That's an excellent beginning to a honeymoon."

"I need to get something." He pressed a kiss to her forehead. "Go on into the den. I'll join you in a moment."

Excited to see what he had for her, Jazz went quickly to the den and stepped inside. Her mind on just what Xavier had planned, she was almost in the middle of the room before she sensed a presence. Looking around, she came to an abrupt halt, her body frozen in place and all breath leaving her in an audible gasp. She knew that face, and she knew those eyes.

"Brody?" she whispered.

"Hey, Little Mighty," he said softly.

With a soft sob, she flew across the room and into his open arms. When they closed around her and he whirled her around like he did when they were kids, Jazz cried against his neck, "Brody, oh, Brody, I didn't think I'd ever see you again."

"I know, Jazzy. I'm so damned sorry for leaving you like that."

She couldn't respond, the emotions so big and overwhelming all she could do was hang on and treasure the moment. Her beloved, wonderful brother was here with her. She had never given up on him, but she wasn't sure she'd believed she would ever see him again.

"Come on, let's sit down. I can't stay long."

She told herself to get her act together. Brody was already planning to leave, and she had so many things she wanted to ask him, so much she needed to say. She let him lead her to the sofa, and she sat beside him but refused to let go of his hand.

"How did this happen? How did you know where I was?"

"Your husband sent me a message." He squeezed her hand. "I wish I could have given you away, but it's best that I stay in the shadows."

"Why, Brody? What do you do? What happened to you?"

"That's a long story for another day, Jazz. I just wanted to see you and wish you happiness. I know I let you down all those years ago, and not a day goes by that I don't hate myself for it."

"No, Brody. Don't say that. Kate told me what happened. You protected me the only way you knew how." She took the hand she was holding and kissed it fiercely. "Thank you for always looking out for me. I'm so sorry you went through hell for me."

And he had gone through hell, there was no question in Jazz's mind about that. The eyes might be the same, as well as his features, but the Brody she remembered as a child was no more. In his place was a scarred, hard-looking man with a fierceness that would have scared her if she hadn't had experience with hard, scary-looking men. Whatever Brody had gone through had changed him in drastic and dramatic ways.

"I'm just glad you're all right, Jazz. Mom and Dad would be so proud of you." His mouth tilted slightly, the closest he'd come to a smile, as he said, "You look so much like our mother."

Our mother. Brody's birth mother had taken off a couple years after he was born, and Papa Mac had raised his son by himself until he'd married Jazz's mom. From the moment Brody had met her, he'd looked upon Eliza as his mother. And she had loved him like he was her own son.

"Do you know what happened to them, Brody? Do you know who killed them?"

"Not yet, Jazz."

"Let me help."

"You help by staying safe. Okay? Make sure that big lug of a husband takes care of you."

When he went to his feet, Jazz's heart wrenched. She jumped up and grabbed his hand again. "Don't go."

"I can't stay, Jazz. I just wanted to see you and tell you how proud I am of you and how happy I am for you. Quinn might be an ass, but he loves you, and that's what matters most."

She could only imagine the conversation Xavier and Brody might have had. She was sure there had been plenty of threats thrown back and forth. Such was the way of tough, grumpy, overprotective men.

"Will I see you again?"

"Maybe not for a while, but I'll try. Okay?"

"Okay."

When he pulled her into his arms, she hugged him as tightly as possible and said, "I love you, Brody. Thank you for being such a wonderful big brother. You're still my hero."

He gave her one more hard squeeze, a gruff, "Love you, too," and then he was gone, striding rapidly out the door. Jazz wanted to run after him. Wanted to demand that he stay and tell her what he was up to and promise her he'd never leave her. But she knew he couldn't do that. Brody had an agenda, and he wasn't going to let anything or anyone get in his way.

"Are you okay?" Xavier stood in the doorway, his expression a mixture of concern and anger. "If he upset you, I'm going to kick his ass."

Unable to speak, she just shook her head. Xavier scooped her into his arms and sat down with her in his lap. A part of her wanted to cry, but another part felt so incredibly blessed.

Today, she had married the man of her dreams. She had seen and talked to her beloved brother. And she had more family than she'd ever dreamed possible.

Cupping her husband's face, she spoke against his mouth, "Thank you, Xavier. For helping make my dreams come true."

"Thank you, Jazz, for being my dream come true."

The kiss they shared was a culmination of both their dreams. Jazz knew that with Xavier by her side, she would always have his love and devotion. Her dreams, both big and small, had come true.

ONLY BY CONCENTRATING on his goals was Brody able to walk away. Seeing Jazz again and talking to her had been the most emotional thing to happen to him in years. He did not do emotions, and this... Well, this had been too much. This couldn't happen again.

She had people who had stepped up for her, loved her. There was no one more deserving than Jazz. The onerous weight he carried on his shoulders for what had happened all those years ago wasn't something he could contemplate. Even as he told himself he'd had no other choice, the memories would never leave him.

But she was happy now. Married to a man who would literally die for her. She had friends who would stand beside her, support her. All the things he'd always hoped for her were now hers.

His hand on the car door, he took one last look at the cottage he'd just left. She'd be all right. Quinn would see to that. An unusual longing had him taking a step backward as he hesitated. Maybe he—

The ping of his phone drew him back to reality. Pulling the phone from his pocket, he swiped the screen to read the text, and his mouth twisted in a rare smile.

He quickly responded, accepting the job. And then he sent off another text, this one to Xavier Quinn to let him know he could call off the people he had following Sullivan.

Brody slid into his car and started the engine. Sometimes, karma came at just the right time. Oscar Sullivan was about to have a very, very bad day.

And Brody was one step closer to his goal.

THANK YOU

Dearest reader, thank you so much for reading Reckless. I sincerely hope you enjoyed Xavier and Jazz's love story. If I could ask one favor of you, would you please leave a review to help other readers find this book? Just a few words or a star review would be fine and very much appreciated.

Next up is Fearless, which is Serena and Sean's story. I'll be honest with you, I've been putting it off for a bit because the story is heartbreaking in many ways, but never fear, there will be a happy ending. I promise. These two may just have to work a little harder for it.

If you would like to be notified when I have a new release, be sure to sign up for my newsletter at *https://christyreece.com/ sign-up-newsletter.html*.

To learn about my other books, please visit my website at *http://www.christyreece.com/*.

Follow me on:
Facebook at *https://www.facebook.com/ChristyReeceAuthor*
X at *http://twitter.com/ChristyReece*

Amazon at *https://www.amazon.com/stores/Christy-Reece/author/B002K8S34A*

Bookbub at *https://www.bookbub.com/profile/christy-reece?list=author_books*

OTHER BOOKS BY CHRISTY REECE

OPTION ZERO Series

Merciless

Relentless

Heartless

Ruthless

GREY JUSTICE Series

Nothing To Lose

Whatever It Takes

Too Far Gone

A Matter Of Justice

Grey Justice Box Set: Books 1 - 3

LCR ELITE Series

Running On Empty

Running Dark

Running Scared

Running Wild

Running Strong

LCR Elite Box Set: Books 1-3

LAST CHANCE RESCUE Series

Rescue Me

Return To Me

Run To Me

No Chance

Second Chance

Last Chance

Sweet Justice

Sweet Revenge

Sweet Reward

Chances Are

WILDEFIRE Series writing as Ella Grace

Midnight Secrets

Midnight Lies

Midnight Shadows

ACKNOWLEDGMENTS

To adequately express my deep appreciation to everyone who supported me in the writing of this book is likely beyond me. However, I will do my best.

To my heavenly Father, who makes all things possible and always answers my prayers in the most amazing ways. To Him, I give all glory, honor, and praise.

To the love of my life, my husband, Jim, who encouraged and supported me in ways too numerous to mention. Thank you for the laughter and all the extra things you do that I take for granted. You are, and will always be, my one and only love.

My beautiful mom, who continually inspires me. How very blessed I am that you are my mom!

My beautiful fur-babies who bring me smiles and more love than I ever thought possible.

The amazing Joyce Lamb whose copyediting and fabulous advice are always on-point and makes all the difference.

Kelly Mann of KAM Designs for her gorgeous cover art and infinite patience.

The Reece's Readers Facebook group, for their support, encouragement, and wonderful sense of humor.

To Jackie, whose friendship meant the world to me. I miss you and hope Serena's aunt Jackie made you smile.

Anne, my super reader, whose encouraging words and kindness keeps me going.

My beta readers and proofreaders, Crystal, Hope, Alison, Kelly, Julie, Kris, Linda, Kara, and Susan. So appreciate all of you!

Special thanks to Hope for your help and assistance in a multitude of things. Your generous heart and kindness are so very much appreciated.

To my all readers, your support means the world to me. Thank you for your patience and encouragement as I continue to learn my way around these OZ characters with all their secrets and complexities. I hope you love them as much as I do.

ABOUT THE AUTHOR

Christy Reece is the award winning, NYT Bestselling Author of dark romantic suspense. She lives in Alabama with her husband and fur-kids.

Christy loves hearing from readers and can be contacted at *Christy@ChristyReece.com.*

Made in the USA
Las Vegas, NV
07 December 2024

13528928R00229